Praise for *The Way of*

"*The Way of the Brave* grabbed me at the first chapter and never let go. Susan May Warren is a master storyteller, creating strong, confident, and compassionate characters. This book is no different."

Rachel Hauck, *New York Times* bestselling author
of *The Wedding Dress* and *The Memory House*

"The first in Warren's Global Search and Rescue series combines high-adrenaline thrills and a sweet romance. Perfect for fans of Dee Henderson and Irene Hannon."

Booklist

"Warren lays the foundation of a promising faith-influenced series with this exciting outing."

Publishers Weekly

Praise for *The Heart of a Hero*

"Susan May Warren whips up a maelstrom of action that slams Jake and Aria together and keeps the pages turning. Twists, turns, and constant danger keep you wondering whether this superb cast of characters can ride out the storm."

James R. Hannibal, multi–award-winning author
of *Chasing the White Lion*

"Warren keeps readers in suspense throughout a Category 5 hurricane and its perilous aftermath with harrowing details. Amid the chaos of this natural disaster, the characters' understanding of heroism is underscored by Christian messages of self-forgiveness, grace, and sacrifice."

Booklist

"*The Heart of a Hero* by Susan May Warren was perfectly woven in a way that had me never wanting to leave the book."

Urban Lit Magazine

Praise for *The Price of Valor*

"Warren continues her Global Search and Rescue series with this enjoyable thriller about a high-stakes rescue mission during a devastating catastrophe. Warren's fans will enjoy this."

Publishers Weekly

"The Global Search and Rescue series by Susan May Warren has been a rip-roaring, action-packed, suspense-filled crazy ride, and *The Price of Valor* is the nail-biting conclusion that wraps it all up."

Interviews & Reviews

"Susan May Warren brings all our favorites from the Global Search and Rescue series in one of the most action-packed stories she has written! With engaging characters, a fast-moving storyline, and little snippets of characters from other beloved Susan May Warren books, this is easily one of the best I have read this year."

Write-Read-Life

SUNRISE

ALSO BY SUSAN MAY WARREN

SKY KING RANCH
BOOK 1

SUNRISE

SUSAN MAY WARREN

Revell

a division of Baker Publishing Group
Grand Rapids, Michigan

© 2022 by Susan May Warren

Published by Revell
a division of Baker Publishing Group
PO Box 6287, Grand Rapids, MI 49516-6287
www.revellbooks.com

Printed in the United States of America

Library of Congress Cataloging-in-Publication Data
Names: Warren, Susan May, 1966– author.
Title: Sunrise / Susan May Warren.
Description: Grand Rapids : Revell, a division of Baker Publishing Group, [2022] | Series: Sky King ranch
Identifiers: LCCN 2021020276 | ISBN 9780800739829 | ISBN 9780800741143 (casebound) | ISBN 9781493434244 (ebook)
Subjects: GSAFD: Romantic suspense fiction.
Classification: LCC PS3623.A865 S86 2022 | DDC 813/.6—dc23
LC record available at https://lccn.loc.gov/2021020276

Baker Publishing Group publications use paper produced from sustainable forestry practices and post-consumer waste whenever possible.

22 23 24 25 26 27 28   7 6 5 4 3 2 1

Soli Deo Gloria

ONE

By the time Dodge got to the hospital, he'd already broken his first promise.

It was a Saturday, the same day the sun turned the Copper River into blades of ice, lethal and brilliant as they shoved and jockeyed out of Denali's shadow south into the Gulf of Alaska. The dawn had broken at the respectable hour of 7:42 a.m., and with it, the sunrise not only brought a southernly gust of warm air that cracked the freezing point and turned the starting line of the Iditarod to mush and grime but also laced the air with the scent of spring.

A balmy 37 degrees in Anchorage, nearly a heat wave this time of year.

Which only brought out the crazies.

As he stalked through the waiting room of Alaska Regional and punched the elevator button, Dodge shot a look at the flat-screen where the news recapped yesterday's celebration, aka the parade through Anchorage of the fifty-seven or so mushing teams. People dancing on icy berms, high-fiving the mushers, tailgaters wearing board shorts along with fur caps and mukluks, children wanting to pet the dogs. Outsiders from the Lower 48 were trying to grab selfies with local celebrities.

The mushers would be starting on their thousand-mile journey from Willow Lake later today, and with that information from the reporter, Echo Yazzie slipped into Dodge's mind.

He wondered—

No. He shook her away, got on the elevator, and rode it to the third, med-surg floor. As he got off, he recognized the smells of a hospital, not that different from Walter Reed, and his insides clenched.

He wouldn't stay long.

Of course, the old man hadn't died in the accident, and maybe that was crass of Dodge, but if he had, maybe it would all be over, the burn in Dodge's gut finally extinguished.

He spotted his sister, Larke, standing at the end of the hall, staring through the window at the blue sky, the muddy streets. She stood with her back to him, so he only guessed it was Larke, her long blond hair in a singular braid down her back. But she also wore a Sky King Ranch flight jacket, the words emblazoned on the back, so that seemed a dead giveaway.

A man sat in a nearby molded chair, his hair cut military short. He considered Larke with worried eyes.

Probably Riley McCord, her SEAL husband. *Perfect.* With Dodge's luck, his brother Range and Riley would have met on some classified SEAL mission, become best of pals, and Riley would have gotten an earful of family dirty laundry over a post-mission debriefing.

Dodge, of course, starring as the villain of the story.

He braced himself. "Larke?"

She turned, and of course she looked older—the last time he'd seen her she'd been eighteen and joining the Army.

And he'd been sixteen and just stupid enough to think that he had his life buttoned up.

"Dodge?" She wore trauma in her eyes, probably fatigue and worry, but also residue from the years she'd served as a medic. Still, he wondered if she had been the one to find the wreckage of their father's DHC-3 Otter bush plane. His friend Moose had been sketchy on that part when he'd called to tell Dodge about the accident.

Glancing at the man in the chair, who rose, Larke put her coffee on the ledge of the window. "Wow. I didn't think . . . I mean . . . how did you find out?"

Dodge wished she'd finished her first thought. She didn't think . . . *what?* That he cared about the old man? That he'd ever return? That he didn't think about his choices nearly every day, especially recently?

"Moose Mulligan, down at Air One Rescue," Dodge answered.

Larke wore a pair of jeans, Sorels, and a wedding ring on her left hand, but he knew that, too, thanks to the *Copper Mountain Good News*'s online portal.

He just kept his subscription for the obits. And maybe the police report. Really. The fact that it listed her engagement to a Navy SEAL a couple years ago was just a bonus line item.

"Have you been in Anchorage all this time?" She seemed to be working her words, trying not to accuse.

He felt it anyway.

"How'd it happen?" He glanced at the other man—Riley—now standing. Big enough, built like a linebacker, he stepped close to Larke and put his arm around her.

Dodge met his eyes even as Larke spoke.

"Otto Smith saw him go down and called it in. Dad was low, coming in for a landing at the Copper Mountain airfield, and his wing clipped a tree. Otto wasn't sure but he thought the wing might have detached before it hit."

"A faulty wing attachment?" His gaze went back to Larke, having found some solid ground in his silent face-off with Riley. Riley loved her—he would protect her, and Dodge appreciated that. Larke might be two years older than him, but she was still his sister.

"It's the only way we can figure it." Her gaze flitted toward the closed door that Dodge guessed was the old man's room. "He's been flying for forty-nine years. He doesn't make mistakes."

"It doesn't have to be a pilot error for accidents to happen, Larke. Weather. A wind gust. Anything can happen in the bush."

Her jaw clenched and her husband tightened his grip on her. He finally held out his hand to Dodge. "Riley McCord."

Dodge met it. "Dodge Kingston. When did you two finally hitch up?"

"Before my first tour," he said. "About a year ago."

Dodge didn't ask if he knew Ranger, figured it would come up if it needed to. "Congrats. Sorry I wasn't there."

"We eloped," Larke said. "You and the boys were too hard to track down, and Dad already gave his blessing, so . . ."

She was being kind with her words. Truth was, he hadn't a clue where Ranger, and especially Colt, had landed on the globe. And he didn't ask. Just because they were triplets didn't mean they were close. At least, not anymore.

"How bad is it?" He gestured with his head toward door number one.

"Dislocated shoulder, broken arm, a couple cracked ribs. One of them nicked his lung, though, and it collapsed. Moose and a team from Air One Rescue flew in to the crash site. Took them forever, but they did save his life." She frowned. "But you know that. What, are you flying for them now?"

Dodge wrapped a hand around the back of his neck. Not really. Maybe. "Moose has my number and he called me."

He left out the part where he'd gotten on a plane in DC and flown eight-plus hours before he'd let his brain kick in.

It wasn't like his father wanted him around. Or like Dodge would swoop in and save the ranch, walk back into the life he'd longed for once upon a time.

Pick up where he left off with the girl he left behind.

Clearly, he needed a shower, breakfast, and coffee—although he'd given up the last one during his stint in Walter Reed, so maybe just tea. He'd promised his docs to keep his heart rate at a reasonable tick going forward.

Still, maybe he needed to offer Larke something of an explanation because she just looked at him, through him, clearly not believing him. But if he kept going with his explanation there'd be more judgment, questions, and who knew what else. He might even end up doing something he swore he'd never do.

Like return home.

Nope. His stupid impulses had done enough damage. "How long are you in town?"

"We've been here about ten days. Riley has about a week left on leave." She wrapped her arms around herself. "I should have gone with Dad."

"Larke," Riley said quietly, "he's been flying by himself for years."

Maybe he didn't mean the indictment, but Dodge's chest tightened anyway.

She glanced at Riley. "What? I know what I'm doing up there."

A muscle ticked in Riley's jaw.

Behind them, the door opened, and Dodge turned just as a doctor in her midforties walked out. She seemed no-nonsense, with short brown hair, seasoned eyes, and a lean frame. She wore a jacket over a pair of scrubs and held out her hand to Larke.

"I'm Doctor Madison. I operated on your father. He's going to be pretty sore, and we're going to keep him here for another day or two, but he's a tough one. He'll be okay."

Dodge's throat thickened with her words.

"Thanks, Doc," Larke said for them both. "Can we see him?"

Doc Madison nodded, and Larke headed for the door.

Dodge didn't move.

Larke stopped, turned. "Really?"

"It's been ten years, Larke. I know you weren't around, but . . . it was bad. He doesn't want to see me."

Her mouth tightened around the edges. "Don't be stupid. You're here. Come in with me."

He held up his hand. "He's wounded. Maybe now's not the time to—"

"See his oldest son? Confirm that you're not dead in some Taliban-occupied valley in Afghanistan? Yeah, you're probably right. He wouldn't want to know that you're okay and standing in the hallway afraid to walk in and say hi to your father."

Oh, she could light him up. He clenched his jaw.

Riley looked away and shoved his hands in his pockets.

"What are you afraid of, Dodge?"

"I'm not afraid, Larke."

She met his gaze, and in hers he saw a woman who'd been through her own trauma and survived. So not the girl who needed to be protected, not anymore.

Fine. "I left for a reason, and that reason hasn't changed."

"Hasn't it?"

A beat passed, and he still didn't move.

She opened the door and went inside.

Riley gave him a thin-lipped smile and followed.

Dodge walked to the end of the hallway and stared out the window.

With the break in the freeze, blackened snowdrifts edged the parking lot, muddy with thawing rivers of ice. Cars splashed mud, and ice floated in the Knik Arm waterway. The view looked out over Merrill Airfield and the hundred or so parked Beavers, Otters, Cessnas, and Piper Cubs that roamed the skies, then extended past the airfield to Joint Base Elmendorf–Richardson, to the north. Beyond it, the ridge back of the Alaskan range razored across the sun-soaked blue sky, bold and white and impressive. Denali and Huntington, Foraker and Russell, were tucked in there, each glacial runnel and granite ridge imprinted in him like the lines of his palm.

The mountains called to him like an old familiar song, a tune embedded in his bones.

One he was trying to forget.

Though he couldn't see it from here, Sky King Ranch was nestled in the foothills of the range, perched on a lake that hosted cabins and a lodge for the family.

They also ran thirty or so head of cattle and a handful of horses.

Barry Kingston, his father, was one of few remaining born and bred Alaskans in Copper Mountain. And his sons were supposed to carry on the legacy.

Dodge crossed his arms, glued there because, of course, Larke was right.

He *was* afraid. Afraid of the memories that still broke free sometimes. And most of all, afraid of the words that he longed to hear and never would.

He should leave. He'd made himself promises, and he'd already broken the first one by standing in this corridor. Yes, stupid impulses.

"Oh, thank God, Dodge, you're here."

The voice jolted him, made him turn.

Winter Starr. Daughter of the legendary bush pilot Sheldon Starr. Her family ran Starr Air Service, northwest of Copper Mountain. She wore her dark hair in two long braids and had on a pair of boots and a Starr Air sweatshirt. She probably ran her own plane by now.

He had no words when she walked right up to him and pulled him down in a hug. "I'm so sorry about your dad."

She'd beat him out for valedictorian by a half point and that had intrigued, if not irked, him enough to like her. But she'd also been Echo's best friend, so that was as far as his interest went.

"Thanks."

She let him go. "I was coming up to talk to Larke, but I'm so glad you're here. We can divvy up his charters, but I can't do his mail route, Dodge. I just can't."

He raised an eyebrow.

"I've already got the mail run to Paxton, plus every homestead east of the Copper River, and if I add the western mail, that fills me right up."

"You're running the mail?"

"And medical and groceries for most of the east side north of Susitna. Your dad has the western run, over the range, to Nikolai and Stony River, and even out to Russian Mission."

Of course he did. An area that would probably keep him in the air for days.

"He also checks in on the homesteads in the area—he's got a schedule."

"I know it." He'd flown that route more times than he could count.

She cut her voice down. "They're talking pilot error."

"No. Otto Smith said his wing was coming off."

"Ernie Wright just did a hundred-hour inspection on the plane. It was cleared." She sighed. "I don't know how much you know, but your dad has had a few close calls lately. Nearly clipped another plane in the Copper Mountain airfield during taxi, and I heard he spooked a recent group by flying too close to one of Huntington Mountain's spires."

"Aw, that's just Barry Kingston showing off."

"The National Air Transportation Board is coming in to do an investigation, and depending on what they find, he could be shut down. At the very least, he can't fly, not for a while, right?" She gestured to his room.

"Larke is here. She knows the routes—"

"In her condition? I'm surprised that Riley let her get in a plane with me to fly them down."

Condition? So that's what the look between them was about.

Winter's expression portrayed concern. "I get it—high-risk pregnancy and all that, but he's a little overprotective, if you ask me. But that's a SEAL for you." Her voice turned sweet. "Where've you been, anyway? Someone said Air Force."

"Something like that."

"Afghanistan?"

"Sometimes."

"I heard your brothers are big-shot military guys too. Ranger made the SEALs."

Dodge nodded.

"And Colt, some sort of special forces in the Army?"

Delta Force, according to Ranger. Dodge lifted a shoulder.

"All a bunch of overachieving heroes, aren't you?" Her eyes shone, maybe a little of their untried past in them. "Glad you're back."

"I'm not back," he said, the words just slipping out.

Winter frowned.

And what was he going to say? That not only had he vowed to never return to Sky King Ranch but he wasn't keen on getting in the cockpit again either?

He shouldn't be here, for so many reasons. But Winter was the last person who should know that. Mostly because if Winter knew, then her sister Shasta knew . . . and if Shasta knew, well it wouldn't take long for the entire town to buzz with the news.

So he found a benign smile. "Never mind. Good to see you, Winter."

"Your dad keeps that yellow Piper 14 you used to fly tuned up. I saw him out in it a few weeks back. You flew that thing like it was a part of you. Like you had wings."

He'd forgotten that. But yes, she was right. Once upon a time, the sky felt like home. Maybe it would again—he just had to get back on the proverbial horse-slash-cockpit.

Or not.

"Well, like I said, I'm glad you're back." She looked at him, paused. Then, "She will be too."

His smile faded. "I didn't ask."

"Sure you did." She winked and walked away, and his heart slammed like a fist in his chest.

"She will be too."

The door to the room opened and Riley stepped out. "Going for more coffee. Your dad is still sleeping. Larke didn't get much sleep last night."

He didn't move down the hall, however, and again Dodge braced himself.

"Listen," Riley said. "I don't know what went down, and she doesn't talk about it, but she can't stay, Dodge." He took a breath, looked past Dodge to the window, his mouth tightening. "She lost our first baby about six months ago, so this one is higher risk. I can't have her up there, doing . . . well, I'm well aware of the perils of being a bush pilot." He shook his head. "We met the summer of the Copper Mountain fire. The one that took out your grandparents' house. She was a daredevil, even then. I can't—"

Dodge held up his hand. "Stop. I get it."

Riley turned his gaze on him. "Get this, then. If you don't fly, he loses his contracts. And if he loses his contracts—"

"He could lose the ranch. I can do the math, Riley. Once upon a time, I was planning on taking over Sky King Ranch."

Silence fell between them.

"You weren't planning on going home, were you?" Riley asked.

Maybe the guy was an interrogator, but Dodge had no secrets, not really.

The entire town knew why he'd left. He shook his head.

"Why are you in town?" Riley asked.

What could it hurt? "I have a job offer with Air One Rescue flying choppers." He'd been sitting on his answer for a while now, not sure of the wisdom of saying yes to a job that might be doomed, but what else could he do?

His answer seemed made when Moose called him.

"I see. So nearby, but not all the way home." Riley raised an eyebrow.

"You should stop right there, because you don't know anything about it."

"I know that I wish, with everything inside me, that I had a second chance to show my pop that I turned out okay. That I finally became the person he knew I could be."

"My father couldn't care less how I turned out." And that came out exactly as bitter as it felt in his chest.

"He has your picture on his mantel," Riley said.

"He probably has my brothers' pictures up there too."

Riley nodded slowly.

Dodge drew in a breath. Managed not to put his fist in the wall. Instead, he sighed and said, "Okay, here's the bottom line. Nothing has changed since the day I walked into the recruiter's office and enlisted. I'm not back. I'll fly his routes until he can take over, but you tell Larke not to mistake any of this for a happy ending. There's no sunrise of hope here." He glanced out the window at the slush and rivers of melting snow. "This winter isn't over, and everyone should just calm down. We have at least one more deadly blizzard ahead of us."

Riley gave a slow nod. "Okay. So how do you like your coffee?"

Dodge looked at him. Right. So much for promises. "Black and bracing."

Echo picked the wrong day to emerge from hiding.

Not only had the temperatures soared to nearly the forties, turning the snow to mush, the roads to mud, and the rivers dangerous, but this day, of all days, her dreams turned out to mock her.

"Who are you rooting for?"

The question came from Vic, who handed her a mug of hot cocoa and a basket of greasy fries as Echo sat at the bar of the Midnight Sun Saloon, trying to ignore the broadcast of the annual start of the Iditarod, the famous thousand-mile trek on dogsled from Anchorage, or thereabouts, to Nome, Alaska.

Outside, the sun fell along the backside of the day, still three hours from darkness but low enough for shadows to lurk along the main street of Copper Mountain. The heat wave had brought out the locals and other homesteaders, and around her, the saloon was hopping. The Bowie brothers, all four of them, played foosball in the back, and Goodwin Starr was holding an arm-wrestling contest near the front. The booths were filled with gold miners, climbers, and homesteaders, not to mention local mushers, who'd arrived to watch the flat-screen.

She probably should have headed straight home after filling her grocery order and propane tanks, but her father wanted to order parts for his 1978 Ford pickup, so while he talked with Otto at his shop, she'd headed over to the Midnight Saloon.

She hoped that was *all* her father was doing. He'd been dry for nearly sixty days now, so maybe it would take.

It might have been better for both of them if they'd stayed home, but she needed to pick up seeds to start under the grow lights. And besides, they were running out of a few staples—flour and sugar, and she'd indulged in a box of Lucky Charms.

Just because.

But with the racers whooping across the television screen, it just dug a trail through her chest.

Once upon a time . . .

"I don't follow the race," Echo said to Vic's question.

Vic wore a Midnight Sun sweatshirt over her bulky body, her thin blond hair tied back. Echo had once seen Vic leap the bar and break up a massive all-bar fight with a baseball bat and her bare hands. A true Alaskan woman, although they came in all sizes and shapes.

Sometimes she wished she was as tough as Vic. A former cop, Vic had come up from the Lower 48 some thirty years earlier and opened up her tiny bar and grill on the road leading into

Denali State Park, the last outpost of food and drink before hikers, climbers, and all manner of tourists lost themselves in the last frontier.

Vic was hearty, brave, and tough. Most of all, she knew how to survive.

She grabbed a glass and held it under a tap to fill it with a foamy brew. "I remember when you and your dad came in and camped out here nearly every day during the race. You were such a Susan Butcher fan."

"Along with every woman in Alaska," Echo said. "Only woman to win the race four times."

Vic put the glass on a tray. "You even named one of your dogs after hers, right? Granite?"

"Her lead dog. Did you know that when he was born, he was the runt of the litter?"

Vic grinned at her. "Don't follow it, huh?"

"Not anymore." Echo picked up a bottle of ketchup and doused her fries.

"I remember when you and Dodge used to run your dogs up and down Main Street for the Copper Mountain Summer Mush."

And this was why she didn't come to town much. Or talk about mushing or Dodge or frankly any of the Kingston brothers.

"Young and stupid, Vic. Why anyone would run the Iditarod is beyond me—eight to thirty days in the wilderness, with wind chills down to minus forty, freezing off your fingers and toes, trying to keep your dogs alive and away from moose and grizzlies, and most of all, alone that entire time? No, thank you."

Vic added another beer to the tray. "So, I'll just turn up the volume on the TV, then?"

"Gimme the remote. I'll do it."

Vic put the final glass on the tray.

"Need me to bring that out to a table?" Echo asked. "I think your waitress is a little occupied." She glanced over to Shasta Starr, who was collecting money for her brother's arm-wrestling gig.

"Hey, Shasta!" Vic yelled, but it didn't carry over the crowd. Echo got up. "I got this."

"Take it to the guys from Remington Mines over in the booth."

Echo carried the beers over and set the tray down on the table of the modern-day miners. They, too, appeared like they hadn't been out of the wilderness since October, wearing beards, their hair matted, their jackets grimy. At least she'd taken a bath and washed her clothes.

It earned her a couple of suggestions and one actual compliment as she unloaded the beers.

"Struck gold yet, fellas?" she asked as she tucked the tray under her arm.

"There's always gold. It's just how much. You should come out to the mine sometime, let us show you around." This from Jude, the youngest of the Remington brothers, a man in his midtwenties.

"I've panned for enough gold in my time," Echo said, "trust me. My dad has a claim near our homestead. Can I interest you in fries?"

She took their order because, well, why not? Then she headed back to Vic.

On the way over, the door opened, and Otto Smith came in. He still wore his greasy coveralls. "Vic. We have trouble. Call Hank and get him over here."

Hank Billings worked for the Alaska Department of Fish and Game, and that had Echo putting down the tray and following Otto outside, her heart thumping.

Because it wasn't only the spring thaw and the day of the Iditarod, but big-game hunters were arriving in swarms to hunt the hungry grizzlies and black bears who would soon start emerging from hibernation.

Please, Dad, don't start a fight—

She pushed her way out of the saloon, into the gravel parking lot. A small crowd had gathered around an open bed pickup truck that contained—her breath sucked in at the sight—the carcass of a full-grown grizzly. The odor of death soured the air, the bear's fur matted and grimy. It had been field dressed—its skull and claws removed from the rest of the meat. So much power destroyed. Skinned, declawed, beheaded, and harvested.

Echo might be ill.

A hunter stood nearby, fielding questions.

A tourist, evidenced by his fancy hunting gear—bright orange shell over a green printed down vest, waterproof pants, and tall boot sheaths. He posed as a friend took shots of him with the kill.

Echo pushed through the crowd to the animal. She didn't see a locking tag, but as she drew near, she spotted a tracking tag on its ear, and, oh no, a tuft of white between its ears.

And worse, it was a female.

She blew out a breath. She needed to get her dad out of here before he saw this.

"You know it's illegal to kill a sow, right?"

Too late.

The hunter turned to the voice, and Echo groaned as her father joined the crowd.

He'd been drinking. She knew him well enough to recognize the sharp, unforgiving tone. Charlie Yazzie was a gentle man, a kind man, a wise man.

A man who lived on his daily dose of pain meds. And when that mixed with some of Otto's moonshine, or even a lonely beer—

She needed to get him home, pronto.

The fading light only added to his look of menace, highlighting the thick scar that ran up one side of his face, into his wool cap, and through his scalp. He wore a dark, gray-streaked beard—had even before the mauling, although now it served to cover up the scars on his face—and a fraying green military jacket and a pair of work boots. He stood with his hands in his pockets, without even a hint of weakness in his bearing.

Her dad might be even more Alaskan than Vic in his toughness, his ability to buck up, survive, and most of all . . . defend what he loved.

He stepped right up to the hunter. "Where are the cubs?"

"She didn't have any cubs with her," Trophy Hunter said.

"You don't know that. She might have hidden them, protected them."

His raised voice shut down the crowd, and a few moved over to watch the altercation. The sun had tucked behind the mountains, and a chill brushed through Echo.

She should probably get a closer look, see if the bear wore a collar.

"Do you have a harvest ticket for this animal?" her dad asked, and although his voice sounded calm, her insides buzzed.

Oh, buddy. He'd better have a yes to that question.

"Of course I do. It's with my guide."

"Who's your guide?" her dad snapped.

Echo wanted to wince when the man named him. "Ray Kelly."

"Dad—" She headed toward him.

But her father's eyes had already hardened. "Idaho."

She reached him, put her hand on his arm. "Let's go." The last thing she needed was for her dad to end up in the local cooler for breaking his restraining order by going after the guide from the Lower 48.

"He doesn't even have a guiding license," her dad said, shaking her off.

"We're leaving now, Dad."

His mouth pinched into a tight line of disagreement. Then he shook his head and stalked over to the bear.

She waited while he looked at the tag, at the carcass, then followed him. "It's not Elsa," she said.

"No. It's one of her cubs." He pressed his hand to the white between the ears.

"Let's go." She put her hand on his arm again, and this time he let her walk him away.

For a moment.

Then he turned and headed back to the hunter.

Someone screamed when the man hit the dirt, bleeding from the mouth.

"Dad!" Ah, shoot. She hoped Vic's extra room wasn't rented.

Her father knelt on the man's chest, his hand at his throat, his fist cocked.

"Charlie!" The voice boomed out over the crowd, and Echo wanted to weep when Hank Billings strode up. He wore his Fish and Game jacket, jeans, and Sorels. "Back off."

Her father didn't move. "He's got a grizzly sow in that truck."

"She attacked us. It was a defensive kill!" Trophy had his hands around her dad's wrist, trying to pry his grip from his neck. Blood still dribbled from his mouth.

Echo leaped forward and grabbed her dad's other wrist. "Let Hank deal with it."

"Where is Idaho?" her dad asked.

"Ray called it in, Charlie," Hank said. "Asked me to seal the kill."

Her father looked up, stared at Hank. "No."

"A defensive kill is not illegal—"

"It is when the mother is just trying to defend her cubs." Echo couldn't believe the words issued from her mouth. Even her dad looked at her, something of pride in his eyes.

And maybe that's why he let go of the hunter and got up. The man scooted away from her dad.

She grabbed his arm and managed to turn him toward their truck.

And wouldn't you know it, right then—like a spark to a fire—Ray Kelly appeared. He wore a grimy down jacket, a wool hat, and a beard, like he belonged in the bush.

"Hey, Adams," Ray said, smirking. Her dad bristled.

Adams, as in Grizzly Adams from the old television show from the '80s. Apparently the main character had a pet bear.

So what? Bears had been known to be tamed from the days of the Wild West shows. It happened. Get over it.

Besides, she knew for a fact that Ray was from Idaho. Or had been. He'd arrived, a cheechako, three years ago. She couldn't prove it, but she'd bet he hadn't survived one full winter here, just south of Denali State Park, in the wilds north of Anchorage.

Which meant that any Alaskan hunting guide license he possessed was a fake. But she hadn't dug, and her dad couldn't prove his words. She needed to get him away before things really got ugly.

"Get in the truck, Charlie," Hank said.

"She might have cubs, Hank," her dad said, but he kept walking toward the truck. "It's too early for them to leave their mother."

He climbed in and closed the door.

She put her hand on the driver's door handle.

Aw, shoot. Her dad was right. She walked over to Hank, who was now examining the carcass while Ray-slash-Idaho told him where they'd bagged it. He claimed they'd spotted the sow in 16a, a section a hundred or so miles west, very near the border of Peters Creek. "We were hunting moose, and the bear just came out of nowhere—"

Idaho pointedly cut off when Echo stepped up to Hank. "Listen. It's one of Elsa's cubs. Not a yearling but maybe three years old. She's been tagged, so we can track her movements and get a fix on where she's been and try to lock down what happened. She doesn't look like she's given birth—her teats aren't swollen. But, if you want to take a look, we can return to the place of the kill—her cubs, if any, would probably be nearby."

Hank pulled her aside. "If they're still alive. Cubs that young would be easy prey. That's wolf country."

She glanced at her father, who was staring hard at her from inside the truck. She'd give him about ten seconds before he got out and tapped back in.

"If I need a guide, you're my first call, Echo." Hank nodded at her dad. "By the way, I'll smooth things over with the hunter, but get him home before things get out of hand and we have to call Deke."

"On my way." The last thing she needed was Sheriff Deacon Starr showing up to haul her dad into lockup.

She climbed into the truck and looked at her dad as she fired up the engine. "How many shots did it take for you and Otto to figure out that part you needed?"

He didn't look at her as they pulled out. "She looked like Elsa."

"But she wasn't. You gotta bring it down to DEFCON 3, Dad."

"We already lost George."

"We don't know that. His collar just went off the radar."

He said nothing as she headed south, took the bridge over the river, then drove back north to their homestead in the woods. By the time they arrived it would be nearly dark, and she'd have to haul the propane tanks in alone, feed her dogs, light the stove, and start dinner.

Her dad let out a snore.

Nice.

The stars came out slowly, arching over the nightscape, the moon an eye, tracking her as she finally turned off the main road and headed along the snow-packed route toward the homestead, a half mile deeper into the woods. She followed the narrow, rutted road until it finally led to the open space of their settlement. The wood cabin had long ago turned into an impressive lodge with two stories, a wraparound porch, a balcony that overlooked the river in the back, and a number of outbuildings. But only because her father couldn't leave well enough alone. He was a jack-of-all-trades when he wasn't under the sauce, but it was his injury that led him to drink, so she gave him grace.

After all, they had only each other now.

Their subsistence footprint had also grown in the years after her mother left. They'd added a permanent greenhouse with hot lights for a longer growing season. A chicken coop housed nearly twenty hens, with chicken wire protecting the large roaming area. She made good egg money at the farmers market during the summer.

Her father had also enlarged the sawmill shed and took in business on the side, cutting wood for a few of the locals. It supplemented his honey business and, of course, paid for the motley crew of rescued and rehabilitated animals he fostered for Alaska Wildlife Rescue. A wolf pup, separated from his pack and caught in a trap, a bald eagle with an injured wing, a coyote who'd been shot, three baby red fox pups, and a pair of black bear cubs. The foster animal pens lay beyond the barn, out of the reach of her sled dogs, who were sleeping in furry mounds in another large pen.

In the barn were their snowmobiles, an ATV, a small Alumacraft fishing boat, and, of course, her sleds.

"I need to check on Bo and Luke," her dad said, rousing as she parked. He had the door open before she'd turned off the truck, heading out to the large bear pen that still bore the sign HOME OF ELSA AND GEORGE.

She watched him as he walked up to the pen. The bear cubs had been deep in hibernation for the past four months, but recently, she'd seen them emerge, and her father had started putting out frozen salmon chunks.

Now it looked like they were back inside the wooden den he had built long ago.

She got out, and her breath formed in the air, a lonely wisp in the night.

Granite came off the porch, looking more wolf than Siberian husky, with his gray-black face, his ruff of white over his shoulders, the perked black ears. She crouched, rubbing him hard around the ears. He leaned into her hand.

Her other sled dogs whined and barked, penned in the massive dog run that also contained their straw-bedded shelters. Granite was the only one she trusted to stick around.

Maybe she was jaded, but a girl with her history had a right to be. Sooner or later, the ones you love leave. Which meant that maybe they never loved you at all.

Her eyes had adjusted to the darkness by the time she lugged the propane tanks to the porch. Granite stayed at her heels as she ferried in the groceries, heated water, then fed her dogs.

She had come inside and pulled off her boots and jacket and left them in the arctic entry by the time her dad finally came in.

He too shucked off his outerwear, then he came into the kitchen, leaned against the doorframe. "Sorry for the commotion in town."

"It's okay. I'll make dinner."

"There are some moose steaks left in the freezer out back."

"Yum." She thought of her unfinished fries. Oh, she liked moose. She was just grumpy.

Her dad started a fire in the stone hearth while she went out to the back pantry and opened the freezer. She pulled out a couple steaks, but it would be hours before they thawed, so she set them in the refrigerator for tomorrow and retrieved a bowl of yesterday's chicken soup.

She put it on the stove to warm, then she unwrapped the homemade bread and sliced it. She found the last of the honey and set it all on the table. Then she put a kettle on to boil and sat at the kitchen table.

For a so-called homestead, the place still bore the impeccable taste of her mother. Her father had added the second story as an anniversary gift, using up all the sunlight one summer to finish it.

Then he'd given her the new kitchen, with a butcher block island, custom-made pine cabinets, hardwood flooring, and furniture she'd had shipped up from Anchorage.

Offerings intended, maybe, to woo her into staying.

It hadn't worked. Effie Yazzie had left him nearly twenty years ago, and yet her *Southern Cooking* magazines still filled the bookshelf, a few of them dog-eared. And pictures of their family still sat on the mantel. Her dad, Effie, and Echo bundled up to watch their first Iditarod, the one by the river with her holding a giant salmon, and one with Echo holding Granite as a puppy. But, of course, that one was taken after her mother had left.

Her own pictures also hung on the walls, photographs in unnecessary frames, but what could she do? Her dad insisted.

And she'd do anything for her father.

The soup was boiling, so she got up and ladled it into bowls.

Her dad sat and she set a bowl in front of him. "I know I shouldn't let him get under my skin."

"Idaho is a criminal, there's no doubt. And I am just as angry as you are. But short of following him into the bush and catching him red-handed, I'm not sure what you can do." She gave him a look. "Especially since you're supposed to be five hundred feet away from him."

He made a face.

"Good thing Hank is on our side," she said.

"I hate cheechakos," he said as he dug into the soup. "Especially the ones who act like they belong here."

She said nothing, because he had his reasons.

Her kettle whistled and she got up, turned off the heat. Pulled down a cup and a box of tea and added a bag of Earl Grey to the cup. Poured in the water.

Then she set it in front of her father.

He grabbed her wrist as she turned away. "Echo. I'm sorry."

She put her hand over his. "I know, Dad. I know."

"You should have left a long time ago."

"Where am I going to go? I belong here."

He picked up her hand and kissed it. "You are more of this place than I am."

She gave his hand a squeeze, and he let her go.

Fixing another cup of tea, she took it out to the back porch, the one overlooking the river, and stood, a sweater wrapped around her, her fingers absently playing with the heart charm on her gold necklace. She stared at the darkness, at the great wash of starlight, clear and bright and gleaming on the dark, jagged horizon.

Undulating ribbons of green and pink folded over each other from the light refracting off the polar ice caps, and as she watched them, she wondered if the mushers had reached the first checkpoint on their journey into the wild frontier.

And what dangers lay beyond, in the darkness.

TWO

I think you're all set." Larke came in from the arctic entry of the lodge at Sky King Ranch where they kept the deep well freezer. She wore a down vest over flannel leggings and wool socks, her hair in a braid. To Dodge's mind, she looked all of eighteen and ready to leave him for the military.

He didn't feel any less abandoned today, really.

Maybe she could read his mind because she came over to where Dodge sat on a stool at the long kitchen bar and stepped right in to give him a hug. She had that way about her—a kindness that probably came from his mother. After all, she had known her the best.

He had a sort of foggy memory of Caroline—or Cee, as his dad called her—Kingston that Dodge tried to associate with the woman caught in photographs on the mantel of the great stone fireplace. In truth, he possessed just smells, impressions, maybe the faintest hint of a voice, but he wasn't sure those didn't belong to Larke, too, so he tightened his grip around her. "Thanks, Sis."

She let him go and met his eyes, her hands on his shoulders. "You'll be fine, both of you. I packed enough casseroles in the freezer to last you through next winter. And there's potatoes in the bin, and—"

"We'll be fine," he said. He glanced at Riley, now coming down the stairs, hauling a green duffel bag over his shoulder. He wore a pair of black canvas pants, a black thermal shirt, and with his sunglasses sitting backward on his head, he reminded Dodge of the last time he'd seen Ranger, at the Bagram Air Base in Afghanistan.

"All set?" Riley said as he set the bag by the door.

"One more look-see on Dad, and we'll be ready." Larke headed upstairs to her father's bedroom, where he'd been recuperating for the last few days.

Riley looked at Dodge, and a beat passed, then he said, "I'll just load our gear." He headed toward the back door.

"Need any help?"

"I got it," Riley said and offered a smile. Dodge liked Riley—especially how Riley loved his sister.

She deserved a guy like him after all she'd been through. He hadn't known the whole of her time in Afghanistan as a medic, hadn't known the losses she'd endured until she'd sat in one of the leather chairs in front of the fire and spooled out her story a couple nights ago.

"Why didn't you tell me?" he'd said.

"I don't know. I just wanted to put it behind me. Come home, fly, fix up Grandma's cabin. But I was stuck, really, until Riley showed up."

She'd also told him about the summer the sky burned across Alaska, how Riley and his smoke jumping team showed up to help fight the fire that nearly consumed the ranch.

Riley had saved Larke's life.

Yeah, Dodge liked him.

Of course, Larke had turned into the spitting image of their mother, with her blond hair, her adventurous spirit, her courage to face her fears. And she was courageous enough to face them again, if she had to, with Riley.

It evoked her words from over a week ago. *"What are you afraid of, Dodge?"*

Maybe she was right—he *had* been afraid. Mostly that his father wouldn't have wanted to see him.

Dodge still struggled to reconcile the look of surprise, the smile his father had given him when he'd woken in the hospital, with the father who had betrayed him ten years ago.

Okay, everybody calm down. His father had been heavily sedated, maybe a little loopy from the pain meds.

He was probably just relieved that the ranch wasn't going to fall apart.

As Dodge waited for Larke, he got up and walked over to the big bank of windows that lined the back of the house.

This view. He never tired of it, the postcard visage embedded in his mind. Even when he flew over the barren brown Kuhi Baba range in Afghanistan, Dodge had seen in his mind's eye the majestic granite spine of the Alaska Range. From here, with the sky clear, the massive hulk of Denali framed the horizon, whitened peaks jutting ruthlessly through the finest wisp of brave clouds, the deadly blue-black granite valleys. At the foot of it all crouched the darkened foothills, and through them wove the fingers of the hundreds of glacial tributaries, now frozen, but in a month or so, lethal as the rivers broke and flushed out the remains of winter. Between the lodge and the park, a vista opened, once upon a time a lush array of black spruce and deep green pine. Now, the snow blanketed the land, newly sprinkled with saplings, like tiny moles peeking through the white.

"I miss it when I'm not here. Florida is warm, but it has a sort of earthy, almost mossy smell that feels primordial. Here, you always smell the mountains, the vast magnificence of the land." Larke had come down the stairs, a bag over her shoulder. "Thanks for staying. You're doing the right thing."

He turned. "Take care of that baby."

She smiled, the finest shadow in her eyes. "Don't let him do too much, Dodge. He's so stubborn."

He lifted a shoulder. "So am I."

"I'm counting on it."

Riley came back inside. "I'll be glad to get out of this cold."

"Wimp. It's nearly in the teens outside." Larke laughed and headed for the door.

Riley had the truck warmed up, and Dodge climbed into the driver's seat of the extended cab. He'd spent the four days before Larke and Riley arrived from Anchorage with their father checking over the vehicles.

He'd also done a thorough check on his Piper PA-14, and indeed, his father had taken care of it. Dodge had even started it up and listened to the prop hum.

He hadn't taken her up, but he counted it as progress.

He'd also given the chopper a once-over. Larke had mentioned it recently passed a hundred-hour inspection.

Dodge had spent the rest of the time chopping a slew of wood and stocking both the house and one of the cabins by the frozen lake. Just in case he had to take refuge.

It was better than fleeing the state. Again.

Dodge, Riley, and Larke drove in silence the forty-five minutes to town, mostly along snow-packed roads, until they crossed the Copper Mountain Bridge and headed northeast to the depot.

He hadn't been to town yet and planned to veer a wide berth.

The last thing he wanted was to run into— Nope. Not even going to think about it. Fate just might read his mind and sabotage him.

"I could have flown you to Anchorage," he said, the words twisting in his gut. But it might have been good for him.

"We want to take the train. The Aurora Winter Train is so romantic," Larke said.

Dodge glanced in the rearview mirror in time to see Riley roll his eyes, but he wore a grin.

As they headed north, Dodge noticed a few changes—a slew of new cabins along the highway, a gas station, a couple small neighborhoods. "I feel like I'm in a suburb of Anchorage."

Larke laughed. "We even have a pizza parlor now. Levi Starr runs it."

"You're kidding me. When did he come back to town?"

"About a year before I left. He got tired of waiting for his big break, hung up his skates, came home, and started tossing pizza. It's good too. And Goodwin runs the gear rental in town—bikes and kayaks and snowshoes, cross-country skis—"

"I thought the Starrs would all be pilots, like their dad. I saw Winter in Anchorage."

"Just Winter, although I think Shasta still flies too. I saw her waiting tables at the Midnight Sun a couple weeks ago."

He passed the Laughing Moose B&B and the small float plane operation near Fish Lake, and then drove by a church, parking lot crowded for the Sunday afternoon service. The area became more populated, plowed roads branching off into neighborhoods. The forest fought back with the heavy cover of spruce and pine, but dusted in white, it seemed more of a wonderland than menace.

He'd give them another three hours of daylight, given the glint of the sun against the mountains to the north.

He passed the Copper Mountain Lodge on the left and noticed new cabins along the Copper River. "The Bowie brothers seem to have turned their luck around."

"Yeah. Rough to lose both their parents at the same time. But Hudson is in charge now, and he seems to have a business mind. He and Malachi opened an outfitter's store and run trips out to Remington Mines in the summer."

"You do a pretty good job of keeping up."

She looked at him. "Don't tell me you don't have a subscription to the *Copper Mountain Good News*."

He said nothing.

"Besides, Winter tells me everything. She has her own YouTube channel too."

Of course she did.

He didn't ask about anyone else. Just kept his mouth shut. And Larke didn't offer. Until, "Hey. You'll be in town for the Rowdy." She looked at him, grinning.

"Nope."

"Dodge, c'mon. You were amazing—"

"Nope."

"What's the Rowdy?" Riley asked as Dodge took the spur to the train depot.

She turned in her seat to face the back. "It's our annual post-Iditarod party. It used to be called the Cabin Fever Festival, but somewhere along the way it just turned into the Rowdy."

"Because . . . ?"

"It gets pretty rowdy," Dodge said, rolling his eyes.

"It's fun," Larke added. "There's a big flapjack feed at the community church and a snow sculpture contest and a three-dog sled race and a breakup dance."

"What's a breakup dance?"

"No one can bring a date. You have to come stag. Even if you're dating someone. That gives everyone a chance to dance."

Dodge shook his head. "It's a way to make the guys bathe and shave."

Larke laughed. "Six months of winter and it's about time. But Dodge is all talk—he doesn't dance."

"Not at all?" Riley said.

"I have two left feet, and I'm not about to make a fool of myself out there."

Larke turned back to the front and smiled at her brother. "Dodge has other skills—he was one of the key defensemen on our high school state championship hockey team three years running. The Rowdy has a big outdoor hockey tournament between the townies and the bush folks. Dodge was always the star of the bush team."

"Larke." He glanced at her.

Larke continued, clearly ignoring his warning look, "He's

amazing. When he was sixteen, he was playing in state tournaments. Dad wanted him to play for a traveling team, but Dodge didn't want to leave home."

Just another attempt by his father to get rid of him.

"I had other plans," he said, and then wished he hadn't let that escape.

Larke put a hand on his knee. "Dodge was always a pilot, in his heart. He wanted to fly. And playing hockey cut into his time in the sky." She bore warmth and maybe a little pride in her eyes when he glanced at her. "And then he went off and became a war hero."

His chest tightened, and he just grunted as he pulled into the depot. No need to start a fight right before she left.

The parking lot of the log-sided depot had been cleared, the pavement glistening with salt, and he pulled into a space. The train, with its festive orange cars, sat at the tracks, warming up.

Dodge got out and helped Riley pull their bags from the bed of the truck, then carried them to the platform, where a few tourists dressed in parkas, Uggs, and fancy fur hats stood taking pictures of the faraway mountains.

He set the bags down, and Larke pulled him into a goodbye hug. "I love you, little brother," she said in his ear. "You're right back where you're supposed to be. You'll see."

He kissed her cheek and let her go, managed a smile.

Riley picked up a bag and loaded it on the train, leaving it in the vestibule near the door. Then he came back. Stuck out his hand. Dodge met it, and Riley held it a little longer than necessary. "Don't get in your own way."

Dodge frowned. "Take care of my sister."

"Tier one priority," Riley said and slapped him on the back. Then he picked up Larke's bag.

Dodge was turning away when—

"Dodge! Wait." Larke ran back to him. "I forgot. Dad needs

a refill of his pain meds. Can you pick these up in town? I already called it in."

She shoved an empty bottle in his hand.

Perfect. "Sure."

He waited in the truck until the train pulled out, the orange container sitting like a grenade on the seat beside him.

Fine. Whatever. In and out, no problem.

He trekked back to the main road and drove the two miles to Main Street Copper Mountain.

At first glance, it had hardly changed. The road was still mostly packed earth, with a thin layer of pavement scraped smooth and salted. Gray, grimy snowbanks lined the sides of the road. At the juncture of Main Street and Seward's Way, the words WELCOME TO YOUR LAST STOP were scribbled on a piece of wood stuck in a pile of rocks. Below it, another sign, similarly scribbled, read JUST KIDDING. WELCOME TO COPPER MOUNTAIN.

He always thought it was funny. Now he found it apt.

He'd ended up back at the end of the world.

From there, his town had been given a makeover. He took a left on Main and drove past the Tenderfoot Coffee and Bakery, the former small cabin transformed into a timber-framed building with a front porch and a drive-through.

Next to that, the old Duncan log cabin had been purchased and shined up, painted white, and turned into the visitors center. He sort of missed Old Gordy Duncan sitting on his front porch, smoking a pipe, yelling at the tourists. A giant copper moose stood in the yard of the center, and he supposed that was better than the real thing.

Across the street, the *Copper Mountain Good News* biweekly paper still shared a space with the radio station, but an upstairs had been built on to the former false-front building, with the name GOOD NEWS MASSAGE added to the listing by the front door.

Probably not a bad way to get the local scoop for the paper.

The only building that looked familiar, really, was the Midnight Sun Saloon, set back in a gravel parking lot. A timber-framed building with a red roof, it still listed their barbecue special over the front door. He hoped Sergeant Vic—the name he and Mal used to call her—still ran the place.

Dodge passed the Blue Moose gift shop, a former blue house-slash-storefront for Miss Henry, the psychic, then Starlight Pizza on the left. He found a smile. Levi's place.

He pulled into the lot between the Lone Wolf Bar—yet another log cabin—and Gigi's Grocery, a former two-story boarding-house that had been gutted and turned into the local grocery and pharmacy. Getting out, Dodge glanced at the sky. The sun had taken a dive and was turning the mountainscape a deep, glorious orange.

He pulled his cap down and headed inside, straight to the back where glass partitioned off what had been the house's back bedroom. He didn't recognize the person at the counter as he handed over the pill bottle.

"Right. Barry Kingston." After a moment, the pharmacist handed him the bag.

More luck—he also didn't recognize the youngster at the register. The kid, maybe sixteen, with the name Carter on his badge, checked him out, and Dodge grabbed the bag and headed to the truck.

"Are you kidding me?" The voice came from across the street, and he looked over his shoulder, startled.

Aw. But— "Mal?"

"Dodge? Seriously?" Malachi Bowie was walking out of Bowie Mountain Gear, a newer timber-framed building, wearing jeans, hiking boots, a black parka, and no hat, his blond hair tied back in a knot. The guy still swaggered as if he owned the world.

Or at least all the local female hearts.

"I can't believe it." He slapped his hand into Dodge's and

pulled him against him, giving his back a pound. Let him go. "What is going on, Forty-Four? Ten years ago, you practically vanish off the face of the earth, and now, poof, you're back?"

"It wasn't quite like that."

But Mal was grinning, and shoot, there was something infectious about Mal and the way he called Dodge by his old jersey number. It could make a guy remember the good times. "But yeah, I'm back. You guys still running the guiding service?"

"Yep, although we opened the outfitter's shop a few years ago, and it's almost doubled our sales. We're running mostly fishing trips. Not much going on right now. A few moose hunts, but we're pretty dry. Idaho has all the work."

"Who?"

"Ray Kelly. He's from Idaho, has his residency here, has sort of taken over the guiding work—we're not sure how, but a few of the guys think he's doing double tagging."

Double tagging—when a guide used their own catch permit to help a client bag more kills than allowed.

"Brought in a grizzly last weekend—a sow—and Charlie Yazzie went off on him. Said he'd killed one of Elsa's cubs, and it got dicey."

Elsa. Echo's bear. Dodge had been in town less than ten minutes and already she'd walked into the conversation. Well, what did he expect? "That's terrible. *Was* it one of Elsa's cubs?"

"Dunno yet. Hank took DNA samples to make sure, but you know how Charlie is."

Yes, he did. Which was why, maybe, Dodge had made such a colossal, impulsive mistake so many years ago.

He feared Charlie's hold on Echo.

But really, Dodge had only himself to blame for the fiasco that had followed.

"So, you back for good? Taking over Sky King Ranch? Oh, how's your dad, by the way? I heard about the accident."

"Getting better. Sleeping a lot. I just dropped Larke and her husband off at the train. I'm taking over starting tomorrow. Doing his homestead route."

A truck rolled down the street behind Mal and turned into the lot for the Alaska Fish and Game office.

"So that's a yes," Mal said. "Good. We need you for the annual hockey tourney. I'll tell the guys you're back."

He wasn't—

And that's when the driver of the truck got out of the cab. A woman. Trim but fit, she wore a pair of black leggings, tall, laced mukluks, and a down jacket. And even from here, he could make out her profile—that pretty nose, the angled jaw that could clench hard with a stubborn streak to rival his own. And long, dark, golden hair that turned almost bronze in the setting sun.

She glanced his direction but didn't seem to notice him, then headed toward the ranger station.

"Dodge?"

He took a breath, looked back at Mal, who turned around to see what had caught his attention.

Mal turned back. "So—"

"I don't want to talk about it."

A stiff wind shuffled down the street, wrapping around him.

"Fine. But practices are Monday and Wednesday afternoons, at the rink. Mostly it's us slapping around the puck and then going out for pizza over at the Starlight."

"I'll see. I gotta stick around the house, make sure my dad is okay."

"If I know your dad, he'll be up making you dinner when you get back, telling one of his crazy bush pilot stories."

Dodge gave him a courtesy laugh, a fist around his heart.

Yes, that had been the dad he'd known.

Maybe that's why the betrayal hurt so much.

"Tomorrow. Or Wednesday." Mal backed away. "And she's still single, by the way."

"I didn't ask."

Mal grinned.

Oh, this stupid town.

Dodge got in his truck and headed home with the setting sun.

"Echo, are you okay?"

Echo turned away from the window of the Fish and Game office, watching as Malachi Bowie walked over to the Midnight Sun Saloon.

That was weird.

She looked up to where Hank stood holding the report he'd printed on the DNA findings of the bear Idaho's hunter had shot a few days ago. "Yes. I'm fine."

"Did you hear anything I just said?"

She blinked at him.

Hank put the report down. Looked past her to the empty street. "What, is there a moose on Main Street again?"

She laughed. "No. Yes. Something like that." She reached out for the report. "I just thought I saw a ghost."

He raised an eyebrow, and she shook her head. "Okay, not a ghost, just a man who looked very much like someone I used to know. But I think he was just a tourist asking for directions or something. Anyway, he's gone now." She directed her attention to the report. "What's going on?"

And again, Hank explained what the report meant. *But what if it was Dodge?* He'd looked like Dodge, with that dark, almost black hair, that solid build, except bigger, maybe. But wouldn't Dodge have filled out? And he had shorter hair, but that's how they wore it in the military, right? And he'd stood like Dodge, confidence in his bearing, almost as if daring the world to push him over. But Dodge hadn't set foot in Copper Mountain for nearly a decade and—

"So, what do you think we should do about it?"

Aw. She looked up again. Made a face.

Hank folded his arms and leaned back against the counter that cordoned off the staff areas. "Okay, who is this guy?"

"What guy?"

"The ghost."

"Oh." She frowned, not sure where to start.

"It's okay if you don't want to tell me."

She looked up. Hank was a lean, handsome man in his early forties, with dark hair and kind brown eyes. He'd moved from the Lower 48 five years ago with his wife, Sarah, and their eight-year-old daughter. She considered him a friend, but not the kind she'd tell, well, the story of her stupidest moment. "It's just, um, a . . . guy."

"I see. Not any guy. *The* guy."

Right. "It's in the past. Bygones. I think that he's probably forgotten about me, and I need to do the same. *Have*—have done the same."

"Except for the ghost."

"Yeah. So, what's the deal with the bear?"

"She *had* given birth."

Echo stilled. "What?"

"But her milk had dried up, so we're not sure if the cub is dead or if she stopped nursing prematurely. It's possible that's why she was out of her den early, looking for food."

"If she wasn't shot in her den."

He lifted a shoulder. "There's no way to prove it. Not unless you have a camera on the den."

"We'd have to look at the footage, and these cameras don't send back a feed—we have to get the recording manually, but . . ." She handed Hank the report. "My dad is driving me crazy. You know he tracks Elsa and her cubs every year. A few of her cubs are tagged, but mostly it's about Elsa. According to the telemetry, she's not moving. I think she's still denning—it's too early for a mama to be out of her den, but my dad thinks it's because she's already been murdered, and her collar removed. He wants to go out and check, but—"

"I understand. He gets too close to a mama bear this early, and if she is awake and nursing, it could be very dangerous."

"He says that if *this* bear was out—like Idaho said she was— then Elsa should be out too. I disagree. I know we've had a warm spell for a week or so, but it shouldn't be enough to trigger a mama bear coming out of hibernation."

"Which means, you think this bear was killed in her den."

"And her cub left to die."

"Those are some pretty serious poaching allegations."

"But I can't prove it." She sighed. "I'd like to get a look at the camera in that area, however. I might be able to catch our dead bear out roaming before she was shot. If not, it's not proof that she was in her den, or of the poaching, but it might help us figure out if Elsa is hibernating or not."

"That's a good idea." The words came not from Hank but Peyton Samson, who came out of the back offices. "I heard you talking about the cameras, and I'd like to check on them too." Peyton wore a black flannel jacket with her Alaska Fish and Game logo on it, her dark hair back in a tight ponytail. Half Native American, half Black, she just might be the most beautiful woman Echo had ever met. And she had the degree Echo had once longed for—a master's in wildlife biology. Even if she had moved away for the better part of six years to study in Seattle, Echo still considered Peyton one of her close friends.

Peyton's three-year grant to study the denning habits of wolves had sent her out into the bush with Echo as her guide.

"I'd like to check on the pack," she said. "Sheila has probably delivered by now. I'd like to see how the betas are faring. I wonder if Neo has tried to come back."

Neo was the loner they'd tracked for miles on the telemetry monitor the first year they'd set up the cameras. A rangy male wolf with a long silvery mane, he was older and tried to mate with Sheila.

Hugh, the alpha, had run him off.

"He's too afraid of Hugh to mess with Sheila," Echo said.

And with that, Dodge again stepped into her brain to haunt her. Sort of like what happened between him and Colt.

Because of her.

Unfortunately, she'd also lost Dodge.

"There's a storm front headed this way in a couple days," Hank said. "Maybe you should wait."

"We'll be fine," Echo said. "We'll head over to Ranger cabin 37 and stick around there if it gets bad. And we'll take a long-range sat radio."

"And register our route," Peyton added. "C'mon, you know Echo is the best guide in the area. I'd pick her over the Bowie brothers any day."

"Not if you want to catch decent salmon," Echo said. "But if you want to grab a picture of a bald eagle or a herd of caribou or a nesting red fox, I'm your girl."

"Your photos are amazing. Are you going to enter them in the Rowdy photo contest this year?"

Oh, that's right. Along with the breakup dance, the festival was just a few weeks away.

"Maybe. I never know what to enter."

"I hear the chamber is bringing in a country headliner this year. Some all-girl band from Minnesota—the Yankee Belles," Peyton said.

"Oh, the guys will dig that. New blood for the breakup dance." Echo walked over to the window again and looked out. The sun hung low, stretching long fingers across the muddy road.

"Such a stupid tradition. Why would you break up with someone for one night just so you could dance with someone else? I wouldn't go to a dance unless I could dance with the guy I wanted to be with."

Peyton was looking at her.

"What?"

"You haven't ever been to the breakup dance, that I can remember."

Because the person she'd wanted to dance with hated dancing. "Yeah, well, I don't like to dance."

"Whatever, Miss My-*Step-Up*-DVD-Is-Worn-Out. I'll bet you still have Channing Tatum posters on your wall."

"Not even close. I'm nearly twenty-nine. I took them down a year ago." She grinned at Peyton.

"Fine. Just promise to go to the hockey game with me."

"Now who is pining?" Peyton had loved Nash Remington from afar for years. She never missed the annual pickup hockey tourney.

Echo couldn't bring herself to go the first few years after Dodge left, his absence like a tumor inside her. But after Peyton returned . . . "Sure."

She walked over to check out a photo on the wall, an amazing shot of a grizzly with a salmon caught in her mouth, two cubs standing behind her in the water.

She'd shot it with her old Canon 5D digital SLR, a shot that took her all afternoon to get.

Well, she'd been mostly mesmerized by watching Elsa, three years out of captivity, adapting so well to motherhood.

She was magnificent—silver-tipped hair along her back, a tuft of white between her ears, and her paw stretched out, as if to catch the fish. Powerful, protective—exactly the way she was created to be.

A fostering success story. At least *something* had gone right after that terrible accident.

"That's an amazing shot," Hank said. "You sure you don't want to go pro?"

"I like my life." Echo looked at Peyton. "We'll leave at first light tomorrow. Meet me at my place."

"I'll be there."

She headed back out to her truck. The sun had fallen halfway behind the mountains, turning the valley to shadow and the surrounding mountains—Foraker, Huntington, Russell—an eerie salmon color.

She made her way down Main Street, then toward Copper Highway, passing Mulligan's Hardware, the Roughneck Roadhouse near the river, and finally the Copper Mountain schools. All three—elementary, middle, and high school—in one building.

Beyond that sat the public rink, edged in a wooden border. At this late hour, a handful of kids slapped a puck around, a pickup game with no pads. Just kids in parkas jostling each other on the ice. Above the rink, a board bore the stats of the Copper Mountain Grizzlies' history. They'd been an all-state team every year Dodge—and Ranger and Colt—had played.

Echo had spent hours warming the bleachers.

In her mind's eye, she could see Dodge dressed in his jersey—number forty-four—intercepting a puck, or even a player, slamming into the boards, recovering, finding the puck, shooting it down to the other end of the ice.

Saving the day.

The hero he was.

Yeah, ghosts.

But what if it *had* been Dodge in the street? Her breath caught, snagged on the old shards of her broken heart. After ten years, surely he would have forgiven her.

They'd been children, really. Okay, old enough to know better.

Oh, she'd been such a fool.

Sometimes she could still see his face, bloodied, some tears, maybe, in his fury.

So shattered.

Maybe forgiveness was out of reach. And really, maybe it didn't matter. They'd both moved on.

Okay, *one* of them had moved on. She'd just dug into a life that made her feel safe.

She shook the most brutal memories away, leaving only the image of Dodge skating to the edge of the rink, grabbing a drink, then searching for her in the stands, those deep blue eyes like the sky before a storm.

Her headlights carved out the night as she headed toward the Copper Mountain Bridge, back to their homestead tucked away in the woods.

Thankfully, the ghost would be gone by morning.

THREE

All Dodge had to do was make it back home in one piece. So far, so good. First of all, he'd made it into the air. And once there, as usual, the scenery and finding his own piece of the sky sucked the fear clean out of him.

He may have panicked for nothing. Maybe his bad luck was in the rearview mirror.

To the north, out his starboard window, the ragged Alaskan range jutted skyward, heavily blanketed with a layer of snow and ice, its granite peaks fierce and lethal. A pale blue sky hinted at the severe chill that had descended upon the Denali valley, sweeping southward into the town of Copper Mountain and the surrounding areas. He could practically write his thoughts in the air gathered with his breath this morning when he'd gone out for his preflight check.

Thoughts that had been on last night's face-off with his father.

He should have known that the détente wouldn't hold.

"What are you doing up?" Dodge had asked last night when he got home with the pain meds.

Yep, just like Mal said, Dodge had found the old man in the kitchen, scrambling eggs. Totally ignoring doctor's orders, like it might be ten years ago, when Dodge came home from hockey practice famished.

Like the past decade had been an illusion.

Dodge didn't mention it to Larke, but it also bothered him that his father hadn't changed Dodge's room even an iota in ten years. His hockey posters of Jace Jacobsen with the Blue Ox were still up, his trophies gathering dust on his dresser.

His leather Sky King Ranch jacket hung on his desk chair. Like he'd never left.

And when his father dished up the eggs, one arm across his chest, catching his breath in a wince, that was just *enough*.

"Sheesh, Dad. Get back in bed." And then he'd gone around to grab the pan and somehow, he'd knocked his dad off-balance.

The old man went down, right there on the kitchen floor, and his grunt of pain roused the exact memory Dodge had run from.

Another person he loved, hurt at his own hand.

So, he'd helped him up—not that his father was especially cooperative—gotten him to his room, and left him there with the eggs.

"Thanks," his father had said, his mouth tight around the edges.

"For Pete's sake, stay in bed."

"I feel fine. I don't need you to take care of me."

"Clearly not," Dodge snapped. And shook his head.

But okay then. He packed up his duffel bag and escaped to one of the guest cabins by the lake. But not until after he'd made sure his dad took his pain meds.

Stubborn old man.

Below him, the shadow of his plane flew across icy fields that drained from the foothills, spilling out in massive runs of untouched snow, undulating over hills and into canyons, and dumping into now-frozen rivers. The lush greens of black pine and spruce were a sharp contrast to the endless span of white.

A quiet escape from his own regrets.

No, not regrets. He'd made his decisions, had to live with them.

"You headed out to the Farleys' place today?" His father's question this morning hung in his head as Dodge banked and headed south along the east fork of the Yentna River, following the rugged channel that traversed the base of Magnus Peak.

"Mmhmm," he'd said, checking his ForeFlight planner. The office of Sky King Air Services was simply an attachment to the lodge his father had added in the last thirty years, and the open door led into the kitchen and dining room. From there, too, he could see the great room and a southward view of their land.

"Looks like there might be some weather coming in later today," Dodge said, writing down his flight plans. "I thought I'd get an early start."

His father came to the door, holding a cup of coffee, clearly trying to prove his words from last night. He'd dressed by himself, the arm of his sweater empty, his casted arm next to his body. How he'd gotten on his jeans, Dodge didn't want to ask. He'd shaved, too, and wore his Sky King Air cap, as if he might be going someplace.

Fine. Dodge was here to fly the planes, not babysit.

"Watch the approach—the wind comes whipping in from the north and the crosswinds from the west can throw you off."

"I know. I'll make dinner when I get home."

"I can put one of Larke's casseroles in the oven. It's a long trip out there."

"I remember." Dodge loaded the updated plan into his tablet and his watch and looked out the window. He'd fly VFR—visual flight rules—but sometimes the best navigation came from his gut.

Clear skies, the ceiling still high. He'd get over to the Farleys' with their load of supplies and back before his window of sunshine failed him.

"I'll put some coffee in a thermos," his father said.

Whatever. Dodge grabbed his jacket. "I'm going to load up." He tucked his chin into his collar as he headed out to the Quonset hangar that housed their Bell 429 chopper—mostly Larke's baby—and his beautiful Piper PA-14 Family Cruiser.

It was over thirty years old, but he'd gotten a deal, and at seventeen, owning his own plane would have just been the start of an empire he hoped to build.

Today, it housed memories that awakened as he did his preflight check. He turned on his master switches and checked his fuel gauges. The fuel pump hummed to life, and in the darkness of the hangar, the lights flashed. He checked his flaps, the connections, the ailerons, and gave the wings a good shake.

"You won't hurt it, son. It's made to withstand turbulence."

He shook his father's voice away, and finished with a tap on the wing, listening for loose rivets. He checked the prop, then the stall tab, and finally the tail cone for any critters who might have crawled inside, trying to keep warm. Outside, the dawn had started to slide over the runway, a deep amber that lit the gravel on fire.

He checked the air pressure on the tundra wheels, hearing his father's laughter echo in his head—*"Those are the silliest things I've ever seen on a plane"*—yeah, whatever, but the oversized wheels allowed him to land on ice, snow, and any manner of gravel beach.

He checked his fuel mix, his oil, his spark plugs and magneto. He tapped his finger on the brake fluid reservoir, listening for the fluid level.

Then he closed up the engine compartment and loaded in the supplies Spike and Nola Farley had ordered from town. The shipment from Gigi's Grocery had arrived yesterday during his trip to town with Larke, which meant he managed to duck out of Gigi's reconnaissance questions—*How long have you been home? What's your brother Ranger up to?* Of course. And the big one . . . *Are you staying?*

Nope.

By the time he returned to the house, the gear packed, his father had filled a thermos and handed him a backpack of food. "Just in case."

He should just give up. "Thanks." Besides, he knew about *just in case*. His emergency pack—a sleeping bag, water, food, flares, a tent and propane stove—was shoved under his seat.

"Fly smart, son," his father said.

"I got this." He didn't meet his father's eyes as he took the pack. "I'll be back in a few hours." Dodge had lifted a hand, glad it wasn't visibly shaking.

He'd fought through the coil in his gut and was skyward before the sun could clear the mountains, heading west, a glare on his instrument panel.

But the day was bright and crisp, the snow glistening, the clouds to the northwest and a day of flying spread out ahead of him, and sometime in all that, his stomach had loosened.

Yes, he had this.

He chased a herd of caribou as they scattered through the snow south of the park line. Followed the river through Cache Creek Canyon, the familiar terrain latching on to his memory.

"You don't want to get too close to the walls—a gust of wind could push—"

"I got this, Dad."

Even when he was sixteen, they'd been at odds.

When he emerged into the flattened area southeast of a massive spur of mountain, Dodge spotted a bull moose standing just offshore in the snow, feeding on rushes. It lifted its massive head and watched the yellow intruder snake through the valley.

Dodge ascended, crossed the ridge, kept an eye on the ceiling, then headed south on the Yentna River, scanning the ground for the Farley homestead.

When Dodge was in high school, Spike, a former military paratrooper, and his wife and infant daughter had moved north, following the dream of so many—gold and the freedom to live as they liked.

Recognizing a spur in the river, where it angled west, Dodge spotted the Farley homestead. The cabin sat on a hill in a cleft in the mountain overlooking the river. A trail had been cut out between the trees that led down to a dock.

They'd enlarged the place to include a barn, a greenhouse, and what looked like a clearing for dogs.

For a moment, Echo slipped into his brain. *"There's no greater freedom than running dogs."*

He wondered if she'd watched that Norwegian racer check in at the halfway point of the Iditarod this weekend.

Nope. Not going there.

On the ground, someone had heard him and come out of the house and was now waving a red flag. He dipped his wings, then banked, checking out his landing on the beach of the frozen river. Despite the recent warmth in Anchorage, the freezing nights still kept the river solid. And today's cold spell had deepened the freeze.

He angled in, adjusted his flaps, straightened her out, and set the PA-14 down on the beachhead.

The plane sputtered to a stop, and Dodge opened the door, stepped out on the strut.

The air smelled of woodsmoke, pine, and a deepening chill. The sun had climbed high—he'd put the time near noon.

A gunshot cracked the air, and in a second he jumped off, crouching down behind his tundra wheel.

What?

"Barry! Sheesh—didn't you see the flag?"

Dodge glanced over the tire to see Spike Farley running down the slope in his green Army-issued parka, red thermals, a pair of boots, and a fur hat. He was carrying his 12-gauge Remington 870.

Dodge put his hands in the air, just in case Spike had a case of cabin fever. "It's me. Dodge Kingston—"

"Dodge?" Spike stopped in the snow, peering against the sun as if trying to recognize him. "What are you doing here?" He didn't cross the beach.

Dodge kept his hands up. "I have mail. And some supplies from Gigi's." He went to open the back door.

"Don't move!"

He stilled. Turned.

"He's still around here, somewheres."

Dodge considered the man. He'd lost weight, but most of the homesteaders did in the winter, especially when they got to the end of their supply of moose, caribou, elk, or even salmon. But Spike bore a strange, almost feral look about him.

"Spike. Everybody okay at the house?"

Spike started creeping across the beach toward Dodge, his back to him, facing the woods. "He's out here. He's been watching us for nearly a week. Every time we go out—"

A crack sounded in the woods, up near the house, and Spike lowered his gun. "You stay there!"

Dodge reached in the plane and pulled his .357 Taurus from its holster behind his seat. Wouldn't be the first time some homesteader lost it and did something terrible to his family. "Spike? Who are you—"

Then he saw it, and Dodge's blood went cold.

Nine-hundred-plus pounds of enraged grizzly, thundering through the woods out onto the beach. Dodge could practically smell the beast from here, feral and rank, his claws digging up the snow as he charged them.

Don't. Run. Somewhere in the back of his head, Echo was screaming.

No, that was him screaming, inside, at least. He leaped for the plane.

Crazy Spike just stood his ground and fired. The animal kept coming.

A bear could clear fifty yards in ten seconds. "Spike!"

Spike's second shot might have clipped his shoulder, because the beast stumbled.

"Get in the plane!" Dodge shouted. Spike turned, glanced at the angry bear, then took off for Dodge.

He leaped inside the opened back compartment, squeezing himself in and closing the door as Dodge fired up the engine. "Hold on!"

He throttled the plane forward just as the bear found its feet. "C'mon, sweetheart!"

The grizzly took off again toward them, loping, roaring, a medieval beast ready to tear the plane from the sky.

Dodge bumped along the beach, the throttle all the way forward, urging speed. "Faster!"

The plane lifted off just as the animal reached it, rising to claw at the tires.

They flew hard out of the riverbed, into the sky. Sweat snaked down Dodge's spine, despite his layers.

Spike was sitting on a crate, his hand clutched to Dodge's seat.

"Something is wrong with that animal," Dodge said, banking.

"You think?" Spike leaned over his shoulder. "He's been camping out at our place for a week. Got into my smokehouse and finished off my salmon and the moose and then went for the outside freezer. He destroyed our greenhouse and would have taken out our door, but I shot at him and he ran."

"So he's wounded?"

"Maybe. Not that it matters. He's the devil, just waiting for us to step outside. Kids are terrified. The wife is hysterical. Had to bring the dogs inside." He leaned back. "You know what it's like to have seven malamutes living inside a two-room cabin?"

Dodge didn't want to imagine.

"We've been living off the supplies in the house, but those are nearly gone. I'd rather gnaw off my arm than eat another can of Spam. Just get me close." He moved over and reached for the door.

"Hold up, Spike." Dodge came around, low along the canyon. "It's illegal to shoot a bear from a plane."

"He's killing us!"

"I know. Let me see if I can chase him off."

Dodge came in low, gunning his engine, and the bear looked over at him, rising now to greet the plane. He swiped at the tires.

"Told ya. He's not afraid."

"Right. Probably spent the summer lunching on the snacks at the Denali campgrounds."

"Just get me in for a shot."

"Let's call Hank, get him out here."

"We'll be dinner by the time he gets here."

Dodge banked and came around again. This time, he flew twenty feet off the beach.

"Are you crazy?" Spike shouted.

"Just hold on to something." Because clearly, he'd lost his mind, but—well, Echo was back in his head. *Bears have a reason for everything they do.*

Below them, the bear landed on all four feet and started to lope.

"It's working."

Dodge slowed, then gunned the motor as he drew near the bear. It spooked and broke into a run.

Dodge pulled up, banked again, came around, and again buzzed the bear. Scared and alive was better than dead, although the thought of the animal wandering around wounded only to be attacked by a pack of wolves seemed inhumane. They should land and track it, put it down.

But first, Dodge had to take care of Spike and his family.

He followed the bear upriver a mile, two, then into the woods and out across the bushy tundra.

Then he turned back and landed again on the shore.

Spike climbed out of the back. Swiped off his fur hat and ran an arm across his forehead. His brown hair was long and matted to match his beard. "That was some flying." Then he grinned.

Oh, yes, the man needed to come out of the bush, preferably for a hot bath and a trip to the dentist. The smell now wafted over to Dodge. But he met Spike's hand. "Let's get your gear unloaded."

Spike hung his gun over his shoulder and reached for a box. "I heard you were over in Afghanistan."

Despite the wide spaces of the north, the community felt as big as a one-stoplight town. "Yep," Dodge said as he unpacked the wooden boxes of supplies—flour, sugar, oil, medicines. "I was a pilot with the 438th out of Bagram."

"F-15 fighter?" Spike carried one of the boxes up the hill, his feet digging into the packed snow.

Dodge followed him. "No. I flew a Pave Hawk."

Spike shot him a glance. "You flew spec ops."

"And combat search and rescue." Dodge readjusted his grip on the heavy box. "What did you order, bricks?"

"Homeschool supplies."

"Have you never heard of the internet?"

"I wish." Spike laughed. "No internet out this far."

Dodge set the books on the deck. Inside, the dogs barked, a cacophony of noise and chaos. The door opened and Nola stepped out on the porch. Noticeably pregnant, she wore one-piece thermal long johns, a flannel shirt, and a stocking cap over her sable brown hair. "Dodge, is that you?"

"Hey, Nola." He met her hug. "You look good."

"I look fat. And grumpy. And I smell. I long for a bath, a pizza, and a beach. No, change that to Chinese takeout and I'll sell you my oldest kid."

"Mom!"

Dodge couldn't remember the daughter's name, but she'd grown, her hair long in a dark brown braid as she came outside in her snow pants and a fraying wool sweater. She glanced up at Dodge, something of an embarrassed smile on her face.

And again, a younger Echo walked into his head, wearing her

hair in two long braids and a smile that could stop his heart. Oh, the perils of finding your true love at the age of ten.

He should have known that coming back to Copper Mountain would awaken his mistakes.

"Hi—"

"Maylene."

"And your brother is—"

"Archie," said the boy. He was a couple years younger and a miniature version of Spike. He followed his father off the deck and down the hill.

"Archie!" Nola put a hand over her belly.

"We ran the bear off. He's miles away," Dodge told her.

"For now." She turned to Dodge even as she watched over his shoulder as her husband hiked back to the beach. "I'm ready, I think, to be done here." She sighed, and one of the dogs slipped past her and ran out, barking. "It's not just the bear. It's the life. It's beautiful and—"

"Exhausting. I get it."

Archie returned, and Dodge lifted a crate from him and carried it in the house.

Spike was right about the smell. But Nola kept the place clean—a cast-iron stove sat in the center of the room, toasty warm, and separated the kitchen from the family room. A worn sofa and chair, clearly handmade with some craftsmanship, faced the stove, and along the wall, books filled floor-to-ceiling shelves. The dogs were mostly cordoned in a back room, whining to be freed. And above it all, a loft overlooked the main room.

"That would be our bedroom," Nola said of the kennel. "We've been sleeping with the kids, so that's fun." She pointed to the loft. "I can barely get my nine-month big belly up there."

"I'll get Hank out here."

"Spike tried to shoot it, but the bear seems unfazed. I know he's wounded—we found blood."

"He probably is, and that's why he didn't leave. Too much easy food around here. He'll have to be moved, if not put down."

"You could have killed him from the air." She folded her arms over her belly.

"I could lose my license that way." He put his hand on her shoulder as Spike came in with the last of the supplies. "Hang tight."

"If the bear comes back, he's dead," Spike said.

"Fair enough, and probably for the best."

"Stick around for lunch?" Nola asked with so much pleading in her eyes he couldn't turn her down.

She needed gossip from the outside world, and he did his best to update her with Larke's information. The Spam stew found the nooks and crannies of his stomach, and Spike updated him on the homestead and his plans to upgrade it.

He ignored a stab of envy—once upon a time, he'd dreamed of a future in this land.

Checking in with the homesteaders, giving the latest news, and even just assessing their mental health was as much of his job as ferrying supplies.

"I'll be back in a couple weeks," Dodge said as he stepped out of the house a couple hours later. He cast a look at the sky. Dark clouds hedged the horizon.

Running a quick check, he climbed back in the PA-14 and fired her up. Lifted into the air.

Angling out of the jagged valley, he circled back to where he'd last seen the grizzly.

It took a few low flybys, but he found the animal on a hillside ten miles east, and it rose, waving a spiked paw at him as he flew by.

He hated to see an animal wounded, but a dead grizzly meant he'd have to skin it and bring it in for Hank to lock, and not without a load of explaining. Bush pilots had rules, and despite the wild frontier rep of the bush, Winter's words had hung around in his head for the past week. *"They're talking pilot error."*

Dodge still couldn't get his brain around that—his father was legendary in the area for his flight record. Still, if it was pilot error, they didn't need any more problems staining their record.

He'd get Hank and take down the grizzly lawfully.

The afternoon sun slung dark, jagged shadows across the glacial spill south of the Alaskan range, and he ducked under the falling ceiling, the clouds thickening. A ring of spidery ice crackled around his windshield, and he guessed the weather had decided to betray him, the storm chasing him home.

He shouldn't have expected any less, really.

He passed Chelatna Lake Lodge, a spiral of smoke rising from the stone chimney, and debated for a moment setting down on the thick pack of ice to wait out the oncoming storm.

"Mistakes get you killed. Fly smart."

At this airspeed, he guesstimated he'd be home long before the clouds closed in. He hugged the foothills, the jagged peaks to his port side, as he flew low, nearly a thousand feet. A voice came over the radio, reporting snow in Copper Mountain, but he could already see it gathering on his windshield.

The clouds started to sink, and he found himself in a wash of white. He gained altitude, now over another glacial run, flying almost from memory, but he knew how the terrain could deceive. *Stay calm.*

He broke free at 3,500 feet, his gut a little jumpy, and saw the rise of peaks ahead of him. Angling to the south, he made out familiar terrain in the fading light. Rambler Creek. He could take it north to his next marker—Cache Mountain.

The clouds hadn't yet fogged in the river valley, so he descended for a better view and followed it. If he needed, he could put down at Cache Mountain Cabins, a tourist mining and hunting operation just ten miles south of the park.

The snow hit his windshield in a fury now. It began to cake, so he turned on the pitot heater. Visibility cut to a half mile, and he wove his way up the creek. He finally spotted the scattering of red-roofed cabins and the long lodge.

Nearly home. He could make it.

He ascended over Cache Mountain, heading for the pass with a latent muscle memory. The clouds fogged him in now, but he held course, his eye on the compass, and in a few moments, cleared the white.

He released his breath, not realizing he'd been holding it.

Above the cloud line the sky was clear, a deep indigo, the sun still a ball of fire behind Denali.

This. This was freedom. This was where he could feel his heartbeat, seize the life he'd longed for.

This was where his dreams lived.

Denali rose eighteen thousand feet to his north, brutal and bold, snow-packed, undefeated. Thick clouds lay in the deep pockets of the range, between Hunter and Moose Tooth and Foraker, and he had no doubt that a few deadly storms raged at the higher altitudes.

He could stay forever up here, in the silence of the sky, waiting for the stars, the aurora borealis to ribbon across the horizon . . .

Ice started to form a sheet over his windshield. And then he felt the plane begin to drag.

Ice on the wings, the struts, the tail. Thankfully, the props didn't seem to be icing up yet.

But he needed to descend, get to warmer air.

He pushed the yoke in, began his descent into the cloud clutter, his eye on the altimeter. If he remembered this area correctly, he was in a corridor of riverbeds and low forests, but he sweat a little when he didn't break through at two thousand, one thousand—

It wasn't unheard of for pilots descending to warm temperatures to fly right into a mountainside, the cloud cover so low.

He broke free at 550.

His heart restarted. Especially when he spotted the lights of the various homesteads of the valley guiding him home.

Starr Lodge, a handful of other homes, and of course his gaze fell on the Yazzie homestead. Lights blazed in the windows that overlooked the river.

He followed that river north until it curved east, and then the tributary south, and at the end of a small lake, he spotted Sky King Ranch.

From the air, he could still trace every inch of what it had been before the big fire had taken out so much of it a few years ago. Gone, at the far end of the lake, was his grandmother's cabin, where Larke had lived after she returned from the Army. The handful of cabins situated on the other edge of the lake remained, however. He'd taken up residence in one of them.

On the hill above sat the lodge, all hand-hewn log with a wraparound porch and a massive stone fireplace. The old red barn that still housed his motorcycle and a few other vehicles sat a stone's throw away, and at the end of a large runway, the Quonset hangar.

He called in his approach, and of course his father confirmed. Had probably been working in his office for hours.

Dodge pinpointed his landing and set the plane down heavy, bouncing a couple times—not pretty, thanks to the icy weight—but a landing without injury to plane or people was a successful landing.

Then, Dodge simply sat on the runway and let himself breathe, listening to the *tharrump* of his heartbeat.

He finally taxied over to the hangar, got out, and surveyed the damage.

The ice lay an inch thick on the airframe. A little more ice and he could have been in serious trouble.

Oh, who was he kidding?

He tied down the plane, grabbed the thermos, then closed

the hangar door and headed inside the office. He recorded his flight time, his fuel used, and the sighting of the bear. Then he brought the thermos into the kitchen.

"There's lasagna in the oven. It'll be ready soon."

His father sat in his recliner in front of the fireplace, a hardback book on his lap. Probably taken from his Louis L'Amour collection.

Dodge unscrewed the lid of his thermos and dumped the coffee into the sink. Washed it out and set it on the rack to dry.

"How was the flight?" his dad asked.

Dodge stood in the kitchen a moment, also staring at the fire, how it licked around the logs, turning them a glowing red, ashy at the edges, eating away at their once-undiminished strength.

"It was fine." He took a breath. "Farleys have a rogue bear near their place. We chased it off, but we'll need to call Hank."

He turned the light on in the oven. The lasagna bubbled away, the smells of tomato, basil, and oregano rich in the air.

He picked up his jacket and headed out into the cold again.

The night was brisk, sharp, the kind that had a man rethinking his commitment to the north, the storm still rolling in from the east. But above the bright mountain peaks to the north, a swirl of magenta and violet made him stand up, made him take in a breath. The aurora borealis. Glorious. A reminder of the harsh beauty of this life. His breath formed in a crisp fog, spiraled out to join the night.

Then he dropped to his knees, caught himself on one hand, and emptied out his stomach onto the frozen, unforgiving earth.

The howl started low, like a moan, then moved up in pitch, turning deafening as it shattered the darkness. Throaty and deep, it was joined by others, a feral music that serenaded the darkness with the call of the wilderness.

Echo stood in her thermals, a fleece jacket, and her mukluks at the doorway of the ranger cabin. She was holding a cup of hot cocoa, blowing on the steam.

The sounds died into the wind, but they could make the flesh of her skin prickle if she wasn't safely harbored inside four sturdy walls tonight. All that vast darkness, frigid and lethal.

"The dogs okay?" Peyton stood at the potbellied stove, shoving in a few of the logs they'd split earlier. She wore her snow pants and a white turtleneck, her curly black hair pulled back in a harsh ponytail, a white wool headband over her ears.

Echo's gaze crept over her sleeping team. Tucked away in the snow, the dogs had been fed, their feet checked, and now they slumbered in peace as the night kaleidoscoped around them. It had stopped snowing, the storm having passed over them, but a terrible wind howled through the trees.

Not a great night to be out in the rough.

She went inside.

From his place on the floor, Granite whined, but she held out her hand. She knew he wanted to be outside, but she worried for him. He seemed depleted after today's run, and rightly so. He might be her lead, but he wasn't the strongest dog in the pack anymore. Soon she'd have to retire Granite and move Maverick to the front.

Besides, she liked having Granite in with her to alert if something threatened her dogs.

"The wind is really whipping up." Peyton stirred the pot of hydrated stew on the stove. "And it's getting cold."

"Maybe our last big freeze," Echo said as she shut the door. "The wind will die down by morning—it's just the tail end of the storm. You kids from the Lower 48 are such cake-eaters."

Peyton laughed. Never mind that she'd grown up in the bush just south of Copper Mountain. "Going to university in Seattle doesn't classify me as a cheechako."

Echo walked over to the table and picked up her new Nikon

D500. She scrolled through the photos on her viewfinder. "I'm glad we stayed until dark. You should see these shots of that grizzly tearing into the moose kill the wolves brought down."

They'd spent the morning checking on Peyton's wildlife cameras, the ones she'd set up to capture the mating and den habits of a pack of wolves she tagged a few years back. The pack had returned to the same den for the past three years, and Peyton's study focused on the long-term mating patterns of two wolves in particular named Sheila and Hugh.

They spent the rest of the day sitting on a snowbank above a riverbed, watching the wolves—Hugh and his two underlings—take down a thin bull moose. The battle ensued for an hour, and she'd caught most of it on film, both video and in photos.

"I have a great shot of Hugh standing on that outcropping, watching the other two wolves eat." He was black, with a strange, yellowish streak behind each shoulder, as if he might have wings. She zoomed in. "Did you know he has a wound over his shoulder? It looks healed, but the hair around it is rusty and white."

"That was from a fight a year ago with Neo, when he attempted to join their pack. Sad that Neo ended up alone."

"Maybe he found another pack."

Peyton handed her a bowl, and they sat at the tiny table. The one-room log cabin was stocked with a couple cots, a table, cookware, and a few condiments as well as snowshoes, shovels, and rudimentary tools to survive a sudden storm. Per her contract with the Fish and Game service, Echo made a point of maintaining all the cabins on her route every fall.

She continued to move through her pictures. She'd gotten a number of great shots of the pack's alpha female. Sheila was thick bodied, short-legged, and generally smaller than the other females, but she had a temper and a doggedness about her that won her top position. Dark gray, with almost an indigo aura, she had the most intriguing blue eyes, as if she had husky in her gene pool. It wasn't unheard of to have a sled dog break from its line and disappear into the woods, only to join a wolf pack.

Hence how Echo had gotten Granite—he'd been rescued by a trapper after the man had accidentally killed Granite's mother, who'd mated with the man's lead dog. The female had hung around her mate and was caught in a trap line and died. The trapper had found the den, retrieved the pups, and given them away to neighbors.

"Here's the one of the bear." She passed the camera to Peyton. "Hugh put up a good fight for that kill, but that big brown wasn't having it."

It was a battle, for sure. The grizzly had come practically out of nowhere, angry, ready for blood. He'd pounced on the kill, ripping the leg off the moose, then dropped it to swat away one of Hugh's cohorts. Hugh had pounced then, grabbing at a back leg, and the bear roared and shook him off, rounding on him.

The battle raged for a good hour, the bear feasting between attacks. Finally, Hugh and his pack settled back on the shore, pacing, watching until the bear wandered off somewhere in the woods, probably close by, to sleep it off.

"He was definitely angry," Peyton said, handing the camera back. "Hugh was smart to wait it out. My guess is that the pack has dismantled that moose and buried the parts in caches for later."

Echo put down her camera. "I should radio my dad. He's not sleeping, and I often find him up at night just staring at the telemetry, checking in on Elsa and the cubs."

"I thought he was getting better."

"He is, mostly. He was dry for most of the winter, but this thing with Idaho, and of course he worries about me when I'm on the trail, and . . . well, that can be a bad thing. He sort of channels it all toward Elsa."

"I don't blame him," Peyton said. "People go missing in the bush every year. Alaska is a dangerous place."

"I can take care of myself, I have for years now. But you're right—anything can happen in the bush."

"Do you think we should go back?"

"No." Echo blew on her soup, took a sip. "He knows I'll be gone for ten days. I asked him to wait until I got back to do anything about Elsa. This is good soup."

"I added my traveling spice packet to it. Oregano, parsley, basil, and thyme. Speaking of spice, did you hear that Dodge Kingston is back?"

And just like that, Echo choked. She put her hand on her mouth to stop her soup from escaping. Coughing, she grabbed a towel.

"Sheesh. I guess that's a no. Sorry."

Echo was still coughing, but she put up a hand. "No. It's fine." She took a drink of her tea. Put it down and cleared her throat. "When?"

"A few days ago. Showed up, and according to Winter Starr, he's flying his father's homestead route until Barry gets back in the air."

So it *had* been Dodge who Echo had seen on the street.

Wow, he looked good. Changed, but good. Maybe, hopefully, also healed.

"I heard about Barry's crash from Otto. That's rough. Clipped a tree coming into the Copper Mountain FBO," Echo said.

"Weird, right? They're saying it might have been structural, but Winter said the wind was less than five knots that day, so . . ."

"How badly was he hurt?"

"Broken arm, a few broken ribs. His pride."

"I'll bet." She took another sip of her soup. "How'd Dodge get into the picture?" See, her voice didn't shake at all. No more coughing, choking, or general seizing up of her heart.

"Dunno. I think Larke called him. But I did hear from Moose

Mulligan that he was joining Air One, so maybe he's been in Alaska for a while."

For a while?

She put down her spoon, no longer hungry. *For a while* and he hadn't bothered to contact her.

Not that she expected it. After all, he hadn't answered even one of her letters. She leaned back and picked up her cup of tea. Outside, the wolves mourned again, and with it, Granite sat up, perked his ears.

"It's okay, buddy," she said.

"Winter said he was still single."

Echo cut her gaze back to Peyton. Lifted a shoulder.

"Please. Not even a little perk of interest?"

"That's long over. Never started, really."

"Echo—he asked you to *marry* him."

"It was a mistake."

"A mistake?"

It wasn't hard to remember the night he'd proposed. "Yep. It was only our second date." Although it could have been a thousand times they'd driven home under the pale night sky, but this night was special.

The night of their first kiss.

She could still remember the way he'd tasted—like cherry Coke—and the smell of campfire smoke on him.

"It was a crazy, spur-of-the-moment question while we were watching the Fourth of July fireworks over Copper Mountain."

"Romantic."

"Impulsive. He'd just kissed me. My first kiss—and probably his—and all around us fireworks were exploding, and it was practically a Hallmark moment, but we got done kissing, and he told me he loved me."

"This *is* like a movie," Peyton said, holding her soup cup in both hands.

"A horror flick, more like. Because he also picked right then to propose."

He'd scared her. The way he slid his hand behind her neck and met her eyes. Then, as if the idea had just taken him, he'd said, *"Will you marry me?"*

"I just stared at him. I couldn't think. Couldn't breathe. Somewhere inside me, I was saying yes, but a bigger part of me thought—'What in the world is he thinking?' And then, I don't know, the word just spilled out. *No.*"

"You said no."

"You know this."

"I've never heard the story though. I'm just trying to wrap my mind around it."

"Yeah, me too, ten years later. He drove me home in silence, and I knew I'd broken his heart. And then I didn't see him for the rest of the summer until . . . well, the rest is history."

"Oh, Echo. No wonder you're choking on your food. Because he looks gooood, honey."

"I know. I saw him in town, except, I didn't think it was him and *what am I going to*—"

Outside, the dogs erupted. Granite jumped off the cot and ran to the door, whining. Growling.

Echo hit her feet. "Something's out there."

Peyton had a hand on her arm before she reached the door. "Take this." She shoved the JM capture air rifle into her hand. "It's loaded."

Hopefully with enough Zoletil to slow down whatever was harassing her dogs.

Echo opened the door, peered out into the darkness. Maverick jerked at the end of his tether, snapping and growling, along with Goose, Viper, Iceman, Jester, and Merlin, all baring fangs.

And at the end of it all was a sight that made Echo's entire body go cold.

Holly was fighting her way free of a giant, angry grizzly.

No!

She already lay in the snow, moaning, growling.

Granite ran out past her, a streak of defensive fury.

"Granite!"

Echo took aim and, without a thought, sent the stinger into the night.

The bear roared as Granite pounced on him, pulling away from her injured dog, and rearing up.

"Granite!" Echo came off the porch, running to her animal.

"Echo!" Peyton ran after her. "Stop!"

Granite ripped at the bear, his growls betraying the wolf blood inside.

Echo raised her gun again, searching for a shot. "He's not going down!"

Suddenly, the bear fell on all fours and fled. Bellowing, scared, possibly hurt, but most importantly, *away* from her dogs.

Echo grabbed Granite before he could follow. "Here!" She handed him to Peyton, who'd run out behind her, the light from her headlamp illuminating the worst.

Holly lay in the snow, bleeding, her leg broken. A gash in her side flayed open her skin, and she was crying loudly.

No, no—

Echo shoved the gun into Peyton's hand, then whipped off her fleece and wrapped it around the dog. She picked up the animal, trying not to struggle under the weight. Holly, miraculously, didn't fight her. "Help me get her inside."

Peyton followed her in, the capture gun trained on the darkness.

Echo put Holly down on the floor. Blood saturated her beautiful white fur, and she whined, in serious pain. A flap of her skin had been half sliced from her body, and her leg hung, bloody and broken. Echo pushed the skin back over the wound, holding it there. "Get my pack. There's a sedative there and first aid gear. But we need a rescue flight in here, pronto."

Peyton grabbed the pack and brought it to Echo.

"Hold her wound."

Peyton took over for Echo, who then pulled out a syringe and a bottle of Novocain. "This won't be enough but at least it'll help." She drew out the liquid and inserted it near the wound, another shot on the other side. Holly continued to whimper.

Echo finished administering the sedative.

"She's starting to clot," Peyton said.

"She needs ice on the wound. I'll get that. You get on the radio to Copper Mountain and see if they can send a chopper."

Peyton was digging through her pack, one hand on Holly, as Echo grabbed a bag and headed outside. She packed snow into the bag, then returned to the cabin and set the bag on the wound.

Holly whimpered under hand. Echo stroked her neck. "Hang in there, sweetie."

Granite crept up beside Holly, nudging her with his nose.

Peyton was still trying to connect to base.

Please. Echo just couldn't bear to put Holly down. Not yet. Not if she still had a chance.

Echo picked up the gun, reloaded it, and headed back outside. The dogs were still on alert, barking, growling. She went to each one, knelt and soothed them, talking in low tones, running her hands along their bodies. Maverick's was taut, every muscle corded and ready. He growled, his eyes focused on the darkness.

"He's gone, buddy. And he'll be asleep for a while. Don't worry. I won't let anything happen to you."

She repeated the words to each of the dogs, then finally returned to the cabin. Holly was resting, emitting tiny whines even in slumber. Peyton still sat beside her, her hand on her neck, speaking in soft tones.

"The snow has socked in Copper Mountain, but they're sending out a call to nearby FBOs. They'll get someone out here."

Echo nodded, took a breath. "I'm going to light a fire. That'll alert the chopper and maybe make the bear think twice before returning. Let me know if her breathing changes."

She went outside again, propped the gun on the porch, and headed over to the woodpile. A rustling in the woods caused her to jerk up, but it was just the wind, maybe.

Hauling the wood over to a place beyond the dogs, she piled the logs up, added tinder and kindling, and tromped back inside for the matches.

Peyton held the radio in her lap.

"How's she doing?"

"She's tough, like her mama."

Echo offered a wan smile and headed back outside with the matchbox. The fire lit on the second match, and she cupped the flame as it took to the curled birch filaments, the flame sizzling as it bit and glowed.

It started to crackle, and she stood, looked at the heavens, at the spray of stars. *Please.* Certainly heaven had a soft place for animals like Holly.

Then she returned to the porch, retrieved her gun, and hunkered down in the snow, staring into the dark sky, her face like flint against the wind. Waiting. Guarding. Hoping for rescue.

And in her heart, she was lifting her own mournful song into the dark night.

FOUR

He was grumpy, edgy and hungry, and probably not fit for human companionship. So clearly that's why Dodge found himself sitting at the counter of Vic's Midnight Sun Saloon, digging into a bowl of her delicious chicken pot pie—Monday's dinner special.

He probably should have taken his father up on the dinner instead of going back to his cold cabin, void of any real sustenance. But dinner would have required him to sit down and venture into conversation.

A conversation that might meander into dangerous territory. Like the past, and maybe what Colt was up to these days, and then, inevitably they'd land on the Epic Family Fight, and suddenly the tenuous peace he'd tried to knit together would be in shreds.

He'd end up on the train south to Anchorage to continue the life he'd returned to Alaska for—flying choppers for Air One Rescue.

But then Larke would be angry at him, and in truth, he couldn't let Sky King Ranch fall into bankruptcy. Even if it would never be his. There was a legacy here. A reputation.

He couldn't be the one to let it die.

Just a few weeks, and the old man would be able to fly again, and then Dodge could restart his life.

Until then, he needed groceries and real grub in his gullet, and when he'd driven by Vic's, an old, errant habit had him pulling into the gravel lot, parking next to the clutter of other grime-streaked pickups, and finding an empty stool at the bar.

He knew a few souls inside—Mal and Hudson Bowie were at a booth, their eyes glued to a hockey game on the flat-screen. And Shasta Starr had come right up to him, given him a hug, and said she'd missed him. So that was something.

"On the house," Vic said, setting down a golden, foamy beer in front of him. She still had short blond hair and that steely set about her that kept this place in shape. But her eyes warmed when they fell on him. "Glad to see you back."

"Thanks, Vic. But I don't drink." He pushed the beer away. "Coffee?"

"You got it." She took the drink away and pulled a mug from one of the hooks behind the bar. She filled it with black coffee and set it in front of him. "You flying for Sky King?"

He took a sip. Still brewed at a thickness that could keep him awake for a month. "Yep."

"How's your dad?"

"On the mend. Angry that he's grounded."

She nodded. "He doesn't come in much anymore. What're Ranger and Colt up to?"

Aw, he knew that was coming. "Not sure. Ranger's a SEAL, but I haven't heard from Colt for a while." He kept his voice easy, hoping she wouldn't pick up on anything.

A while meant ten years, and the last time he'd seen him, Colt was in a hospital bed. They hadn't talked, but Dodge had looked through the door window to make sure he was still alive.

Their Dad was parked at Colt's bedside, and that was all Dodge needed to walk away and down to the recruiter's office.

"Glad you're home," Vic said. "I'm sure Echo will be glad to see you when she gets back."

"Back?" He dismissed the other part.

"She's out in the bush with Peyton Samson, stalking wolves."

He raised an eyebrow.

"Peyton's on a three-year grant to track a pack of wolves,

study their mating patterns or something. She'll be glad to sit you down and wax on about it for a few tedious hours."

He laughed. "She likes to warm up one of these stools?"

"She likes my chili fries." Vic headed down the row to serve a couple guys who'd ventured in from the cold. The snow had started to drift from the sky, the weather pattern he'd outrun. The one that nearly took him down had found its way to Copper Mountain.

His stomach had calmed, the pot pie settling like a warm hum inside, along with his nerves. See, he'd be fine.

No one died on today's flight. It just took a bit to get back into the perils of bush flying again.

No, to settle back into the cockpit again, if he was truthful. He took a breath and cast a look at the game.

The Minnesota Blue Ox were playing the Colorado Blades, Wyatt Marshall at goal. The Blue Ox were up by two goals.

"Dodge?"

He turned and it took a second to place the face. Bearded, with long brown hair tunneling out of his wool hat, the man wore a thick canvas jacket, jeans, and work boots. A Remington Mines emblem on his jacket added a hint, and the recognition slid into place. "Nash?"

"I thought that was you. Wow." He held out his hand. "When did you get back?"

"A few days ago. How's the gold business?"

"Full of dreams and enough hits to keep hope alive." He slid on the stool beside Dodge. "Taken?"

"Nope. Still trying to figure out who I remember in this town."

"Yeah, well, the town remembers you."

"Thanks for that."

"Hard to forget—"

"Let's try."

Nash lifted a hand to someone behind him, and Dodge turned

to see Mal headed their direction, holding a couple empty beer glasses. He put them on the counter.

"You missed a good practice." He glanced at his brother Hudson, who jerked his chin in greeting. Mal must have updated him. Dodge returned the gesture.

A couple years older than Dodge, Hudson had taught him a few things when they'd played hockey together.

"Not sure if I'm in yet," Dodge said to Mal as Vic filled the glasses. Although the idea of slapping the puck around had stirred something deep inside him. And it wasn't just about hockey.

"Worried you're too out of shape?" Mal made to give Dodge a friendly gut punch, but a self-protective instinct had Dodge knocking his fist away. All in fun, but Mal still frowned.

Oops. He probably shouldn't be so jumpy. He'd healed just fine.

"I'm in shape enough to take you," Dodge said, covering up.

"Sure you are. Show up for practice Wednesday and we'll see. No pads." Mal picked up the beers.

"Hey," Dodge said, "did they ever find out if that bear killing was poaching?" He didn't know why he asked, but something about the grizzly today at the Farleys' didn't sit right.

Mal shook his head. "Hank said no, but I guess Charlie isn't satisfied. He thinks it was a den killing. But you know how crazy Charlie is about his bears."

"You'd think a guy who'd survived a mauling wouldn't be such a fan of grizzlies," Nash said.

"He blamed the mauling on himself." Dodge took another sip of his coffee. "He ran his dogs right into the sow as she and her cubs were feeding on a moose. If Sheldon Starr hadn't happened to be flying overhead, Charlie would be dead instead of the bear."

As the story went, Sheldon chased the bear away, set down, and still had to shoot the animal when it charged again.

The story was legendary, mostly because Charlie had survived, his arm nearly torn off, deep wounds in his legs and torso, his scalp nearly severed from his head.

Dodge still remembered flying out with his father to rescue Echo, who'd been left behind with their dogs. He'd mushed the dogs back to her house, his first time alone with them. "The cubs needed a home, and Charlie took them in."

"Elsa and George," Mal said. "We used to go 'round their place when they had dog litters. Got a number of dogs from Charlie, but really, we were there to see the bears. I'd never gotten that close to a grizzly, never mind petting them."

Dodge finished off his pot pie and was contemplating an order of those chili fries to take home. "Reminded me of that television show—the one with the tame bear."

"*Gentle Ben?*" Nash said.

Malachi frowned at him.

"Hey. My dad had every episode on VHS. What can I say? We loved it."

Dodge shook his head. "Not Gentle Ben. That's in Florida with a black bear. I'm talking about the one with the grizzly."

"Idaho calls Charlie Grizzly Adams," Mal said.

"That's the one," Dodge agreed. Yes, definitely he'd need the fries.

"Charlie tagged the bears and freed them into the wild a few years ago," Mal said. "Rumor is that George is lost, but Elsa is still around. Charlie has some research grant to study her and her cubs. People say he goes out into the bush and tracks her. That they have a *connection.*" He finger-quoted the last word.

"That's what happens when you don't have a wife," Nash said, and Dodge gave him a look.

"What? My dad said Charlie went a little crazy after Effie left. He and Echo all alone out there—"

"They weren't alone," Dodge said and got up. He didn't need the fries.

Silence, then Nash smirked. "Right. I forgot. They're the closest homestead to your outfit, aren't they? No wonder you and Echo were so tight. Hard for a guy to wedge between you two."

Huh. Hadn't been that hard for Colt. Dodge dug into his pocket. "That was a long time ago. Water. Bridge."

Mal said nothing, and Nash had the decency to turn to the bar and order. That's what Dodge got for venturing back into a town that couldn't forget.

He pulled out a ten and dropped it on the counter. "Thanks, Vic."

"Don't be a stranger, Dodge," she said and took his bowl.

He put his hand on Nash's shoulder. "By the way, there was a crazy grizzly out near the Farleys' place. Ate all their winter stash, was terrorizing the dogs. We chased it away, but it was acting strange. I know your land runs near theirs, so it could be headed your way."

"Thanks for the heads-up."

Dodge nodded.

Mal glanced at Dodge before he headed back to his table. "Wednesday afternoon around four. Don't be a coward."

Dodge was about to decline when the door opened, letting in the brisk night air, and with it, Deacon Starr, garbed up in his county sheriff uniform, his wool hat dusted with snow.

He stopped, his eyes adjusting to the light, and scanned the room.

When his gaze landed on Dodge, it stuck. Deke came over. "Well, look who the storm dragged in."

Dodge met his grip. "Guess I know who to stay clear of."

"Only if you break the law." He didn't add *again*, so Dodge counted that as a positive. "Your dad's accident bring you back?"

"Still first in the class, Deke."

He grinned. "Your dad said you were some kind of hero, fighting over in Afghanistan. Flying choppers?"

Huh. How the old man found that out, he hadn't a clue. And he clearly didn't have the full story. "Not a hero, but yeah, I did a couple tours. Got out about a year ago." Deke didn't need the details, not when Dodge was trying to put it all behind him.

"Hope you're sticking around."

Dodge was trying to find an answer when Deke's radio squawked. He picked it off his belt and stepped away, answering it.

This was probably his cue. "See you 'round, Nash." He headed toward the door.

Outside, the snow had begun to pile on the cars, the warm weather clearly a faint memory. The chill bit at his ears, and he turned up his collar as he stalked out to his truck.

"Dodge!" Deke's voice turned him around. The sheriff was jogging out toward him. "Hey. Just got a call. Bear attack, out at one of the ranger cabins. They need an emergency chopper."

Dodge stuck his hands in his pockets and stared at Deke. A beat, then, "Wait, *me*? What about the Copper Mountain SAR?"

"What Copper Mountain SAR? We ran out of funding a long time ago. Nearest SAR crew is Air One in Anchorage."

Aw. Dodge made a face, looked at the sky.

"Aren't you some hotshot chopper pilot?" Deke asked.

Dodge angled a look at him. "Not fair, and no. Taliban rebels are no match for a Denali snowstorm."

But still . . . grizzly attack. Someone had to go. And Sky King Air was one of the few outfits that had a chopper as well as planes.

"I'll get home and take a look at the ceiling. Where's the cabin?"

"Ten miles west of your place. Cabin 37."

He knew it. "I flew that area a couple hours ago. Lots of ice. Nearly took me down."

"I hear that, Dodge," Deke said. He looked at the sky, the

layering of snow. "I guess we're all grounded until this weather clears." His mouth tightened, and he looked back at Dodge. "The call came in from Peyton Samson. The victim is Echo."

Dodge stared at him, a fist closing around his chest. "Tell her I'm on my way."

No one was coming and Holly was going to die. Echo threw another log on the fire, watching as sparks leaped into the sky, swept away at once by the wind. The snowstorm had passed, leaving a fresh-fallen layer over her now-sleeping dogs, but as the sky cleared, a terrible wind from the north swept through.

No one could land in these conditions.

She should pack up the dogs and head out into the night. Eight hours of running, and they'd be home by dawn.

By the arc of the moon, it was well past midnight. She'd heard what she thought had been a plane thunder by hours ago, but no one had appeared on the trail. Her guess was the high winds, the snowpack, and the darkness had aborted the rescue mission.

She pulled her sleeping bag around her. Ice rimmed her balaclava despite the glow of the fire. The bear hadn't returned, but her capture gun sat within reach.

Please, get here. Echo clung to the tiny hope that someone would find a weather pocket and swoop in. Save them all.

"Dodge Kingston is back."

She'd be lying if she didn't hope that someone might be six feet two, have dark curly hair, blue eyes the color of a stormy sky, and bear the smile that she couldn't forget.

Maybe even with it, forgiveness.

Sometimes, she went back to that night, replayed it. Made different choices.

Said no to Colt and his charm before she got in over her head. Before she caused the Kingston Family Feud.

Before she lost the only man she ever loved.

"Echo?" The voice drifted out over the cold.

Peyton stood in the door, her jacket on. "I think Holly is going into shock."

Echo got up, shot a look at the darkness, at the fading fire, then grabbed the capture gun and headed inside.

Holly still lay in front of the potbellied stove. Granite had moved away but perched on the cot, his eyes on his offspring.

Echo knelt beside Holly, felt her pulse, put a hand in front of her nose. "She's breathing okay." She lifted her lips. Pale. She pressed on her upper gum and watched how fast the color returned. Shoot.

"You're right. She probably needs blood. Any news from Copper Mountain?"

"The sheriff's office said they were sending in someone. But that was—"

"Hours ago. I know. And the wind has really kicked up. I thought I heard a plane earlier, but they probably turned around."

She got up. "I should hitch up the dogs." She walked over and poured herself a cup of coffee that was simmering on the stove.

"It's fifteen below out there," Peyton said. "I get that you want to wait for help, but going out there in the wind is going to burn your dogs' lungs and freeze off your fingers."

She warmed her hands on the coffee cup. "She is from one of Granite and Nanook's litters." Echo could still remember Holly's birth, the first time she'd bred her own dog team.

And with that memory came the image of Dodge, learning with her the basics of running a team so long ago, training her father's dogs before they were sold. He'd been about fifteen then, same age as her, also gangly and wild-headed.

Perfect in every way.

If only she'd figured that out sooner.

"Echo," Peyton said, "I know you don't want to think this, but . . . she's suffering."

Echo turned to her, her breath caught. "No. Not yet. There's still hope."

"Is there?" Peyton's eyes had filled.

"I'm going back outside to wait." Echo put her mittens back on over her gloves.

"You should stay inside," Peyton said softly. "No one is coming."

No. She would not give up on Holly. Not yet. Besides, "There's a bear out there. I made my dogs a promise." She pulled on her goggles.

If she couldn't keep the promise to Holly, she intended on saving the rest of her pack. Still, her throat closed, her eyes burning as she fought tears. Her eyes could freeze closed.

Tromping back outside, she picked up a log from the pile on the porch and added it to the fire. Then she rearranged her nest in the snow, packing up the wind break. The sleeping bag kept her warm, and the fire had melted the area around her enough to create a cocoon despite the vicious cold. Still, the trees shivered in the darkness and the wind moaned. Any creature with sense would be tucked into a den somewhere.

And maybe Peyton was right. Holly was suffering.

No. Not yet.

Besides, that grizzly was still out there. It had to be injured to attack a dog on a tether. Maybe it was the grizzly they saw fighting the wolves.

George.

The thought had crossed her mind earlier—she thought she saw a white tuft between its ears, but it was dark out, so she couldn't know for sure. And with the snowfall, she couldn't track it.

Wishful thinking. In all reality, George was probably dead. Her father just didn't want to admit it.

That's what they did at the Yazzie homestead—lied to themselves. Told themselves that everything would be okay. They could survive the winter, their animals would live, and people wouldn't break their hearts.

Told themselves, at the least, they were tough enough to survive anything.

She was such a liar. After Dodge left, she'd put herself back together with anger and blame, and then good old-fashioned denial. They were never meant to be. He didn't want what she wanted.

He wasn't the one.

But that was the thing with lies. Eventually they break apart and you're left with nothing but the ugly truth.

She'd had her happily ever after and had blown it. And there was no putting it back together again.

So, even if Dodge did show up, there was no happy, hot-chocolate ending waiting at the end of this not-so-Hallmark blizzard.

No. Instead, come spring, they'd find her frozen body gripping a cold capture gun, her beloved dog dead, and her dog pack abandoned in the snow.

Except for Peyton. She'd make it back. Hopefully.

See, there was a reason Echo didn't stay in the cabin. She was oh-so-fun to be around.

And tired. So very tired. And hungry. And maybe a little achy, right to the center of her body.

"Stay alive, Echo."

The voice drew her up, made her realize she'd closed her eyes. She looked out into the night, but of course, it was just her father in her head.

She picked up a stick and poked the fire. Sparks bit into the night.

Tired. So . . .

What? She sat up, listened.

The night pulsed with a rhythmic chopping of the air, growing louder, a hum, and then the roar of an approaching engine.

"Peyton!" She got up and flicked on her headlamp.

In the clearing just beyond the cabin, the snow kicked up in a terrible whirl. She threw her hand over her face, the snow biting, stinging her eyes.

The dogs woke up, climbed out of the snowy hovels, and started barking.

Out of the sky, like some ephemeral beast, descended a deep-blue, beautiful Bell 429 chopper.

The wind pawed at it, but the chopper fought, turning in the air, steadying back on course.

Whoever helmed it had more guts than brains, but she was nearly in tears by the time they set down. The skids were fitted with wide skis and the chopper settled on the snowpack.

"Hello!" She hiked out beyond the ring of light and fire, shining her light on the snow, her heart thundering. "Peyton! Get Holly!"

She turned back just as the chopper door opened.

Briefly, she imagined that Barry Kingston might be emerging—the pilot was tall and wearing thermal windbreak pants and jacket and a wool hat. He had a sure gait about him, earned by his forty-plus years flying the Alaskan bush. Or maybe Sheldon Starr. Or someone from Anchorage?

And yet, as the pilot unlatched his snowshoes from the skids of the chopper and strapped them on, as he straightened and trekked toward her, strong and fierce and determined, her heart knew.

Oh *no.*

Only one person had that singularity of mind, and frankly, the crazy steel-boned courage to fly a chopper into this wind.

She stiffened, found the place inside her that reminded her she knew how to survive anything the Alaskan winter dished out. Including needing the help of the man she'd destroyed.

Dodge Kingston.

He stalked toward her, his dark blue eyes on hers, his black hair peeking out of his hat, almost an angry expression on his face. She wasn't sure he recognized her—not yet, because he didn't even blink as he came near. Then again, she wore her balaclava, her wool hat, goggles, and an insulated snowsuit.

"Where is she?" he said as he came closer.

"Inside," Echo said, practically shouting over the wind. She turned and led him onto the steps. He stopped, unstrapped his snowshoes, and set them near the deck. She went inside.

He followed her.

She couldn't really explain what happened next. The silence as Dodge stared at her dog, struggling for life on the floor next to Peyton, who got up, wide-eyed. The way he then looked back at her, reached out, and grabbed at her face mask. The hard yank he gave it to reveal her face.

He stared at her a long moment, and she, like an idiot, said nothing, because just seeing him here, back in her world—

Yeah, it was akin to a north wind taking out her breath.

Oh, he looked good. Grown up. A man—filled out, thick shoulders, lean body, tall. A dark swath of whiskers layered his face, just slightly touched with snow, and those eyes—those dark blue eyes were older too. Fierce. Knowing.

Steely.

Now they fixed on her, his chest rising and falling. "Thank God."

Huh?

"You're not hurt?" He stepped closer, looking her over, and she had to admit just being around him hurt very, very much, what with her regrets rising up to choke her, to tighten a steel band around her chest.

"No," she whispered. "I'm fine. It's Holly."

It took him a second, then he turned away from her, and it was like a fire being snuffed out, the sudden chill that layered the air.

"What happened?" He knelt beside the dog, putting his hand on her body.

"Grizzly attack."

He lifted the snow pack, lowered it. Glanced at her leg. "Right. Okay, so we need to leave, right now. Let's pack up."

"I'll bring the dogs home," Peyton said, meeting Echo's eyes.

Echo watched as Dodge grabbed Peyton's sleeping bag, put it on the floor, then lifted Holly onto it. He wrapped her up in the bag, then took her in his arms.

He looked at Echo. "Are you coming?"

Peyton must have read her mind. "You don't have to stay, Echo. I'm okay."

But—

And maybe she saw the past alight in Echo's eyes, because she stepped up and touched her arm. "I'll be fine."

"I can come back tomorrow on a sled, if we need to," Dodge said, looking at Peyton.

"I can run the dogs on my own, don't worry. I know the way." She looked at Echo. "You're not the only one who can read the forest."

Dodge headed for the door.

Peyton was right. Really.

"My gun and sleeping bag are outside. If the bear comes back—"

"I'll have Granite with me."

The older dog had come off the bed and now whined. Dodge turned around at the door. "Hey there, old buddy." He knelt and Granite came over to Holly. Nudged her. "I'll do the best I can," Dodge said.

Then he got up and headed into the night.

"Go," Peyton said, and Echo scrambled after him.

The wind whined in her ears as she followed Dodge out to the chopper, carrying his snowshoes. He waded through the snow, then opened the door with one hand and put Holly inside. He jumped in to secure her on a litter.

Echo climbed up on the skid and hoisted herself inside. Dodge leaned over and grabbed her jacket to help her in.

"You need to strap in. It's a bumpy ride."

He closed the door behind her and climbed through to the cockpit.

"I should stay with her—"

"Get up here and strap in."

She bit back words and obeyed.

"It's going to be dicey getting up, but once we're in the air, the wind isn't quite as rough."

He was turning on the controls, his movements practiced from the way he grabbed the cyclic in one hand, the other on the collective between the seats, his feet on the pedals.

"I didn't know you flew helicopters."

He said nothing as they began to move. The wind took the bird and they spun. He fought it with his foot pedals and the cyclic. The tight-jawed expression on his face under the dim light of the cockpit instruments betrayed his focus.

She glanced back. Holly hadn't moved.

Below, near the cabin, the campfire sparked into the sky, and she spotted Peyton retrieving her sleeping bag and gun.

Then Peyton stood and watched, waving as the chopper left the earth, trembling, spinning, fighting its way into the sky.

They cleared the trees, and he continued to ascend. Darkness spread over the land, but she could make out the shadows, the undulating hills, the glimmer of the river. And finally, the lights of Copper Mountain.

Dodge hadn't spoken once, but with the wash of the rotors and the howl of the wind, she didn't either.

He flew them over town, past the highway, past Main Street, into the neighborhoods beyond. "Aren't we landing at the airport?"

"We're going right to the clinic."

"Right to Anuk's place?"

"Yep. She's still practicing, right?"

Echo nodded, and in a few minutes she recognized the compound of the Copper Mountain vet clinic, aka Anuk Swenson's place.

Dodge put down right in the gravel driveway just as the porch light flickered on.

He unbuckled and climbed into the back, unstrapping Holly.

Echo opened her door and slid to the ground.

By the time Dodge got Holly out, Anuk had emerged, dressed in a thick parka and boots.

"It's Holly," he said, as if it might be his dog.

"She got attacked by a grizzly," Echo added, running after Dodge's long strides.

Anuk headed to the clinic and opened it up, then went right to the back, to the surgical area. "Set her down on the table."

Dodge gently put the animal down.

Anuk shed her jacket. Her black hair snaked down her back in a braid. "She's going to need blood, and I'm going to need an assistant. Dodge, go wake up my husband. Echo, you hold Holly while I assess her wounds."

Dodge left.

Holly moaned as Anuk removed the sleeping bag, then the snow pack. "Good job keeping this cold. You slowed down the bleeding. She's lost a lot of blood."

"Will she live?"

Anuk was examining her leg. The dog whined. "I know, baby," Anuk said. "We need to get her under—oh, thank God."

Her husband, large and blond, came into the room, followed by Dodge.

"Gunnar, type her blood. Dodge, get Echo out of here."

"No, I—"

"Echo, come on," Dodge said, and he wrapped his arms around her. "Let them work."

Her eyes filled. "No—"

"Yes," he said, a softness in his tone.

She closed her eyes and let him lead her from the room.

He walked her to the sofa in the lobby, helped her onto it, and sat down next to her.

And then, because she didn't know what else to do, she put her hands over her eyes, leaned against him, and wept.

FIVE

The problem was that the dream ended the same way every time. With her standing in the field, in front of a bonfire, watching her future implode.

This was not how it was supposed to end. In fact, it wasn't supposed to end at all.

Echo knew she was dreaming, knew it because outside the veil of her memories, she could still smell the faint antiseptic plus animal odor of the vet office. Could still feel the rasp of Dodge's Gore-Tex thermal pants, the weight of his hand on her shoulder, offering some sense that everything would be okay.

But it *wouldn't* be okay. And that's what she kept screaming as she watched herself walk through the boreal forest to the bonfire in the back of the Bowie family's Northwoods estate, where her friends, classmates, and more had gathered for the end-of-the-summer party.

Woodsmoke haunted the air as the massive flames shot sparks into the sky, still light from the long daylight hours. They'd all be leaving soon—some to the Lower 48 for college, some for Anchorage, a few others getting married. In her class of twenty-eight, most of the graduates had plans beyond Copper Mountain.

Not her. Sure, she'd played with the idea of going to Anchorage to pursue a biology degree, but how could she leave her father alone on their homestead after everything he'd been through?

"Just the Way You Are" by Bruno Mars pumped out from a

nearby speaker. The sky overhead had turned a deep lavender, not dark, but with a hint of twilight that would just slightly deepen then burst back to life in a few hours. She'd parked in the gravel lot of the beautiful log home, poised on a tiny lake south of Copper Mountain, and hiked back through the woods to their recreation area. Her guess was that Malachi's parents were probably in Anchorage or beyond, maybe even in DC, for him and his brothers to be holding such a rager. A giant trash-bag-lined garbage barrel held a brew of alcohol and punch that made her head swim just from the fumes.

Don't do it.

"Echo!" The voice carried from across the glow of the fire. And for a second, her heart simply stopped. She didn't expect to see him—not after the fiasco she'd made of his proposal. But surely he'd be here. It was his party too.

Except, as he came closer, through the glow, her heart re-started.

Not Dodge, but *Colt.* Just ten minutes younger, but he could have been years apart for the differences in personality. He looked similar, of course, with dark hair, now long and behind his ears, and the similar tall, rangy build. But Colt had brown eyes, a smile that could charm a girl out of her common sense, and a laugh that told most he didn't take life too seriously. He lived for the moment, dove in with his whole heart, and didn't care about the consequences.

Nope, not a smidgen like Dodge, the guy with the five-year plan, a to-do list, and forethought before every word that left his mouth. And Dodge's smile might be hard-won, but when it happened, all the darkness fled.

"I didn't think you'd be here. You never come to the bon-fires," Colt said, a dangerous twinkle in his eyes.

She played with the charm on her necklace, fitting her thumb into the small heart. "I just thought, since it was the last one . . ."

No, really, she thought maybe she'd see Dodge. But, of course, he wouldn't be here. Dodge didn't drink, didn't live outside the lines.

Colt, however, had no problem leaping right over any confines, and now he wrapped a muscled arm around her shoulders. "You picked the right party to come to. C'mon. Let's get you a drink."

He took her hand, and she didn't know why—maybe because Colt was everyone's favorite, the life of the party, and perhaps just a little of the boy she wanted—she followed him over to the toxic punch. And when he'd shoved the drink into her hand, she took a sip.

It didn't taste awful. Mostly sweet.

In her brain, outside the dream, Echo was waving semaphores. *Don't do it!*

"Let's dance."

Barefoot in the cool grass, she found her arms around his shoulders, his around her waist. He smelled good, and she liked the way he held her. She finished her punch, and he got her more, and then she danced by herself, the stars bright and spinning. She fell, and he laughed, then he picked her up and helped her over to a bench.

"I've always thought you were so pretty, Echo." Colt touched his hand to her cheek. His eyes were sweet in hers. "I know you and Dodge are—"

"We're nothing. Not anymore. Dodge hates me." She didn't know where those words came from, but maybe they were true.

After all, she'd broken his heart. He hadn't said as much, but she saw it in his beautiful eyes when she told him no. What she should have said was that he was moving too fast. That she needed time.

That he was scaring her.

Sheesh, he had them married, her strapped down with a kid before the end of the year. And look what that did to her parents.

Hello. So she'd said no, and Dodge took it like a punch to his chest, refusing to listen, ignoring her.

Pushing her out of his life.

And here was Colt, telling her that he thought she was pretty, and smiling at her, and suddenly Dodge was pushy and bossy and suffocating and—

Colt kissed her. He tasted sweet, like the punch, and smelled a little smoky. But his kiss was firm and determined and it felt good to be wanted, and when she put her hands on his chest, she kissed him back.

Why not? Colt was fun, and it was just a night under the stars, a last hurrah, nothing serious.

Nothing serious?

Please stop, Echo, before it's too late—

Except, it was already too late because she heard the voice even before she looked up.

"What the—"

Dodge. And even now, as she was dreaming, she wondered if this might be fiction. Maybe he hadn't just shown up, caught Colt with his arms around her. Seen them kissing.

But for the look on his face, the backdrop of the flames behind him, and the way Colt jumped up in defense, she might have simply blinked it away.

Woken up at home, hours later, with nothing but a splitting headache.

She didn't know how it happened—her brain was sloshy and gray around the edges—but she did remember hot words exchanged, and then snapshots of a between-brothers brawl that had everyone backing up.

Real bones being broken, real blood being shed, real pain as Ranger tried to get in the middle.

And then the cops. Teenagers scattering as Dodge was tackled to the ground. Cuffed. His face bloody, his eyes reddened. He might have even been crying.

She stood in the circle of light, watching, her hands over her face as she sobbed.

"Echo, wake up, you're having a nightmare."

Dodge's voice peeled through the layers, brought her into the light.

Back to the vet's office, where the sunrise broke through the window of the waiting room. The light skirted across the wood floor to the closed door that led to the back.

She pushed herself up.

So, it was true—she *had* fallen asleep with her head on Dodge's leg. Nice. Please let her not have drooled.

He appeared not to have slept, his eyes tired, his hair ruffled. He wore it shorter than he had in his teenage years, but still longer than a high and tight in-the-military cut, his curls turning over behind his ears.

"Sorry."

He drew in a breath. "It's okay. It's been a long night."

She sat up, pulled her hair out of the messy holder, then reworked it. "How's Holly?"

"She's out of surgery, but that's all I know. You were asleep, and they said you couldn't see her yet, so I didn't wake you."

But he'd stayed. In the daylight, he didn't look nearly as formidable as he had last night. More of a tired warrior with the dark scrape of whiskers, fatigue in his blue eyes. He'd taken off his jacket but wore a fleece under it.

"You must be exhausted."

"I slept."

"Sitting up?"

"You get used to it."

It took her a second. "In the military." Which is where he'd gone without saying a word to her after that fateful fight. Not even goodbye.

His mouth pinched and he gave a nod.

The door opened and she turned away from the words that

wanted to spill out. Like, When did you get back? And, Why didn't you call me?

Maybe she didn't want to know the answers.

Anuk came out to the lobby. She too looked tired, her hair rebraided and pinned back under a surgical cap. "She's out of the woods. We gave her a transfusion, stitched her back up. And her leg is set, but . . ." She shook her head. "I don't think she'll be up to mushing again."

"Ever?" Echo asked.

"We'll see, but I doubt it. It puts a lot of strain on a dog to mush."

"She loves running," Echo said softly. "Can I see her?"

"She's still sedated. Why don't you go home, get some rest, and come back later? We'll keep her under watch."

"I don't want her to be scared." Echo picked up her scarf. "Can you tuck this in next to her?"

Anuk smiled and took the scarf. "We'll call when she wakes."

Echo stood there, just breathing. *Holly will live.*

Next to her, Dodge was pulling on his jacket and grabbing his hat. "Do you need a ride?" He stood away from her, his blue eyes cool.

"Um . . ." She didn't know why, but she thought . . . maybe he'd . . . "I think I can get a ride. Thanks for your help last night."

"Yep." He headed for the door.

Wait— "Dodge?"

He turned, a quick look.

After a moment, where she tried to find words—

"What?"

"So, are you really back?"

He raised a shoulder. "Until my father is back on his feet."

Oh. "Are you okay?"

He raised an eyebrow. "Yeah. Fine. Why?"

"I just thought . . . maybe we could talk?"

His chest rose and fell. "I don't think there's anything to say, Echo."

"But . . . you were so . . . you comforted me."

"Your dog was hurt."

Yes. Right, but, "Don't you think we should air things out?"

"I think by now anything worth saying is gone. There's nothing to air out."

No ire in his voice, no emotion at all. Just words. Words between strangers. And nothing in his eyes either. Icy blue, cool, detached.

She swallowed past a fist in her throat. "I'm sorry."

His lips thinned to a fine line. Then, "I forgive you."

Her mouth opened, and stupid tears burned her eyes. "Oh, Dodge, thank you. I've felt so terrible for so long—" She closed the gap, put her arms around his waist, leaned into him. "I don't know how it went so wrong, and knowing how I hurt you . . ."

He didn't move. Didn't put his arms around her. Didn't pat her back. Nothing.

She finally released him and looked up. He was looking away, out the window. "Feel better?" He looked at her.

She stepped back. "Not . . . really."

"Yeah. Well, let it go, Echo. I have. It's over. Good luck with your dog."

He opened the door and walked outside.

She stood there, watching him go and . . .

No. No, it wasn't supposed to be this way.

She ran out after him, across the gravel driveway. The wind chill had loosened, but the cold still struck her like a slap, her throat burning. She wrapped her arms around herself. "Dodge!"

He stopped, turned. Frowned. "Go back inside. It's cold."

"You said you forgave me!"

He stared at her. "What do you want, Echo?"

Him. She wanted *him*. Had always wanted him, right? She'd spent ten years hoping he'd return, hoping she could fix it between them. But those words just couldn't emerge from her mouth, not with him staring at her with so much acrimony.

She preferred the cold, maybe.

"Nothing? Fine. I'll tell you what I want." He stalked back toward her. "I want to forget you. I want to forget this town. I want to forget that I gave you my heart—my entire stupid heart—and you spit it back at me. And then you set fire to it and turned it to ash. You mocked me in front of our entire town with my brother. My *brother*." He looked away. Took a breath.

"I never loved Colt," she said quietly.

He looked at her. "You never loved me either. And it's taken me ten years to get that through my brain, but now it's there, and I got it, Echo. I wasn't the brother you wanted, obviously. So, I need to forget you. Do I forgive you? Yes. Do I want to be with you? Not even a little. I'm over you."

She brushed the sting of his words away, seeing past them to the storm in his eyes. "Then what was last night? I cried, and you held me. You came out in the blizzard to rescue me."

"Like I said, your dog was hurt." His voice was cool, but he swallowed hard.

Her eyes narrowed and she retraced his reaction to her at the cabin. Wait one second . . . "You thought *I* was hurt. That's why you came. And... maybe you sticking around was you trying to deal with the fact you still have feelings for me. That you meant it when you said I was the only woman you'll ever love."

His eyes narrowed around the edges.

And, bingo. Because despite his cold front, she *knew* him. Knew when he was fighting hard to dodge the truth.

So she smiled. Crossed her arms. "You're *not* over me, Dodge. And I'm not over you. And like it or not, you're going to have to deal with that."

He drew in a breath, then sighed. His voice turned quiet, as if settling into some kind of resolution. "You stay away from me, and I'll stay away from you, deal?"

Not even a little.

She said nothing, still smiling as he shook his head. Then he walked away, got into his chopper, and flew off.

But he'd be back. Because he couldn't stay away from her any more than the sun could stop shining, even in the darkest Alaskan winter.

───⌣───

She was absolutely *not right*.

He was over her. Full stop, no problem.

The sun had risen, turning the snow on the mountains a deep gold. Dodge flew over the winter wonderland that was Copper Mountain, stores lined up along Main Street, houses nestled into the tiny community, surrounded by black spruce and white pine. Snowmobile tracks led out of town, and pickups and all manner of vehicles, from trucks to snow machines to dogsleds, were parked in front of the Midnight Sun Saloon, Gigi's Grocery, Starlight Pizza, and the school. A few kids played outside, swinging and throwing snowballs.

He angled west, toward Sky King Ranch. The wind had cleared the clutter of clouds, the sky an imperial blue, the mountains majestic and breathtaking.

Just calm down. He listened to the steady beat of his rotors, the collective in one hand, the cyclic in the other, Echo's words in his head.

"You thought I was hurt. That's why you came. And maybe you sticking around was you trying to deal with the fact you still have feelings for me."

Fine. Maybe he *had* thought she'd been hurt. But sticking around at the vet's office had more to do with the fact that he'd just nearly killed them flying through thirty-knot winds, and he just needed to be on the ground for a bit. Let himself breathe and ratchet his heartbeat to less than stroke levels. And wait, of course, until it was actually *safe* to put the bird in the air again.

And sure, what was he going to do—leave her when her dog might be dying? So yeah, he'd stuck around. But not because of his *feelings*.

"*You're* not *over me, Dodge. And I'm not over you. And like it or not, you're going to have to deal with that.*"

Despite her smile and her annoying confidence, he was over her. For example, when she leaned against him, crying, he put his arm around her, but he didn't lean down and smell her hair or kiss the top of her head. Didn't lift her chin to meet her beautiful green eyes—oops, okay—but that was just a fact, not something that was flitting about his head. So he hadn't met her eyes. And hadn't given more than a thought—okay, a couple, but not more—about kissing her. About pulling her into his arms and telling her it would be okay.

And for sure he hadn't noticed the way she slept so sweetly against him, as if she trusted him. As if she'd been waiting for him.

"*I never loved Colt.*"

Yep, he knew that. Of course she didn't. He figured that Colt was more to blame for what he'd walked into than Echo.

But it surely didn't look like she was putting up a fight, did it? And not even one visit to the county jail the entire week of his incarceration.

No, she didn't love Colt. But she hadn't loved Dodge either. Not really.

Not like he'd loved her. Because she'd been right about one thing . . .

She was the only woman he would ever love. And she'd taken that from him, leaving only darkness behind.

He *was* over her. He didn't exactly know what to do with her other statement about not being over him, but it didn't matter.

Another month, and he was out of here. Maybe sooner if he could talk someone into taking over his father's homestead route. And between now and then, he meant his words . . . he planned on staying far, far away from Echo Yazzie.

Now if his brain would stop replaying the smug look on her face when he'd walked away from her.

From the air, Sky King Ranch looked like a postcard—snow layered the roof of the barn and the lodge, smoke curled out of the stone chimney in welcome. Scrub pines dotted the fields beyond the runway, new growth after the fire, and down by the lake, the red roofs of the cabins glistened in the sun.

The perfect wintery retreat.

Once upon a time, he'd loved this view. Had plans to expand the operation with snowmobile tours in the winter and fishing expeditions in the summer. He'd mapped out an addition to his grandma's place, although he'd heard that Larke had remodeled it before it burned down.

The runway near the hangar had been plowed, so clearly his father was on the mend.

He landed the bird in the gravel and turned it off. He'd tow it into the hangar later. For now, he strapped it down and headed inside, his gaze falling on an unfamiliar red Silverado in the drive.

He stopped in the office and logged his hours, his flight, the fuel—he'd need a refill soon—and a few other details.

Voices lifted from the room beyond.

"We couldn't find any structural defects, Barry. The plane was sound."

"Ernie gave it a hundred-hour test a few weeks earlier, but I can't account for how it slapped that tree." Dodge heard his father's voice and stepped nearer the door.

"Otto said you were coming in pretty low. You sure you didn't just nick it? Wind was less than five knots."

"I've flown that route a thousand times, coming in from Denali. I could fly it with my eyes closed."

"That might be against regs." Laughter. Then, "I hate to do this, but right now, we need to put Sky King's operation on probation. No incidents for six months. Otherwise, we'll have to pull your FBO license."

Nothing from his father, and Dodge leaned out of the office to get a look. The old man was nodding, his hand behind his neck, massaging a tense muscle back there.

Dodge didn't recognize the other man, but he wore a shirt with a NATB badge on the breast, so he did the quick math. National Air Transportation Board.

"Well, thanks for coming out, Dwayne." His father held out his hand.

"I hear your son is back and is flying for you."

"Dodge. Out of the Air Force. That boy sure knows how to fly. My best student. Did you know he flew a combat chopper over in Afghanistan?"

Dodge stiffened.

"Wow."

"Yeah. Even got shot down. Got a Purple Heart. Scared me to death." Barry was walking Dwayne to the door.

"I'll bet. How's he doing?"

"Seems fine. Quiet. You know how it is, right? After war."

Dwayne nodded. "How are the other boys?" They reached the door, and Barry opened it, turning to Dwayne, but Dodge didn't hear his words.

His father knew about the crash. *And* his injury.

And he'd never written. Never come to see him. But what did Dodge expect? His father had made it pretty clear how he felt about him long ago.

The door closed, and Dodge moved back into the office to check the schedule. His docket was clear for now.

"I saw the chopper outside. Didn't hear you come in." His father stood at the door, and Dodge turned.

"Yeah."

"Deke called this morning to check on you. Said you'd brought in a dog to Anuk last night."

"Echo's dog. Got attacked by a grizzly."

"Oh no. How is she?" He wore a University of Alaska sweatshirt, a pair of baggy jeans, and his worn, blue Sky King cap. He'd shaved, showered, and frankly looked more ready to hop in a plane than Dodge did. Except, of course, for the cast and sling.

"It was a little dicey," Dodge said. "Had a terrible gash, a broken leg. But she had surgery, and Anuk says she'll live."

"That's good, but I meant Echo." Barry raised an eyebrow.

"Fine, I guess."

"You guess? You didn't talk to her?"

"Of course I talked to her. We . . . talked." Smells of last night's lasagna still embedded the kitchen. He wondered if there might be leftovers.

"You talked? Really?"

"There's nothing really to talk about. We said some things, but it doesn't matter. It's in the past. I'm tired. I'm going to bed." He turned to head out.

On the way, his gaze caught the picture in the office, the one with all of them, minus their mother, of course. But Larke, Ranger, Colt, Dodge, and his father all stood in front of his beautiful orange-and-white de Havilland Otter, the mountains green in the background. To his memory, it was the day Larke had finished her first solo.

They were grinning, and his father had his arms around Ranger and Colt.

"Son."

Oh, it was the tone, a soft warning, the same tone he'd use when Dodge would overcorrect or might be about to miss his landing. He probably shouldn't have, but he bristled. "I didn't come back here to be lectured."

"You need to forgive her. She was young. And Colt was—"

"Stupid? A jerk?"

"Yes," his father said quietly. And that turned Dodge. He just stared at the man. "Then why did you side with him?"

"I didn't side with anyone—"

"I *sat in jail* with a couple drunks waiting for you to bail me out! I sat there like a fool, and you never showed. Do you have any idea what that felt like as an eighteen-year-old kid? To know your father chose your stupid, arrogant, irresponsible brother over you?"

"I didn't choose him, Dodge. I just didn't bail you out."

"Really, Dad? C'mon. Just admit that you picked Colt over me."

"He was injured, Dodge. Seriously injured."

"Because he was drunk!"

"And you weren't injured."

"And whose fault was that?"

His father held up a hand. "You needed to think about your actions—"

"You let me sit in jail for a week. A *week*."

"It was better than for the rest of your life."

Dodge's mouth tightened, and he looked away.

"If the charges hadn't been dropped, you would have gone to prison for assault. And then who would you have become? Certainly not the man of honor that you are today."

He wasn't a man of honor, but he skipped that and went right to, "And I'm supposed to be thankful?"

"No. But that perspective might help you forgive him. And her."

"I've already forgiven her."

His father cocked his head. "Really?"

"Yes. She apologized. It's over."

"You've got a pretty big chip on your shoulder to call that over. It's gotta be getting heavy."

"I'm fine."

"Dodge. Be honest. It's not close to over. You've been nursing this wound for nearly ten years, working it off over there in Afghanistan, trying to forget the girl you've loved since you were ten. There's *no way* this is over. There is so much bitterness sitting in your heart you can't even see it. But maybe that's why God brought you back—for her. And to set you free from all that darkness."

No. Dodge rounded on him, his voice low. "I'm back because you needed help. If you don't—fine. I've got a job lined up with Air One Rescue. I can pack my bags in an hour."

His father took a breath, his jaw hardening.

"Oh, please. You didn't think I was staying, did you?"

"I've been praying for ten years for you to come back. God has bigger plans for you. A destiny if you'd just stop fighting it."

Of course he had to bring God into it. Too bad God had abandoned Dodge long ago. "There's no destiny, Dad. All the big plans have turned to ash. There's nothing left." He turned away. "As soon as you're able to take over, I'm out of here."

His father's soft voice stopped him. "I see."

Nice. He rounded. "Now who's bitter?"

"No, Dodge. I get it. Really. I wouldn't want to go back to hauling mail after I'd flown combat helicopters either. Thank you for your help with the ranch."

Oh. He hadn't expected that. "Sure." He put his hand on the door handle.

"You could stay at the house." It almost sounded like a request, and it slowed him down.

"I don't think so."

"C'mon, Dodge. You have to forgive me eventually. It's not good for your soul to hang on to anger this long."

Not good for his—he took a breath. "You've never asked."

Silence, and he waited for his father to say it . . . *I'm sorry, son. Please forgive me . . .*

"I guess I haven't." His father met his eyes. "I did what I did because I thought it was for the best. I can't change the past."

"Sounds like you're not sorry."

"I'm sorry you were hurt."

"That's not what I'm asking."

His father took a breath. "I felt like you needed a wake-up call. And you did. You left and became a hero."

"I'm not a hero, Dad." He turned away and opened the door. "You have other sons for that."

Then he walked out into the cold.

SIX

She was tired of the bloodshed. Echo stood outside the chicken wire of her coop and grimaced at the sight of two more of her laying hens dead, half-eaten before the killer had been scared away.

She blamed the snowfall—it had shorted out the Christmas lights she used around the pen and inside the coop to help with laying during the dark hours of the winter. And, emboldened, the coyote had ripped open the fencing from one of the fence posts, gotten in, attacked, and escaped with one of her precious hens.

The others were bunched inside the coop, snuggled in for the night, still traumatized.

Blood pooled in the fresh hay she'd set down before she left and splattered a trail outside the fence, all the way to the woods.

"Sorry, honey." Her father came over, lugging a bucket of water to add to the water heater for the chickens. "I came out as soon as I heard the fuss, but he'd already killed two of them. I chased him away, but he'll be back, I'm sure."

"No matter what I do, he finds a way in." She'd practically built Fort Knox for her hens—a huge six-by-twelve fenced area with a roof and tight chicken wire, a raised insulated house with laying beds, a heated tank for water, and lights to mimic the sunlight. Her Barred Rock hens laid beautiful light brown eggs year-round, and she sold them at the farmers market in the summer. "If Granite was here, he would have heard him."

But he was still out on the trail with Peyton, and given they hadn't returned yet, Echo guessed that Peyton had continued her route.

Echo had been at the vet hospital most of the day, deciding to wait, after Dodge left, for Holly to wake. Anuk let her shower at her home, fed her, and Echo had even grabbed a couple more hours of sleep before she helped Anuk tend a couple patients—a French bulldog named Bandit, recovering from soft palate surgery, and a sweet husky named Mo, undergoing chemotherapy.

Holly finally woke and Echo sat with her, feeding her by hand and settling her. Holly lifted her pretty blue eyes to Echo when her dad showed up to drive her home. "I'll be back, sweetie," she had promised.

Her dad was thin-lipped as she described the events of the night.

"You sure the grizzly had a white tuft between its ears?"

"Not even a little. It wasn't George, Dad. He wouldn't have attacked."

"George is used to humans. He grew up with us feeding him from our hands. He is also used to dogs and wouldn't have a fear of them either."

She'd looked out the window of the truck, not wanting to feed her father's worry. The sun hung low, the night already descending behind Denali, turning the ice-packed spires a deep amber, the descending valleys a rich violet. Nothing compared to a sunset in Alaska, regardless of the time of year.

Probably one of the reasons she'd stayed.

Her dad had turned on the radio, listening to the weather report from KTNO, the local station. Norm Dahlquist's resonant tenor predicted a dip in the temperatures, a storm brewing from the north. Apparently, last night's blow was just the appetizer.

"That was some fast thinking, to dart him," her dad said, looking over at her. He wore a hint of worry in his eyes, touched her knee with his hand, giving it a squeeze like he might have when she was a child, and she knew exactly why she'd stayed.

They'd pulled up to the house without the familiar greeting from the dogs, and she hoped Peyton and the dogs were safe. But then she'd spotted the mess with the chicken coop.

Now, she cleaned up the bloody straw, laid down a fresh layer, and added feed to their buckets inside the coop. The chickens squawked at her but didn't move. Their firm little bodies would keep the place warm.

Her own fingers were nearly frozen by the time she entered the arctic entry, stomped off the snow, shed her coat and hat, and headed into the kitchen. She pulled down a couple plates from the cupboard and walked over to the table to set it.

Her father had made a stew from moose meat, and the scent of garlic, oregano, and thyme filled the great room. Flames flickered in the hearth, the crackle stirring up her night in front of the campfire.

And the arrival of Dodge Kingston as if from heaven.

Or maybe somewhere else, given his response to her this morning.

She could still hear the hurt in his voice. *"I want to forget that I gave you my heart—my entire stupid heart—and you spit it back at me."*

She could see how it felt like that, but it had been nearly a *decade*, and they were different people now.

Maybe too different. She didn't recognize the Dodge with the cool blue eyes, the stiffened demeanor. With one blink she could see him as he'd been as a teenager, helping her train her dogs. Or taking her flying. Or even when he'd finally stirred up the courage to ask her out.

"You okay, honey?"

She turned to see her father holding the pot. "Yeah. I guess." She let go of the charm she played with on her necklace. She should probably take it off. What a fool to hang on to it this long. Bygones.

Her dad set the pot on the table. "Bowls?"

Right. She grabbed those too, and he dished up the stew. He'd made bread, too, and added that to the meal.

She could probably eat an entire moose, but for some reason, the food didn't sit well with her.

"Okay, spill. It's not just Holly, or the chickens—"

"Dodge is still angry with me."

She didn't know why that came out so easily, but her father had always been less of a father and more her best friend. "He told me to stay away from him."

Her dad had picked up the homemade mayonnaise to add to his soup, and now put the jar down. "I see."

"I get being angry, but after so long, it feels childish."

"A broken heart takes a long time to heal."

"But I apologized. And I'm here, *still* here." Which made her want to cringe.

Maybe she was a fool. Because deep in her heart she'd thought that someday Dodge would return. The fear had crossed her mind, more than once, that he might find someone else, but . . . *"You're the only woman I'll ever love."* Yes, he'd said that. Hadn't even denied it.

So, she'd had good reason to believe that someday they might end up past this. And then, she'd finally accept his marriage proposal.

Her dad picked up his bread, smeared mayonnaise on that too. Sighed. "I know it's because of me."

She frowned at him. "Dad—"

"No. I know something happened, Echo. Something you've never wanted to talk about, but one minute Dodge was practically the son I never had, helping you run your team, planning for the Iditarod, him hoping to start his own pilot service, and the next . . ."

"The next he's sitting in the Copper Mountain town jail for assault."

"No, next you're upstairs trying not to let me hear you cry."

He made a face. "I knew it was because you didn't want to leave me—"

"It wasn't because of you." She didn't mean to say it so abruptly, but, "He asked me to marry him, Dad. I was eighteen, and I just . . . I freaked out." She pushed her bowl away. "He had our lives planned out, and I . . ." She looked out the window, toward the darkness. "I didn't know what I wanted."

"You wanted to leave. And he wanted to stay."

"I wanted the freedom to figure it out before he had us building our own cabin and making babies in the woods." At least that was the story she was telling herself.

Her dad's lips tightened, and he nodded. "You're more like your mother than I thought."

Her breath caught and she stared at him, her mouth open. "Wow."

"I didn't mean it like you're thinking. Just . . . you're smart, like Effie. And yes, you deserved a chance to figure out what you wanted."

"I wouldn't have abandoned my husband and my child for a life in the Lower 48."

"She's in Anchorage."

She had nothing for her father's words.

"She started a practice there." He looked away. "I was so angry, Echo. I should have told you, but she—"

"She walked out on us." Echo folded her hands over her chest. "I don't want to know anything about her."

And just like that, she got it. Why Dodge hadn't replied to her letters. He didn't want to know anything about the person who'd torn him asunder.

Maybe he was right. They just needed to stay away from each other. Besides, hadn't he said he was leaving?

Despite how she felt about him, the last thing she needed was to find her way back into his arms, only to have him walk away.

Her dad picked up his spoon, blew on the soup, then took

a bite. "I should have known, even in the beginning, that your mother didn't want this life. I wooed her into it. I told her we'd only be here for three years, on my research grant. Sure, she liked the woods and hiking, but she never expected to live rough, out in the bush, with the nearest neighbor three miles away by snowmobile."

His voice dropped. "She never expected the hardships." He sighed. "But then she got pregnant with you, and three years turned into five and then nine, and she sort of forgot all that, at least for a while."

He left out the part where they were happy. Where Effie grew her garden and made herbal remedies, and he studied bears and ran guiding trips. And in the deep of winter, they kept each other warm, entertaining their daughter with games and stories and so much love it still pained Echo to think about it.

No, she wouldn't have wanted to hear from her either.

"Why didn't you go with her?"

He took another sip of soup. "I was made for the bush. What was I going to do in the city? Drive a snowplow?"

"You were a professor once."

"I hated teaching."

"Maybe you could build houses. You built this one."

"Now you tell me."

She laughed.

"Do you still think about leaving?" Her father's voice turned quiet, almost fragile.

"Dad. C'mon. Two against the world, you and me. I'm not going anywhere." She put her hand on her dad's.

He ran his thumb over her hand. "I'm so glad you weren't hurt in that grizzly attack. Even if it were George, I would have put the animal down."

"It wasn't George. And thanks."

He pulled away and picked up his spoon. "It was a pretty

windy night. Rough for a chopper. Dodge took quite a risk for your dog."

She didn't suggest that he'd gotten faulty information.

"You left Peyton with the dogs?"

"Yes. She'll be okay. She has three more cameras to check—we planned to be out in the bush for at least ten days, so I don't expect her back for a while."

He made a face and nodded, not saying what she was thinking. She should have stayed with Peyton. Or maybe, head back out to find her.

"She'll be okay," he said, repeating her words. "Eat your soup."

She picked up a piece of bread.

"By the way, did you talk to Hank?" he asked. "He said that mama sow had given birth."

"You gotta let Idaho go, Dad."

"I know he's out there, poaching bears. I feel it in my gut." He picked up his own bread and dunked it in the soup. "But I picked up Elsa's signal. She's awake and roaming near the Cache Mountain area."

She touched his arm. "See. Everything's fine."

He gave a laugh, and it warmed her through. Yes, two against the world. She didn't need Dodge.

Even if he was the only man she'd ever love too.

She finished her soup, then gathered up their bowls. She was filling the sink with water when she heard a screech outside.

Her dad was already on his feet. "That's Gregory."

Her rooster.

"I'll bet the coyote is back," Echo said, reaching for a towel. Her dad grabbed his capture gun by the door and headed out the back.

More screeching, now joined by her hens. She slipped on her boots and grabbed a jacket.

"Echo! You'd better get out here."

She pushed open the door, the cold a slap, and ran outside to where her father stood under the floodlights.

What—?

Granite stood in the driveway. He was without his harness, collarless, as if he'd been freed from the gangline.

She crouched and he ran into her arms, jumpy, upset. Snow caked his paws, without his booties.

She ran her hands down his body, trying to keep her voice from shaking. "Where is your team?"

She stood. "Maverick! Goose! Iceman!" The wind swallowed her words. Overhead, snow drifted down, lazy, a hint of the northern storm.

"Peyton!"

She listened, her heart thudding. Granite whined, sitting, then leaning against her.

No answer in the endless darkness.

Dodge probably deserved the frigid gush of water that woke him before the sun arose.

Mostly because he had been re-dreaming his angry words with Echo, his stupid decree.

"You stay away from me, and I'll stay away from you, deal?"

He didn't know when he'd turned into a full-out jerk, but he cringed at the memory, trying to escape it as he tossed and turned—

And then his cabin ceiling decided to come down on him. It started with a drip, something he swatted away in the folds of sleep, then a drizzle, a ripple of chill that brought him awake to stare at the dark ceiling. With so much gauzy darkness, it was tough to guesstimate the time, but he'd pin it around 6:00 a.m.

After the first drip—which he thought he'd imagined—he'd lain there, thinking about his day. Before, on a day like this, he might have gone hunting with his father. Or maybe checked on the herd.

He couldn't believe his dad had sold the cattle. He'd asked about the herd, casually, wondering if Dad had hired a ranch hand.

Sold. All thirty head.

"Bygone days," his father said last night over the plate of Larke's famous chicken divan casserole he was eating alone, at the kitchen island.

The smell of garlic and broccoli had nearly broken him. Some of the leftovers were going bad in the fridge and still Dodge couldn't bring himself to eat at the lodge.

He didn't know why. It just felt like it was one more layer of his anger sacrificed.

A guy had to have his principles, right?

And then—right in the middle of his thoughts—the roof gave way. Not just water but snow chunks plummeted onto his bed, and he rolled away a second before a sheet of ice rained down.

What the—?

He jumped up, his feet bare, wearing only his thermals. He pulled on his Sorels, grabbed his parka and headlamp, and headed outside.

The weather hovered a millimeter above freezing, the wind nipping at him as he hiked out to the toolshed. The sun had begun to tinge the range in fire, casting deep lavender shadows into the valleys and across the vast white terrain that surrounded their property. Behind him, wind carried snow dust off the lake, sprinkling it onto his jacket.

Inside the toolshed, an extension off the Quonset hut, he grabbed a ladder. The shovel he picked up down at the cabin.

He noticed a light on at the house, and through the window, he spotted his father in his recliner, reading, his glasses low on his nose.

His morning routine—coffee, Bible, prayer. Dodge used to

find a sort of comfort in that, as if, with his dad at the helm, all would be okay. He wouldn't crash in the bush somewhere, leaving them orphans. To him, Barry Kingston had been the wisest of men, the person he looked to for learning not only to fly but also to live life.

Dodge's thoughts drifted to his father recapping his military service. *"Scared me to death."*

Nothing scared Barry Kingston. Dodge didn't know what to do with those words.

He propped the ladder against the side of the cabin and climbed up.

The snowpack had been allowed to accumulate, and now he stepped down onto the roof, and it came nearly to his thigh.

Well, that was the first problem.

He dug in with his shovel and began to throw the snow from the roof, over the side.

The sun slid higher and turned all of the peaks bright pink, the base a deep blue, the foothills a lavish green, the snow that blanketed the valley a light robin's-egg blue. Sweat dripped down Dodge's back, but he stood to watch the glory for a moment, the stripping of the darkness to reveal the scars, the crevasses, the dangers, but also the stark beauty of a land that endured. Survived.

Thrived with the sunrise.

He had the roof half shoveled when he discovered the problem. The heat wave last week had melted some of the snow, but the cold snap had refrozen it into layers of ice. The liquid had been trapped under that layer and found the unsealed rivets in the roof.

The rivets had then rusted and weakened, and the weight of the snow and ice that had built up underneath had simply collapsed the roof. Hence, Niagara in his bedroom.

He finished shoveling, ignoring the growl in his stomach, and then climbed down, got a sledgehammer, and used it to gently tap at the ice buildup under the snow. He cleared the roof of that too, and the sun began to heat the rest, turning the roof a rich, beautiful red.

Except for the gaping hole over his bedroom.

Okay, it wasn't *that* bad. He could patch it until spring.

He climbed down the ladder, returned to the toolshed, and found a tarp.

At least it would stop the snow from getting in. He'd go to town, pick up some sheet metal, and get the gap repaired by tonight.

In truth, however, the entire roof needed to be replaced. And probably the roofs on the rest of the cabins. And snow guards added.

And while he was at it, he'd replace the insulation in the ceiling, and maybe add an instant water heater to the bathroom. He was tired of lukewarm showers, the hot water heater making a mere dent in the frigid cold from the lake.

All the cabins needed new decks, too. Most of them sagged with the snow weight.

At the thought, he cleaned off the deck of his cabin.

His stomach made him call it quits, and he went inside and opened the fridge. Of course he was out of eggs. And milk. Maybe he should swing by his dad's place and see if he was running low on perishable grub too.

He went in his cabin and put on a pot of water to boil. At least he still had ramen noodles. He'd upped his game at ramen over the years, adding fried bacon, onion, mushrooms, and an egg to the mix, but it still felt like bachelor food.

While he waited, he cleaned up the mess in his room, stripping the bed. He'd made a meager but decent home of the small cabin. With one bedroom, a woodstove, a small kitchen, a tiny bathroom, and a sofa, the place was also stocked with books and got cell reception most of the time.

His water boiled, and he moved the pot off the stove, added

the pack of spicy noodles he'd found at Gigi's. He put a top on the pan to let them sit and walked over to the window.

The sky seemed clear, but he spotted a dark thickening of clouds stirring over the mountains.

Storm.

And if he didn't get the roof repaired in time, it could be a long, cold few days, socked in.

Shoot. Truth was, he should just move back in.

He ate his noodles quickly, then went to the back room and tossed his clothes into the duffel. Finally, he grabbed his current book—*The Way of Kings* by Brandon Sanderson—and the pillow he'd hauled from his childhood bedroom and trekked up to the house.

His father wasn't in his recliner anymore.

He didn't know if this boded well or not. "Dad?"

No answer, so he slid off his boots and his parka and headed upstairs to his bedroom.

The upstairs was more of a long loft with two bedrooms, one at each end, and a walkway in the middle overlooking the great room. In the early days, the boys' bedroom took up one side of the loft, all three of their beds in one giant area.

The rest of the room had been a mess of Ranger's plastic soldiers, Colt's LEGOs, and Dodge's comics.

He'd finally convinced his father to build a wall in their room so he could have his own space. Small, but his to keep tidy and read late into the night without having his brothers rat him out.

He entered his room, his gaze falling on the Jace Jacobsen poster. Defender for the Minnesota Blue Ox. He'd retired years ago, but Jace was the toughest guy on the ice for a while.

Dodge had wanted to be just like him. Tough. Bold. The guy who didn't sit on the sidelines.

The guy who didn't let emotions cloud his vision.

Maybe he'd just keep the poster up.

Dodge dropped the duffel on the floor and threw the pillow

on the single bed. Admittedly, it was warmer here, and he didn't have to feed the woodstove every three hours.

He might actually get some sleep tonight.

So maybe he had been a little bullheaded.

He came downstairs and was making a mental list of needed supplies when he spotted his father outside in the Quonset hut. The door was open, probably to let in light as he worked, and the nose cone of Dodge's Piper PA-14 lay on the ground.

It looked like his father was working on the prop bolts. He wore a stocking cap, his lined canvas jacket, and his readers.

He kept pulling the glasses off his nose, adjusting them, backing up, then pulling in close as he tried to adjust a bolt.

Dodge couldn't really tell from here, but the way the old man kept fiddling with the bolt churned something inside.

Okay, he'd just go check. He pulled on his Sorels and his jacket and headed outside. "Dad, what are you doing?"

The man still wore his arm in a cast, but his other hand held a safety wire.

"I'm just finishing up changing the bolts on the prop. It's been on my to-do list for a while, and I thought while you were home, and the sky was clear, I'd get it done."

Of course he did. Again, Dodge watched as he tried to insert the safety wire into the tiny hole in the bolt, a precaution against losing the bolt.

"Dad. You're not even near the hole." He stepped up to him, reached out for the wire.

"I got this," his dad said, glancing at him. He wore his spectacles down on his nose, and it aged him. In fact, in this light, his father looked downright old. He had deep lines around his eyes and his hair had whitened. And he wore a thick scratch of white whiskers.

It unseated Dodge.

"I've been changing prop bolts since before you could walk." He made another stab at the hole.

Not even close. Dodge stepped back, watching him struggle, not saying anything.

Finally, "Dad. Can you *see* the hole?"

"I don't need to see it. I usually feel for it—it's so small, but—"

"If you had two hands, it might work better."

His dad's mouth tightened into a thin line. "Maybe."

"Can I try?"

With a sigh, his father handed him the thin wire. Dodge inserted it into the bolt hole and wound it tight, then attached it to the adjoining bolt, yet another layer of safety. From here, he could see the other safety line had been already tightened down, albeit messily. A one-handed job.

He could fix it when he got home from the store, before he took the plane up again. "I'm going to run into town and pick up some groceries, as well as some tin. The roof came down in my cabin this morning."

"Are you okay?"

Huh. Not the question he'd expected. "Fine. But there's a hole, so I'm going to try and patch it before the storm gets here. For now, I moved back into the house. I hope that's okay."

His dad was tightening another bolt, not looking at him. "Yep."

No emotion, but that was probably the best thing.

Somehow, however, something in Dodge chipped away, broke free. Felt lighter.

"I'll be back later."

"Don't worry about me. I have a year's worth of lasagna in the fridge." He looked at Dodge and gave a wry grin.

And before he knew it, Dodge was grinning back.

Okay, whatever.

He turned on the radio as he drove into town.

Norm Dahlquist's voice came over KTNO. He was doing a rundown of the week's events, ending with a callout to all the homesteads. They called it the bush pipeline, a way to communicate with all the homesteaders who didn't have ham radios.

"To Spike and Nola, your doctor from Anchorage will be out on Friday next, for a checkup."

Dodge wondered if he'd be the one flying them. Hopefully. He was a little worried about the family out there in the bush.

The thought of flying didn't rattle his gut so much. He'd handled his recent flights without incident. Nothing to get sweaty-palmed about. And he no longer felt like retching every time he landed.

See, he could kick the demons.

The thought of flying out to Spike's place turned his thoughts to the rogue bear.

And Holly, Echo's dog.

And then, of course, Echo.

Maybe he should apologize. Just to clear the air, nothing more.

The radio turned to a mix of country and folk, and he tapped his fingers to a song by the Yankee Belles, an all-girl country band that had found some favor among his fellow pilots overseas.

One of their hit songs was about a soldier who'd lost his life and the girl who couldn't forget him.

He turned off the radio.

He crossed over the Copper River, then turned north toward town, passing the suburbs, the new cabins and lodgings, the Fish Lake floatplanes, then the Roughneck Roadhouse, which had him thinking about their sourdough flapjacks. He passed the school, where a group of kids slapped their sticks around.

He finally pulled into Mulligan's Hardware on Seward's Way and got out.

The sun had reached its apex—high noon, a good six hours of daylight left. Funny how he'd again started orienting his days around the sunrise and sunset, bracing himself to endure the darkness.

Ace Mulligan, Moose's father, stood at the counter as Dodge walked in. A big man, Ace had a smile and an answer for nearly any problem, be it construction or politics. He'd even served as mayor for a while until he was beaten by a write-in voter wave for a local bulldog named Stubbs.

To Dodge's knowledge, Stubbs was still in charge.

"I heard you were back, Dodger." Ace called him by his old hockey nickname. "Moose said you're going to fly for him with Air One."

Ace wore a bushy red Fu Manchu mustache, a gimme cap backward on his head, a pair of Carhartt overalls, and a black thermal turtleneck. "He's coming up in a few weeks for the Rowdy. He's going to play in the annual pickup match, for the townies. Are you hopping in on the game too?"

Dodge would be on the other team, the guys from the bush, with the Starr brothers and the Bowies—who technically lived in town after their parents were killed, but no one argued—and of course, the Remington brothers. Moose Mulligan had rung his bell a few times on the ice, and his kid brother, Axel, was even bigger. But it was Topher Dahlquist who had nearly broken Dodge's collarbone his senior year.

"We'll see," Dodge said to Ace. "Had a cave-in today in one of the cabins. Snow load. I need some sheet metal."

"No problem. We'll get it ordered."

"You don't have any in stock?"

"Used to. Sold out. How much do you need?"

Dodge outlined the project and put in the order. He walked out with a bag of sealant, a thicker tarp, and orders for a couple homes on his route—the Sattlers, west of Spike and Nola's place, and Erv and Joann Nickle, not far from Remington Mines.

He was loading up his truck when his name in the air caught him.

He turned to see Goodwin Starr walking up to him. Brown hair, blue-eyed like his sisters, and fit, Goodwin wore a vest with DENALI SPORTS on the breast pocket. "I thought that was you I saw the other night at the Midnight Sun. You here for practice?"

Practice. Right.

He noticed that a pair of skates hung over Goodwin's shoulder.

"These babies are new, just in time for the game. Getting them sharpened." He gestured to the hardware store. "I still have my old pair, the ones I wore when I beat you in lines."

Goodwin was a couple years younger than Dodge but had played with a ferocity as forward that had netted him a varsity position.

Dodge couldn't account for why he said it, but, "I'll bet I can beat you now."

"Really," Goodwin said, grinning. "I'll take that bet. Get your skates."

"Sorry. Left them at home."

"No problem. We have a slew of secondhand skates in the shop. Freshly sharpened. Go pick a pair, on the house, and I'll meet you on the ice, Forty-Four."

And that's how Dodge found himself, thirty minutes later, sitting on a bench next to Mal in the rink's warming house, lacing up a pair of broken-in size elevens.

"I have extra gear in my locker," Mal said. He had given Dodge a fist bump when he'd walked in, saying, "I have a good feeling about this year."

Okay, that felt good.

The sun hung high, the day bright, a hint of anticipation in the air, and everything inside Dodge buzzed as he stepped out of the warming house onto the ice. He took a swing around the ring, stretching, listening to the scrape of his blades carving out his line.

He turned around, skated backward, an eye over his shoulder, then flipped back around, glided close to the boards, and grabbed a stick. Mal, Hudson, Goodwin, and even Jude Remington, Nash's kid brother, had joined them, along with a few younger players that Dodge didn't know.

They slapped pucks around, and for a second, Dodge missed Ranger's voice, calling to him to pass it out to him. And Colt, swinging around to grab the puck. Colt always had amazing stickhandling.

Levi Starr waved before disappearing into the warming house. And then Axel took the ice at goal and suddenly, they had a pickup game, practicing with shots on goal, passing the puck around.

Dodge started to sweat, his lungs opening up, his body turning loose, the old adrenaline and skills returning like a sweet song inside him.

More cars pulled up, a few people took the stands.

Kids lined the boards, calling out.

"Ready for that race?" Goodwin shouted. He leaned over, his hands on his knees, gliding around the ice.

Dodge shot the puck at goal, then headed over to the side and handed his stick off to one of the kids, who took it with wide eyes. "I'll be back for that," Dodge said.

Then he skated down to the end of the ice.

"Lines?" Goodwin said.

"You bet."

The others had cleared off to the sides, and for a moment, Dodge was seventeen and trying to hold his position as fastest on the team. Fastest, strongest, fiercest.

He glanced at Goodwin, who was grinning.

"What's the bet?" Dodge said.

"Loser buys pizza."

"No prob—"

"For everyone."

And it was then that Dodge's gaze traveled to the gathered spectators. He always had a sense of when she was around, as if his heart just knew it, a radar that centered right on Echo Yazzie.

Now his eyes fell right on her. She wasn't hard to miss. She had climbed the bleachers up to the fifth row, ventured out to the middle, her usual spot, only this time she was standing, as if trying to decide whether to stay and watch.

She wore a red jacket, her hair in two bronze braids tucked back by a headband. And wouldn't you know it, she was looking right at him.

A strange and unfamiliar heat rose from deep inside, building, until it roared through him.

He looked at Goodwin. And smiled. "Hope you brought your wallet."

SEVEN

How Echo found herself in the stands, cheering for Dodge as he outskated Goodwin Starr, she had no idea.

One moment she was driving into town with her dad after checking on Holly, intent on confirming Peyton's whereabouts with Hank.

The next she was walking over from the city parking lot to the rinks and climbing the stands to watch Dodge warm up.

Oh, he still had moves. Only these were stronger, bolder, more powerful moves. She knew he'd filled out. She well remembered the way he'd held her at the vet's office, but seeing him skate, handle a stick and puck, listening to him laugh—

Oh, his laugh. It found the dark places inside her and filled them up with a light, a desire that could nearly choke her.

She should run. But like the lure of a car accident, she couldn't help but stare, even if she had a head-on collision with the man.

It might be worth it to see him play, just this once.

He'd lined up for some kind of race with Goodwin, the wind playing with his hair, his smile wide as he and Goodie probably talked trash.

And then it happened. He looked up in the stands and spotted her. Stripped her of any defenses with his blue-eyed stare. She couldn't look away. Her breath caught.

Oh, she loved him, and she was such a wimp for letting this man take so much of her. For not trying harder to erase him from her heart.

For being so easily wooed by her own sad dreams.

She should leave. She told herself that, loudly, practically waving warning flags in her head. Instead, she stayed planted.

Someone shouted "Go!" and Dodge took off like he was on fire. They ran lines—skating to the first line then back, then the middle and back, the third and back, and finally the full length and back.

Dodge beat Goodie by an entire half length.

She'd never really seen him skate that way, with such tenacity, such drive.

As if nothing would beat him.

Or maybe that had always been Dodge. She'd just forgotten.

He was breathing hard afterward, bending over to grab the boards. She thought maybe he'd hurt himself, but then he banged fists with Goodwin and grinned, and see, he was just fine.

She, on the other hand, might be having a full-out heart attack, so she tucked her head down and hustled away toward Hank's office before she did something like stand up and cheer.

Pitiful.

She nearly took out Shasta on her way down.

"Whoa, Echo. Hey!"

Shasta was wearing a white down jacket, leggings, her brown mukluks, and a hat with a pom-pom. With her dark hair down, she was practically an Alaskan cover model. "Where are you going?"

"Uh—"

She hooked her arm around Echo and dragged her back up the stands. "Sit. Watch." She sat next to Echo. "I can't believe that Dodge is back. He looks good out there." She leaned into Echo, gave her a nudge.

As Winter's kid sister, Shasta had been privy to many of Echo and Winter's apparently not-so-private conversations about Dodge, as well as Winter's heartthrob, Malachi Bowie.

"Yeah, well. He told me to stay away from him." Echo didn't

know where that came from—it just sorta spilled out, and along with it the hurt that had been floating around her heart like acid.

"What? Why?"

Echo gave her a look. "It probably has something to do with the fact that I broke his heart."

"Ten years ago. Sheesh. Tell him to grow up."

Echo smiled. "Maybe I'm the one who should grow up. I used to think he'd come home and I'd be here, and he'd just sorta forget about what happened. But maybe I'm the one holding on to something that I should let go of."

Dodge was out on the rink, playing defense, a formidable opponent to the motley crew who tried to get the puck past him. He slammed Goodwin into the boards, although admittedly, not with the force he had when they were kids. They scrabbled for the puck.

"I'm going over to talk to Hank," Echo said.

"You should stay and watch practice."

"Say hi to Winter for me."

She climbed down and didn't look at the rink as she headed over to the Fish and Game office.

Hank wasn't there, but his assistant was, a girl named Clementine, with long black hair and Native blood in her features.

"Hey. Has my dad been in?" Echo asked. "He wanted to talk to Hank."

"Yeah. They went over to the Starlight with Ace Mulligan for lunch."

Her father was probably bending Hank's ear about the need for more fish and wildlife enforcement, and most particularly a scrutiny of Idaho's so-called guiding license. She didn't disagree.

"Has Peyton checked in?" she asked. "I think she is still in the bush, but Granite came home alone yesterday, so I'm a little worried."

Clementine walked into Hank's office, looked at a chart. "He's got her pinned here as out, and she's listed as green, so it doesn't look like anything's amiss."

Hank kept track of all his rangers' whereabouts when they traveled the bush. No doubt he'd checked in with her.

So Echo wouldn't worry either. She checked the guiding schedule and signed up for a couple trips later in the month. She also checked the weather report—a storm was headed down from the mountains.

And then, just because, she decided to send a text to Peyton on the sat phone. She was for sure out of voice range by now, but she could text back.

The smell of pizza had invaded the office, and by the time she finished, her stomach demanded satisfaction. Maybe she'd just duck into the Starlight, grab a piece of pizza, and talk to Hank herself.

Quite a few pickups had pulled up in front of the place as she went inside.

And immediately, she realized why.

Levi and Goodwin Starr were feeding the hockey team who'd shown up for practice.

The tiny pizza joint was packed. When Levi took it over, he'd gutted the small house, replanked the wooden floor, washed the paneling, and shoved together long yellow tables and stools down the center of the room for community dining. A purple sign over the back of the long bar listed the specials, and the regular menu was chalked on the opposite wall.

The view to the kitchen was open, with a ramp for kids to watch from, their noses pressed against the Plexiglas as Levi and his team flipped pizza dough and slathered on rich red sauce.

Despite the chilly afternoon weather, the doors to the deck were open, with tall heaters blasting out warm air. Edison party lights lit up the area, and music played throughout the place—

"Arms," by Christina Perri. *"You put your arms around me and I'm home . . ."*

The team had congregated outside, but a few stood inside, and of course, like she had some eerie Dodge radar, Echo's gaze fell right on him. He stood near the door, dressed in his jeans and an open parka, a wool cap, his dark hair just visible around the edges. He was talking with Malachi and laughing.

That laugh again. It curled inside her and tugged.

Yes, she should probably run. But Goodwin was behind the bar, serving up beer and sodas, and called out to her. "Echo!"

She turned her attention to him, and he nodded toward the nook by the back door. She spotted her father talking with Hank and Ace.

Her dad didn't see her, evident from his animated hands. Hank sat back in his chair, his arms folded over his chest, nodding.

She didn't want to get anywhere near that conversation.

Instead, she walked up to Goodwin. "Got any lonely pieces of pepperoni back there?"

"I'll see what I can find. Want something to drink?"

"Just a Coke."

He scooped up ice and filled her glass. "Did you see our boy out there take me down?"

Maybe he'd missed Dodge as much as she had. Once upon a time, he'd practically worshipped the guy. Apparently, over the years, the town lore had swung back in Dodge's direction.

"He smoked you," she said and took the Coke.

"It'll be a good tournament. Now, if we can just get Range and Colt home."

Echo gave a tight-lipped nod. She had a feeling, given her conversation in the vet's office yesterday, that might not go down quite as well as Goodie thought.

She moved down the bar, watching the news on the flat-screen. The first of the Iditarod runners had come over the line. A Norwegian in first place, a fellow Alaskan in second.

"Still thinking of running it?"

The voice made her freeze, and she stood, wordless, as she looked up at Dodge. His dark blue eyes settled on her, and he smelled of sunshine and fresh air. He looked downright woodsy with the finest layer of grizzle on his chin. He set his drink—also a Coke—down on the counter. Up close, and without all the anger that had hued his face at Anuk's clinic, he was downright breathtaking.

At least, *she* couldn't breathe.

Maybe he saw her expression because his smile vanished and his own turned solemn. "Echo, I wanted to apologize for what I said to you, um, before." He swallowed. "I was a jerk. I agree—we were both young, and it was a long time ago and . . . maybe I was tired. I don't know. Just . . . I'm sorry."

She blinked at him. "So you don't want me to stay away from you?"

His eyes widened. "Oh, uh . . ."

A chair tipped over, and a shout rose from the nook in the back.

Echo turned and groaned.

Idaho had joined the party, and now he and her father were nose to nose, shouting over the top of each other.

Her dad looked very much like he wanted to put Idaho through the front window. She'd never considered her father a powerful man. Lean and wiry, he'd never put on much weight after his mauling, and now, compared to the burly mass of Idaho, he looked very much dwarfed. Except for his fury. He stepped right up to the guide and pointed a finger at him.

Idaho pushed him. Her dad went tumbling over a table and onto the floor.

"Hey!" Dodge said, and before Echo could move, he'd waded right into the fray. He slammed his hand on Idaho's shoulder before he could go after her father, who was scrambling up from the floor.

Then he put his hand on her dad's chest. "Take a breath there, Charlie."

Hank was trapped behind the table, but he too found his feet. And Ace looked like he wanted to take a piece out of Idaho. Goodwin joined them, stepping up beside Dodge, and in a second, Deke Starr had also arrived.

"Let's just calm down," Deke said, and Dodge didn't move as Deke led Idaho away.

"He violated his restraining order!" Idaho was yelling, but Deke didn't seem concerned.

Echo was shaking as she walked over to her father, edging up next to Dodge. "Dad, what's going on?"

Her dad was still shouting after Idaho. "He's a poacher. He killed a denning mama bear, and that's not the first time!"

He'd been drinking.

Dodge separated him from the crowd, his arm around him as he walked him out. "I know, Charlie. I know. Let's just go home, get some sleep."

Echo walked behind, aware of every eye on her, on them.

On Dodge, saving the day. Her throat burned.

Her dad got outside, then tore away from Dodge. Bent over, breathing hard, he looked up at Echo. "Sorry, honey. I don't know what got into me."

"How much did you have, Dad?"

He stood up, his eyes hard on her. Then he walked away, across the street to where he'd parked the truck in front of the Fish and Game office.

"No way is he driving," Dodge said. He took off after him. "Charlie. Give me those keys!"

He reached him, grabbed his arm, turned him around. Her dad yanked away from him, but Dodge took him by both arms and backed him up to the truck. Strange to see them face-to-face, the size Dodge had on her father.

Echo didn't know what he said to him, but her dad pulled

the keys from his pocket and slapped them into Dodge's hands. Dodge nodded, and then maneuvered her dad around the truck to the opposite door. Put him inside.

She approached the truck. "I'll drive."

He pulled out his keys. "I'm driving him home. You follow in my truck." He handed them to her and pointed at his dad's Ram truck.

He met her eyes, held them. "I got this, Echo."

Then he got in.

Yes, yes he did.

And she wanted to weep.

———〜———

Dodge simply wasn't sure Charlie wouldn't force Echo to turn around and take him back to the Starlight to finish off whomever he'd been fighting with.

He turned on the wipers as the slightest drift of snow hit the windshield, melted, and slid off. The afternoon sky had turned a deep pewter, the landscape a wash of gray and white, the trees a mottled dark green.

"Want to tell me what happened back there, Charlie?"

His prisoner sat in the passenger seat, staring out the window, arms crossed over his jacket. The ultimatum he'd given the man flashed through Dodge's mind.

"I don't want to make a scene, but I will take those keys from you. Don't go down in front of your daughter."

Maybe he could have been kinder, but Charlie had called him a couple ripe names as he'd backed him into the truck, so he'd decided to get to the point.

Now, however, he glanced at Charlie, and a shard of compassion separated him from his frustration. "What did that guy say?"

"It's what he did. He's a poacher, and he killed a denning sow, left her cub to die."

Right. He'd heard that story a few days ago. Dodge glanced into the rearview mirror. Echo followed him a few car lengths behind.

He wouldn't be here except for the stricken look that crossed her face in the pizza place when Charlie went down. All Dodge's instincts had lit, and he'd found himself across the room and hauling Charlie to the street before he came back to himself.

He refused to look too deeply at that. Just old habits.

Still, it was one thing to apologize. Quite another to find himself at her house, in the quiet hour, when all ill-fated conversations about the past could rise between them.

Not going to happen. He'd drop off Charlie, then leave.

His goal was peace, not a happy ending where they reignited some long-cold romance.

"I heard about the bear," Dodge said. "You're worried about Elsa."

Charlie lifted a shoulder. "She's a bear in the wild. I know things can happen. I just don't want it to be by a couple poachers."

Dodge nodded.

"I think George was killed a few years back, although I can't prove it. His GPS collar stopped working, but when I went out to the last known location, I couldn't find it. If he'd died of natural causes, the collar might have been with his carcass."

"Honestly, Charlie, I can't believe Elsa's still alive. She's nearly fifteen years old."

"It's not unusual for bears in the wild to live twenty, even twenty-five years." Charlie glanced at Dodge. "I thought you were gone for good. Echo cried over you for years. Are you back in her life, or what?"

The words brought him up and he stiffened. But if Charlie was going to shoot straight, so would he. "I'm just in town for a few weeks, until my dad gets back in the cockpit, then I'll be flying for Air One in Anchorage." The words cemented inside him. Yes, now that he'd worked out the kinks, he'd call Moose and officially accept the offer. "So, no. I'm just here as a friend."

Charlie's mouth tightened into a knot. He looked away.

Cried for years?

"You stopped being her friend at age sixteen when I saw you two working that sled dog team together. I knew even then what your intentions were, son."

Dodge glanced at him, but he didn't argue. In truth, he didn't know when friendship turned to love, to longing, to dreams.

"Just don't hurt her," Charlie said. "I can't watch her go through that again. She's had enough people leaving her."

Bitterness laced his voice, and Dodge had nothing as he crossed the bridge over the Copper River and headed north. The water was angry, gray, and frothing up cold chunks of ice and debris.

He turned up the windshield wipers. Behind him, the lights on his truck carved out two blades in the deepening storm. The flakes came thicker now, like the shooting stars hitting the *Millennium Falcon*.

His grip tightened on the steering wheel. "Charlie, I haven't told anyone this, but I was shot down in Afghanistan. Got pretty banged up. Did some time at Walter Reed. Lots of rehab. I know about pain." He looked at him. "I also know how it feels to drink it away. I warmed a stool at a local bar near the base for a while after the accident, trying to forget. I just ended up with a headache and more regrets. There are other ways."

He didn't look at Charlie, but he'd seen the scars. The one through his scalp where the bear's teeth had clamped down and separated flesh from skull. And the long thick scar down Charlie's arm bore the legacy of the grizzly's claw. From the look of it, he still couldn't close his fist on that hand.

Dodge's body, too, carried a few scars, and for a long time, the docs wondered if he'd walk again.

Charlie looked at him. "You don't know anything about it."

He tried to sort out the words as he turned off the highway, back through the winding, rutted road that led back half a mile to their homestead.

It. Being betrayed by the woman he loved? Yeah, he knew plenty about that kind of pain too.

His father's words to him rose, clung. *"You have to forgive me eventually. It's not good for your soul to hang on to anger this long."*

Maybe Dodge had no right to lecture Charlie on letting go. Still, "Just think about Echo. She hurts too, every time she sees you like this."

"Echo is my business, not yours. Not anymore."

Right. He looked over at Charlie. "For what it's worth, you taught me how to survive in the wilderness, and that toughness kept me alive in Afghanistan. So there's that."

Charlie said nothing for a long time. Finally, "Glad you made it home in one piece, son."

Home. As Dodge pulled up to the homestead, blanketed in a layer of fresh snowfall, a well of memories opened. Him with the dogs, hitching up the sled, or attaching one of Echo's dogs to his harness and skijoring with her through the pine-scented, quiet forests. Helping her feed the goats in the barn, the scent of fresh hay layering the air, and changing the straw amid angry, bleating goats. Gathering eggs in the coop, like hidden treasures, stealing them from scolding hens. Smoking fish and caribou meat in the tiny smokehouse.

Chopping wood—oh, so much wood—and stacking it in the massive woodshed.

Yes, this land had felt as much his as Sky King Ranch. More, maybe, because the ranch had had Ranger and Colt to tend it.

He'd felt vital here and helping run this place had been as much a hope as flying for Sky King Ranch.

"You added on to the house," he said to Charlie, noting the new side entrance to the log home. As at many of the homesteads, snowshoes were tacked to the wall outside. Over the front door hung a pair of skinned moose antlers that Dodge knew Charlie had probably found rather than harvested.

"Echo's idea. And she made me build an office to keep all my books."

No one read like Charlie, a reminder that, once upon a time, he'd been a professor of biology in Wisconsin, where he'd met Effie and dragged her to Alaska. *"If it's in a book, you can learn it, son."* Charlie's words to him, long before the mauling, back when Effie taught Echo how to garden and create her own healing balms.

Frankly, if any couple could have lasted, it should have been Effie and Charlie.

No one knew why Effie had left, really. And Charlie didn't talk about it.

Dodge pulled up to the house, the lights on, and an old dog got up and walked toward them, barking.

Granite? What was he doing here?

As Charlie opened his door, Dodge got out his own side and caught the dog. "Hey, bud. I thought you were out on the trail." Maybe it had been a different dog at the cabin. Crazy, but his eyes burned as he rubbed the dog behind its ear. Granite leaned into it, groaning, and then gave him a kiss on the chin. "Yeah, I missed you too."

Dodge spotted Charlie grunting and limping up to the house. He must have been hurt in the fall. He got up and hustled over to him as Echo's lights cut into the drive.

Dodge put a hand on his arm, but Charlie yanked it away. "I got this."

Dodge didn't take it personally, just followed him and opened the door.

Charlie didn't look at him as he tromped inside, kicking off the snow, then sat on the bench in the arctic entry and toed off his boots.

Dodge was stuck on a picture that hung on the wall of the entry. Clearly taken from a bluff not far from here, it captured the land in summer, where the green fields and deep pine forest rose and fell, split by glimmering blue rivers, an endless cerulean sky. To the west, a ragged horizon captured the deep purple of the foothills, and farther, a hint of white-capped glaciers nested into mountain canyons. A thin layer of cirrus clouds suggested a lazy, warm day. And at the center of the picture, standing in a field of deep pink dwarf fireweed and yellow poppies was a massive grizzly, a lone sentry in the middle of a vast beauty.

"That's George," Charlie said. "Our last picture of him. Echo took it a number of years ago."

"It's beautiful."

Charlie made a noise of agreement and got up. Dodge refrained from grabbing him when he groaned and reached out to prop his hand on the wall.

Echo came in behind him. "Dad. You okay?"

He didn't look at her. Just shuffled out of the entry toward his office.

She glanced at Dodge. "Sorry about that. He'll fall asleep in his recliner and be okay in the morning. He sleeps better sitting up anyway. His shoulder doesn't hurt as much." She bent to take off her boots. "Thanks, Dodge, for bringing him home." She dropped her mukluks onto a boot warmer. "Do you want some coffee?"

He should say no. He'd done his good deed, brought Charlie home, a peace offering of sorts to cement his apology.

"Sure." And suddenly he was taking off his shoes and jacket and following her in his wool socks into the house. As he walked by Charlie's office, he noticed he was already in his recliner, his head back, a snore emanating.

Echo closed his door. Glanced at Dodge. "He was dry all winter. Then this stuff with Idaho started and suddenly he's drinking beer with Hank and picking fights." She walked into the kitchen and grabbed a kettle. "It's his pain meds. They interact with the alcohol and suddenly he's three sheets to the wind. Pie? I found a can of pumpkin from last fall and didn't know what to do with it."

"I like pie." Really, what was he doing?

She laughed, and it was both so familiar and unexpected that it blew past all his defenses and landed inside, lancing something open, almost a welcome pain.

He fled to the fireplace, grabbed a couple split logs, noted that she probably needed a couple loads before he left, and added the logs to the hearth. Then he tucked in some birch scrapings and sticks from the kindling bucket and struck a match.

In a moment, the fire lit, crackling through the birch. He stood, his gaze on the pictures on the mantel—Echo with Granite, one with a salmon. A family picture, dust on the frame, showcased beautiful Effie and Charlie holding Echo by each hand, lifting her in the air. Echo wore a red cap with bunny ears, a smaller version of the cabin behind them.

"She's had enough people leaving her."

He heard the indictment. But whose fault had that been?

"Here you go." Echo came up behind him and handed him a piece of pie and a cup of hot coffee. She'd put it through her French press.

He inhaled. "Now this is coffee." He took a sip and turned to a set of pictures on the wall, wildlife shots. A gorgeous red fox sitting in the snow, its fluffy red tail curled around itself, yellow-gray eyes fixed, staring at the camera. A coyote in a field of wild lavender irises, ears alert, staring into the horizon. A shot of two black bear cubs wrestling on a rocky river shore.

"These are amazing."

"Thanks." She took a sip of the coffee. "Those are some of the animals that my dad has fostered."

"You're a real talent, Echo."

She smiled. Lifted a shoulder. "Just a hobby." She sat on the worn leather sofa, drew a leg up under her. The firelight flickered on her face, a warm glow. Outside, the snow had thickened, fell harder, turning the world white. He should probably get home before he was stuck here.

He set his coffee down on the coffee table, a beautiful piece of live-edge alder, and sat on a matching worn leather chair. Then he dug into the piece of pie. "This is really good."

"Thanks."

"So, did you get your biology degree at the University of Alaska?"

She shook her head. "It never seemed right to leave."

He frowned. "I always thought you'd be some big-time researcher, written up in *Sunset* magazine or working for the DNR."

"I take guiding trips out. But I like it here. And I can't leave my dad."

She looked at the fire. "The homestead always needs work. Gardening, canning, raising the dogs, fishing—you know the drill. He can't run this place by himself. And he's busy with his wildlife research." She took another sip. "He still keeps tabs on Elsa. Goes out early in the season, when she wakes up, and gathers hair from her cubs so he can keep their DNA and track them if people bring in kills. He's tagged a few, too, although he doesn't like to do that. It affects them, you know. To be wounded and watched. It's like the bear knows he's not quite free anymore. Or he's been forever altered."

He hated to admit how much he understood that.

The fire crackled, popped.

"Remember when your dad used to make popcorn in the fireplace?" he said.

"He only did that for you, because he knew you liked it."

"I did." He sighed. "You ever run the Iditarod?"

She shook her head.

He didn't know why, but he felt a shame, deep inside him. "So, you've just been here, working the homestead, for the past ten years?"

"Is there something wrong with that? Once upon a time, you had the same dream, Dodge. I remember you talking about flying for Sky King Ranch. Why do my dreams have to be grand to be important?"

He held up a hand. "Sorry. I just—"

"I couldn't run like you did. I had to stay. I had responsibilities and a father who needed me." She let those last words sit on him.

He drew in a breath, meeting those pretty green eyes, the color of the pine trees. If he looked too long, they could hold him hostage. Yeah, this was a bad idea.

Because in them he saw the dreams they'd both shared.

"Did you get my letters?" she asked.

He said nothing. Outside, a whine sounded at the door, and Echo must have heard it also, because she got up and opened it. Granite came inside, shook off the snow, and came over to settle in front of the fire.

Dodge finished his pie and set the plate on the table.

"He's an inside dog now?"

"He deserves it, after all these years. Are you going to answer my question?"

"Yeah, I got them."

She looked away, at the window, the gathering storm. He blinked.

It occurred to him then. "Wasn't Granite out with you and Peyton?"

She nodded and walked over to the dog. Knelt next to him. "He came home yesterday, alone."

"Weird. He should be on the gangline."

"Yeah. But I checked in with the station, and Peyton texted in, so maybe she let him go. Or he ran off. I don't tether him when we're out and he might have slipped away when we picked up Holly and found his way home." He couldn't tell if she was worried or not. But Peyton had grown up in the bush. She knew how to take care of herself. Maybe she'd let Granite go, knowing his heart was turned toward home.

Clearly. The animal groaned happily as Echo rubbed behind his ears. "He loves me."

And for a moment, Dodge was sitting with her in front of the fire, doing a puzzle with her on the coffee table, caught inside the quiet cocoon of winter, their fingers brushing now and again as they fought for pieces.

Yes, this was a very bad idea. "I should go. The storm is going to sock me in." He stood to leave.

She looked up at him, and he startled to see the wetness in her eyes.

"Echo—?"

"I'm okay." She stood up as well, wiped her cheek. "Just worried about Peyton."

Oh. "I'm sure she's fine. She's an Alaskan. She knows how to survive."

"Yeah." She took a breath. "I'm glad you're back, Dodge. I did worry about you overseas."

"Thanks." He turned, trying not to run.

Because he very much wanted to pull her into his arms, tell her that everything would be okay.

That he'd not only received her letters—thirty-eight of them, to be exact—but read them, tucked them away, and read them again, over and over until they turned creased and thin.

Wanted to let himself believe them.

He took his dishes to the sink, then went into the arctic entry for his boots and coat.

She came in and leaned against the door as he got dressed. "Thanks again, Dodge."

"Sure." He looked at her. "Take care of yourself, Echo."

There. That was a better version of a goodbye, something he could live with without digging up the past, the regrets.

The skeleton of their happy ending.

He could walk away and never turn around.

He let himself out, started the truck, and while he waited for it to heat up, he went to the woodpile, filled the wheelbarrow, and wheeled it over to the door. Restocked the woodbox outside the step.

Then he cleared his windshield, got in, turned on the lights, and backed around.

He glanced in the rearview mirror as he pulled away.

She was standing at the door, her hand on Granite's head, the snow falling softly on the cabin nestled in the woods.

EIGHT

The grizzly came out of nowhere.

Fourteen-year-old Echo and her dad had just come around a curve, the late-afternoon shadows thick between the alder and pine on this stretch of the trail.

Her father knew it well—could mush it with his eyes closed, and maybe they were. They'd gotten up so early, the kind of early that required her father to wear his headlamp, the light carving out a path for their twelve-dog team.

That day, they'd caught three river trout—she still remembered it. Then he'd tucked her back into the sled, the sun starting to slip away.

She slept, the warmth of the furs that covered her settling deep into her bones. She didn't see the bear until the team had already crashed into it.

Her first real memory was falling into the snow, the sled dumping over as the dogs tried to flee.

Even now, under the swaddle of sleep over a decade later, she could taste the tinny blood as she bit her lip.

Mostly, however, she could hear the howling. Dogs crying, her father yelling. The batter of her heartbeat against her chest as she scrambled out of the furs, away, watching as the beast swatted one dog, then another.

Then her father raising his bear spray. He didn't bring a gun on the trail—never had—but he wasn't stupid. He knew what a bear could do to a team, a man.

His daughter.

"Dad!" The roar of the bear ate her words, and she clung to

the sled, watching as the animal batted away the spray, as it bore down over her father, his head practically in the bear's mouth.

He was going to die, and in her sleep, she whimpered, her body thrashing.

The bear would kill him while Echo watched. And still, she hid.

Run! Her brain pulsed the word, but she couldn't move, her bones stiff. She'd closed her eyes to the gore and wailed, the noise keening up from inside her. It morphed into a droning sound, then a shot cracked the air, and she knew it was almost over.

The belly of a ski plane swept past her.

The bear dropped her father's body and stood, pawing at the plane. Another shot and it ran, bellowing.

Leaving the bodies of three dead dogs, more battered, and her father unmoving.

She was still crying, her breaths huffing out as the plane landed. She threw her hands over her ears, not able to bear her father's cries, the gurgle of his voice.

Then feet crunching on snow, and a man dropped down in front of her. "Echo! It's okay. He's gone. You're safe."

She looked up at the man. Wool checkered hat, the furry ears tied up, a lined face—she knew him, maybe.

Safe. Her breaths tumbled over each other. Yes, safe—

The roar lifted her from her body, her bones shaking free, and she looked behind the man.

Not safe.

The grizzly rose behind him, its claws lethal, the stench of the animal feral and casting death over them. Echo screamed.

"Echo!"

She just kept screaming as the man turned, as he fired.

"Echo!" Hands on her shoulders.

The bear fell to all fours, charged.

The man shot again.

"Echo. *Wake. Up!*"

She opened her eyes to the darkness, the sounds, the smells still a stench in her nose, still hearing the screams echo. Hers. Sheldon Starr's.

Her father sat on the bed, the night thick around him, his hands on her shoulders. He'd been up for a while—she could smell the clean shower on him, the coffee on his breath.

She closed her eyes, covered her face with her hands. "Sorry."

"The grizzly attack?"

She nodded. Looked at him. "I haven't had one of those in years."

"It's probably me. Sorry. All this business with Elsa and Idaho." He took her hand. "Sorry, honey. I try. I just—"

"It's okay, Dad." She wore her thermals under her flannel, but the house still felt cold. "Did the heat go out?"

"I don't know. I was in my office, reading."

"What time is it?"

"Early. Five, maybe." He got up. "Go back to sleep. The storm is getting worse."

She should tuck back in, try and sleep, but the images of so much gore hung in her brain, and after he left, she rose, pulled on a bathrobe and her wool slippers, gathered her hair into a hat, and headed downstairs.

The fire had indeed died out. She poured herself a cup of coffee, gave Granite a pet, and then let him outside.

The world had turned white, the snow thick on the chicken coop, the shaggy pine limbs heavy with frosting. The animals were all huddled in their dens, leaving a thick silence. An ethereal luminance lifted off the snow, turning the ground almost an indigo blue.

Granite bounded out into the dark.

She glanced at the woodshed, dreaded hiking out in the knee-deep snow. She should have filled it before she went to bed. Except, as she glanced at the woodbox, she saw that her father had filled it.

She dragged in an armful of wood and dumped it in the copper box by the fire.

She stoked the flames back to life, the memory of Dodge doing just the same thing the night before vivid in her mind.

What was he doing here? She couldn't scrape the question from her mind. He'd driven her father home, stuck around to accuse her of not living a bigger life, and then left after admitting he'd gotten her letters and simply didn't care.

Weird.

Still, something about him being back here had felt, at least for a moment, right.

And maybe that's why the nightmare had found her. Because just when everything was right and good, a grizzly stepped out onto the trail.

Okay, that was a bit dramatic, but still, accurate.

Or maybe the dream came from his question. *"So, you've just been here, working the homestead, for the past ten years?"*

She hadn't needed to be so defensive. Except, the question needled her.

She had wanted to leave. More than once. Had wanted to run the Iditarod and study biology and take pictures and maybe travel beyond Anchorage, even to the Lower 48. But every time she thought about it, she simply felt paralyzed, the scream still clogging her breath.

No, she wasn't like her mother. Not one bit. It sorta irked her that her dad had said that the other day.

The fire flickered to a warm glow and she got up. Her dad was back in the kitchen, his cast-iron pan on the stove, bacon sizzling. "Eggs?"

"Please." She slid onto a chair, one foot up, her hands wrapped around her flanneled knee. "Do you ever think about her?"

He wore a pair of baggy jeans and a sweatshirt. His hair was short—he didn't have a lot of it anyway. After they'd stitched his scalp back together, his hair came back spotty and stark white.

His shoulder was hurting today, from the way he held his arm against his chest.

"My mother," she added when he didn't answer.

"I know who you are talking about. And yes. Often. Probably too often." He looked at her, and in the wan light of the kitchen, he looked old and tired. "Why?"

"I don't know. I just . . . you never talk about her."

He sighed. "They say you only get one great love. Effie was mine." He looked at her. "Still is."

She understood the ache behind that confession.

"I have one really vivid memory of her. We're playing Sorry! in front of the fire. You're making popcorn—"

"Oh, no. Your mother was the one who always made the popcorn. I learned from her. No one makes it like your mom—I still can't get it right."

Huh. Somewhere in the back of her brain, she thought she remembered that too, maybe. "There were happy times, right?"

"We were very happy, Echo." His voice was soft, as if he hadn't wanted to admit it.

"Did you know she was going to leave you?" She had never asked him this before, never wanted to bring it up. But maybe, if she knew, then . . .

Well, then she could prepare her heart for the day Dodge left again.

Her dad was quiet as he cracked eggs into the pan. "Maybe. There were signs. She hated the dark and cold and would pore over medical books, trying to keep her brain sharp. She'd left Wisconsin without finishing her residency, and that wasn't fair to her, but she did it for me. But I know it tugged at her, this longing to become the woman she'd left behind."

"Did you fight?"

He shook his head. "Not really. She just sorta . . . slipped away. We stopped saying yes to each other, I guess. Yes, I see you. Yes, I need you. Yes, I trust you. And then one day, she simply said no and walked away."

He slid two sunny-side up eggs and some bacon on a plate and gave it to her.

She got up, grabbed a fork, filled her coffee, and sat back down. "I always thought it was me."

"I know." He plated his own eggs. "Scared me to death when you went after her."

He met her eyes, but she looked away.

"She loved you."

"She just didn't love me enough."

He sat down. Picked up his coffee. Studied her. "That's why you said no to Dodge, wasn't it?"

She stilled, a forkful of eggs halfway to her mouth. "What?"

"Why you told him no when he proposed. Because, when you've lost someone, you fear giving yourself to someone else."

She stared at him.

"Your mother's betrayal uprooted everything you knew about love, threw your life into chaos, and suddenly you didn't know who to trust." He poured ketchup on his eggs. "You were scared to be vulnerable again. To let someone have any control over your heart."

She wasn't sure now if they were talking about her . . . or him. But it didn't matter. "It was a long time ago. I'm over it."

"Her leaving blew up your entire life, Echo." He picked up his fork, then met her eyes. "You might have healed from the event, but you continue to bleed from the impact."

She had nothing. His words raw, brutal.

True.

Outside, a sharp bark bit the silence. She put down her fork. "That's Granite. I forgot he's out there in the storm." She practically fled to the arctic entry and opened the door.

But Granite wasn't waiting at the stoop. He barked again, a warning, in the dark.

The cold air rushed in, cooling the heat in her chest. "I think the coyote is back." She lifted her jacket from the hook, slipped on her mukluks without tying them, and grabbed her capture gun and a headlamp.

Granite was still barking, louder now, a few growls, and she called to him as she flicked on her headlamp.

The night was starting to lift but clung to the forest and slunk out into the yard. Her light peeled back the darkness some fifteen feet ahead of her, awash with snow. It pelleted her face, her open jacket. Her hands turned to ice in the wind. She should have grabbed gloves.

"Granite!"

She tromped out to the driveway—the snow had accumulated a good ten inches in the night, nearly to her knees, and she fought through it, seeing Granite's prints. They led out to the barn.

Oh no. Maybe it wasn't a coyote but wolves, maybe daring to take one of the goats. She picked up her pace, slogging hard.

Granite burst into the glow of her lamplight, running hard for her. He stopped, barked, and took off again.

"I'm coming!"

She shined the light on the barn, but the doors were closed. And Granite's gray form lit out down the driveway. "Granite!"

Oh, she hoped he wasn't on the trail of a moose. The last thing she needed was to run into a bull moose and get trampled.

Or a grizzly.

Suddenly her gut dropped.

"Granite!" She stopped, shouting for him, her voice shrilling. "Granite!"

Barking, coming closer, more warning, and she stilled, held up the gun, trying not to shake.

Granite burst into the light again, only this time, another animal followed him, a dog, black and gray. For a moment, she thought it was a wolf.

Then as the dog came into the light, she lowered her gun.

"Jester?" She knelt in the snow and the dog ran up to her, caked in ice and snow, breathing hard. She ran her hands over him and found the harness and the cord that attached him to the gangline torn, fraying, and hanging from his body. The pads of his feet were bloody, the paw protectors gone.

She caught his face, found his golden eyes. "What are you doing here? Where is Peyton?"

Another bark. She stood, her breath catching as Merlin arrived, also dragging her harness. She bore a long scratch on her body, dried blood, and limped, her paws raw.

"Echo?"

Her father had run out into the storm, his coat open, his mukluks dragging their laces. He was also carrying a dart gun.

"It's Merlin and Jester," she said. She stood up as her father called to them, looked at their wounds.

She called for the rest of her pack. "Goose! Viper! Iceman!"

Nothing, her voice swallowed in darkness.

"Maverick!"

The wind howled back.

"These harnesses look like they've been cut, Echo," her dad said. "We need to get these dogs inside and tend to their wounds."

He started to herd them into the house.

But Echo stood out in the storm, the snow pelting her face, and all she could hear was the roar of the grizzly.

———

Cold. She'd never been so cold. But the fact that she still felt the cold probably worked in her favor, right? She burned, her entire body shivering, so she had to be alive.

The cave had probably saved her. That and the dog who'd crept in, curled around her, and finally found warmth next to her. She'd feared it was one of the wolves who she knew tracked her, but they wouldn't have ventured in.

She and the dog had kept each other alive as the wind howled.

Her arm hurt—she knew she'd probably broken it in the crash, but she could still move her hand so maybe it was just her wrist. It didn't hang at an angle or anything—at least from what she could see in the wan light.

She couldn't know how far she'd hiked—she couldn't remember the map, hadn't a clue where they'd traveled. North, for sure, but they'd gotten lost in the storm.

She remembered the world spinning, and maybe it was adrenaline, or fear, but just like that, she found herself in the snow, flung wide of the disaster, pieces of the cargo strewn around her.

And then, the smell of blood.

She couldn't find him, the animal who had stolen so much from her, but she didn't look hard.

All she knew was that she was alone.

She got to her feet, the light fading, and remembered her survival training.

Shelter. She'd figure out warmth and water later.

She followed tracks through the snow—could have been dogs, or wolves, but they led into a ravine and then up a hill, and by then the night had nearly pitched around her.

The place was so vast—so much white—she'd forgotten, really, how big Alaska could be, the mountains brutal, majestic, and unforgiving.

She spied the shelter—no more than an overhang over the ravine, but when she crawled up inside it, the place was protected, the floor free of snow. She ventured out again for pine boughs, returned and found the dog.

So maybe he'd been following her.

It hit her then that maybe *he* was also following her. But with the wind whipping down, and the cold dropping fast, what choice did she have? She put down the pine boughs, tried to cover up the entrance, then worked on coaxing the dog toward her.

It was dark before she felt his furry body against hers. She lay down, curled up with him, and told herself that this was better than dying.

Maybe.

But please, God, she wanted to live.

Had to live.

Lives, besides hers, were depending on it.

Dodge did what he always did in a storm. Chopped wood. Hauled water. Built a fire. Shoveled the deck.

Studied the sky.

It was how a guy survived in the north when the snow and wind trapped him inside his house. But maybe he had turned into a lightweight, because after two days, Dodge was going stir crazy.

He'd even sat down and played a game of chess with his father. A three-hour, silent game that the old man won.

Of course.

Now he was heating up the last of Larke's lasagna in the microwave before it went bad.

His father was in his office, eating the last of the chicken divan, probably reading yet another Louis L'Amour novel. A couple quiet bachelors surviving the winter.

Dodge was halfway through *The Way of Kings*, and by the looks of the storm, he might be able to finish all eight hundred pages by the time he was set free.

Problem was, Echo kept creeping into his mind, distracting him from the story. *"You're not over me, Dodge. And I'm not over you. And like it or not, you're going to have to deal with that."*

Words he'd tried to forget, but going over to her house had raked them up. Stirred them to life.

She was probably right.

She'd only gotten prettier in the last ten years. Sure, at age eighteen she'd been sweetly cute, with her long golden-blond hair, her youthful face, young curves.

But the woman who'd made him coffee was confident, settled into herself. Beautiful more than pretty, with a strong, tempting body, and eyes void of the stars they once held. *"I had to stay. I had responsibilities and a father who needed me."*

He would have expected nothing less of her. In fact, that loyalty was what he'd loved perhaps most about her. What he'd needed, really.

And yes, once upon a time, he had dreamed the same dreams. He had their life all planned out.

Maybe that had been the problem. Not his plans, but hers.

He had no business deciding her life for her.

He walked over to the giant picture window that looked north. The storm had cleared, mostly, and the sun just barely peeked through the troubled clouds. The wind had sheeted up the snow into a bank on the far side of the lake and skimmed off a layer, sneezing white into the air. The quiet, powerful beauty of the north never ceased to stop him. The pine trees that dotted the whitened fields, the rugged granite spires, the harsh wildness of the mountains.

The microwave beeped and he retrieved his breakfast-lunch-dinner—whatever time it was—brought it to the island, and sat on a stool.

He picked up his book.

And of course, Echo walked into his brain and sat down. *"Whatchya reading?"*

He'd looked at her over the top of his book. Around them, the sound of basketballs on the wooden floor and shouts as kids worked off the lunch-hour steam flooded the small area. She wore her hair in a long ponytail, a golden mane that always mesmerized him a little. That and her eyes—so impossibly green—could make him a little dry mouthed.

"Harry Potter." He turned back to his book.

"Which one?"

"*Prisoner of Azkaban.*"

"I love that one. Wait until you find out who Sirius—"

"Don't."

She had this way of leaning on her hand and smiling at him that made his insides clench up and his skin tingle.

"Don't what?" She pulled the book down.

"Tell me the ending."

"Only if you promise to come over and help me. Nanook just had another litter and Dad says I can help train them."

"Cool." He looked at the book again, but the words were all jumbled.

"Someday, I'm going to have my own gangline, and I'll name them after that movie you like."

"What movie?"

"The fighter pilot one."

"*Top Gun*? That's an old movie."

"I liked it." She smiled again.

Heat burned his face. They'd watched it once when she was at his house. He'd found it in the stash of old VHS movies his father kept. Had wanted to run in embarrassment when Maverick had taken that girl to bed.

"C'mon. You said you would help me in the summer race. I teach you to mush dogs, you teach me to fly, right?"

Wouldn't that be something? To fly his own plane. His dad had been letting him take the yoke now, and he'd even landed once. Someday Sky King Ranch would be his and—

"Right, Dodge?" Echo looked at him. She wore a flannel shirt and a pair of jeans, but something about her had changed this fall. Sure, they were thirteen now, but something about her . . .

She was prettier, maybe. He swallowed, and it stuck in his throat. He nodded.

"Great. My dad is picking me up. He can drive you home afterward."

He'd always been a little intrigued about Echo and her dad. They were practically neighbors, and sometimes his dad helped hers with homestead chores, like repairing a roof or changing a car engine. And he'd been the one to hang out with Echo. He thought her a little strange—cool, really. She raised her own chickens and goats, and they lived on an off-the-grid homestead with solar power and wood heat. And her dad was some kind of grizzly master.

Most of all, she didn't have a mom either.

He'd have to tell Colt and Ranger that he had a ride. He spotted Ranger shooting baskets, surrounded by a group of other seventh graders. Colt—who knew? He was probably off with some kids smoking. Dodge had caught him twice with a cigarette and threatened to tell their father. He'd think Colt might care a little about not dying from cancer like their mother.

But Dodge had kept his mouth shut because that's what he did. Protected his stupid brother. He didn't know why.

The bell rang.

"See you later." Echo got up and he watched her walk away. Prettier and maybe taller. That was it.

He got up, stashed his book, and headed for class.

And he'd thought of nothing all afternoon but Echo Yazzie and the way she walked, that pretty hair shining in the sun, and the way her eyes turned magical when she smiled.

Now, sitting at the kitchen island a lifetime later, he read a sentence for the third time, blowing absently on his lasagna. She still had magical eyes. *"I'm sorry."*

He closed his book. *"It's not close to over. You've been nursing this wound for nearly ten years, . . . trying to forget the girl you loved since you were ten. There's no way this is over."*

Shoot, the old man was right too.

Ten years hadn't burned her away, despite the miles. And he had forgiven her—really. He'd been a child when he'd left. And besides, he'd had no claim on her.

She had every right to kiss Colt.

Especially since she'd made it clear she wasn't going to marry Dodge.

"No, Dodge. I . . . can't." He still couldn't believe that she'd turned him down so fast—not even a hesitation. Sure, he didn't have a ring—*way to think that out, Dodge*—but he'd thought for sure . . .

That was what happened when he acted on impulse, without a plan. People got hurt.

Lives were ruined.

If only he'd learned his lesson then.

"Maybe that's why God brought you back—for her."

Aw shoot. He needed to get outside, do something before he started agreeing with the old man.

He finished off his food, washed his dishes, and put them on the rack. Then he put on his coat, boots, hat, and scarf and stepped out onto the deck.

Snow had accumulated on the steps since his last pass, and he picked up the shovel by the door and cleared a path out to the drive that went from the lodge to the hangar.

The sky had calmed, but with the cloud cover it still wasn't safe to fly. He had a request from Remington Mines to use the chopper to move some equipment to an inland stake. He'd go out in the morning if it was safe.

Meanwhile, he'd plow the runway.

He hiked out to the barn and fought his way inside. The smells of oil, gasoline, and the faintest hint of hay from the days when his grandfather used it as a cattle barn filtered into his nose as he fumbled for the light.

He found it, flicked it on. The place was unchanged—still a collection of his father's machinery. A tractor, a disc mower, a small collection of minibikes, including Dodge's old motorcycle, just waiting for the summer months. A slew of old snow machines sat near the entrance, some of them recently used. He spotted the plow attached to the old Dodge truck sitting near the big double door entrance. It was his father's favorite truck—a blue and white 1972 Dodge D100—and most importantly, Dodge's namesake.

At least it still ran. His father's '78 Ford Ranger sat on wheel jacks in a dusty corner of the barn. And the little '82 Dodge Colt his mother used was covered with a dirty tarp.

Clearly his parents had been under duress for names when the triplets were born. He couldn't imagine having to fly his wife to Anchorage while she was in labor, but then again, his father had lived a wild life here with his true love, Cee.

He opened the doors, got in the truck, and plowed his way out. Then around to the runway. He scraped away the snow in great swathes, then cleared a path down to the cabins by the lake.

The daylight was hanging on, turning a waxy gold along the horizon by the time he put the truck away. He was stamping out the snow and closing the door when he heard it—the sound of whining lifting from behind the row of cars, near one of the old haymows.

He crept back, squeezing past the Colt until he came to the empty stall in the back of the barn, still cluttered with hay.

The doors of the stall sagged at an angle big enough for an animal to get through.

In the dim light, he made out a dog. It sat in the corner of the mow, curled up, licking an open wound.

"Hey there, buddy. You okay?" He made a few noises, and the animal stuck his nose out to smell his outstretched glove. He took off his glove, offered that, and the dog licked it.

He took a step inside and crouched in front of the dog. Touched his fur.

The dog wore a harness. Dodge reached under it. "I'm going

to pick you up, pal," he said and grunted as he moved the animal into his arms.

The dog moaned. "It's okay, buddy. Just going to get you into the house to see what's going on." He picked his way out of the barn, past the cars and machinery, and then into the sunlight.

And headed straight for the lodge.

He opened the office door and carried the animal through to the kitchen. The lights were on, and something savory was baking in the oven.

He set the dog down on the kitchen floor.

"Son?" His father came down the stairs.

"Found this dog in the barn." He soothed it with his hands and checked out the wound the dog was tending. Four inches long, a half-inch deep, it sliced open the dog's haunch. Seemed to be a gash of some sort— "This looks almost like a knife wound."

His father took a look at the wound. "Or a bullet. See how there's bruising along the edges, and the wound isn't clean—as if it's torn. And there's still tissue connecting the wound in places."

The dog moved, trying to bite his father, and Dodge held his head. "A bullet wound?"

"Or he might have been hit by something. A shovel?"

The dog had settled again, putting his head down. Dodge ran his hands over him, closing his eyes. A beautiful husky, with blue eyes, a gray body, and a full muscled chest.

He looked at the harness. Echo always marked her dogs with—yes. The name Iceman was inked into the back of the harness.

"This is one of Echo's dogs," he said.

His father got up and was fishing through the pantry for his first aid kit. Now he turned. "How did he get here?"

"I don't know. We left Peyton a few days ago with the dogs up at Ranger cabin 37. Echo said she was okay, but this isn't looking good."

His father came over and knelt next to the dog. "I can clean this and tend him. You should get ahold of Echo and see if they've had any trouble over there."

Yep.

He pulled up the ham radio and sent out a message to the Yazzie homestead.

No answer. He tried again.

Nothing.

"I'm taking a sled and heading over there."

His father looked up from where he was washing Iceman's wound. "Pack a bag in case you get hung up. And, take a sat radio."

Twenty minutes later, Dodge loaded his pack onto the back of one of the Ski-Doo Expeditions, added gas, and pulled out of the barn. His father came out onto the step, his jacket wrapped around him. "I'll keep calling them on the ham."

Dodge lifted a hand, put down the shield on his helmet, and took off toward the Yazzies'. Ahead of him, the clouds had turned the sky a faded, smoky blue.

And behind him, the wind began to howl.

NINE

For two days Echo had stood by the window of their home, pacing, watching the sky, listening to her father trying to connect with Copper Mountain on the ham radio. They'd gotten through to Deke Starr, but he couldn't offer any help in this whiteout.

Peyton, where are you?

The sky had finally cleared enough for her to see the horizon, and with half of her team still missing, she dug out the Polaris snowmobile from the shed, added another gas can to the back, along with supplies, and took off into the blue-gray day.

The snow blew up around her, pelleting the visor of her helmet and dusting the air as she plowed a track down the road, and then into the deep snow of the fields and wooded areas that led out to Ranger cabin 37.

She'd start there.

The drone of the machine settled inside her, eclipsing her thoughts as she drove. Around her, the air was crisp. To her guess, she had a short window of time before another blizzard socked her in. But such was the way of Alaska in March—temperamental weather as winter wrestled with spring.

She was ready for the summer sunrise. Ready for spring, and the seeds under her grow lamps to sprout, be transplanted into the greenhouse. Ready for the high winds to die, the smell of wildflowers to scent the hills, to hear the river roar behind her house.

She was ready for life.

The thought struck her as she came upon a ridge that over-looked Moose Creek. The west branch of the creek snaked into the forest, nearly all the way to the cabin.

Still, what took her dogs eight hours, she could accomplish in about two on a snowmobile, depending on the terrain.

She gunned the sled down the ridge, riding it with one knee on the seat, looking for drop-offs and debris that might be hidden in the snow.

Yes, she was ready for life. She didn't know what it was, maybe just the longing for spring, but the storm, the worry had dug into her, turned her heavy.

Not to mention her dad's words—*"You might have healed from the event, but you continue to bleed from the impact."*

She had never considered that her mother's leaving could cause her to be stuck in a sort of darkness, afraid to move.

Yeah, she needed the sunrise like she needed breath.

Landing on the creek bed, she found it solid, protected almost, from the raging wind that would have swept up drifts, and she settled down into the drive, her eyes peeled for Peyton's green jacket.

She would have trekked the dogs this way, if she could. With the shallow creek solid with ice, it was the easiest way to travel. The storm, however, obliterated any sign of her dogsled, or even the telltale packing of the snow from a team.

The wind scurried through the trees, along the banks of the creek, sheeting up white, stirring it with the plume her machine churned up. She shivered. She also didn't work up a sweat on a snowmobile like she did on a dogsled.

Her hands were frozen by the time she found the cutoff that led up to the cabin. The tiny timber-framed building sat on a ridge that overlooked both Moose Creek and Seventeen Mile Lake.

If Peyton wasn't here, she'd continue on to their next sched-uled stop, the cabin some ten miles away at Peters Lake.

As Echo drew near, she spotted the faintest wisp of smoke circling out of the chimney, and a fist eased in her chest.

Peyton had found her way back here, holed up, and built a fire.

Echo stopped in front and glanced toward the field where Dodge had landed his chopper so many days ago.

Maybe she should have stayed with Peyton.

Pulling off her helmet, she left it on the snowmobile and tromped up to the house. The snow lay thick on the deck, only trampled near the door.

She kicked some of it away, headed to the door, and pushed it open.

Someone lay on one of the cots in the room, trussed up in a sleeping bag, a pack on the floor next to boots and snow clothes.

The stove glowed, the fire turning to coals inside, but a hint of a chill laced the cabin. Snowshoes leaned against the wall, and on the table sat a gas stove and a bucket of water, probably melted snow.

It didn't look like Peyton's gear, but, "Peyton?"

The body stirred, and she took a step closer.

"Stop." The body sat up, and Echo's gaze froze on the ten-inch buck knife that protruded from the sleeping bag. "Don't move another hair."

The man wore a fur hat, his brown hair long to match his matted beard, a thermal shirt, and, she guessed, long johns, but he didn't sally out of the bag, thankfully.

Probably because she obeyed and put her hands up. "Idaho. It's me, Echo Yazzie."

She probably should have used his real name—Ray—instead of the local nickname, but it just sort of emerged. The guide looked at her, as if trying to get a fix on her.

"Yazzie?"

"Yeah. Echo. Charlie's daughter."

Aw, she should have probably left that reminder alone.

However, he put his knife away. He peeled out of his bag, and to her relief, he wore a pair of fleece pants.

"What are you doing here?" He got up and walked over to the stove in his stocking feet, opened it, and added a block of wood.

She backed away, and only then noticed the small bottle of whiskey on the table. "I'm looking for Peyton Samson. She's a researcher with Fish and Wildlife? She's been missing for a few days."

"That Black girl?" Idaho said.

Actually, Peyton was half Native American, half Black, but she wasn't going to argue. "She was here a few days ago and left with my dogs. But something happened . . . a few of the dogs made it back to the house, but Peyton's missing."

"I haven't seen her." His eyes, however, dragged over Echo. "You're an awful long way from home. You're by yourself?"

Idaho had a reputation for his loud opinions of women made during his between-trip visits to Vic's place. Vic usually chased him away when he got out of hand, but now Echo saw something in his eyes that ran a chill through her. "If you see Peyton, just . . . can you call it in?"

"Radio's down, sweetheart." He smiled at her, and the smell of his breath turned her gut. "But I have food. And there's another storm coming." He glanced at the window. "You're not going back out, are you?"

She took another step back. "I need to go."

He lunged and his hand palmed the door as she tried to open it. "I think you should stay."

She turned, her back to the door. A terrible stench washed over her, whiskey and body odor from days in the bush without a bath. "My dad will be expecting me."

"Charlie's at home, drunk, having nightmares about the bear I'm going to kill." He leaned closer. "Maybe you want to help me."

She stilled, closing her eyes against his halitosis. "You're out here to kill the grizzly that attacked my dogs?"

He laughed and leaned away. "Naw. I'm just doing some scouting. Getting ready to meet my next group." He ran his tongue along his teeth. "But I'll be ready, if he decides to attack." He reached up then and brushed snow off her jacket. "I heard he nearly killed one of your dogs."

"I need to go." She put her hand on the doorknob, trying to quell her insides.

She wasn't a victim. She knew how to handle a handsy guy, thank you. But the fact she was out in the middle of—

He put his hand on her shoulder. "Echo. You're staying." His grip tightened on her.

She whirled, her arm up, and cut his grip off. "Back off, Idaho."

He held his hands up as if in surrender, laughing. "That's what I like about you. You've got sass. These girls from the bush—they're tough on the outside." He put his hands down and leaned near her ear. "But what are they like on the inside?"

She pushed him, but he caught her wrist. "C'mon. Can't we be friends?"

She tried to jerk it away, but he tightened his hold to the point of pain. She refused to cry out. "Get your hands off me!"

Her gaze dropped to the knife, sheathed in the strap on his thigh. She tasted her heartbeat as it climbed up her throat.

"Sure, sweetheart." He let go of her wrist but grabbed her by her jacket lapels. "As long as you stick around—"

Behind her, the door opened. It hit her, and she bumped hard into Idaho.

He let her go and fell back, caught her from falling, too, his hands on her upper arms.

"Let me go!" She tried to jerk away from him, but his grip was strong. She turned.

Blinked.

Dodge was standing in the doorway, staring at her. He wore a blue jacket, his dark hair under a wool cap, his scarf covered in crusty snow.

He shot a look at Idaho, who let go of her.

Something in Dodge's dark gaze on Idaho ran a cold finger down her spine. "Echo. You okay?"

Her heart thundered as she stepped away from Idaho, toward Dodge. "Yeah." But her voice was sharp and thin.

Maybe he read her face, or maybe he was just that perceptive, but his eyes narrowed at Idaho. "What are you doing here?"

"I have every right to be here."

"I thought Peyton might be here," Echo said quietly, glancing at the door. She dearly wanted to know how Dodge had appeared, but right now, she only wanted out. "Clearly, she's not." Then she left, barely stopping herself from sprinting from the cabin.

She didn't know what Dodge said to Idaho, but after a moment he joined her as she stood outside, breathing in the clean, pine-scented, crisp air.

Stay calm. She was fine. Just *fine*.

Dodge's snowmobile was parked next to hers. Now he came up to her, his expression dark. "What happened in there?"

"Nothing . . ."

"Echo—"

"Idaho's a jerk."

His lips tightened, and he drew in a breath. "Do you need me to go back in there and settle something?" He met her gaze again.

And the look in it didn't match the boy she knew, the one who loved books and flying and running with her dogs and . . .

This looked very much like the man who'd leveled his brother ten years ago. Angry, protective . . .

Fierce.

"Peyton's not here, and that's all that matters." She frowned. "What are *you* doing here?"

He was frowning too. "What's this about Peyton?"

"Oh, I thought . . . maybe . . . Did my dad get ahold of you?"

He shook his head. "Actually, I spotted you from the hill over Moose Creek. I've been following you for about an hour. I was headed to your place to tell you we found Iceman in our barn."

The words took a moment to form. "Iceman? At your barn?"

"Yes. And we think he was shot."

"What? Oh my—"

"Take a breath." His hands landed on her shoulders. "He's fine. My father is tending to him. It's just a scrape, but I was worried so . . ." He made a face. "I know I said we needed to avoid each other, but—"

"Thank you, Dodge."

She said it softly, a little more relief in it than she had intended, but maybe that was okay because it slowed him down, and he swallowed as if he wasn't sure what to do.

Finally, he nodded. "What's going on with Peyton?"

"I'm not sure. Some of my dogs came home without her, and now Iceman, and . . ." She grabbed her helmet off her snow machine. "I'm just worried that she's lost out here, or in trouble. I need to find her."

He caught her arm just as she made to put on the helmet. "Echo—it's been at least two days of a storm that no one should be in . . . maybe we should call search and rescue."

"We *are* search and rescue, Dodge."

He shook his head, and she couldn't help it. Maybe it was the aftermath of her encounter with Idaho, or maybe just Dodge's grim tone but—

She put her helmet down and took a few steps away from him. "When did you become the guy who gave up hope? You always believed in more, and now you're . . . I don't even know you!"

His mouth tightened. "No, you probably don't. But I'm also just trying to be real here. Peyton is—"

"Not. Dead." She met Dodge's eyes, her own filling.

He sighed. "Aw, Echo." Then he walked over and pulled her against him.

And he was just so solid, and here, and she couldn't stop herself from moving her arms around him and hanging on. "I can't leave her, Dodge. I can't. What if the bear got her? It's just like—"

"Charlie. I know."

She drew in a breath, hating how it seemed too terribly close, the raw-edged fear. "I'm scared."

There, she said it. Really scared. And not just about Peyton, maybe.

He held her a moment longer. "Okay, Echo. Where do we look?" He pushed her away. Met her eyes. And she saw in them the Dodge who'd been her friend.

Her *best* friend, especially when she'd needed one the most.

It made her want to weep, again. But she didn't have time to fall apart. Not now, not probably ever.

"We're going to the cabin on Peters Lake. It's on our route, and there's a camera there that is trained on another legacy den. She could have gone there and maybe something happened."

He was picturing it. She could see the trek mapping in his head. "There's that ridge there, it overlooks the cabin."

"And a ravine that runs from Peters Creek to the cabin. It's rough ground around there. Easy to turn over a dogsled."

"Okay." He glanced at the cabin. "You don't think she was here and . . . something else happened to her?"

She didn't want to think it, but she was still shaking a little, her adrenaline dipping, leaving only the what-ifs. "I don't think Idaho is a murderer, despite his faults."

Still, the question lingered . . . What if Dodge hadn't come along?

Nope, not going there. She grabbed her helmet and climbed back on her sled. Dodge did the same.

She fired up her snowmobile and lit out toward the deepening shadows.

What was Dodge supposed to do—leave her out in the wilderness?

Besides, he had a clench in his gut at what almost went down in the cabin, and he just couldn't live with himself if anything happened to Echo.

So, of course he followed her through the thick snow. He stayed just far enough out of the spray of powder as she wove in and out of the forest on her way to cabin 63.

In his gut he knew—just a rundown of the facts would confirm it—Peyton was dead. She may have been thrown and was suffering from a broken leg or arm or even ribs. And she might have survived the cold, but with the storm . . .

But Echo had looked at him with such hope, and frankly it had dredged up so many memories—

The loss of his mother, and hers. Summers spent training her dogs, winters spent mushing. Flying with her under the shadow of Denali, through canyons, along rivers, over mountain peaks. Winter nights watching old movies, driving her home in the truck, the heater blasting, her sitting under a blanket, them singing to some country song.

But it wasn't just the memories. No, as he'd held her, he felt her tremble, and his brain went to what he'd seen in the cabin. No, what he'd *felt*.

Idaho wore a look in his eyes that suggested Dodge had interrupted something, and maybe just in the nick of time. Dodge had very much wanted to go back in that cabin then and put a little fear in him about how to treat women.

And sure, Echo could take care of herself. But frankly, the entire package—the memories, the look of both relief and fear on Echo's face when he'd walked in, and even her dragging up the terrible accident with her father—conspired to ignite something inside him that he'd never been able to escape. Protect Echo.

Which was how, like an old habit, he ended up in her wake, snow hitting his helmet.

She glanced behind her and waved her arm for him to come up next to her. He pulled up, still standing on his sled. He sat as he cut the throttle.

"We usually cut through this canyon, across the lake, then around the creek." She pointed out the route, and in the distance, he made out the ridge.

"I remember," he said. "I went hunting with my dad and the boys in this area, and we stayed there."

"Then you know that the approach is up around the backside. Be careful. It's pretty craggy around there, with lots of overhangs and crevices."

Ice clung to the wisps of hair that strayed outside her helmet, her cheeks bright with cold, despite the covering. "My hope is that Peyton was heading there and somehow overturned the sled. Maybe she cut the gangline to let the dogs free and then made it to the cabin."

He longed to put a fire to her hope. "That's sounds like a reasonable scenario."

She met his gaze, offered a smile. Then she put her face guard down, stood up, and throttled forward.

Of course, he followed her.

They were running out of sunlight, the gray-blue mountains rimmed with a fading fire as they descended into the canyon. He'd flown over this creek bed so many times that he could probably trace the route, the way it curved south, then north again, and finally broke into two more branches, one of them turning into the bigger Peters Lake.

As they turned out into the creek, he lifted his visor and breathed in the crisp air. They reached the lake, and he sat down on the sled, gunned it across the open ice, hard on Echo's trail. She'd also upped her speed.

He nearly caught up to her as she reached the shore, but then dropped behind as she climbed out of the lake, ran along the creek bed and up a ridge.

This, too, he knew—the ridge ran west, along a narrow lip that fell to the north into a deep crevasse.

He guessed this was the crevasse in which she feared she'd find her sled.

They slowed as they topped the ridge. The view could steal his breath, even from the ground. A thick stand of spruce edged the lake ahead, the snow a pristine layer of frosting, the sky to the south a deep purple. He loved Alaska from the sky, but here on terra firma it was just as breathtaking.

He followed her tread as it chewed up the snow, aware of the slope of the earth dropping away to his right.

They finally found the log cabin, nestled into a pocket on the hill, the snow thick on the roof, drifts up to the windows. In the glow of their headlights, it looked uninhabited.

She pulled up in front of it. Took off her helmet. Glanced at him. "No tracks."

"She might have gotten here before the storm." But his gut clenched even as he fought his way through the drifts to the door.

It was frozen shut, so he put his foot into it and nearly went down the steps when it just shuddered. But he'd managed to break the ice free, and when he tried the latch again, it opened.

He stepped inside.

The place had been recently visited. There was an ancient hint of smoke in the frigid air. Clean and dry firewood was stacked next to the potbellied stove. A small table in the corner was clean of any debris. Near it a small sink stood next to an icebox, a few condiments in baggies on the counter.

A handmade sofa with denim cushions faced the stove. And in the back, two bunkbeds, no mattresses.

But it was safe and would be warm, and here they could spend the night.

"Is she here?" Echo stood in the doorway, such a broken expression on her face that he thought, for a moment, she'd suggest pressing on.

"No, and it's too dark now. We can't keep going."

"I thought for sure she'd be here." Her jaw tightened. "She's out here, somewhere, freezing to death."

He refrained from reaching out to her again because, well, his heart was already breaking promises, and he didn't need any more catastrophes. "I know. We'll find her. But we need to stay."

She sighed.

"I'll unload the sleds."

She followed him out.

They unpacked their gear in silence. He was turning toward the cabin with his pack when he spotted something out of his periphery.

"Echo, look." He pointed toward the end of the lake.

A grizzly meandered out of the woods, trekking across the lake, as if it knew where it was headed. Dodge hoped it wasn't toward them.

He would have gone inside, but Echo dropped her pack, then pulled a monocular from the side pocket and trained it on the bear. He stepped up to her. "What are you looking for?"

"A little white spot between the ears." She lowered the eyeglass. "I can't tell."

"Lemme see." He took the monocular from her, closed one eye, and trained the view onto the bear.

Big son of a gun. Well over a thousand pounds, probably. It didn't look like the grizzly he'd chased from Spike's place, but he couldn't be sure.

"Let's get inside," he said and picked up her pack too.

She let him. Inside, she turned on a flashlight, then dug out her cookstove and unscrewed the top pot. She went outside and filled it with snow.

When she returned, she set it on the table, and closed the door behind her. Night filled the windows beyond their cozy enclave.

It struck Dodge that this might be exactly the opposite of saying goodbye to Echo Yazzie.

"I'll make a fire," he said, his throat tight. Who thought this was a good idea? He knelt in front of the stove and began to pile in the wood—birch shavings for a starter, and then he broke off kindling from the logs, using the axe from his pack.

Meanwhile, she had assembled her camp stove and lit it, putting the pan on top.

He soon had a fire lit, and it added an orange glow to the room. "We'll be warm soon."

She glanced at him, giving him a smile, but it didn't reach her eyes.

"Echo." He came over to her. He touched her arms. "I know what you're thinking. But this is not your fault. You offered to stay with her, but Peyton practically ordered you away. She said she could mush the dogs herself. And she could. Sheesh, she grew up out here. She knows what she's doing."

She was nodding, but by her torn expression, it wasn't sinking in. And he, of course, knew why.

"This is not you, Echo. This is not you left in the woods, alone."

She looked at him, swallowed.

"Okay, listen. Here's how this is not the same. First, Peyton's not a child, left alone with the dogs while Sheldon Starr flies her father, who is fighting for his life, to Anchorage. Second, we know where she is—she's out checking her cameras—we don't have to search the entire county for her armed with a sketchy PLB signal. Thirdly, you, Echo, are not alone."

She nodded, but he touched her chin, lifted it. "You're *not alone.*"

She smiled. "Yeah." She blew out a long breath and pulled away. "Thanks, Dodge. I know that I'm probably the last person you want to trek out into the bush with, but—"

"I'm here because I chose to be here, Echo." Because, surprisingly, his father was right. *There's no way this is over . . . Maybe that's why God brought you back—for her. And to set you free from all that darkness."*

Yes. To get closure. To have that conversation he probably should have had in the vet's office.

The one that would set them both free from the past, where he could leave Copper Mountain behind without the stings of regret.

That's all.

He unpacked his bag and set the sleeping bag on the upper bunk, along with a small pad that he partially inflated.

"I have some jerky noodles," he said.

"Really?" she said, looking over his things. "Peanut butter, beef jerky, and ramen. You never change." She shook her head.

"What? It's good. I'm a ramen master."

She laughed and he was like Granite, leaning into it. Oh brother. "Fine. What did *you* bring?"

"Leftover stew." She pulled a baggie from her pack, still frozen, and waggled the bag. "I brought enough for two just in case . . ." Her smile fell.

"In case you found Peyton." He turned to her. "Breathe."

She nodded. Blinked away tears.

"We'll leave at first light."

The water boiled on the stove, and she got out her water bottle and poured it in. He opened the stew bag and she put it into the pot. The smells of thyme and garlic scented the air.

His stomach suddenly emerged from hibernation and roared.

She laughed, clearly trying to dig herself out of despair. "Methinks your little ramen packet wouldn't feed that beast."

"Probably not. I didn't plan for a big meal—just something in case."

"In case what—you found me, hurt?"

His mouth tightened, and he lifted a shoulder. "Things happen to people out here."

"Yes, they do," Echo said quietly.

It was definitely getting warmer in here. He walked over to his bunk and pulled off his jacket, then his fleece. His thermal shirt came with it, and he was just pulling it down when she gasped.

He turned.

Her eyes were big, stuck on the scar that ran from his lower back, around and up his rib cage.

Oh.

"I'm sorry." She turned away. "I'm sorry." She was stirring the stew, staring hard at it.

"Echo."

"It's none of my business." But her voice shook.

He threw his fleece on his bunk and turned to her. "I was shot down."

She glanced over at him. "I didn't know that."

So, although her father had known, he hadn't told her. Interesting.

"It was two years ago. I was flying combat SAR and our team got called in to rescue a team of SEALs who had gone off the grid. I found them holed up in a riverbed and set down to evac them. They started running for the chopper, and suddenly, they were ambushed by some Taliban forces hidden in the hills."

He sat on the bench, the smell of the gunfire, the sounds of the chopper, the shouting like yesterday in his head. "I had five guys aboard, and I lifted off, just to get away from the gunfire. But I had every intention of hanging around and going back as soon as I had a chance."

"Then I saw where the Taliban were shooting from, and I had this impulsive, stupid idea to do a flyby, let the guys on board take them out. They were all in, and we executed it perfectly. The SEALs barraged the nest and destroyed it. Or we thought we did. I was coming in to pick up the rest of the team when I spotted a stinger heading right for us. I managed to move the chopper enough for it to only take out the tail rotor, but we hit the dirt, and hard."

He hadn't realized he'd reached around and rubbed his wound, the scar numb but still itchy sometimes.

"It killed two onboard SEALs. I was thrown free. The rest of the team got me to safety, but I was pretty torn up. Another Hawk came in to get us, along with air support, and they took care of that nest of terrorists. I don't remember anything after the stinger, but apparently, I had a lot of internal bleeding. Someone did some field surgery on me." He turned and showed her the scar. "Lost a kidney and my spleen, had a concussion, broke my arm, and bruised my spine."

He delivered this information as officially as he could, with no emotion. He especially left out that moment in Germany, at Landstuhl, when he'd been told that he might never walk again.

But he had. After months of PT and sheer will.

But he'd never fly a combat chopper again for the Air Force. Maybe he didn't deserve to after the reckless decision he'd made that had killed two warriors. Like he'd told Charlie, he tried to soak it away, and when that only ended up with him feeling emptier, he channeled his fury into his PT.

But he skipped that and boiled it all down for her into an easy statement. "I did a stint in Walter Reed, and after I was discharged, Moose asked me if I wanted to fly for Air One."

"How did Moose find out you wanted to fly for him?"

"He wrote to me. Said he heard I'd be getting discharged. Offered me the job. I was still thinking about it when I heard about Dad's accident. Again, from Moose. I got on a plane."

He also left off the fact that he hadn't been exactly sure he could sit in the cockpit again.

All this time, she'd been listening, stirring, nodding, a pinched look on her face. When the stew came to a boil, she grabbed her cup from her bag.

He retrieved his too. And when he put it on the table, he saw her wiping her eyes.

"Hey. I'm okay."

"Yeah, I know." She didn't look at him, though, as she ladled up the soup and set his cup in front of him.

"Echo. Really. I'm okay—"

"But you might *not* have been, and that's all my fault." She was still crying softly.

"What? Hardly—"

"Yes." She looked at him, those green eyes alight. "If I'd said yes, or at least told you . . . why . . . If I'd come to the jail and explained . . ."

And of course, here it was, the conversation he'd wanted to dodge. But maybe not anymore.

"I was in no mood to listen to you," he said, slipping into a chair at the table. In fact, he hadn't been for the better part of ten years. But now . . . He picked up his spoon. "So, why did you—"

"Kiss Colt?" She sat into the other chair. "Because I was drunk. And sad. And he was sort of you, but not you. And it was the end of the summer, and . . . because I was young and stupid. And—and you'd asked me to *marry* you!"

He stared at her, trying to compute all that.

"Did you even have a plan? Where were we going to live? I just . . . it was all so fast and—"

"I know. I did it all wrong."

"No, Dodge." She sighed. "You did it right. You always do it right. It's not you. It's me." She looked down. "I got scared. I thought of all the things that could go wrong . . ."

Oh. "Like your mom leaving your dad?"

She drew in a breath, like he'd wounded her. "Yes. She dove into a life she wasn't ready for and look what happened."

"She had you." He offered a smile.

"She got in over her head and left my dad devastated when she went off to pursue another dream." She stirred her stew, the steam rising. "And maybe I am just like her. I dream of things, but never do them. Like the Iditarod. And my biology degree. And even my photography. But most of all . . . you." She met his eyes. "I wasn't ready to go all in, Dodge. To give you a yes for something that felt so . . . unplanned." She nodded as if agreeing with herself. "It scared me."

Oh. He hadn't expected that.

"I loved you. Of *course* I loved you. You were part of the air I breathed, the smell of the pine, the majesty of the mountains, my best friend. But . . ." She looked away. "Sometimes I still think about what if—what if I ran the Iditarod or went to college or published my pictures beyond the *Good News* or . . . I don't know. Left here for the Lower 48."

"You want to leave?" And now his chest hurt.

"No. Sometimes. I don't know." She blew on a sporkful of stew. "And that's what scares me. What if I dive in . . . and then it goes south?" She looked away. "I need to know that we're not going to end up hurting each other again. I need to know that you won't leave."

Oh.

Right.

And maybe he didn't have the answer, but suddenly, he knew exactly what *he* wanted. And shoot, Echo was right. Always had been.

He *wasn't* over her. Had never been over her. And that truth had been simmering since he'd raced through a storm, fearing she'd been hurt.

Outside a wolf's howl rose, mournful, filling the room with the sound of sorrow, then dying into the night.

Echo swallowed. "It's all silly, anyway, because I have my dad. He needs me."

She dug into her stew, and he ate in silence, not sure what to say.

Her voice turned quiet. "I should have come to see you at the jail. I almost did, a couple times. But I was so ashamed of myself. I never dreamed you . . . well, that you'd leave and not come back."

She said it without blame, but he winced anyway. Him either. Another impulse he wished he could take back, at least sometimes.

"When I heard you were back, I hoped that maybe you had forgiven me," Echo said softly. "That I could explain to you what happened. But I don't . . . I don't expect things to ever be fixed between us, Dodge. Not really. I tore your future from you. And sure, I used to think that maybe, someday, you'd come back . . . but nothing has changed. I'm still stuck, and from my vantage point, I'm not going anywhere."

She gave him a smile, something sweet, yet sad.

And for the life of him, he didn't know why he reached out and touched her hand, squeezed. "As it were, it looks like I'm not either. At least for a while."

She stared at him.

"Don't tell anyone," he added, "but we have to have six months free of accidents or we'll lose our FBO license. I can't let that happen. So I'm going to need to take over Sky King Ranch, at least for a while."

She leaned back. "Dodge. You're finally getting to run the ranch. What you always wanted."

Huh. He hadn't quite realized that, not until it tumbled from her mouth.

Shoot. Suddenly feelings, or maybe dreams, ignited that hadn't been alive for a very, very long time.

He might call it desire, but it was deeper than that.

Home, maybe.

But, most importantly, almost all of those dreams included Echo.

He met her gaze, unblinking.

Maybe they could start again, right here, right now. Tonight. And tomorrow they'd figure out the rest. "Echo—"

"Look." Her gaze went past him to the window. "The aurora borealis is out." She put down her spork and got up, opening the door.

The cold swirled in around her, but he followed, stepping up behind her. So close he could put his hands on her shoulders, turn her around . . .

Remind them both of what they'd walked away from. He could almost taste her lips on his, an old memory that sometimes haunted him with how real it felt.

Tonight, it could be—

What? *No. Stop, Dodge.*

He took a breath and looked out. Indeed, the sky washed with waves of light—lavender and mint, magenta.

"I never get tired of it," she said. "This, I know I would miss."

Aw, who was he kidding? "Echo?" He put his hand on her shoulder, turning her.

She looked up at him, and his gaze roamed her face. "Can I—"

A bark sounded from across the lake, warning, and then, behind it, a roar that thundered through the forest and lifted the hair on his neck.

Echo jerked around. "I know that bark. That's Goose—or maybe Maverick. It's one of my dogs, for sure."

He stared out into the cold. And then grabbed his outer gear and started pulling it on. She reached for her jacket.

"Oh no you don't. You stay here. I'll find him."

He picked out the .357 Taurus he'd put into his pack. "I'll be back, I promise."

Then he headed out into the night.

And for the first time in years, he meant to keep that promise.

———

She just had to keep running. Because running meant she would stay warm, at least on the inside, and maybe she'd stay ahead of him.

Behind her, the dog barked, maybe waging war with the beast, but she couldn't know. The snow pulled at her feet. They were almost numb anyway, despite her expensive boots and the fatigue burning through her.

Rest. She longed to stop, to sink into the snow, to close her eyes. But her heart pummeled in her chest, pressing her forward, the memory of his hot breath on her pushing her into the night.

She could so easily imagine what he'd do to her if he caught up.

She shouldn't have left the cave—she knew that now. But hunger and cold and the memory of the cabin pressed her out into the open, where the sun had emerged, and the blue sky had beckoned.

The cabin was around here somewhere—she'd seen it. And the dog seemed to know, too, because he danced around her, ran forward, then back to her, urging her on.

It was her fault—all of it, really, but especially the fact that she'd ended up lost, so far from *anything*.

From help, from home, from rescue.

Tired.

So tired.

The night had dropped from the sky like a lantern snuffing out, and she could barely see her mittens in front of her face. She kept her good arm out, however, because the spruce limbs could hit her in the face. Besides, she needed to hold on for support.

The dog's barking seemed distant now, faded.

Don't leave me.

The world around her turned quiet, just the crunch of her feet in the deep snow, the huff of her breath, the crackle of trees. The night sky soaring above her.

Oh, the night sky. She pushed through to a break in the forest and stood, eyes upward, watching the beauty. Waves of light, pulsing from the earth's northern pole, magenta, a deep green, a turquoise blue, all of it magical.

She had this, at least. Beauty. The quietness of her last hour.

No. She had to live. Must live. Must tell—

Barking behind her and a sudden roar made her turn.

He'd found her.

She fled.

Tripped.

As she landed, the earth broke away under her. Her scream rent the night, but the cold gobbled it. She landed softly, not brutally, despite the distance, just her face in the snow, her hands and knees dug into the deep snowpack.

She fought her way free from the grip and rolled over. Only then did she feel the pain radiating up from her ankle. It pulsed and burned, and she must have twisted it.

Oh.

She caught her breath, staring up at the sky, watching the warmth from her core form in tiny clouds above her.

A wolf howled, its cry rising, and she sank into it, reached out for more when it ended, the sound of it familiar.

Her own.

In the back of her head, she heard a hum. No, a buzz . . . no . . .

A *motor.*

She sat up. "Here! I'm down here!" But the darkness and wind ate her voice.

"Here!"

The motor dimmed.

Maybe she'd dreamed it. Longed for it.

She sank back down in the snow.

She'd just stay here for a moment. Rest. Just stay, listen to the mourning of the wolves and watch the waves stretch out over her, light refracted from the bitter palette of ice.

There was a metaphor there, she knew it, but her brain had slowed along with her body, and she couldn't think.

But the beauty of it. So much beauty.

Maybe she'd just close her eyes.

And then, in a bit, she'd get up and keep searching for that cabin.

TEN

Oh, Echo was in deep trouble. She'd veered so far off the path of safety into the crazy what-ifs that she'd found herself in a cabin, alone, with the one man who could make her forget the future and surrender to the now.

And everyone knew how *that* turned out. Impulsiveness only ended up with you alone in the cold.

Dodge had been about to kiss her. Echo knew it from the look in his eyes when he'd turned her, the way those blue eyes roamed her face, fixed on her lips.

"Echo? Can I—"

Even worse—she would have said yes. Lifted her head and let him kiss her. Like they didn't have a sled full of baggage between them, as if she hadn't left a gaping wound in his heart.

How could he just *forgive* her?

But her own words, her own accusations, came back in answer. *"You meant it when you said I was the only woman you'll ever love."*

And that made her betrayal that much worse.

He deserved a woman who could give him her whole heart—and not look back. Who knew what she wanted.

And sure, okay, yes, she wanted Dodge. Had *always* wanted Dodge. But that didn't stop the what-ifs from churning in her heart. Didn't stop her from fearing that one day she might hurt him again.

And then he'd leave, just like before, taking all of her with him.

Nope, nope, nope. She would not end up like her father.

Besides, Dodge didn't exactly say he was staying for good.

He had a job, a future that didn't include her, and she had to get used to that. Which meant no kissing, thank you.

Even if she longed to curl her arms around him, draw close to that solid frame and hold on.

She closed the cabin door behind her after the tenth time she'd opened it to the darkness, searching for him.

He'd been gone over an hour.

She added another log to the fire, glanced at the dwindling pile. The cabin had turned toasty warm, and she was walking around in her fleece jacket, a pair of fleece pants, and her wool socks.

To her guess, the temperature had dropped into the single digits, maybe now even into the negatives.

She should have never left Peyton alone. She hired Echo because she needed a guide, because frankly, no one should be out alone in the Alaskan bush.

Echo got up again and went to the door. She grabbed her jacket, slid her feet into her boots, and donned her cap. She pulled the jacket around her and stepped outside.

Overhead, the northern lights waned, dissolving into the sky, leaving behind a scattering of stars, a waxen moon. The night bore mysterious sounds, the wind, a crack of a tree.

Dodge, where are you? Come back.

As if summoned by her worry, she spotted a light out on the lake, a tiny spot of hope.

He had come out of the faraway forest and now headed up toward the ridgeline where he could ascend to the cabin.

Please.

She watched until he disappeared out of view, then went back inside to warm herself. She'd already cleaned the dishes, and now put on water to heat up some cocoa.

It was just coming to a boil when he walked in the door. Snow-caked and stiff, he pulled off his helmet and set it near the door, then freed his hands from his snowy mittens, working them, blowing on them.

"What did you find?"

Dodge brushed the snow off his coat, a light dusting from his ride.

"Nothing. I thought maybe the dog was in distress, so I headed out to where we last saw the bear. I found tracks. It's a big one. I don't think it's the one who was tormenting Spike or who attacked your dogs. That bear was smaller, in the nine hundred range. This one is a good hundred pounds larger." He dropped his hat on the table, his dark hair tousled and glistening at the edges.

He made a ring with his hands. "Prints are a good six or seven inches wide, and the back paw is a foot long. And deep." He unwound his scarf. "I saw evidence of the dog too. Could have been a wolf—it circled the bear a few times, but didn't attack, then took off through the woods. I followed its trail, but it cut into the trees and . . ."

"And with that bear out there, you didn't want to get off the sled."

He made a face. "First thing in the morning, we're back out there."

She nodded. And couldn't blame him. It might have been a wolf—clearly she'd heard one out there, and they were close to the wolf pack that Peyton studied.

Echo warmed herself in front of the fire as he shucked off his outerwear, down to his fleece pants and shirt.

Then he came to stand behind her. "Echo. I've been thinking—"

"I can't bear the thought of her out there, by herself." She stepped away from him.

He frowned but nodded. "Peyton is smart. She'll find some place to hole up, get warm."

She folded her arms over herself. "You don't get it, Dodge.

To be out there, by yourself . . ." She drew in a breath. "You don't get the thoughts that run through your head, that feeling of being completely abandoned, over your head, helpless to the elements . . ."

He closed the gap between them, his strong hands on her arms. "Stop what-iffing."

"It's not a what-if!" She pulled away from him and headed to the window. Played with the charm at her neck as she watched Dodge's reflection in the glass, the way he turned, the worry on his face. "If you hadn't found me, I would have died out there—"

It took him a second, but his voice quieted. "You're talking about when you were nine, and you went looking for your mother."

Her eyes burned. "I was stupid and impulsive and . . . I didn't have a plan. I probably deserved to die out there."

"No, you didn't. You were upset—your mother had left you. *Of course* you went out to find her."

She gave a harsh laugh. "My plan was to mush the dogs to Anchorage." She shook her head. "I had Susan Butcher in my head, maybe, but I thought . . . I was so naive."

"I thought you were brave."

She turned back to him at his words.

He just stood there. Gave her a small smile. "And smart. You figured out how to survive until we could find you."

For a second, the memory flickered in his eyes, and she saw it from his vantage point. A girl with a broken sled, surrounded by her dogs, trying to keep warm in the dead of night in front of a meager fire, thirty miles from the nearest town, the temperatures dropping fast.

"I still can't believe I spotted your fire," he said. "My dad said it was a miracle, and maybe it was, but we found you, Echo. And we'll find Peyton too." He kept his voice quiet, stayed where he was by the stove.

And shoot, now she desperately wanted him to cross the room and put his arms around her. The firelight lit his face. His dark whiskers had deepened with the hour, and his thermals outlined the body he'd cultivated in the military—corded shoulders, muscled arms, a core that bespoke a warrior, with the scars to prove it.

"I can't bear to think of you wounded, in Walter Reed, all alone."

His mouth pinched. "I should have written to you."

So many should haves. "I thought of you almost every night. I'd look at the stars and wonder where you were."

"And I'd look at the stars and think of you on that balcony overlooking the river." His mouth tightened. "Although sometimes I wondered if Colt was there with you."

Right. "You know he left for the military a couple months after you did. And Ranger too."

He nodded. "Ranger is a SEAL. He served in Afghanistan, and I saw him once, in my first deployment. Larke wrote to me and told me that Colt was in Delta Force, but that was a few years ago. I don't know where he is now."

"I hate it."

"What?"

"The fact that I exploded your family. That there is still a gaping wound because of me."

He shook his head. "It's not because of you. It just ripped open over you, but Colt and I had been . . . well, let's just say that Ranger had his work cut out for him keeping us from killing each other."

She did have a vivid memory of Ranger getting between them at the bonfire, emerging with his own bloody nose. "Why? What happened between you two?"

Dodge raised a shoulder. "Dunno." He knelt and grabbed a log, used a hot pad to open the stove, and shoved the log in. Sparks escaped and he shut the door. "When we were kids, we were all close. But then my mom died, and I guess . . ." He stood and slapped the debris from his hands. "Colt didn't handle it the way I wanted him to, I think. He got moody and reckless and started living sloppy."

"Sloppy?"

"You know . . . outside the lines. And my father never seemed to care." He picked up his coat from the chair, shook off the remaining snow, and hung it on a hook near the door. "When we were about fourteen, my dad left on a run for three days—left Larke in charge of us and me in charge of the cattle. We had about thirty head at that time." He turned, walked toward her. "There was this grizzly that was harassing the cattle. We lost a cow to it, and Colt decided to hunt it down. He left early in the morning and was gone for two days. I was worried out of my mind. Even went looking for him. My dad arrived home, and . . ." He shook his head. "I thought he was going to kill me and Larke. He was out of his mind with worry, and right about then the jerk shows up with the bear loaded onto his four-wheeler, field dressed and locked. There was no taming him after that."

"Everybody deals with grief differently." She could smell the woods on him, pine and fresh air. He stood close enough for her to reach out and touch. She folded her hands around herself.

"It would help if the way he lived his life didn't hurt other people."

She met his eyes. "That's what I'm afraid of, Dodge. There is no guarantee that we're not going to hurt each other again, and . . . I don't think I can bear it." She shook her head. "We're at peace again. Friends again, I hope. Let's leave it there."

His mouth tightened. "Problem is, Echo, we're beyond that. I can't be your friend without thinking about how you smell and taste and . . ." He took another step toward her. "Without thinking about how the color of your eyes deepens when I touch you." He reached out, hesitated, and when she didn't move, he touched her face, his thumb caressing her cheek. "Or how your breath draws in when I kiss your neck."

She closed her eyes and he leaned down and whispered his lips across her neck. Yes, she caught her breath.

Oh boy. She put her hands on his chest. "Then maybe you should stop thinking."

He smiled then, and it wheedled through the shadows lurking inside her. "I stopped thinking awhile back, when you started playing with this." He tugged out her necklace. "You still have it."

Her hand closed around his over the charm, and her throat dried.

"For all the what-ifs you're throwing at me, for all the I'm-afraid-of-diving-ins—you still have my necklace." His gaze darkened. "Echo, I think you should stop thinking too."

Her entire body heated. He was no longer the boy with big dreams, the unwavering, sweet friendship in his eyes. He'd grown up in the intervening years, turned into a man, solid, with wide shoulders, thick arms, a lean body, and a different kind of desire in his eyes that lit something deep inside her.

The man she always knew he'd become, deep in the back of her brain. A man she could trust.

Until, of course, he walked out of her life. Again.

"Dodge . . ."

His voice softened, a huskiness to it. "I missed you, Echo. Every day, every hour, every second. And I tried to forget you. Tried to move on, but . . . you're like Alaska. You're in my bones, my cells." He moved his hand behind her neck. "You are still the only woman for me."

He paused, and she swallowed, and then his mouth captured hers.

Oh. His kiss wasn't exactly soft, but not bruising either, and for a moment, she just stood there, overwhelmed. He tasted different and yet the same. There was so much certainty in his touch, she could hardly believe this was the same man who'd told her to stay away from him.

Yeah, well, she hadn't believed it then either.

Maybe she should stop thinking. Stop what-iffing. Stop fearing that she'd somehow break his heart.

And that in the end, he would break hers.

Dodge. She let her body mold to his, relaxing into the sweet safety that was the boy she'd always loved.

He moaned, a tiny rumble of desire, and it ran a thrill through her. She gripped his shirt, then wound her arms around his neck, pulling him down to her.

His arms went around her, the strength of them radiating through her, and she simply held on.

And kissed him back.

Oh. *Dodge.*

His hands tangled in her hair, and he deepened the kiss, and it lit a fire right down to her core, one that she'd tried to forget.

But how could she ever forget this man and the way he made her feel? She sighed, a sweet sound of surrender, of hope maybe, lighting deep inside.

Around her the night turned soft and cozy And for the first time since she could remember, she didn't worry about what lay beyond the horizon.

～

Oh boy.

With that little sound, Echo made everything inside Dodge turn to fireworks and heat.

Echo was softness and home and everything he'd longed for since the day he'd stupidly walked away from her.

Since the day he'd proposed.

He was in big trouble. His heart thundered, and a sweat had broken out across his body, completely lit with the fact that, oh, he'd missed her. Missed the smell of her, the taste of her, the feel of her against him.

Missed her laughter, her smile, the way she took him seriously.

He'd been such a fool—for all of it, from leaving her to suggesting they spend the night in this way-too-small, now sweltering cabin.

Thankfully, his brain kicked in before he did something foolhardy and ended this night in a place they might both regret.

So, despite his impulses, he tore himself away from the heady lure of Echo's touch.

He drew in a hard breath.

"Are you okay?" She looked up at him.

"Yep," he said, taking a step away. She'd taken off her hat, her long blond hair loose, and he could still feel its silk between his fingers. Still feel her in his arms.

He practically sprinted to the door.

"Dodge?"

"Just trying not to get us in over our heads here, E." Then he stepped outside.

The night was crisp, the stars winking from the heavens. He just needed to clear his head.

She opened the door. "What are you doing? Have you lost your mind?"

"Yep. And now I'm trying to get it back."

"Oh."

He looked at her. She was frowning.

"That didn't come out how I meant it." He was shivering now. "I didn't lose my mind, Echo. I knew exactly what I was doing. Which is why I'm outside, trying to remember why I don't spend the night in a cabin with you."

"Right." She smiled, and her green eyes twinkling nearly brought him back inside. "I forgot. You and your God have an agreement."

He'd never thought of it that way . . . more of a pledge, really. But he nodded, unable to speak.

"You mean to tell me that you've never—"

"Have you?" A sort of horror went through him.

"No."

Oh, thank you, God. "Why not?" But maybe he hadn't a right to ask that of her.

She lifted a shoulder. "No one else . . ." Then she shook her head. "Actually, I like what you believe. That there's only one, ever. And that guy was always you, Dodge. Even if I couldn't have you."

He met her eyes. "Go in. Close the door. I'll be back in a moment."

"I'm going to bed."

"Even better."

She grinned and closed the door. And yes, maybe he was an idiot, but he'd made a mistake the first time, asking her to marry him on impulse, before she was ready.

He wasn't about to make another impulsive mistake that could derail them again. No. This time he'd be smart about it all. Make plans.

Not destroy his entire life by a stupid misunderstanding that one simple conversation could have solved. Except, it didn't feel simple—not back then. Back then, it felt like his world had blown up.

So he'd run.

But now, for some reason, he was back.

Ranger would say that God brought him back—he could practically hear his overzealous brother's voice now. *"You don't know what plans God has for you—but they're good ones."*

Yeah, they hadn't felt like good ones while he'd been sitting in the Copper Mountain jail.

But maybe God *had* brought him home.

What if he stayed? Worked this out with his father. Created for himself the life he wanted, finally?

The breeze lifted and curled in through his thermals, raising gooseflesh. Maybe he was coolheaded enough to venture inside.

Echo was curled into her sleeping bag. He fed another log into the stove and climbed up onto the bunk over her, zipping himself into the bag.

"Good night, Dodger," she said quietly into the darkness.

"Good night, E," he said, his voice low.

It was the first time in years that he slept the night through. Without the nightmares and the replays and the sense that if he just did things differently, then maybe he could face the guy in the mirror.

And, even better, he woke to the smell of—coffee? He rolled over, and Echo was crouched by the fire, a pot of grounds bubbling. She looked up, the early morning sun in her hair, turning it golden, her eyes bright. "You snore."

"You know this," he said, sitting up. He needed a toothbrush, a razor, and a shower, not necessarily in that order.

He hopped down.

"I forgot. You sound like a locomotive is driving through the cabin."

"Yeah, well, you still talk in your sleep. Little muffles of groans and weird shouts." He dug through his pack for his toothbrush.

"No I don't."

"You did at the vet's office." He put toothpaste on the brush. "But that's okay. You often don't make sense."

She narrowed her eyes at him, and he laughed as he threw on boots and his jacket and stepped onto the porch. The day had broken clean and bright, high cirrus clouds near the apex of the mountains, a day without storm or high winds—it felt like hope.

He cleaned his teeth with the snow, then used it to rub his

face, waking himself up. His breath formed in the crisp air as he stretched.

Oh, he felt good. The kind of good he hadn't felt in years.

The kind of good that had led him to propose to Echo, all those years ago.

Okay, that wasn't entirely true. He'd proposed out of panic after Charlie had told him that Echo had been accepted to the University of Alaska.

If he were honest, he'd proposed because he'd been afraid.

And maybe a little selfish. Turning him down was probably exactly the right thing to do.

His dad was right—the last ten years had changed him. Scraped away a little of the cockiness, he hoped.

Made him ready to come home and be the guy Echo deserved.

Okay, so calm down. Rein it in. But still—maybe, finally, he'd realigned the path he'd screwed up so badly.

He could talk to his father, see if there might be room for him at Sky King Ranch.

And then he'd take his time with Echo. Prove to them both that this time, there was nothing to fear.

He was turning to go back inside when he heard a dog's bark, the same from last night, carry in the air.

The door opened. "Did you hear that?" Echo came out, bringing the smells of coffee with her. "That's Goose, I'm sure of it."

She stuck her finger and thumb into her mouth and whistled.

More barking.

She whistled again.

"There!"

A dog burst from the tree line near the house, snow flying up around his black-and-white body as he struggled toward them through the drifts.

"Goose!" Echo came off the porch, and Dodge went inside and grabbed her jacket.

By the time he came back to drape it over her, the dog was nearly in her arms.

He tackled her, kissing her face, pushing her back into the snow. She laughed and pulled him down to her. "You rascal. What are you doing here?" She sat up and he bounced away, barked at her.

"I know, I missed you too," she said and got to her feet, pulling on her jacket. He wasn't wearing his harness, but she reached out for him.

He bounced away again, set himself, and barked again.

"I think he's trying to tell you something," Dodge said.

She glanced at him, nodded, then turned back to Goose. The dog took off, running ten feet, then looked back.

"Okay. Let me get my pants on, dog," she said.

Dodge followed her inside and they pulled on their outerwear. "Let's leave the packs. We'll come back for them," he said, and she agreed.

He grabbed their helmets on the way out, and in a moment, they were on their sleds, firing them up.

Goose barked, running in circles, trampling the snow.

He turned and ran, and Echo shot off.

Dodge gunned after her, following in her track.

Yeah, he was hopeful too. Because it was that kind of day.

They followed Goose into the woods, along the ridgeline, slowing to duck under trees or move around tree wells.

And then they were out, motoring along the edge of the ridge. Goose stopped, barked, and worked his way down the side, into the gully below.

"Dodge!" Echo had already dismounted and was walking over to where Goose had alerted. "There's someone down there!"

He stopped his sled and ran over to her. "Is it Peyton?"

"I can't tell. She's wearing a black parka—I think Peyton had a green one. But I could be wrong."

He looked over the edge. Some twenty feet down, a woman lay in the snow, wearing a knitted cap, her furred hood up, her back to them.

He descended the cliff, finding footholds where the dog had gone, and in a moment, he was down and crunching over to her.

Please, God, don't let her be dead. He knelt next to her and rolled her over.

A white woman, with blond hair, her makeup smudged, her lips a pale blue. "It's not Peyton!" He took off his gloves and pressed his fingers to her carotid artery. Weak and thready. "But she's alive."

He shook her shoulder. "Ma'am? Wake up."

She didn't move.

He held his hand under her nose. Barely a breath.

"I think she's hypothermic." He stood up. "I'm not sure how to get her out of here."

Echo was already headed down. She tromped over the snow to him. "We'll tie her to your back, piggyback style, and you can climb up."

"That's the trick." He shucked off his coat, and knelt again as Echo propped the woman up. He got under her, pulled her arms around his neck, and Echo moved her legs to straddle him. She tied his coat under the woman's backside and legs, then around his waist.

He stood, bending over, and grabbed the sleeves of the woman's jacket with one hand. "You gotta stay behind me in case she slips."

"All the way."

He moved up to the wall. Under the snow, the tumble of rock created steps, and he managed to drag himself up one step, then the next.

Echo stayed behind him. "Just a few more steps."

She wasn't that heavy—maybe a hundred twenty or so—but her weight shifted, and he fought not to tumble back.

Echo put her hand on the woman to steady her, and he finally crawled onto the deep snow at the top.

Echo joined him a few moments later. She helped move the woman off him and lay her on the ground. She didn't rouse.

"She doesn't look wounded," Echo said.

"Who knows, Echo. That fall could have caused some internal bleeding, maybe a broken bone. We need to get her back to the cabin, get her warm, and call for help."

"We're too far out. The radio won't reach this far."

Of course it wouldn't.

"Okay, let's get her back, tucked into a bag, and I'll go for help."

She met his eyes. "I know this is wrong—but she's not Peyton . . ." She shook her head. "I can't believe I even said that."

He pressed his hand to her face. "I know. But we have to save the ones we can. Back in Afghanistan, we had a motto—'That others may live.' I let myself get crazy and forgot that and got two people killed. Not today."

"What about no one left behind?"

"We won't stop searching for Peyton, I promise. But this woman needs help now."

"Yes. I know—I'm sorry." Her eyes filled. "I just hoped . . ."

"It's okay, E." He grabbed her arm, squeezed. "Let's get her back to the cabin."

Around them, Goose was barking, rowdy in the snow.

Dodge picked up the woman and sat down on the sled. Then he draped her in front of him, put his arms around her, and negotiated the sled back to the cabin.

Echo pulled up beside him and helped him carry her inside. Echo spread her sleeping bag on the lower bunk, and he set the woman into it.

Goose came inside, too, and lay down, whining.

"I can take it from here. You need to go," Echo said. She stood up.

He glanced at the woman, then Echo. "Are you sure? Maybe we should try the radio."

"I will. But I know it doesn't work this far out. Just go, Dodge. Take the lake south, and it will connect with Remington Road. It'll be at least trekked by some of the big trucks. You'll cut your time in half. Remington Mines recently got a de Havilland Beaver. Take that—you can land on the lake—"

"Okay, okay. I got this." Then he reached out and pulled her to himself and gave her a hard kiss. "That's so you don't forget that I'm coming back."

Her eyes were still wet. "I'm counting on it. Hurry."

As the sun started to climb into the sky, he took off, the snow turning to spray in his wake.

ELEVEN

By the time he reached Remington Mines, Dodge had his happy ending all mapped out.

Okay, sure, he'd take it slow with Echo, not propose for a few more weeks—okay, months—but there it was . . .

The life he'd come home to find. As he plowed through a drift, snow salting the crisp air, the sky endlessly blue, his father's words fell upon him.

"I've been praying for ten years for you to come back. God has bigger plans for you. A destiny, if you'd just stop fighting it."

Destiny. The word lit inside him. Maybe.

A sweat had formed under his parka, his teeth loose from the hum of the snow machine. He'd come out onto the road, just like Echo said, and followed it west until he came to the cutoff for Remington Mines, a rutted dirt road that jerked and fell and tried to topple him. He hurtled peaked drifts, found old ruts from a plow, and finally came out to the land owned by Remington Mines.

The old log buildings of the first stakeholder, Jack Remington, still stood, shuttered up for the winter. In the summer months, tourists came out to walk the pathways, peek inside the old sluicing huts, try their hand at panning.

The real operation was over the hill, spread out over fifty acres of mud and tumbled rock and piping and river all circling the Remington pit, now some hundred feet across and two hundred feet down, clear to the bedrock, where Ox Remington and his boys were churning out enough gold to keep hope alive.

More than that, actually, given the homes that were built a couple miles away from the mine on a hill overlooking Remington Lake. A large log home and two smaller ones, with electricity and plumbing.

Dodge sped past the old encampment, over the rise, and down the valley toward the compound. The operation had expanded, with a massive power plant that powered the various buildings. The Quonset huts-turned-summer-accommodations seemed abandoned, but a wisp of smoke curled from a metal pipe in one of the permanent metal buildings, probably the office. A sign of life.

Next to it, a giant garage door was open to the machine shop, lined with excavators, dump trucks, a crane, bulldozers, and an assortment of four-wheelers and pickup trucks, most of them covered in a layer of grime.

Gold mining was dirty, hard-labored work, but now snow lay upon the ground, a lumpy blanket of grace, as if forgiving the destruction of the land.

Echo's father hated the place, but Alaska was so vast, the wilderness nearly indomitable, Dodge had to give props to the Remington boys for holding fast to their dreams.

Now, he just hoped that one of the brothers was around.

He pulled up next to the office and was getting off his snow machine when the door opened. Ox stood in the frame. The years of enduring this hard life were etched into his face, in his seasoned eyes. He wore a cap over his whitened hair, and an old flannel shirt, a leather vest, and jeans.

And held a shotgun.

Dodge held up his hand. "It's me, Dodge Kingston. I need help."

He lifted the goggles off his face and pulled down his scarf, and Ox lowered the gun. "Dodge?"

"What's going on?" Jude Remington pushed past his father, wearing a puffy black jacket and a pair of work boots.

"Echo and I found a woman in the woods—she's half-frozen and I need to use your plane."

Jude looked at Ox, then back to Dodge.

"Echo said you have a plane?" Dodge added.

"Yeah. A Beaver. Nash picked it up last summer. But—"

"Does it run?"

"He flew it here, so yeah."

"Can I borrow it?"

Dodge knew what he was asking—it wasn't like borrowing a truck, but maybe—

"Of course," Ox said and strode toward the machine shed. Dodge followed, Jude beside him.

"Who is she?" Jude asked.

"I don't know. She's hypothermic, and Echo is trying to help her. But she was barely breathing, her heart rate slow." He looked at Jude. "Actually, we were out looking for Peyton Samson. She was out with Echo's dog team, but they broke their gangline and a few of them have made it back to the homestead."

"In the storm?"

"Yeah. And if Peyton hasn't holed up somewhere . . ."

Jude shook his head. "I like her. Smart. I think Nash has a thing for her."

"Where is he, by the way? I would have thought he'd be at practice on Wednesday."

"He's putting up a spike cabin at a stake we have near Cache Mountain. Likes it up there. He probably got socked in by the storm."

Nash had always been the one to strike out to new places. Not the oldest, he was still the most likely to someday helm the Remington legacy. At least hold down the Alaskan branch. The legal side, though, was left to Pearl, their sister. Their oldest brother, Trace, ran the family's investments, probably back in Montana where their mother lived.

Ox pressed a button outside another massive door, and it whined as it opened on the cold runners.

Inside sat a beautiful, yellow-and-maroon de Havilland DHC-2 Beaver, a high-wing, propeller-driven bush plane.

Not only that, but she was an MK III Turbo, with a PT-6 Turbo prop engine.

"This is a collector's item," Dodge said. "She's gorgeous. Why did Nash get it?"

"To haul supplies. And tourists."

"For fun," Jude said, glancing at his father. "Nash is a sucker for nostalgia. He says Han Solo has this plane."

"Han—"

"Harrison Ford," Jude said.

"Sounds like him," Dodge said. "You boys must have gotten an increase in your allowance. Sheesh." Dodge ran his hand along the plane's sleek body on hydraulic wheel-skis. She could carry up to eight people, or 2,100 pounds, opened on both sides, and allowed for a full forty-five-gallon drum to be loaded into her belly.

The workhorse of the sky.

The forty-foot wingspan was nine feet in the air, and he walked under it, looking for trouble spots. "What year is she?"

"'67. Last year they made them."

"When was she last inspected?"

"Nash had her inspected before he flew her here. But she needs her hundred-hour inspection. He says it needs a new fuel system," Jude said. "But he's out of money, so it'll have to wait."

Ox had climbed in and turned her on. "Fuel says it's good."

"What's wrong with the fuel system?" Dodge walked over to the access panel and lifted it. "Crank the engine, Ox."

Ox turned it over, and Dodge leaned in, listening. "I hear a buzzing. The pump is working."

Dodge checked the timing belt, then closed the panel.

He did a quick check of the rest of the plane, the wings, the tail, the struts, the ailerons.

Ox got out of the cockpit and Dodge got in, checked the magneto, the lights. Then he idled the engine back and adjusted the fuel air mixture.

It purred.

"We're going for it, Ox."

Jude got in beside him, in the passenger seat. He had donned insulated pants, a hat, mittens, and a ski jacket. "I'm assuming Echo has a snowmobile too?"

Dodge nodded.

"I'll bring it in, so she can go with you."

Because that's what people did up here.

Ox had hooked up the plane to a four-wheeler. "I'll get you out to the runway. I cleared it yesterday, in hopes you'd be bringing your chopper in."

Right. "I'll be back tomorrow for that load."

Ox gave him a thumbs-up, then stood on the running boards of the four-wheeler, and the plane rolled forward.

He motored them out of the shed, into the sunlight.

I'm coming, Echo. Hang on.

They reached the end of the runway, and Ox unhooked him.

Dodge opened the door and called out to Ox. "I'm bringing her right to Anchorage. Call and tell them to send an ambulance to the airport. I'll radio in when I get close."

But first, he had to land on the lake and get Echo.

Dodge fell in love with the Beaver at first rumble, the solid feel of her, the way she lifted off as if she'd been itching for air. He settled in, and it reminded him of the Otter his father had crashed. Same maker, different model. The Otter was a granddaughter of the Beaver. A bigger short-takeoff-and-landing plane, it could hold up to nineteen passengers.

He liked the solid power of the Beaver better.

The prop hummed as the ground dropped away. He banked and headed for the cabin.

This was why he loved flying. The trip that had taken him two hours was reduced to a mere ten minutes as he flew over the ridge that separated them from the cabin.

He spotted Peters Lake and the small ranger cabin, smoke spiraling up into the blue. Echo came out as he landed on the pristine white surface of the lake. By the time he'd motored the plane around to the trail, she'd brought down the snowmobile.

"How you doing?" he asked as he jumped down into the deep snow. She rode close to pick him up.

"She's still breathing, but barely." He noticed she had been crying, probably for Peyton, but also for the girl. He put his arms around her, pulled her close. "Told you I'd be back. It'll be okay, Echo."

Because he had a plan. They just had to get through this, and everything would be fine.

Jude got out the other side, and they picked him up, too, and all three rode up to the cabin.

Inside, Echo had packed up their gear, the woman wrapped tight in her sleeping bag. Jude and Dodge carried her out, and Jude held her as Dodge drove them back down to the plane.

Then, while Dodge settled the woman into the plane, Jude picked up Echo and brought her down. "What do I do with the dog?"

Goose stood on the ridge, barking.

Echo stood on the skis of the plane. "He's coming with us." She whistled, and Goose ran through the snow, kicking up a plume of spray behind him. He scampered inside the plane, and she closed the door behind him.

"I'll take the sled and get it back to you next time we come into town," Jude said. He sped up to the cabin to put out the stove and close it up.

Dodge got in and turned on the prop. "Buckle in, Echo. We're going all the way to Anchorage."

They took off in a spray of glistening, crystalline powder, striations of thick clouds hanging over the mountains in the robin's-egg blue sky.

He rose over the ridges. Pine trees covered the foothills in deep green fir, and the flat white plain of the river cut through the landscape. He followed the river south, the white-peaked mountains to his back.

The lower trees were frosted white, like cotton swabs, with cutouts for houses and vehicles.

The clutter of the engine noise made talking difficult, but he reached out and squeezed Echo's hand.

Wow, it felt right to be here, right here, right now, with her, doing what he loved to do.

Destiny.

Yes.

The Lewis and Clark Wilderness Preserve rose, tough and bold, to the west, the creeks and rivers starting to flow free as he flew them the one-hundred-plus miles south. It wouldn't be long before the sun would awaken the north and set them free of the grasp of winter.

His gaze fell on the temperature gauge. It had started to fall.

He pushed the plane higher and felt a sluggishness.

"I think the fuel is running rich," he said, and glanced at Echo. She was wearing headphones also, but he hadn't clicked the mic. Now, she looked out the window.

In the brisk air of the cockpit, he thought he could smell the acrid base of the engine fuel.

He adjusted the fuel air mixture, trying to make the engine run better.

That helped.

See, they were fine—

The engine misfired and Echo jumped. She looked at him, her eyes wide.

And then the engine died.

The sound of it was so abrupt, just a cutting out of the hum, that he heard the tail end of Echo's scream.

"I got this!" He'd just flooded the engine, was all. He glided for a bit, glanced at Echo. "It's okay. Just breathe."

Then he restarted the engine.

It popped back to life. He'd clearly have to control the fuel flow manually by flipping the pump on and off.

He turned it off.

The plane began to climb.

"That was scary!" Echo shouted at him.

He left out the part where, in a few moments, the engine would die again.

And then it did.

He had gained altitude, so he let the plane glide, then he turned on the fuel pump and restarted the engine.

Echo had her hands fisted around the seat handle. "Dodge?"

"I got this."

The plane flew for another five minutes with no mishaps, and then the engine backfired. He turned off the fuel pump and flew another ten minutes until the engine died.

"What is going on?" she said in the vacuum of the silence. "Are we crashing?"

"Not if I can help it. The fuel pump isn't working right and it's clogging the engine, but if I can keep turning it on and off, we might be able to nurse the engine along . . ."

She stared at him, her eyes wide.

They'd dropped to two thousand feet.

The engine sputtered, and he waited a moment longer, then gave it another go. *C'mon.*

The engine coughed to life.

Echo gave him a wan smile.

They were thirty miles out of Anchorage—another fifteen minutes was all they needed. Already, however, he was veering toward Highway 3, just in case he had to put down. He pulled back on the throttle. They needed altitude if his guess was right. Four thousand, maybe five. He got the Beaver up to six thousand feet before the engine misfired again. He turned off the fuel pump, climbing until his rpms started dropping. Then he flipped the pump back on. *C'mon, don't die on me*—

Nope. Silence filled the cabin as they leveled off, descending gradually.

"Dodge?"

He said nothing as he tried the pump again.

This time, the engine took three tries to restart.

"We're going to die."

Nope. But he didn't want to tell her that this dance was going to continue all the way to Anchorage.

If the fuel pump lasted that long.

It didn't.

The engine died fifteen miles from the Anchorage airport. He could see Merrill Field in the distance, past the Air Force Base, past the railroad tracks, parked right in front of the hospital.

The wind caught the plane, was bumping it as he worked the ailerons.

He pitched down, picking up speed, then pulled out of it, leveling out, slowing.

"What are you doing?"

"In order to keep us in the air, I need speed. But in order to maintain speed, I need to descend. But not too quickly, or we run out of air, and not too slowly, or we'll stall."

"Stall? As in drop out of the sky?"

"Breathe, Echo. I—"

"I know. You got this." Her eyes were wide. "I'm just going to sit here and pray."

"Good idea." He watched the altimeter, his speed. They had

dropped to two thousand again, with plenty of room, he hoped, for a glide path into the field.

He coasted as far as he could, leveled, again nosed down to pick up speed, then pulled back on the yoke to level off again, lengthening his glide.

The ground came closer, and he debated dropping onto the highway or following the crow's path straight on, over the Knik Arm. But they could end up in the freezing water, Nash's plane at the bottom of the sound.

The woman in the back wouldn't be the only one with hypothermia.

He decided on the straight route and dropped to a thousand feet.

"You could land on Big Lake." She pointed out the window to the frozen lake below them.

"We're too high, and the angle is too steep."

He got on the radio and identified himself to the Merrill tower, apprising them of the situation.

"Okay, we got a runway," he said to her, his eye on the altimeter. Oh, this would be close.

He flew over the port of Anchorage, with the long docks and the ocean-going ships, the container shipyard, the many buildings, like round disks, that held oil from the Tesoro Pipeline.

A light came on and, with it, a beeping.

"Dodge—"

"It's the stall warning. But I've run out of air, so just hold on. We'll make it."

They passed the fuel tanks, dipping down over a small neighborhood, and passed eight hundred feet as they glided over the railroad yards. Seven fifty over an industrial center, and six by the time he overlooked the correctional facility, with its high walls and wires.

Echo was glued to the window, probably willing them to stay in the air.

She sucked in a breath as they dropped to five hundred over the highway. He was really losing speed fast, the stall warning still beeping. But there, just a thousand feet ahead, was Merrill Field.

He nosed down, picked up just enough speed, and flew over the gas station at two hundred, narrowly missing the high electrical wires.

He radioed again, and the tower had him on their radar. "You're clear for landing, N-89740." He nosed down again for the tarmac, a nice smooth ribbon of black.

He pulled up just as the wheels touched down. He flipped up the flaps to slow them down and applied the brakes.

They rolled to an easy, pretty stop.

Echo's fists were white on the door handle. She looked over at him, her eyes wide. "Are we alive?"

He smiled, nodding, his body buzzing with adrenaline. Very, very alive.

And then she threw her arms around him, holding on to his neck. "Please let's never do that again."

Goose jumped between them and licked his face.

"Okay, everybody, calm down. We're okay." A siren sounded, and he looked up to see an ambulance heading toward them. "Tower, I'm going to need a tow," he said into the radio, but already he spotted a cart heading their way, probably to clear the runway.

Echo untangled herself and jumped out, grabbing Goose and then stepping back as a couple EMTs came over to retrieve their patient.

She was quiet—breathing, but unresponsive.

Dodge got out, went around, and took Echo's hand as the EMTs strapped the woman onto a backboard. "We did the right thing bringing her in."

She squeezed his hand. "Yes."

"Unfortunately, we'll have to find another ride home." The ambulance pulled away, sirens blaring.

Meanwhile, an airport attendant hooked up the plane to move it off the runway.

Echo still hadn't let go of his hand. "There is a reason I prefer mushing."

He laughed, and it felt so freeing, so . . . alive, cleaning out the dark crevasses in his soul.

He was back. Back in his land, back in the cockpit. *Back.*

And not even the slightest urge to hit the dirt and unload his—well, practically empty—stomach.

He wanted to fist pump or something, but the last thing he needed was Echo knowing how he'd been fighting his own rising panic.

"We should go to the hospital and talk to the doctor," Dodge said. "Tell him how we found her. See if we can help track down any next of kin."

"Dodge Kingston, dead-stick landing over the sound. That was something." The voice came from behind him, and Dodge turned to see Moose Mulligan headed out of a small building near the tarmac. A red-and-white Air One chopper sat outside the building, along with a truck emblazoned with the same name.

That's right—Air One Rescue headquartered here.

"Hey, Moose," Dodge said and met his handshake.

Moose turned to Echo, then looked at Dodge. Grinned. "About time."

Dodge had to agree.

"I'm going to use the facilities," Echo said, and gave his hand a squeeze before she left.

Moose folded his arms over his chest. "So, what happened out there? I was in the office when your call came in but didn't get the details."

"Fuel pump is shot."

"On that old Beaver? Big surprise."

"I checked it before taking it up, but . . . probably. The plane belongs to the Remingtons. I need to get on the phone to Nash, find out what he wants to do, but he's out in the bush. For now, can you help me tie it down?"

"You got it," Moose said. He was a big man, a good six three, dark brown hair, bearded, and proud bearer of his nickname. He and Dodge tied down the plane while Goose barked, running around them.

Echo was still inside.

The air filled with the redolence of fuel, and the creosote smells of the rail yard not far away. Grimy piles of snow edged the runway, and the air held the brisk swill of the ocean, damp and clingy.

He should rent a car, drive them back the one hundred twenty miles to Copper Mountain, and let Deke know that they still had a missing woman on their hands. Except, Dodge hadn't thought about bringing his wallet with him when he'd left on the snowmobile yesterday.

He called to Goose, crouched, and ran his hands down the dog's body. "I think we're going to run over to the hospital and check on our Jane Doe. Can you hang on to Goose for a while?" he asked Moose.

"Sure. I'll have Grady keep an eye on him. Need a lift to the hospital?"

"That'd be great. But really, you don't have an extra set of wheels around here, do you? I need to get back. Peyton Samson went missing."

"Oh no." He frowned. "Yeah. You can take one of the company pickups. You can return it when you start work."

About that . . . "Moose—"

"I can't tell you how excited the guys—and the ladies—are to have you aboard. We've been hearing about your escapades from your dad for years, and to have you choppering for Air One . . . it's a real privilege, man."

Dodge stared at him. His *escapades*? But it didn't matter. "Actually, I was thinking of staying on at Sky King Ranch. At least for a while, or . . . maybe for good." He hadn't worked out all the kinks, but yes, those were the right words. "I'm taking over the flight service."

A beat, and Moose blinked at him. And he couldn't tell if it was surprise or disappointment or just shock. Then, "What are you talking about? I just got off the phone with my dad. He said that Sky King Ranch is up for sale."

And now Dodge went silent. Surprise, disappointment, *and* shock.

"Yeah. In fact, I pulled up the listing. It's such a nice spread, I really can't believe your dad is letting it go. The lodge, the cabins . . . everything, although I have a hard time thinking he'll get one point four mil for it, but I'm sure it's worth it."

A strange sound came out of Dodge, a sort of groan, a cough of confusion, and then, "What? One point four million *dollars*?"

"I'm sure it's not in bales of hay."

He stared at him. "No, that's not . . . what is he *thinking*?"

And then his own voice sluiced through him. *"There's no destiny, Dad. . . . As soon as you're able to take over, I'm out of here."*

He couldn't breathe. Oh no. He looked at Moose. "Listen. I'm going to go home and figure this out, but . . ." Well, his dad had betrayed him before, hadn't he? "You know I'd love to fly for you, Moose. What you do—rescuing people in the wilderness—your offer is the one thing that held me together during my PT. It's a dream job, for sure. So, listen, can you hold my spot? Because I'd love to fly SAR."

Moose grinned. "I hope so. Let's get you to the hospital."

Dodge turned and spotted Echo petting Goose. She got up

and grinned at them, a tight smile. "Let's go check on our Jane Doe."

———⌒———

She was supposed to be smarter and tougher than this. But it was happening all over again, just like she knew it would.

Echo sat in the cab of the truck, trying to erase Dodge's words from her head. *It's a dream job, for sure. So, listen, can you hold my spot?*

The grimy slush splattered as they drove through a puddle, jerking the truck to the side, and she banged against the door.

"Stupid Alaska potholes. You can't even see them and suddenly they're taking out your axle." Dodge sat in the driver's seat. He'd turned weirdly dark and pensive since his conversation with Moose. Maybe trying to figure out a way to tell her that everything that had happened in the cabin was a mistake.

Calm down. He hadn't made her any promises, and maybe she needed to remind herself of this.

Well, just the one about coming back to the cabin, but he'd kept that.

Their slate was clean.

And really, what *had* happened in the cabin? Some kissing— and why not? It was late, she was scared, and they'd simply revived an old friendship.

It didn't mean that they had a fresh start. Even though during the endless three hours she'd waited for him, she'd dreamed up exactly that. Him flying for his father. Them living—where, she didn't know, but she'd told herself that maybe she didn't have to know. Maybe being with him was enough.

"Your offer is the one thing that held me together during my PT."

Sheesh, he never intended to come home in the first place. One twenty-four-hour camping trip wasn't going to change that.

Except, she could still feel his kiss on her mouth, hard, sure. *"That's so you don't forget that I'm coming back."*

The man could break her heart a thousand times over.

Yeah, she had to be tougher than this.

They pulled into the parking ramp of the hospital and got out, the cement structure cold in the late afternoon. She hated the smells of the city. The odor of oil and gasoline and dirt and so much congestion made her choke.

She followed Dodge inside the brown concrete building, the windows reflecting the dark orange of the sun.

They took the walkway and entered on the second floor.

The instant quiet had her hearing her heartbeat as she walked next to Dodge. He didn't look at her.

The place was immaculate, the walls painted a calming blue, the flooring a white linoleum. Large picture windows overlooked the ocean, the small airfield, and the tangle and chaos of the city.

She was instantly sweltering, the contrast to the outside temperature brutal. She unzipped her jacket, realizing she still wore her insulated pants and mukluks. Her head sweat under her wool hat.

They walked past people in scrubs and clogs, and others in jeans and shirts holding jackets, and finally found a sign for the ER and took the stairs down to the first floor.

The lobby was awash in more soothing colors—blues and creams—the furniture patterned, soft music playing overhead.

A few people looked over at them, and she unwound her scarf as Dodge went right to the ER desk and asked about Jane Doe.

He was told to sit down, and Echo left him and walked over to a large directory.

Her eyes scanned down the listing of doctors, not sure why she was drawn to it, but her father had said—

There she was. Dr. Evaline Yazzie, ob-gyn.

Second floor.

Echo put her hand to the wall, inhaling a breath.

"Echo?" Dodge had come over. "You okay?"

"I'm fine." She turned, her back to the directory. "Just . . . hungry, maybe. I'm going to go find the cafeteria."

"Yeah. I could use some coffee."

"I'll pick you up a cup." She practically fled.

She found herself down one corridor, then another, up the stairs, and then sneaking through to the OB unit when doors opened for a woman in labor. Echo kept her head down and walked down the corridor of the maternity ward, her heart thundering.

What. Was she. *Doing?*

She stopped in front of the glass wall to the nursery, staring into the room with a handful of newborns swaddled in blue or pink blankets, their footprints and names on their bassinets.

Olivia Saul. Emmet Perkins. Harper Benjamin. Gabriel McCarthy. Others.

She pressed her hand to the glass.

"Ma'am, are you okay?"

Only when the nurse came up to her did she realize she was crying. She nodded.

"Can I help you?"

She opened her mouth, searching for the words. *I'm looking for my mother.* "No."

The nurse, midthirties, had short brown hair and was a bit on the heavy side. She glanced down to Echo's open jacket, her gloves and mittens, her loose scarf. "I don't see your visitor badge."

She looked down, as if surprised. "Ah, I . . . must have lost it."

"You should get another one," she said, and it didn't sound like a suggestion. "Who are you here to visit?"

"Actually, I'd like to talk to the doctor. Um . . . Dr. Yazzie?"

"You want to talk to the head of the department?"

"Mmhmm."

The nurse took a breath. "Okay. I'll buzz her. She might be in the middle of something, but—"

"I'll wait."

Good grief, she was in it now. She followed the nurse past the rooms of laboring women, others who were sleeping, having already delivered, and finally down to a corridor of offices.

The nurse showed her a chair in a smaller waiting area. "It looks like her office is dark, but she's probably still in the building."

Probably still in the building.

"No hurry." Echo peeled off her jacket, then her hat, and dropped everything in a pile on a nearby chair.

The nurse left.

The corridor held three smaller rooms, all with names on the doors—head nurse, an administrator, and department head.

All the doors were closed.

She walked over to her mother's office and knocked. She didn't know what she expected, but after silence, she gripped the handle.

It turned.

She took a breath and slipped inside.

It wasn't fancy. An L-shaped desk was shoved against the window, filled with papers. The desk portion faced two black chairs stationed side by side. A tall shelf behind the desk held a wall of textbooks, and a number of certificates and awards hung on the wall opposite the window. Excellence in Medicine from the OB-GYN National Board, The Haffner Award for care of Alaskan Native Women, the Dr. Anne P. Lanier Meritorious Health Service Award.

A picture of Dr. Evaline Yazzie with shoulder-length blond hair, wearing a white dress and black glasses, standing next to a tall, middle-aged man in a suit in front of a banner for Alaska Women's Health. She held a plaque, another award.

Echo leaned in, trying to see the woman she remembered.

No. *Her* mother had long blond hair and a smile that turned her eyes a vivid green. And she was taller. This woman seemed worlds away, her eyes hard, focused. Her smile tight.

"Oh my gosh."

She stilled, then turned to the voice.

A woman stood in the doorway. She wore her hair short and tucked behind her ears and was thinner than the woman in the picture.

But the eyes. The green eyes she knew fixed on her.

"Echo?"

"Uh." She swallowed, nodded. "I . . . uh . . ."

"Echo." The woman walked into the room, straight toward her, and pulled her into her arms. "Oh my gosh. What are you doing here?"

She stood stiff, not sure how to break free of the chill that bolted her to the spot.

The woman—her mother—*smelled* the same. She remembered the scent of that cream she used on her skin, homemade from lavender and mint. And the way she said her name, softly, like she did when she would tuck her in, kiss her good-night—

This was a terrible idea. "I—"

"Wait." Her mother held her at arm's length. "Has something terrible happened to Charlie?" Her smile had vanished, a twist of worry on her face.

"No . . . I mean. Not since . . . Effie, you do know he was mauled, years ago—"

"Of course I do. But he's okay now?"

If Echo ignored his broken heart, the way he struggled every day with pain. And she wouldn't mention the drinking. "He's fine."

"Then . . . what are you doing here?"

That's about what she expected. "Nice, Mom—" Shoot. She

hadn't meant for the word to leak out. It wasn't even a habit. Just, maybe, a dark, forbidden want.

"Oh, Echo. I didn't mean it like that." Effie sighed. "I'm glad to see you. You're so . . . you're so grown up. Look at you. A woman. Are you married? Do you have kids? What . . . are you hurt?"

"No. To everything." Echo stepped back, her heartbeat loud in her ears. "I . . . Dodge and I found a woman in the woods. Hypothermia. We brought her here."

"Dodge. Kingston, right? That boy next door?"

"Yes . . ." She couldn't call her Mom, not again. "The boy next door."

"You and he . . . are you—"

"We were searching for Peyton Samson. She's gone missing."

"Peyton? Oh, poor Alena and Gordon."

"She just went missing a few days ago. How do you even *know* them?"

"The Good News radio." Her mother frowned. "Echo. Are you okay?"

Not even a little. "Yes. I guess so." She should go. Dodge was waiting downstairs, and maybe she'd gotten what she wanted. Her mother, alive and clearly well. Echo wasn't even sure Effie had missed her.

She looked at Effie. She'd started calling her mother by her first name after she left. As if it might hurt less to take away the connection.

Right.

And suddenly, she just had to know. "Why, Effie? Why did you leave? I went to school, came home, and you were gone. Not even a note—"

"I left supper."

"Oh, please."

She sighed. Folded her arms. "I got accepted for a year of residency here, at Alaska Regional, and . . . I needed to take it."

"And Dad?" *And me?* But she didn't say that.

"He said he understood. That it was okay if I was gone for a year, and he wanted to tell you, so I let him. I wanted to come home, but we were so busy, and it was just exhausting and . . . I sent you a birthday present."

Echo blinked at her. "I have no memory of that."

"I guess I deserve that."

Echo should leave. *Run.* Because with every word, her soul felt freshly skewered. Talk about open wounds. "And after your residency?"

"I got the chance to go to Annette Island in Southern Alaska and work alongside the Native doctors there, helping the women for three-plus years. It was a chance to really make a difference, Echo."

"I saw the award."

"You were fourteen. I remember because that was the year your dad was hurt."

"You mean mauled within an inch of his life."

Effie sucked in a breath. "I came to the hospital, you know. I heard about the accident and flew up to Anchorage. I saw you outside the door, and I . . ." She sighed again. "I guess I was ashamed."

And that, Echo didn't expect. "What?"

"I knew I could never make up for leaving you. You needed me, and I wasn't there. And—"

"So you decided to never return? That makes no sense."

"You were so brave standing there outside the ICU. You had the backpack and that grizzly bear I sent you—"

"My dad gave me that bear."

"Right. Maybe he thought it would be easier if you thought I wasn't coming back."

Her mouth tightened. "So I could get used to being alone?"

"Oh, please. You weren't alone. You had Charlie. He was a great father. And I knew it." She walked over to the window, stared out at the landscape, the mountains a deep amber. "I knew it would be best for you to stay. Charlie raised you on the homestead. He taught you how to survive. How to thrive. I couldn't do that."

"So you gave up."

She rounded. "I made a choice to let you go. But I *did* pay for his medical bills. And I sent money to Charlie, to help. He mentioned a camera for your eighteenth birthday?"

Her mother had paid for her first SLR? Echo opened her mouth, closed it. Then, "He never said anything."

"I suppose not. I got another fellowship, in Seattle, and almost didn't come back, but then he wrote and said you were going to go to the University of Alaska, and I thought maybe we could be in Anchorage together."

"He *wrote* to you."

"We stay in touch." Her mouth tightened. "I still love him, Echo. I just can't . . . I can't live there. Every moment I'm there, I feel like the world is closing in. Getting darker." She shook her head. "I believe now that I was clinically depressed in the winter. Some people call it SAD—seasonal affective disorder. I was better in the summer, but every year, the sadness got a little worse. I thought that someday it would simply consume me, and I'd be lost to myself."

Echo just stared at her, trying to piece together the words.

"I'm not like you, Echo. I don't revel in that world. That life is . . . it's too big. Too . . . wild. Too alone." She worked up a smile, something fragile. "But you love the homestead, you always have. You love to mush and to work your garden and can and guide, and your photography is amazing."

She walked over to her desk and picked up a picture, then handed it to her.

It was a copy of the one in their entryway, of George and the view from the bluff near their house.

"Where did you get this? Wait, no, don't tell me. Dad."

"He couldn't leave. I couldn't stay. But we still love each other. And we both love you."

The breath escaped from Echo. "I can't . . . I don't even know what to say to that."

"Maybe . . . that you forgive me?"

Echo put the picture down on the desk, backed away from it. "Do you know that I tried to find you? I was nine years old, and I took my dogs and I tried to *mush* to Anchorage! My sled was damaged, I was hurt, and alone . . . and you *weren't there.* You were *never* there." She shook her head. "I don't even know how to begin to forgive you."

She shouldn't have come here. She headed out into the hallway.

"Echo." Effie followed her. "Try and understand. My work—it was important. My dreams—they were important."

"More important than me? Than Dad?"

Effie swallowed. "Sometimes."

Yeah. "That might be the first truthful thing you've said." She walked out into the waiting area and picked up her jacket, her hat, her scarf. Then she turned to her mother, every muscle in her body tight. "You know, I feel sorry for you. You have awards, but you don't have me. *Or* Dad."

Her mother stood in the doorway, and her jaw tightened, her eyes hardening. Yes, this was the woman she'd seen in the picture. "Don't be so selfish, Echo. It wasn't about me. Or you. Or your father. It was about something bigger than me. I *help* people."

"I'm sure you do, Doc. But let's not kid ourselves. All of *this* was about you." She headed toward the door, stopped, turned. "You know, I used to think you left because of me. That I wasn't enough for you. And yes, maybe that's true. But really, *you* weren't enough for you. You weren't content with the life, the *person* you were. That was the real problem."

She walked down the hall, exited through the doors, and hit

the button of the elevator. The doors opened and she walked inside.

She stood, her breaths tight. The doors closed, and she gritted her jaw against the urge to cry.

Dodge was pacing in the waiting area when she returned, shaking his head, as if he might be talking to himself. He looked up when she came over, blinking at her. "You okay?"

"How's Jane Doe?"

"She's unresponsive. I don't know. I gave them my information . . . if she wakes, they'll call me."

"Perfect. Let's go."

He looked at her. "Echo?"

But she'd had enough of promises, of people who said one thing and did another. If she wasn't enough for him to stick around, then it was his loss.

She'd find Peyton on her own. She didn't need him coming after her, protecting her, or making her feel like he cared.

In fact, he *should* follow his dreams. The last thing she wanted to do was be second place.

She headed for the door. "I'm getting my dog and going home." She turned, walking backward. "Do you want to drive, or should I?"

TWELVE

To make matters worse, they nearly hit a moose on the way home.

Dodge was driving, and the road ribboned out, sleek and dark, the snowbanks a wash of endless white. And to be honest, sleep crept over him like the tide, slow, enveloping.

He spotted a hulk in the road from afar, leaned up, trying to make out the form in the darkness, until suddenly the animal formed in his headlights, staring at him, defiant.

Dodge crunched his brakes. The skid woke up Echo, who'd curled up on the passenger seat beside him, not touching him, a gulf of chill between them. She slammed her foot on the floorboard, bracing her hand on the dash—

And didn't scream. Just watched in silence as he zigzagged toward the beast, who froze, anticipating the tragedy.

They were going to hit it. And at this rate of speed, not only would the moose be killed but it would total the truck, too, and the beast might end up in the windshield.

They'd be crushed.

But, as if a hand reached out of heaven to grab the truck, they spun right around the moose. They missed it by a hair, and if Dodge looked carefully, he could probably see the animal's snot on the passenger window.

They glided out to a soft landing in the ditch, not even raising a plume of snow.

He sat there, barely breathing, staring out into the dark at the moose. It considered them, then headed for the snowbank, its long legs like toothpicks breaking through the crusty top until it vanished into the dense pine.

"Grizzly," Echo said.

He looked at her. "Moose."

"Yep."

He frowned. "You okay?"

"Mmhmm." But she was unbuckling herself and turning around to check on Goose in the back seat. He'd been knocked to the floor, but now got up and shoved his pretty black-and-gray face between the seats as if to say, *What's all the fuss about up here?*

Goose licked Echo on the chin.

Dodge turned the truck around and headed north again, now fully awake.

Echo stared out the window.

"Are you angry with me?"

She glanced at him. "Why?"

"No reason. Just . . ." He reached across the seats for her hand, trying to puzzle back together the picture of their life, the one he'd worked out so long ago this morning.

Maybe he'd freaked her out—not just with the moose but with today's near-plummet from the sky. He still couldn't believe he'd cobbled together that landing from nothing. He squeezed her hand. "I promise to get you home in one piece."

She squeezed it back, then let go. "I know you will." But her voice contained a sadness in it. Or maybe it was just fatigue, because she leaned back, closed her eyes.

And he couldn't forget that she was probably worried about Peyton.

But then she opened her eyes and looked at him. "Why did you forgive me?"

He glanced over at her. "What?"

"At the clinic. You said you forgave me. Why?"

He kept his eyes on the road, the beam of lights peeling back the darkness. "Okay, in truth, I don't know that I had, then, really. But . . . I do now."

"Why?"

"Because . . . I love you, Echo. And all the reasons I was angry just seem small in light of how much I love you."

Thank you, God, for the darkness. Because it felt a little like he might be undressing in the wild.

He'd expected a smile. Instead, her mouth made a grim line, and she nodded. As if he'd just told her he had to give her a rabies vaccination for her own good.

Yes, definitely angry. Or at least upset. She was sitting with her arms folded around her, looking small and tired and beautiful, and because he couldn't figure out what else to say, he added, "I do forgive you, Echo."

She wiped a hand across her cheek.

What—? "Echo—"

"What if I wasn't sorry? Would you still forgive me?"

Huh? "Are you *not* sorry?"

"Of course I am, but . . ." She looked at him. Her eyes glistened in the moonlight. "What if I weren't?"

"What are we talking about here, Echo?"

"Nothing." She looked away.

He couldn't help but feel like a moose had just walked into the road again. "Okay. My dad isn't sorry, and yet, I forgave him."

"Did you?"

He frowned. *"You have to forgive me eventually. It's not good for your soul to hang on to anger this long."*

"Okay, maybe not, but sometimes I think I want to." He turned his beams to low as a car passed. "I thought I was over everything that happened, but being back has turned up all these . . . I don't know—"

"Feelings," she said. "Like the tiny shoots of spring, breaking through the ice."

"Maybe, sure." At least until Moose dropped the news. Sky King Ranch, *for sale*.

Talk about *feelings*.

Yeah, no, it was hard to forgive a guy who just kept betraying him.

Beside him, Echo had fallen silent again. And he kept winding through his mind the conversation-slash-fight awaiting him at Sky King Ranch.

They reached the spur for Copper Mountain. "Are you hungry?"

"It's late. And I'm worried about my dad."

She said nothing more as he took the highway toward her home. The night soared above them, and the sky had cleared, the moon bright upon the snow, illuminating the dark swath of road that cut through the forest. A wash of stars swept off the mountains, a jagged purple-black outline, tipped with silvery white.

So magical, and again he heard the old song in his heart, urging him home.

Sky King Ranch had been in the family for two generations. How could his father simply sell it out from under him?

Dodge missed Echo's road and had to bypass it instead of slamming on his brakes. Turning around, he headed down the unplowed drive. Twenty feet in, he realized his folly. "I'm going to get stuck."

She leaned up to look at the road, the way the light carved out the darkness, the shaggy whitened arms of black spruce shivering, closing in on the far end.

It was a half-mile walk.

She reached for the door handle.

"Stop." He looked at her. "I'm not letting you off here to walk a half mile through the snow."

"I can take care of myself. I'm a wilderness guide."

"It's dark and cold and—"

"I have a headlamp."

"No. You're not going alone."

She sighed. "I have somehow managed to survive for years without you, and I will continue to do so in the future."

Huh? Wait—

She didn't meet his eyes.

"Did I read this all wrong? Last night—"

"Last night was me being tired—we both were—and maybe I was a little scared, too, about my friend, and I didn't want to be alone. But I'm a big girl. I have been in the forest by myself plenty of times, and besides, Goose is with me." She reached for the door handle again.

And he reached for his. "Great. I'll go with you."

"No, you won't. Go home."

"You think I'm just going to leave you here, watch you go, knowing that something could happen to you?"

She stared at him. "You didn't think about me for ten years! Why would you suddenly start worrying about me now?" She held up her hand, lowered her voice. "Let's just call this before we find ourselves getting really hurt."

He had nothing, the punch of her words sucking out his breath. "I worried about you *every single day* I was gone. You never left my thoughts—"

"Forgive me if that's a little hard to believe. I wrote to you—"

"Thirty-eight letters."

Her eyes widened, her shoulders rising and falling, her breath a tiny cloud between them. "Yes. And you didn't answer even one."

That was fair. "I didn't know what to say."

He looked away from her, out into the darkness. Goose shoved his head between the seats. He found himself rubbing the dog's ear. "After the anger wore off, I was ashamed of myself. I couldn't believe I'd let myself get that far away from who I wanted to be, and I had no words."

"For ten years."

He drew in a breath. "Your letters stopped coming—"

"Three years I wrote. Every month. More at the beginning."

"When you stopped, I figured you'd moved on."

She looked away. "I probably should have."

Oh. His jaw tightened, a terrible searing in his chest. *"No, I won't marry you."* The moment in the truck flashed back, and he was again staring at her, going numb.

"Listen. I'm glad we're friends again. I'm thankful that you've forgiven me. And I love you too. But I've been thinking about what you said, back before the storm. About going after your dreams." She pulled on her mittens.

No, it was not going to end this way. "Stop."

"I'm proud of you. You're a real hero, just like I always thought you were. Go, live your dreams."

"Echo!"

"Listen, like I said, I have a headlamp. And Goose. I'll be okay."

"But *I* won't!" He didn't know where that came from— maybe the words he should have said so long ago. He softened his voice, not wanting to scare her. Or himself, frankly, but, "I won't be okay." He scrubbed his hands down his face, then turned to her, trying to keep his voice even. "I read every single letter you wrote to me so many times I could recite them." His throat thickened. "My dad was right. I came back for you, E. And I'm not going to lose you again."

She was just tired, and maybe he was too. They weren't thinking clearly.

Her gaze was on him, her eyes wide. "Oh, Dodge, you don't have to prove anything to me."

Maybe not. Maybe he needed to prove something to himself.

He was here to stay, thank you. With the woman he loved. And he let that thought slide in, cement. "Please come home with me. Tomorrow, I'll plow you out and bring you home."

He was about to back out when barking erupted out of the darkness. The headlights illuminated an animal bounding through the snow, a gray-black blur that danced through the headlights.

"It's Granite!" She looked at Dodge. "He heard the truck. And if I leave, he'll just keep looking for me."

He gave her a look, stymied.

"I'll be fine, I promise. I don't need babysitting."

Of course she was right. Still—

"I need to check on my dad. I'm sure he's worried sick about me too."

She could call him from Sky King Ranch, but if her father didn't answer, they'd be revisiting this conversation.

"Fine," he said darkly. "Call me on the ham as soon as you get home."

She offered him a small smile. Then she opened her door. Goose scrambled up to the front seat and out behind her. Granite ran up, leaping at her. She shut the door, pulled out her headlamp, and turned it on.

He watched her until she disappeared into the darkness, the dogs running and barking beside her.

"I'm not going to lose you again."

He couldn't help but feel like she'd just walked out of his life.

Take a breath, Dodge. He was just tired. She'd call him, and tomorrow they'd talk. Work out the kinks in his plan.

He drove through the darkness to the main road and toward Sky King Ranch.

The outside light was on when he pulled into the driveway. He parked in the Quonset hut and noticed the nose cone of his Piper PA-14 was reattached.

Inside, the house smelled of tangy garlic roast stew, and his stomach roared in need. He dropped his outer gear in the arctic entry and headed inside.

His father's office light was on.

From the floor near the fireplace, where the cinders glowed a rich red, Iceman looked up at him.

"Hey, buddy." Dodge walked over to the dog and ran his hand through his pretty icy-gray fur. The dog's wound seemed to be healing well, his father having doctored it with a salve.

Iceman licked his hands, and Dodge rubbed his ears. He'd have to take the dog home tomorrow. Which, maybe, would give him time to figure out what was going on with Echo. "Go back to sleep, buddy."

Dodge went to the refrigerator and found leftover stew inside. He scooped some out into a bowl and set it in the microwave.

"It's such a nice spread, I really can't believe your dad is letting it go."

Dodge took a breath.

He knocked on the open door to his father's office. His father was sitting at his desk, his laptop open, working out something on paper. A cup of coffee sat on an old envelope on the desk. He wore a flannel shirt, a five-o'clock shadow on his chin, and his reading glasses low on his nose.

Dodge had always liked his father's office. It held a mishmash of pictures taken with fishing charter groups, homesteaders, legendary bush pilots, and a few family photos. But the best part was his mother's watercolors. He had framed most of her originals—bears climbing trees, a moose standing in a river, the Alaskan range, a bald eagle, a grizzly holding a fresh salmon in its dripping jaws. In her pictures, Dodge felt like he could know her, see what she loved about this land.

His favorite picture, however, was the one she'd painted of him and his brothers standing in a field, an orange-and-white bush plane lifting into the sky, the ranchland giving way to mountains in the backdrop. The boys wore knitted caps, blue coats of various shades—she didn't dress them alike, despite the trend to match triplets—and each seemed to embody their personalities in their actions.

Colt held a stick out to Boss, their cow dog, playing.

Ranger was crouched in the dirt, digging at a rock or maybe something he spotted alive under it.

And Dodge stood with his hand raised, waving to the departing plane.

He always sort of saw it as sad, a picture of goodbye. But maybe it held something he hadn't seen before.

His mother had *known* them. Seen the men they'd become, maybe.

He'd like to think that, at least.

His father had looked up at his knock. "Dodge. I was worried. Ace Mulligan called and said that Moose had seen you in Anchorage." He got up from his chair. "Did you find Echo?"

Dodge looked at him, not a hint of remorse on his dad's face, and he didn't know what to do with that. He shoved his hands into his pockets. "Yes. She was out looking for Peyton. We didn't find her, but we did find another woman. A Jane Doe. No identification on her. Not sure if she'll make it."

His father came around to stand in front of his desk. "Wow. Out in the woods?"

"Just lying in the snow, as if she'd dropped out of the sky. But Echo's dog Goose was with her."

"Huh."

"I know." Dodge walked over to a picture that sat on one of the bookcases and picked it up. A shot of their family in that last year before Mom got so ill. His parents leaned against a boulder, his father's arm around his mother. Larke stood in front of her mother, clasped in an embrace. Colt stood in front of their father, and Ranger and Dodge stood on the rock behind them. Ranger's arms were looped around his father's neck.

Dodge's were around his mother. He had tried so many times to tunnel back to that day, to find the memory, the smell of her skin, the feel of her touch.

Nothing but white. As if it had been erased.

He picked up the picture. "I never said goodbye."

His father was quiet.

"That last day—Ranger and I were out with the cows. I'm not sure what we were doing—I think we were branding with Grandpa. Larke came running out of Grandma's house, down to the field, and told us that Mom's condition had worsened and you were taking her to Anchorage."

His father stuck his hands into his jeans pockets. "Yes. That was a rough day. I wasn't thinking very clearly. I never thought that she'd"—he exhaled—"that she'd go that quickly."

Dodge nodded. "You took Colt with you."

"That was probably a mistake. You and Ranger were with your grandfather, and I couldn't leave Colt alone, so I just told him to get into the plane. He . . . saw her die." He shook his head. "It's a hard thing, watching death take a person. She fought it. She so wanted to stay for you. You and Larke and Ranger and Colt. All of us. She loved you so much, it was part of her every breath, until the end.

"She wasn't afraid, you know," his father continued. "She didn't want to leave us, but she wasn't afraid to die. She leaned into God's love for her, and in the end, she was singing." He swallowed. "'Turn your eyes upon Jesus. Look full in his wonderful face. And the things of earth will grow strangely dim . . .'"

"'In the light of his glory and grace.' I remember that song. I think I even remember her singing it." The memory filtered in, faint, and Dodge's throat filled. He put the picture back. "I wish I could remember more of her. I have snippets—the sound of laughter, and a memory of her reading to me—*Goodnight Moon*, I think. And I still have one of her shirts."

"You do?"

He nodded. "I used to take it out sometimes and put the arms around me, just, you know, like she was there." He didn't know why he'd said that, and looked away before he did something stupid, like tear up.

His father said nothing.

"I don't get it. Why does God do that to a kid?"

"Oh." His father looked down, then toward the wall at the picture of the trio. "The circumstances of our lives aren't just random, Dodge. There is no such thing as chance when we're in the hands of God. And that's a good thing, because it means that we're part of something bigger, something that has an eternal purpose."

"I don't see how my mother dying and leaving you alone to raise four children has an eternal purpose."

"Of course not. That takes faith, and it's a hard request of a six-year-old boy."

Dodge drew in a breath.

"But faith changes things. It gives you perspective. It allows you to breathe through the grief. And, if you let go of needing reasons and let God work his will through you, you might even see joy on this side of heaven."

"I have faith. I believe in God."

His father turned, met his eyes. "But do you believe that God loves you?"

Dodge's eyes narrowed.

"I know you're angry. You have been for most of your life. I know you have moments when your anger gets the best of you—"

"I think that's understating what I did to Colt."

His father held up his hand. "But for the most part, you've tried to lock that anger away by doing everything right."

"Because if I do, then maybe God won't steal someone I love from me again!"

Oh.

He didn't know where that came from and blew out a breath. "Sorry."

"Dodge, you're a good man. Of all my sons, I know you'll do the right thing. You are stalwart and determined and I would trust you with my life."

Dodge stared at him, the words landing like a burr.

"And I owe you an apology."

Dodge couldn't move.

"I saw Colt's brokenness, and I did too much to protect him from himself and not enough to protect you. I should have seen your fear, saw how helpless you felt—"

"I'm not a coward."

"Dodge." His father's voice softened. "I'm not calling you a coward. But you *are* afraid. You're afraid of God not doing things your way. Of being helpless, and of the worst happening. You always have to have a plan because you're terrified of making a mistake that could screw up your life."

Ha. "Already done, Dad."

His father walked over, stared at the picture Dodge had put down. "The day your mother died, I was standing in the ER, beating myself up that I hadn't brought her in earlier, that I had given in to her desire to go home after those treatments, to be with you all. I thought, maybe if I'd been stronger, braver, or just . . . I don't know—smarter—then she'd still be alive. But nothing I could have done would have changed God's plans for her. For our family. And nothing you did would have changed God's plans for you."

Dodge shook his head. "I don't believe that. I could have *not* pushed back when Colt attacked me. I could have not run off to join the military—"

"And God would have taught you everything he did a different way. Made you into a pilot who could coax a dying plane in from fifty miles out. Made you into a man who would risk his life to save the lives of seven SEALs."

"What? How did—"

"Master Chief Chester Nez, one of the men you rescued, wrote to me. Said what you did saved the lives of his team."

"No, two SEALs died in that stinger strike."

"And he said they would have been pinned down, overcome,

and killed if you hadn't found and helped take out that nest of fighters. That even the strike that took you down alerted the team to the position of the fighters. They were able to call in an air strike and the rest of the team was rescued." He put his hand on Dodge's shoulder. "I am so proud of you."

"It was an impulsive, stupid move."

"Or, it was an impulsive, Spirit-led move. You know, so many times we get the urge to do something and don't act on it. But what if those impulses—especially the ones to reach beyond ourselves and do something dangerous—are from something bigger than us?"

Dodge just looked at him, his breath rising and falling. "I went to the hospital, you know. After I got out of jail. After Colt dropped the charges. And I saw you in there with him. He was sleeping, and you were just . . . you were praying." His jaw tightened. "He was so hurt. He had a tube running out of his mouth, and . . . I was sick. I couldn't believe I'd done that to my own brother. To you."

"To yourself."

Dodge looked away.

"You ran, but that doesn't mean you ran out of God's hand. You cannot outrun God's love for you." His dad offered a smile. "Or mine. In your anger over Colt, and maybe even your mother, you've conjured up a lot of lies, but the biggest is that I don't love you. That I don't want you. And that's why I'm sorry. I should have reminded you just a little bit more."

Dodge's pulse filled his ears.

"I do love you, son. And I'm sorry I hurt you. One thing you don't know is that Colt didn't drop the charges. I did. I told the sheriff that he wouldn't be pressing charges, and Colt never knew a thing about it. By the time he was well enough to think that through, you'd enlisted. What you also don't know is that my buddy works at the recruiter's office and he called me after you showed up."

"You knew I enlisted?"

His father nodded slowly. "I knew you had to take the long way around to become the man you are today."

The man he was today. He met his father's eyes. *I forgive you, Dad.* "Why are you selling the ranch?"

"Oh." He drew in a breath. "Because . . . it's time."

"Dad—"

"You have the offer to do something amazing with Air One, and this ranch shouldn't hold you back." He returned to his desk, sighed, and sat down. Adjusted his glasses. "I've already told Larke, and she agrees."

She *agrees*? "But . . . I thought . . . Don't you want to fly anymore? This ranch has been in the family for generations."

"Dodge. It's not sacred land. It's just a place. You all have bigger lives now, and Sky King Ranch doesn't fit into them."

Didn't it? His breath shuffled out. "I don't understand. You're going to get better and . . ." *What if I don't want to leave?* He nearly said it, but it felt so . . . childish.

The ranch didn't belong to him. It was his father's, and he had the right to do what he wanted with it.

Give it to his children.

Sell it and move to—Florida?

"I thought God brought you back here just in time," his father said. "But maybe it was to show me that I was holding on to something I need to let go of. We've had a couple offers . . . maybe it's time to say yes."

No. Dodge's voice thinned. "What if I want to take it over?"

His father leaned back and took off his glasses. Stared at Dodge. "That's not the question. What does God want you to do? Is this your destiny, or not?"

Dodge's brain turned very quiet. "I . . . I don't know."

His father picked up his coffee cup, looked at it. "What I want is for you to have all that God has planned for you. I thought it was this ranch, but maybe it's not." He got up. "Maybe stop telling God what you want, and let him work his will in you. You might find answers."

Then he walked out, into the kitchen, where Dodge's stew had stopped heating.

But Dodge was no longer hungry.

Echo could be her own worst enemy when she wanted to be. And even when she didn't want to be.

Sheesh, what was her problem that she practically fought the man who wanted to protect her for her oh-so-brilliant right to walk home, a half mile in the dark? In a subzero windchill.

With just a flickering headlamp for light.

And really, it was the final chapter to what she knew—*just knew*—would happen.

She'd simply gotten off the bus a stop before *"I'm sorry, Echo, but I'm moving to Anchorage."* And it would be an *"I'm sorry,"* because she wasn't going with him. Because she wasn't like her mother. When she made promises, she intended to *keep* them.

"Dad . . . I'm not going anywhere." Yes, that was her voice, and she meant it.

Granite ran out ahead of her, nipping at the snow his romping stirred up. Goose played with him, the two nudging each other, growling, running in circles, always back to her as she trudged along.

The trees creaked around her, the snow reflecting the luminescence of the moon, giving the night a silvery sparkle, the stars voyeurs upon her stupidity.

Really, it had started with her impulsive decision to find her mother. Yeah, that had been a winner.

She'd chewed over her mother's brutal, truthful words to her all the way home. She hadn't even seen the moose, although frankly, if they'd run into it, it felt like the right physical ending to the tragedy playing in her heart.

Why would she believe that Dodge would ever choose her? Sure, once upon a time he'd knit their lives together in his dreams. But . . .

Yeah, she sabotaged that too.

Maybe she *was* just like her mother.

Perfect.

But shoot, maybe she shouldn't have been quite so frosty toward Dodge.

"Let's just call this before we find ourselves getting really hurt."

Yes, that was harsh and born from the hurt welling up inside.

He hadn't said one word, not one, about moving to Anchorage in a few months the entire ride home. And she couldn't fit her brain around that. And sure, she could have said something, but she didn't have the energy to open up her wounds and let them bleed out. Her encounter with her mother had wrung her dry.

But one thing was glaringly clear—Dodge had a different definition of *"It'll be okay, Echo."*

In the distance, the light from her house spilled into the darkness, a beacon.

She hadn't a clue what to say to her dad. Had raked versions of that future conversation around in her head, too, for most of the drive home.

"She wrote to you, Dad. Wrote to you and you never told me."

She could picture him, sitting in his chair by the fire, his mouth tightening. Maybe rubbing his shoulder, or even holding a cold pack on it to keep the swelling down after a day of chopping wood.

"Did you think it would be better for me to think that she outright abandoned me? Maybe regretted it and couldn't come home?"

Maybe.

"I guess I was ashamed."

Not ashamed enough to come inside and comfort a child whose world had been shaken.

"You weren't alone. You had Charlie. He was a great father."

Lame. Effie had simply dumped her on her dad. But he *had* been a great father. And she *had* thrived. Become a part of the big wildness that was Alaska.

Her feet crunched on the snow, her breath fogging out in front of her.

She had not only thrived but built a life that, frankly, she loved. Sure, she'd never run the Iditarod, but she knew the joy of running a team, slicing through a quiet, snow-covered forest of birch and pine.

She'd never gone to college, but she knew how to care for the animals of Alaska, how to find them, observe them, capture their moments.

She'd never traveled to the Lower 48, but what could Seattle offer her that outweighed the majesty of her backyard?

"I'm not like you, Echo. I don't revel in that world. That life is . . . it's too big. Too . . . wild. Too alone."

Yes, she had dreams. She'd simply already found them.

And sadly, just let them drive away.

Her eyes slicked, and she blinked the moisture away before it froze.

She reached the house. Jester and Merlin began to bark in their pen, and she wondered whether—hoped that—her dad had fed them. But when she went to the pen and shone a light on their bowls, they were empty, along with the auto feeder. Their water bucket, fed to them by the heated water barrel, looked full, so she went into the nearby shed and scooped out kibble into a large container. She added vitamins to it and a few frozen chunks of salmon that would thaw with the warmed water. Then she added the heated water and opened the pen.

Goose shoved in past her, anxious for dinner—he, too, hadn't eaten since she fed him breakfast at the cabin that morning.

And who knew how long the other dogs had gone. Funny that her dad had let the auto feeder go empty. She glanced toward the house. No trickle of smoke from the chimney, but it was hard to see in the darkness. Still, the main light burned. He was probably in his office.

She poured the kibble concoction into bowls, and the dogs dug in, snuffing and chewing and wagging their tails.

She ran a hand down Merlin's sleek brown-gray body, and it occurred to her that Iceman was still at Dodge's house.

In good hands, no doubt.

She closed the gate, then walked over to the chicken pen.

Oh no. One of the chickens lay dead in the pen, frozen, a bite out of its neck.

She didn't see any other foul play, but maybe the coyote had gotten in before Granite had chased it away. Going inside, she grabbed the carcass off the ground and threw it into the woods. Weird that her father hadn't noticed it, but maybe it just happened.

Gregory, her rooster, squawked at her as she closed the pen, as if to say, "I got this."

She smiled, hearing Dodge's voice today in the plane.

"I got this."

Yes, yes he did. And frankly, if there was anyone born to be a rescue pilot, it was Dodge.

Let him go. Let him live his dreams. She did the right thing. She knew it in her heart.

"Charlie raised you on the homestead. He taught you how to survive. How to thrive. I couldn't do that."

Maybe, in a way, her mother had let her go too.

She shook the thought away. No. Parents were supposed to sacrifice for their children.

Except, what about her dad? *"You had the backpack and that grizzly bear I sent you—"*

Oh, Dad. Maybe he didn't want to give her hope.

Or maybe he'd let his anger steal from Echo the last affection from her mother.

She blew out a breath as she gathered up some freshly chopped logs and added them to the bin by the door. Then she stepped inside the arctic entry, letting Granite in with her, and stomped out her boots on the rug.

The house was warm, although no fresh smell of dinner greeted her, but maybe her dad had heated up some leftovers. She stepped out of her boots, shed her jacket and her insulated pants, and walked by his closed office door. A light shone from under the crack, so she stopped. Knocked.

"Dad?" No answer. Maybe he'd fallen asleep in his recliner. And honestly, she wasn't quite ready to face him yet.

"We stay in touch."

Now, that just wasn't fair, was it?

She stopped by the ham and called Sky King Ranch. Barry answered, and she delivered the okay message Dodge requested, a little relieved she didn't have to talk to him herself.

She walked back into the great room. The fire still smoldered in the hearth, on its last breath. She stirred it to life, added kindling, then a log.

Granite flopped down on the floor, and she couldn't help but think of Dodge, here, just a few days ago, trying to figure out how to build a bridge between them.

"I came back for you, E."

She could almost feel him standing here in the room with her, the smell of him, his very presence nearly taking up all the breathable air.

"I read every single letter you wrote to me so many times I could recite them."

But he hadn't written back. Maybe because he knew, deep inside, their worlds had broken apart.

"I couldn't believe I'd let myself get that far away from who I wanted to be, and I had no words."

She got that. She did.

But he'd figured out who he was now.

And their world was still broken apart.

Her last words to her mother pinged as she headed to the kitchen to check on dinner. Leftover stew, still in the fridge.

"You know, I used to think you left because of me. That I wasn't enough for you. And yes, maybe that's true. But really, you weren't enough for you."

Her mother simply wanted more than this world. More than Echo. More than her father.

More than this life.

And Echo refused to compete with that. With her mother. With Dodge.

Because, in the end, she knew she'd lose.

She went upstairs to the tiny bedroom that took up most of the loft, grabbed clean clothes, and went back downstairs to the bathroom. The overhead water tank was in a room next to her bedroom, and they filled it regularly from the river.

The water was heated by an on-demand heater, and now she flicked it on and waited for it to warm. She stoppered the tub, not wanting to waste the water. It spilled out cold, then warmer, and finally hot enough for her to get in.

She sudsed up her hair and was just rinsing when the water died to a trickle.

Oh no. How had the tank gotten this empty?

She rinsed her hair with the water still in the tub, then let it out, shivering.

Winding her hair up in a towel, she pulled on sweatpants, a thermal shirt, and wool socks. Then she headed out to the kitchen.

Outside, night had descended, thick and cold. Somewhere in the darkness, a wolf howled.

Maybe she wouldn't trek out to the river in the pitch-darkness, open up the thermal plug in their river outlet, attach the hose, and run the pump to fill the tank in the below-freezing temperature.

But tomorrow she was going out after Peyton again, even if Dodge didn't want to, so . . .

She walked back to her father's office. Still, the light bled out under the door. She knocked again. No answer. "Dad?"

Nothing.

"Um, we're out of water. And I need to go back out on the trail tomorrow . . ."

Nothing. She put her hand on the knob, debated—sometimes he got so engrossed with his tracking software that he didn't hear her—and then, slowly, so as not to wake him if he was sleeping, she opened the door.

The recliner was empty. A half-finished coffee cup sat on the desk, and the computer was dark.

Charts were spread out on the desk. She walked over and studied them. Patterns of Elsa's movement over the past three years. And below that, a map. She pulled it out. Her dad had marked the area of Elsa's most recent telemetry, including the place where he supposed her current den might be.

Perfect. She sat in the chair. "Oh, Dad. What have you done now?"

At least she was warm. Agonizingly so, with the pain starting in her feet and moving through her body. But warmth, all the same, and she sank into it, letting it cover her.

She remembered the house, some. Remembered sitting by a fire or a stove or maybe she'd simply dreamed it, having wanted it so badly.

Noises. And then a voice. A man's voice, and she leaned into it, wanting it.

Or not, because then *he* was back.

Her breaths came fast, and she could almost feel his hands

on her, imprisoning her. And, as if she were back there—the drone of an engine.

She could almost see him laughing at her as she tried to flee, to fight him, despite the cost.

The crash was her fault. Of *course* it was her fault. Anything to get away from him.

Oh, she hoped that she hadn't already cost lives.

Especially since now, the whiteness had her trapped, like layers of cotton, filmy, suffocating. She could hear the voices, feel the warmth, but couldn't dig herself out—

I'm here! I'm here—

Now, darkness filtered in like the burned edges of an old-time film.

No! She wasn't done. And if she didn't wake up, then they would win.

Sergei and his comrades, the ones who chased her all the way from Seattle, would win. They'd find her, finish her off.

And people would die.

So much for believing that Alaska might be safe.

That here, in the massive expanse of forest, she might hide.

She fought the darkness burning away at her consciousness. *No!* She didn't want to sleep—

"It's up to you." Another voice, and she knew this one, calm, serious, deadly. *Roy—*

"It's up to you or we all die."

THIRTEEN

Before the sun had fully lit the sky, Echo was up, harnesses in hand.

Granite was jumping around her as she came out of the house, her feet crunching on the snow. The dawn cast over the mountains in a wash of deep pink, the valleys pewter. A cloudless, crisp day. Her breath formed as she went to the barn, refreshed the feed for the goats, then pulled out her old sled, the small one, with just enough room for supplies on the front. She and her father had hand-peeled the boards, made of white ash, molded the brush bow, created the tilt handle for better control on the turns, and bolted it all together. The sled used a standard claw brake, and as she pulled it out, of course Dodge was in her head, riding the ski tails or sitting in the body of the sled as they flew through the white.

"I have somehow managed to survive for years without you, and I will continue to do so in the future." She was such a liar. But she *was* a survivor.

She attached the sled to the fence with a quick-release knot.

Then she unraveled the gangline, the long cable that attached the dogs to the sled, and untangled the tug lines that attached to each dog's harness.

Granite was going berserk beside her, riling up the other dogs who'd emerged from their houses, barking, nipping, jumping on the fence.

"I know, I know. Calm down." Her head told her that her

father was just fine. But she couldn't help but worry—not just about him, but Peyton too.

Granite nearly leaped into his harness, shoving his snout through the head hole and stepping into the leg openings.

She attached him to the front of the gangline, in the lead position. He held the line taut, his entire body shivering with excitement, barking encouragement to the others.

Merlin jumped on the fencing, and Echo shooed her away as she entered. She harnessed Merlin, then Goose and Jester, and hooked them up to the gangline before clipping their tug lines and neck lines.

Although a team dog, Merlin was snapped in next to Granite at lead, and Goose and Jester at wheel positions. She dearly missed Iceman, Maverick, and Jester in the team dog positions, but these four could easily pull her tiny sled.

She strapped in her gear—dog food, a sleeping bag, a tent, a bag of dried chili, an axe, a cook pot and stove, extra fuel, snowshoes.

The dogs were jerking at the sled, launching themselves in the air. The power of the animals filled up the brittle exhausted places inside her that said, *"Stay inside, it's futile."*

As Echo affixed booties onto the dogs' feet, she mentally retraced the map on her father's desk. The area he'd circled was west of here, maybe thirty miles, and ten miles west of the cabin at Peters Lake.

Peyton kept one more camera at a former hunter's cabin near there, aimed at a den of younger wolves. When they checked it last fall, the den had been abandoned, but it was possible that Peyton had been heading that direction. It was rough country—more ridges, canyons, foothills, cliffs, and ledges to get thrown from.

Echo would swing by Dodge's place, check on Iceman, and, okay, talk to Dodge, maybe apologize about . . . well, she knew she'd hurt him.

"I won't be okay." His words, torn from a place inside, had emerged soft but a little broken. And they'd sat in her heart all night.

Because maybe she wouldn't be okay either.

In fact, their entire conversation had unspooled as she watched the moon wax her floor, as she worried about her father and Peyton.

"I'm not going to lose you again."

Maybe she'd been tired and had jumped to conclusions about his words to Moose. Because those words didn't sound like they came from a man who planned on walking out of her life, did they?

Granite turned, barking, as if to say, *"Let's go already!"*

She pulled down her goggles, then untied the quick knot. "We're going to Sky King Ranch," she said to Granite, as if he could understand. Maybe. The dog seemed to read her mind.

Then she lifted the brake. "Hike! Hike!"

The dogs shot off, and had she not been hanging on, she would have tumbled right off the sled, for the power. She adjusted her feet on the runners and settled into the familiar rhythm of the sled, the peaceful hush over the snow.

It was an easy twenty above zero and getting warmer, the perfect day for mushing, and as they lit out cross-country, onto the familiar path up the river, over the ridge that crossed it, and into the bush, she felt herself at one with the movement of the sled, her eyes on the land.

A wide expanse, deepened by the frozen river, cut a swath into the forest. They mushed through a thick grove of pine, then out onto a field that in the summer was covered with pink dwarf fireweed and yellow poppies, wild lavender. The dogs yipped as they ran, excited now to stretch their legs.

They crossed over a ridge, then along a valley, and in the distance, she made out the ranch, some two miles to the northwest, sitting in a pocket of land that unfurled over hill and valley like a white, pristine carpet. On a hill overlooking the lake, rimmed with a handful of cabins, was the beautiful lodge built by two generations of Kingston men and women. It was a sort of kingdom, to her mind, a place of refuge and safety. Sure, Dodge didn't have a mother, but his grandmother had lived at the opposite end of the lake, and they never seemed to lack for anything. No running to the lake for water, no heating their house with wood. More, there was a peace here, despite their losses. She envied it.

She should have said yes to Dodge, all those years ago, when he asked her to be part of this.

Granite must have understood their destination because he made a beeline for the lodge, Merlin following his lead. The sun was up now, the peaks to the north and west clear and white against a brilliant blue sky. The unblemished snow glistened, adding a sparkle to the day and the quiet of her ride. The power of the dogs carrying her swept through Echo.

This was where she belonged. She knew it as she knew her dogs, the pattern of her hand, the song of the mountains.

"He couldn't leave. I couldn't stay. But we still love each other."

Oh, Dodge. What was she going to do?

"Easy, dogs," she said as they drew near, and she stepped on the brake to slow them down. The dogs ran her right into the driveway, and she noticed that the door to the Quonset barn was open, the chopper missing.

They stopped at her command, and she tied up the sled. The dogs stood panting, still hyper after their sprint.

The front door opened, and Barry Kingston came out onto the massive porch. "Echo? Is that you?"

She waved.

"I'll bring some water for the dogs."

She met him at the arctic entry and carried the bucket of water to the team. The dogs gathered around, slurping it up. Then she headed inside.

Barry was waiting for her. He wore a cast on his arm, although it seemed more of a nuisance than correcting anything as he held open the door for her.

"How's it feeling?" she said, stamping off the snow.

"I'm about to take a Skil saw to it," he said with a grin.

She had always liked him. Barry Kingston was tough, strong, and embodied the land he'd been born on. He had a way about him—straight shooting, the kind of guy who kept his word, strict, but also fed out enough line to his kids to let them taste freedom. He'd taught Larke to fly when she was thirteen, and then Dodge, around the same age.

Dodge had taken Echo up for the first time when he was sixteen, right after he soloed.

"I feel like that would be a bad choice," she said, laughing. "Is Dodge here?"

She thought she already knew the answer, but her stomach fell when he shook his head. "He headed out early to Remington Mines to do some hauling work for them. Said he wanted to get back early—I think he had plans to go to your place."

"I wanted to talk to him about . . . well, a conversation we had last night. I wanted to clear the air."

"You two get in a fight?" Barry smiled, an eyebrow up, and she felt about thirteen, remembering that time he'd caught her with Dodge's named doodled in one of her notebooks.

"Actually, I was wondering how my dog was doing."

Maybe he'd heard her, because Iceman got up from whatever pampered bed the Kingstons had made for him and nosed his way past Barry, into the arctic room. He licked her face as she crouched in front of him.

"Come in, Echo. I'll radio Dodge and see when he's getting back, and you can check on Iceman's wound." He called the dog inside and closed the door to the cold while she took off her outerwear.

By the time she came in, he had a pot of hot water heating on the stove, a couple mugs out. "Coffee?"

"Make my wildest dreams come true."

He laughed. "We're all about happy customers here."

She crouched again in front of Iceman, endured a kiss on her chin, then turned him to look at his haunch. The wound was healing nicely, a reddened gash where something had grazed him, tore a quarter-inch-wide streak along his body. "He seems to be walking fine," she said. "I'm not sure I should take him out with me though."

The kettle whistled and Barry poured water into a drip coffeepot. The aroma woke her up, drew her to the counter. Barry set down a mug with the words I'D RATHER BE FLYING on it.

"Where are you headed?"

"I'm going to a hunter's cabin west of Peters Lake, near Cache Mountain."

He poured her a cup of coffee and set it in front of her. "That's rough country out there. You're in the foothills of Denali."

"I know, but Peyton said she wanted to check all her cameras, and she might have included that one."

"Radio reception won't reach that far."

She shook her head. And didn't mention, either, that her father had vanished, taking the last of the radios.

If she was lucky, he'd be where he'd indicated on the map, just southwest of Cache Creek.

"Let me check on Dodge," he said before heading into the flight office.

She slid off the stool and walked over to the fireplace. It wasn't yet lit, but her gaze fell on a picture over the mantel, one of Barry and his family, minus his wife.

She guessed the boys were around fourteen, Larke easily sixteen and, of course, beautiful with that long blonde hair. Barry stood in the middle, with Ranger and Colt on one side. Ranger stood like a soldier, even then, his hands clasped behind his back, his grin solid and warm. Beside him, Colt wore a gimme cap backward on his head, and she couldn't tell if he was looking at the camera or beyond it. He gave a thumbs-up to the camera, however, his grin slightly crooked, as if he might be hiding something.

Probably. Colt was the middle of the three, the one who couldn't seem to find his footing.

Dodge stood at the end, flanking Larke, arms folded, staring into the camera, a sort of smile tweaking his face, as if he were still considering his options. He wore a pair of jeans and a T-shirt, the wind blowing his dark hair, his body already filling out, a hint of the man he would be.

"That was our last family picture before Larke left for the Army. I should have gotten another one, but the boys always were hard to wrangle." Barry had come out and was standing behind her.

"I love this picture. Dad and I don't have even one together. He doesn't like them. Our last family picture was when I was nine, I think, although I can't find it."

Barry nodded. "It's hard when you know there's a missing piece. We didn't take one for years, and then I realized that Cee loved this land as much as I did. Wanted us to raise our family here. She would always be a part of this life, so any picture I took would include her."

Echo took a sip of her coffee. Strong and bracing. She would have expected nothing less from a Kingston. "My mother hated it here."

Barry frowned at her. "I knew your mother. She was a strong woman, and she could appreciate the beauty of Alaska."

"She fought depression, and it was worse in the winter." For the first time, she really heard those words. *"I thought that someday it would simply consume me, and I'd be lost to myself."*

That, probably, Echo could understand.

"That's why she left?"

"I guess. And she had a dream she wanted to pursue. Dad wanted to stay, so she made the choice for him."

It felt a little rough to say it that way, but in the end, that was the easy math. "Funny, I always told myself it was an accident, as if she didn't *want* to leave me. That maybe Dad or I did something to make her go."

"And you feared making that same mistake, doing something that would cause someone you loved to leave."

She looked up at Barry. "I did do that, if you recall."

"Dodge made his own choices. Sure, he was hurt, but don't you blame yourself for his mistakes or . . . your mother's."

"Maybe they weren't mistakes. She's won awards and is the head of her department down in Anchorage."

"Oh?"

She didn't know what it was about Barry Kingston, but she could never lie to him. "I saw her. Yesterday. When Dodge and I brought in that Jane Doe."

"You saw your *mother*?"

"Spoke to her."

He crouched and began building a fire in the hearth. "Hmm."

"I know." She handed him some tinder from the woodbox. "I don't know why—I just suddenly found myself in her office. She had a picture I'd taken hanging on her wall. She was just as surprised to see me."

"Really?"

"She apologized—sorta. Asked me to forgive her."

He said nothing, just kept building the fire.

"I probably already have. I mean, I'm an adult now. I don't need my mother anymore."

"You don't?" He added paper, the tinder, the kindling. Just like Dodge had done it at the cabin, of course.

She handed him a long match from a box on the mantel. "No. I have my dad, and . . . myself. I don't need anybody."

The fire lit, crackled. "I don't know anyone who doesn't need *anyone*."

Probably, that was true.

"Forgiveness isn't for the person you're forgiving, Echo. It's for yourself. It's what you do to be set free."

"I'm free—"

"Are you? Anger is like a virus. It steals hope, tells you lies, makes you vulnerable to more anger. It keeps burrowing deeper until it burns into your soul. But forgiveness is the cure. It's how you start to heal."

"She doesn't deserve it."

"Nope. But that's not the point," he said.

"I was *nine years old.*"

"Yep." He stood. "Young enough to believe the lie that it was your fault. But don't let your mother's betrayal tell you that you don't deserve to be loved. That you're better off alone. God didn't make us to be alone."

Oh, right. She'd forgotten. Barry was a man of faith.

Or maybe, she *hadn't* forgotten. Maybe that's why she'd gravitated here for so many years. Prayer before meals, and before his kids left on flights, or on trips inland. Words of encouragement or even tough love.

Barry picked his coffee mug off the mantel, took a sip, his blue eyes considering her, something of fondness in them.

The fire continued to crackle, pop, burn.

"I know your mother's betrayal hollowed you out. It's different than grief—but it's still grief. You lost the mother you should have had—and you deserved a good mother. But you are not alone."

His words raked heat into her eyes. "I know. I have my dad."

"You have God."

She stared at him. Then drew in a breath. Looked away. "I used to believe that. But after my dad's accident, I stopped believing God cared, I guess."

He nodded. Walked over to a side table and set his coffee down. "Let's just walk through that for a moment. I get you feeling alone and being scared. Sheldon had just packed up your father and flown him to Anchorage, trying to save his life. And he left you alone with your injured dogs, terrified. You were what—fourteen?"

She nodded, needing no help to recall that day.

"Sheldon called me on the way. Dodge insisted on going with me. I figure it took us about an hour to find you."

"The longest hour of my life."

"One of mine too. It was getting dark, the sun going down, and we nearly didn't see you. But we did—"

"And your point?"

"My point is that *we found you*. Practically a miracle. In the attack, your dad's personal locator beacon had been torn off. It was still beeping, left behind."

Iceman came over and nudged Barry's leg. He crouched in front of the dog.

"Are you saying that God used my father's attack to save my life?"

"I'm saying that we don't know how God protects us. How he is there for us, but he is. We live our life seeing only our perspective—seeing our circumstances and judging God by what happens to us. But what if we judged God by what *didn't* happen to us? What if we started asking . . . God, what is your view? What did you protect me from?"

Oh. A strange warmth spread through her.

"There's a story in the Bible about a servant of a great man of God—Elisha. Elisha had made an enemy of a terrible king. And one morning, his servant got up and saw the king's forces surrounding them. But Elisha said, 'Don't be terrified. Those who are with us are more than those who are with them.' And then he prayed for the servant's eyes to be opened and there in front of him, surrounding the king's army, were hills full of horses and chariots of fire."

Barry stroked the dog's head, finding the place behind his ears that Ice liked. The dog groaned in a sort of happiness.

"God is for you, Echo. There is nowhere you can go that he isn't already there. That doesn't mean that bad things don't happen, or we don't get hurt, but even then, we are not alone. The Lord himself watches over you, and you can trust him."

She wanted to believe him, and the way he spoke—softly, caring for her dog—she almost could.

Barry got up. "I called Dodge. He got an emergency call from Spike and Nola Farley. Apparently, she is in labor. He had to abort his mission at Remington Mines and fly her down to Anchorage. I'm afraid he won't be back for a while."

Too long of a while. "Okay. I'm going without him."

"I figured you'd say that." He walked into the flight office.

She knelt in front of Iceman. "Stay here and get better, okay, buddy?"

He licked her face.

"I'm not sure if that's a yes or no," she said, laughing as Barry came out of the office.

"Let him stay here. I'm a little worried that cut will get infected. But I'd feel a lot better if you'd take this."

He held out a small orange radio. "It's one of our personal locator beacons. It can track your GPS and send messages. Out there, a radio might not reach, but if something happens, we can find you with this."

She took it. Smiled at him. "The apple doesn't fall far from the tree."

"I hope not." He sighed. "Are you sure you don't want to wait for Dodge?"

It was probably time to face the truth. "Yes. Dodge has other responsibilities. I got this."

She headed toward the door. *"The Lord himself watches over you."*

Maybe, but really, she was just fine on her own.

"Please don't give birth in my chopper!" Dodge might have screamed it over the thunder of his rotors, but he couldn't be sure. Maybe it was just in his head.

It wasn't like Nola *wanted* to give birth to her third child on the deck of the bird. But from his perspective, she wasn't trying very hard. She lay on her back, on a blanket Spike had grabbed from the house, not even strapped in.

Below them, in the beautiful clear skies, the mountain had washed out into the watershed of the Yentna River, with an endless plain of snow and pine and tiny tributaries that led south to the mighty Susitna. He skirted a mountain, flying along the sharp ridgeback, and spotted the mouth of Knik Arm.

It was worse than flying into combat, what with Spike, who was also unbuckled and completely against regs, sticking his head between the seat and pulling on the ear to Dodge's headset. "Hurry, man!"

"I'm topping off at nearly one hundred knots. Just tell her to breathe!"

"I'm breathing!" Nola shrieked.

Perfect. He shot a look at Maylene and Archie sitting on the bench seat, a front row to the action, their eyes wide as their mother struggled.

There was a memory they'd never wipe.

His father's words about Colt lifted as Dodge passed the tiny town of Skwentna below, population thirty-seven. *"He . . . saw her die."*

Yes, that could scar a kid. Clearly Colt had his own demons he'd been trying to outrun. Dodge probably should have seen that instead of focusing on his own anger. Or, as his dad put it, his fear.

"You're afraid of God not doing things your way."

Maybe.

But what was so wrong with wanting things to turn out his way? And maybe nudging things that direction?

Well, maybe because it never quite turned out how he hoped. *"What if I want to take it over?"*

He'd put it out there, and he'd sort of thought his father would jump on it. After all, just a few days prior, he'd told him he'd prayed for him to return.

Instead, *"What does God want you to do? Is this your destiny, or not?"*

Shoot. He hadn't a clue what God wanted.

Or, frankly, if he should care.

"We're part of something bigger, something that has an eternal purpose."

"Dodge, I can see the baby's head!" Spike yelled, and Dodge heard him just fine through the headset.

"Ten minutes, max," Dodge said, and called in to Alaska Regional Hospital. He informed them of his situation, and they directed him to the heliport at Merrill Field.

"No good, Anchorage. This baby is coming in hot, and we need immediate assistance. I'm putting down in the southwest parking lot, near the maternity clinic. Meet us there."

He heard the resistance but ignored it and aimed the chopper over the sound, descending over the railroad, the highway, the airport—he couldn't believe that he was back here so soon—and around the backside of the hospital.

The lot was half full, and as he came around, scouting a place, he spotted an empty portion in the southeast corner, on the other side of the lot. Close enough.

He put down, curbside garbage blowing up, snow lifting with it. He spotted a couple orderlies and nurses, maybe a doctor, carrying a gurney, running out from the building.

The rotors were still spinning as he shut off the chopper, unhooked his belt, and got out. He opened the door, then stepped back and wanted to avert his eyes.

Oh, his chopper was a mess. Thankfully, most of the blood and fluid was on the blanket, but—

Spike picked up his wife, enduring a yell, and got out, meeting the team.

He plopped her on the gurney. A couple nurses covered her in a blanket, and they took off.

Suddenly it was just Dodge left with two wide-eyed kids.

They sat there, unmoving, watching.

"Hey," he said to Maylene. "It's going to be okay."

She looked at him. Under her wool cap, her hair was down in a rat's nest. She wore leggings and an oversized flannel shirt, a pair of bunny boots, a parka.

Her brother, Archie, looked similarly disheveled in a pair of jeans, work boots, and a sweatshirt and jacket. He too wore a hat, his hair long.

Um. "You guys want some food?"

Maylene seemed to be coming back to herself. "Yeah."

Archie nodded.

"C'mon." He'd deal with the mess later. They climbed out, and he closed up the chopper and they headed inside.

The smells raked up memories of Walter Reed, and more recently, his one-on-one with Larke in this very same hospital, not to mention yesterday's delivery of Jane Doe. But he followed his nose and found a small cafeteria.

He bought the kids each a Subway sandwich and one for himself, and they sat in the chairs, nursing hot cocoas.

"I think it's a girl," said Maylene. "I hope so. I really want a sister."

"And I want a brother. Someone I can boss around," Archie said.

Dodge grinned. "He might boss you back."

"Naw, I'm bigger."

"But you gotta watch out for your brother. That's what big brothers are for—taking care of their little brothers."

Archie eyed him. "Do you have a brother?"

"Two of them," he said. "We're triplets, actually. But I was born first."

"So you're the oldest."

"If you don't count my older sister. She was the boss of all of us."

"See," Maylene said. She elbowed Archie.

Archie gave her a face. Then, to Dodge, "Do they fly too?"

Hmm. "Dunno. I was the only one who really liked flying. But maybe."

And for the first time since he could remember, he wished he knew the answer. Maybe he should write to Larke, see if she knew where Ranger was.

And Colt.

"I saw Colt's brokenness, and I did too much to protect him from himself."

And maybe Dodge hadn't done enough.

"Let's see if your mom has had that baby yet."

He obtained visitor passes, and they headed up to the second-floor maternity center and were buzzed in.

They walked up to the nurses' desk, and he asked about Nola and Spike.

"Oh, yes. She had her baby in the elevator," the nurse said.

That was better than his chopper.

"She's down the hall. They're getting her settled in."

Maybe he'd hang around in the corridor.

"What was it?" Archie asked.

"A little boy," said the nurse.

Dodge held up his fist and Archie bumped it. They headed down the hallway, past rooms with closed doors, and finally to the last room. A cry lifted from inside, and Maylene perked up. "I guess a brother isn't so bad."

The kids went into the room, but Dodge waited in the hall, still holding his hot cocoa. He should probably get the chopper over to the heliport, see if he could wash it down, but his father's call, just as he'd gotten into the chopper with a frantic Spike, lodged in his head.

"*Echo is here. She's wondering when you'll get back.*"

Echo. At his house. Maybe to pick up Iceman, but frankly, he saw it as a good sign after last night's weird conversation. "*Let's just call this before we find ourselves getting really hurt.*"

Not on her life. She'd called and left a message with his father while Dodge was showering last night, so he didn't get to talk to her after their fight.

So yeah, he wanted to get back to the ranch, track her down, and talk. Tell her about Moose's offer and his conversation with his father and . . .

Shoot. He didn't know if he wanted to stay or fly for Air One.

"*Stop telling God what you want, and let him work his will in you. You might find answers.*"

Yeah, whatever.

The curtain in front of the door moved on its track, and he looked up to see Spike heading for him. He was grinning. He'd shed his green Army parka and now wore his flannel over his thermal shirt, the sleeves pushed up past his elbows, and a pair of grimy jeans. He'd pulled his hair back, knotted it, and put a cap, backward, on his head.

But he'd shaved since the encounter with the bear, and maybe bathed too.

When Dodge had shown up, the dogs were back outside, inside their pen, so maybe that instigated some cleaning up.

"Thanks, man!" Spike said and stuck out his hand.

Dodge met it. "You scared me to death."

"Word in the bush is that you don't scare easily. I heard you dead-sticked the Remingtons' new Beaver into Anchorage."

"That was *yesterday*. How—"

"Nash Remington stopped by. Said he'd just come from the mine and Jude gave him the news. Nash is camping on the north-

west edge of their claim in some spike cabin. Came by to drop
off some caribou."

That's right, Dodge had mentioned the news of the ravaging
of the Farleys' cabin to Nash a week ago.

"He doing okay?"

"Seems like it."

"It's just, a couple weeks alone in the bush can make a guy
a little crazy."

"Didn't seem that lonely," Spike said. "Hey, wait here—I got
something for you." He walked into the room. A moment later,
he came out holding a couple cigars. He gave one to Dodge.

"Where did you get these?"

"About a week ago, before the blizzard, we had some hunters stop by. International guys. Probably hunting big elk or
moose. They traded some candies and these cigars for some
frozen salmon. Kids loved the candy. I thought I'd save these."
He winked and stuck the cigar in his mouth.

"Oh no you don't," said a woman, coming out from the
room. "No smoking in the hospital."

She wore a lab coat, a stethoscope around her neck, and
a pair of pink scrubs. She had short bobbed blond hair and
fatigue in her eyes. Something about her made Dodge pause.

And then he saw her badge. Yazzie.

Effie Yazzie?

"C'mon, Doc. I'm just celebrating with my pal Dodge here.
He flew us in. Saved Nola and Eugene's life."

Doc Yazzie's gaze fixed on him. "You're Dodge? Kingston?"

He nodded, met her eyes. Cool green, nothing of Echo's
warmth in them. But he did see Echo's strength, her intelligence.
"Hello, Dr. Yazzie."

She looked like she might correct him, but then just nodded.
"Good to see you, Dodge. How are you?"

"I'm good." His heart jackhammered against his ribs. Effie
Yazzie was a doctor? Here?

And then . . . wait. "Did you . . . does Echo know you're here?"

Dr. Yazzie frowned, glanced at Spike, then back to him. "Yes. We talked yesterday."

She could have slugged him with less effect.

"You talked to her *yesterday?*"

Oh, Echo. No wonder she was quiet on the way home.

Except, she'd seen her mother—after what, *twenty years?*—and said nothing to him.

Why not?

"What did you say to her?" He didn't mean it quite like it emerged—more accusation than quiet question, but he felt that way.

She recoiled. "Our conversation is between me and my daughter."

"And me," he said. "Because . . ." And it didn't matter. The entire valley knew how he'd felt about Echo. "I love her. And yesterday, she all but told me that we were over. After she talked to you. So . . . what did you say to her?"

Effie said nothing, her eyes hard on him. "Maybe she realized that she wants more than the world you want to offer her. We talked about dreams and a bigger life and . . . maybe she realized that it's time for her to move on."

He stared at her, a stone dropping through his heart. What—? He couldn't breathe.

Echo was *leaving?*

"By the way, Echo said something when she left. When you see her, could you give her a message from me? Tell her that she was right."

Right about what?

He just looked at her.

Effie pursed her lips, then cast another look at Spike. "I mean it. No smoking in here. Or near that baby."

Spike slipped the cigar into his pocket.

She smiled then and patted his arm. "Congratulations. You have quite the wife in there."

"I know," Spike said, grinning.

She walked away and Spike looked at him. "Gotta get back. But thanks again, man."

"No problem," Dodge said, and Spike headed back to the room.

Dodge stared at his cocoa, his mind churning.

He needed to talk to Echo, sort this out. Because what if she was leaving . . .

Just when he'd decided to stay.

He finished his cup of hot cocoa, headed downstairs in an elevator, and was getting off when he heard someone call his name.

Moose came down the hall. He was wearing his red Air One Rescue jacket, the emblem on the chest. "I thought that was you. What are you doing here?"

"Had to bring in Nola Farley. She had a baby."

"You're turning into your own rescue service up there."

He lifted a shoulder. "A day in the life."

"Maybe," Moose said, but he stood back, folded his arms. "What if it wasn't? We cover a lot of territory, from the Chugach National Forest to the Kenai Peninsula, even over to the Yukon Delta and all the way up your way to Fairbanks. It can get complicated. What if it didn't have to be?"

Dodge was doing the math too. "Are you saying Air One could have a northern branch?"

"Why not? Did you talk to your father about the ranch? Is he selling?"

Dodge's phone buzzed. He pulled it out and looked at the number. He didn't recognize it, but it said it came from this hospital. Strange.

He swiped it away and put the phone back in his pocket. "Dunno yet," he said to Moose. Frankly, he didn't know if *he* was staying.

"We could figure it out," Moose said. "Gotta run." He lifted a hand. "Got a call from the Coast Guard about a guy they found on his fishing boat, beaten and in bad shape. Apparently, he's been out on the sea for a while."

"Yikes."

"Yeah. One of our pilots is bringing him in now." He was already backing away as he spoke. He turned and headed for the doors.

Dodge pulled out his phone and listened to the voice mail left by the unknown caller. "Hello. This is Sissy Oolanie from Alaska Regional. I thought you'd like an update on the woman you brought in." She left her number.

He checked his watch. Still six hours of daylight. Plenty of time to get home and get to Echo's place.

Fine. Heading back upstairs, he tried to call Echo, but her phone went to voice mail. Yeah, it bugged him.

He found the second-floor nurses' station and gave his name, asking for Sissy. She was the nurse on call, a middle-aged Native woman who brought him down the hall to a woman's room.

"She's out of danger with her hypothermia, but she hasn't woken yet, and we don't know why. We thought if she heard a familiar voice . . ."

"I don't know who she is. I just found her."

Sissy looked at her notes. "It says here to contact you in case of emergency."

"I didn't want her to be without anyone."

Nurse Oolanie gave him a smile. "Okay. Do you want to see her? Maybe you'd recognize her?"

He doubted it, but maybe. She led him into the room.

She looked better, of course. Less pale, her blond hair swept back from her face. She was pretty, early thirties, maybe five three, and caught in a deep, exhausted slumber, the covers pulled up around her. She wasn't hooked up to a breathing machine, just an IV in her arm.

"The doctor ordered an MRI. She might have had a traumatic brain injury—we just don't know. She should have woken up by now."

"If she does, and you haven't located next of kin, let me know." Then Dodge headed out to his chopper, hopped in, and headed home.

The sun had fled to the backside of the day by the time he set down at Sky King Ranch, darkness quickly seeping over the land. He got out, and his father met him, coming out of the house. The wind had whipped up, the edge of a cold chill headed down from the mountains. Dodge turned up his collar.

"Hey!" he shouted over the wind.

"How'd it go?" his father asked as they headed to the Quonset and retrieved the ground-handling wheels.

His dad grabbed one, Dodge the other, and they brought them back out to the chopper. "Good. Nola had her baby. A boy." He attached the wheel to the skids, then walked over as his father was trying to fit the wheel assembly into the notch. He missed, then finally wiggled the assembly in.

Weird. It was starting to seem like his father might be losing his touch.

Then again, he was working one-handed.

He secured the ground-handling wheel, then Dodge went around to the tail, grabbed the stinger and the gearbox, levered the chopper back on the wheels, and pushed it into the hangar, making sure the rotor blades didn't hit.

"It's low on fuel and needs a wash," Dodge said when they got it inside. "Nola nearly had her baby on the deck."

"Oh boy." His father grinned. "That wouldn't be the first close call. We barely made it to Anchorage before you boys were born."

"Yeah, this was her third. I think she went early. By the way, what did Echo want?" He kept his voice casual, no panic at all.

And most definitely he wouldn't do something impulsive and race over to her house demanding answers.

They walked back to the house. "She stopped by to check on her dog. She's headed back into the bush to find her friend."

He stilled. "Alone?"

His father nodded.

Perfect.

"She said she was just fine on her own."

"I'll bet she did." But Dodge turned to look out over the hills, the sun sending long shadows into the valley, and a chill, the fingers of the pervading cold, sneaked through him.

For some reason, the memory of Jane Doe, quiet, asleep in her bed, alone and trapped inside her head, settled into his brain.

Dodge couldn't shake a sense of doom, deep in his bones.

FOURTEEN

Peyton was out here, somewhere, hopefully alive, and Echo planned on finding her. And maybe, please, she'd find her father along the way.

Because it was easier for the dogs, Echo kept to the riverbanks, the frozen lakes, and the trails cut by caribou, deer, and moose.

She and the team wove through thick forests on paths between bushy, snow-laden spruce and tall, silent birch trees that stood sentry over the breaths of her dogs and the whoosh of the sled as it glided over the snow.

She lunched near the cabin at Moose Lake, feeding the dogs a snack and water, then headed in a straight line for Cache Mountain, crossing Peters Creek to the north of cabin 63, and down a frozen tributary. She found the track of a snowmobile on the river, crusted into the ice, and followed it up onto a ridge, skirting the river, then back into the forest.

Overhead, the sky was a quiet, easy blue, the wind only occasionally whipping up and pebbling them with snow.

The dogs ran silently, with Jester occasionally nipping at Goose in his excitement. She whistled to them and shouted encouragement as they settled into a trot. Through the cutout of trees, a mountain ascended, bold and beautiful, hidden deep in no-man's-land.

"We don't know how God protects us."

She let Barry's words drift through her head and stir up that long hour she'd sat in the snow with her dogs after the grizzly attack, trying to doctor the wounds of the two dogs who'd lived, crying over her dad, huddling with the animals, as scared as she was, as the shadows fell.

The bear's body had lain just a few feet away, and she'd kept her eyes on it, afraid it might suddenly shudder to life.

She'd finally heard the Sky King plane rumbling overhead, but it passed her three times before it touched down in a field nearby.

And then, somehow, Dodge was there, dropping to his knees in front of her. Grabbing her up to hold her as she wept.

"*My point is that* we found you. *Practically a miracle.*"

Or just desperate luck.

She and the team now came out of the woods, and the trail fell down the ridge, opening into a valley below, another tributary of the river, although larger. The great Cache Mountain range rose in the distance.

She yipped to the dogs as they ran, following the snow machine tread toward the vast riverbed.

In the distance, she spotted an eagle, who soared low then landed on a brown mass on the ground. It scared away what looked like a wolverine, which clawed at it. The eagle took to the air again, a piece of meat in its beak.

Echo slowed the dogs, then pulled out a monocular.

A moose lay dead on a hillside, as if it had been running to escape to the nearby woods. Brown-red blood stained the ground, the kill relatively fresh. The cavity of the body was open, animals eating at it. The snow around it had been trampled, and snow machine tracks, as well as wheel tracks, circled it.

And then she saw why—the moose antlers had been shorn from the head.

Poachers. They'd killed the moose, harvested the antlers, and left the meat to rot.

Illegal, and disgusting.

She routed her dogs into the valley, away from the kill, and ran along the river's edge, upstream.

Maybe her dad had seen the moose and lit out after the poachers—she wouldn't put it past him, really, and the thought turned to a fist inside her.

She headed across the great white valley carved out between sloping foothills, toward the giant V in the land where the river narrowed. Here, the wind had swept the ice clean.

She didn't like to travel on water, especially rivers, this late in the season. The warm snap and the snow could insulate the ice and turn it brittle, creating thin ice that a team of dogs could fall through.

As they came closer to the V, she made out running water and shouted to turn the dogs away from the crusty, snowy bank.

The wind lifted, swept snow across the land, and carried the faraway drone of a motor.

Dad?

Maybe he'd stopped at the hunter's cabin, but her guess was that he'd been patrolling this area, searching for Elsa and her cubs. The sound of an engine urged her on.

"Yip, yip," she called to the dogs, and they went from a trot to a run as the snow turned to ice, the skids slick. They drove on, toward the narrowing gap, and the sound of the motor rose, and with it a cacophony of other motors.

And behind that, a bellowing, heavy, breathy grunt.

Then a roar lifted through the valley. It raised the hairs on her neck, sent a ripple down her spine. "Easy, Granite."

He slowed, and she lifted her monocular again.

Not her dad on his snowmobile, but three men, dressed in white camouflage, on ATVs. They circled a mother grizzly, about fifty yards away from the animal, as she charged, then howled, roaring as they stung her with spray and a cattle prod.

Nearby, her cubs screamed.

Echo also wanted to scream, especially when she spotted the white tuft between the bear's ears and a large GPS collar around her neck.

Elsa.

No. The poachers would torment her until she finally charged, enraged, uncaring of the pain.

Someone would die, but in the process, so would Elsa.

Echo pulled out her capture gun. If she could put Elsa down, asleep, maybe the poachers would abandon their sport.

She couldn't think of anything else.

"Hike! Hike!" She just needed to get closer—enough to secure the shot.

The poachers were at the far end of the river, past the open water, where Elsa had probably been fishing with the cubs. Two hundred yards. Then a hundred. The dogs, as if sensing danger, pressed on, no yipping, their approach almost stealthy.

"Whoa up," she said, standing on the drag, and Granite stopped, urging Merlin to settle beside him. They stood, breathing hard.

The scene in front of her had unraveled. Elsa had become braver, angrier. She nearly caught up to one of the poachers, but he gunned his ATV away, and the others chased after a cub, who shrieked.

Echo propped her elbow on the handle of the sled, brought up the gun, and set the sights on Elsa.

What she really wanted to do was shoot the stinger into one of the men, but that would be a crime.

The irony filled her chest with acid.

Elsa chased the men from her cubs, roaring, dancing back and forth, desperate. Then, she turned to her cubs, giving Echo a beautiful view of her back haunch.

"Sorry, Elsa." She pulled the trigger.

The bear roared, rising up on two feet. The sound of the gun echoed, but with the noise from the motor, maybe they hadn't heard.

Or maybe they had, because as she peered through her scope, one of the poachers rounded.

Looked at her.

She stilled. Of course.

Idaho.

He pointed at her.

Elsa dropped, woozy, now trying to run with her cubs into the forest.

Run. Echo didn't know if she was saying it for herself or Elsa, but as the animal took off, she held her breath.

And then, suddenly, the ATVs were headed her direction.

Uh-oh.

At least Elsa was safe—except any animal tranquilized in the forest was in predatory danger.

Shoot, shoot! She should have thought through this better.

Echo stuffed the gun away and jumped on the treads. "Hike! Gee! Gee!"

Granite led them to the right, away from the riverbed.

Idaho and his cohorts were motoring on the far bank, heading toward a snow bridge.

She clung to the driving bow as Granite and the team lit out toward the hill that led into the forest along the river.

Almost miraculously, the snowmobile tread appeared, and Granite took to it like a paved highway, urging Merlin with him.

Echo glanced behind her. The ATVs had found the snow bridge.

No way her dogs could outrun an ATV. And given her last encounter with Idaho . . . "C'mon, kids!"

She turned back just in time to see Granite and Merlin leap a berm. No—no—

Jester and Goose were right behind them and suddenly the sled hit the berm, flying into the air.

Echo screamed, went airborne, and landed hard, ten feet from the sled, still being dragged by the dogs. "Whoa! Whoa!"

They were stopping anyway, whining, worried.

She got up—nothing broken—and limped over to the sled, picking it up and breathing hard.

The motors grew louder, and she took a quick look, her jaw tight. Idaho and his cronies had started to cross the snow bridge.

She righted the sled and climbed on, her body aching. "Let's go. Hike! Hike!"

The team started again but, without the momentum, the slope fought them. They eased into it, and she got off, trying to push.

She chanced another peek at her pursuers. The ATVs were nearly across the river to the other side. Two hundred desperate yards separated them—

A crack sounded, echoing through the air, and suddenly, one of the ATVs crashed through the snow bridge. The driver flew over the handlebars and landed in the flowing, freezing river.

She gasped and faced her dogs, breathing hard. "Giddyap, team!"

Miracles. Or someone watching out for her in the woods. Whatever the case, she didn't look back until they reached the edge of the forest.

The two other ATVers had stopped to fish their man from the river, who was struggling to find shore.

He'd be cold, and if they didn't stop to warm him, he'd die.

She had time to get to . . . where?

She couldn't go to the hunter's cabin—it wasn't well known, but it was on every backwoods guide map. Idaho would know.

But he wouldn't know about one of Elsa's old under-ledge dens. Echo had helped her father tag cubs there a few years back, but Elsa had abandoned the den long ago. They'd even stayed there once, she and her father, during an especially stormy night.

As long as it wasn't reclaimed by some other desperate animal . . .

She pulled out her map and found her location, along Cache Creek, maybe eight miles west of the Peters Lake cabin.

The den was only a few miles south, near Remington Mines land. And beyond that, Cache Mountain. She glanced at the sky. The sun had fallen, casting deep shadows along the basin of the valley she'd left behind, darkening the forest. She'd be lucky to make the den before nightfall.

Her adrenaline fell, her heartbeat settling back into place. She thought about the personal locator Barry had given her. She'd clipped it to the edge of her pack after she left his place.

She wanted to check the GPS.

Okay, and maybe even send a note to Dodge.

She couldn't deny the urge to tell him about the poachers. And maybe . . .

No, she had to stop hoping Dodge would come to her rescue.

She felt around her pack, then searched the pocket.

Gone.

It must have fallen off in her crash. She couldn't go back—and besides, she'd hardly find it in the snow.

Apparently there were no more miracles for her today. But she didn't need them. She knew this land, had traveled it in both summer and winter with her father for years.

She mushed the dogs along the ridgeline, then down across a tiny frozen gap in the river, and south through the forest, along deer paths. She turned on her headlamp as the night crept around her.

The dogs were tired. She shouldn't have run them so far today, she knew that, but again, she'd gotten in over her head.

The den was located under a ledge in a rocky wall that edged up from a valley, chiseled out from an ancient glacial river. She left her sled in the valley and climbed up through the dense forest in the near darkness.

The cavern was maybe eight feet deep and four feet high at the mouth, taller inside. Lying on her stomach, she shone the light inside and found it empty.

She came back down to her team and grabbed her pack.

Unhooking the dogs, she dragged the sled into the forest, covered it with brush, then called the team inside the cave.

They whined at the entrance, but she coaxed Granite inside, and the rest crept in after him.

In the darkness, the wind was starting to whip the snow. Maybe her tracks would be covered. And the dogs would keep her warm.

She dragged in snow, heated it, fed the dogs their kibble mash, then rolled out her sleeping bag onto a mat. She could have set up her tent, but she feared the orange fabric would alert the poachers. Maybe she was overreacting, but . . .

Okay, she was scared. The kind of scared that bore through her and knotted her insides, and frankly, she just needed . . .

Dodge. Shoot, yes, she needed Dodge.

She should have waited for him.

Stop. She was going to be just fine. She pulled up her legs in her sleeping bag, the smell of wildlife and wet granite around her, the dogs starting to warm the space with their body heat. She had turned on her headlamp, but now flicked it off.

The sound of occasional snoring and her own breathing filled the space.

Alone.

She breathed out. *Just calm down.* She was fine. No one was going to—

Outside a crunch sounded on the snow. Another. Then limbs breaking.

Granite had shoved in next to her, and now he lifted his head. She touched it, finding the hair on the ruff of his neck raised.

More branches breaking, then a huff.

Probably it was a wolverine. Or a wolf.

Or even a bear.

She reached for her spray.

Then, boots scuffed on the granite, and light sprayed against the cave walls.

She'd brought her capture gun inside and now grabbed it. She flicked on her light and aimed it at the door. "I'm armed. Stay back!"

The light shone on her—bright, blinding. She drew in a breath. "Stop!"

"Don't shoot, Echo! It's me!"

She stilled as her intruder's form emerged, crawling from the entrance. Snow crusted his hat, he had whitened eyelashes and wore a green hunter's jacket, the kind he used to stay concealed for hours as he studied wildlife— "Dad?"

He rose on his knees, his bivouac bag in his hand, his head-lamp shining on her dogs, now awake, some on their feet, barking.

He looked tired, a grizzle of whiskers along his chin, his scarf edged with ice. But his eyes—they pinned her with such a look of worry, she couldn't breathe. "Are you okay?"

She nodded. "What—how—"

"I thought you'd be here." He groaned as he crawled farther inside. "I was there on the ridge. I arrived just after you did, I think. I saw you on your sled, in the river."

"You saw what they did to Elsa?"

"Just the end of it. I had gone to her den, tracked her back to the riverbed."

"I tranqed her."

"I know. And I shot out the tire on one of the poachers' ATVs."

"That was you!"

He nudged one of the dogs aside and flopped down, breathing hard as he pulled off his mittens. "I missed."

"Dad."

He didn't smile, and she wasn't exactly sure he was kidding. He was fumbling with his jacket zipper now. "I would have been here earlier, but I followed Elsa into the forest and watched over her until she woke up."

Only then did she see the darkness staining his coat. "Is that blood?"

He managed to get the zipper open and made a face as he eased off the coat.

"Dad!" She jumped up and helped him work it off. He groaned. "Oh—you're shot."

"Yeah. It happened a while ago—I think the bleeding has slowed. I startled them as they were hacking the antlers off a moose. They took a shot at me, and I got away into the woods, but they winged me good."

He was pulling up his shirt.

Her breath caught. "They did not just wing you. This is a gut shot—you've lost a lot of blood."

"It's a through and through. I'll be fine . . ."

"Dad—"

He held up his hand. "I'll be fine, sweetheart. I just need to rest."

She opened the sleeping bag and helped him inside.

"We need to get a dressing on that wound."

"Yeah, yeah." But he let her examine the wound.

The shot had torn through his lower body, down by his hip. "They shot you from behind."

"Yep." He winced and grabbed her wrists as she probed the wound. "Take it easy there, honey."

"I'm going for help."

He didn't let go of her wrists. "Nope. You're staying right here. Idaho and his crew aren't here to hunt. They're here to terrorize. And you're next on their list."

She sat back. "Why?"

"Because he's the devil," her father said, his eyes closed.

She knew he was just being facetious. Maybe.

She sat back on her sleeping bag, her eyes on her father.

If ever she needed a miracle . . .

Dodge didn't like the look of the Yazzie homestead when he stopped by the next morning, and it only conspired to add to the knot in his gut.

Echo was in trouble; Dodge knew it. And it wasn't only the fact that all her chickens lay dead in the yard, blood strewn around the pen, or that the dogs were gone—he didn't know if they'd run off or not—but something in his gut told him . . . she needed him.

And he wasn't there.

He'd spent the night staring out the window at the waning moon, wishing she'd answer his text to her personal locator beacon.

Not a peep.

He should have gone out last night, his conversation with his father still ripe in his head. *"What am I going to do? It's too dark to go looking for her."*

"You're going to take a breath. Eat something. Stop jumping to conclusions and remember that Echo knows how to survive."

He'd looked at his father. Right. No problem.

That's when he'd started texting her PLB and pacing late into the night.

He was up before the sunlight tipped the mountains.

His father met him in the kitchen with fresh, dark coffee.

Then, just to make sure she hadn't returned home, even though she still wasn't answering her ham, he'd headed out on the snowmobile, crossing overland—faster than on the back roads—to her place.

Now, with the rising of the sun, the warming of the land, the river had started to break free behind her house, icy chunks finding their way along the shore.

He checked on the animals in the pens—the foxes were gone, the bears in their dens, although they were probably stirring from hibernation. He fed the coyote and thought his leg looked healed enough to free.

Then he got back on his sled and motored home, a plan forming.

He'd take the chopper to her PLB location and get eyes on her. Probably, yes, she was . . . Just. Fine.

No need to panic. Most likely, it was like his father had said—his fears trying to convince him that it would all explode in his face if he wasn't in control.

Which sounded exactly like what was going to happen.

The sun was up by the time he pulled into the driveway. He headed into the house, not bothering to take off his shoes or outer clothing. His father sat at the counter, listening to the *Good News* radio show, Norm Dahlquist talking about a warm front heading from the southwest.

"Her place is a mess," he said to his father, whipping off his hat. He set that and his gloves on the kitchen table. "The foxes got out of their pens, and I think they ate her chickens. The place is abandoned. I can't shake this idea that she's in trouble."

His father slid off his stool. "You still haven't heard back from her?"

"No. I'm going to take the chopper out and see if I can track her PLB. Maybe the texts aren't getting through."

"You said you were low on fuel."

"I have enough to get out as far as Cache Creek and back. But that's dense territory in there—it'll be hard to find a place to land. The chopper is easier." He'd been kicking himself for not checking on the refueling tank out back earlier. "But I'm not even sure she's that way. I think . . ." And he winced, not really wanting to go there, but . . . he had to. "Would you take my Cub up and scout south of Cache Mountain? She might have gone to the cabin at Peters Lake, maybe trying to pick up Peyton's trail from there."

His father made a face. He looked away, out the window. "I'm sorry, Dodge. I can't."

He stared at him, the words dropping through him like a stone. "What?"

His father met his gaze. "I want to . . . but I can't."

"You can't."

"No."

Something dark and hot threaded through him. "Of course not. What is it, Dad? Another lesson about trust? Letting God be in charge?"

His father was shaking his head.

"Then you simply don't want to help me. Again."

And the truth of that burrowed deep, turned to acid. No wonder he always had to find his own way out.

"I'm going blind, son."

Dodge stared at him. "What did you say?"

He sighed, looked away, then back to Dodge. "I can't see. Or it's getting that way. I have big black spots in my eyes, and my peripheral vision is gone."

Dodge reached for a stool, then slid onto it.

"It's called macular degeneration, and it's hereditary. Your grandfather had it, only it hit him much later."

He remembered that—his grandfather had slowly gone blind. Dodge had always thought it was old age. "When did it start?"

"About a year ago now, but it's gotten worse recently."

"It's why you crashed into a tree."

"I don't know. I don't think so, but after hearing the NATB report, it's possible. It's getting too dangerous for me to fly."

"No doubt." Dodge ran a hand behind his neck, letting the words sink in. And then—wait. "That's why you're selling the ranch."

"Mmhmm."

"Why didn't you tell me? You know I would have stayed."

"I do." His dad met his gaze. "But I didn't want to get in the way of what God wanted for you. This ranch was my life. It doesn't have to be yours."

His own words to Moose filtered back. *Are you saying Air One could have a northern branch?*"

"Or it could be, Dad." He put his hand on his dad's shoulder. "I'm sorry about what I said. Maybe God answered your prayers, after all."

He smiled. "Oh, son. God always answers. It's just a matter of how."

Right. "Stay by the radio."

Dodge walked out and rolled the chopper into the runway area, unhooked the wheels, did his walk-around, and started it up.

Quick math told him that yes, he had enough fuel for a trip out to Echo's PLB location and back.

If she wasn't there . . .

He powered up the chopper, tested the radio, and his father confirmed, then waved to him from the office.

Blind.

He couldn't think about it now, but the word sat inside him like a rock.

He ran a final check on his instruments, then set his course for her PLB location and lifted off.

The day was bright, and the chill that had ridden in on a northern draft had died last night, leaving only the warming sun, the sparkling snow, and the majestic peaks to the north cutting into an endless blue sky.

He followed the river south, then cut over to the ridge that led to Moose Lake and cabin 37, where he'd put down to rescue Holly so many days ago.

Not a whisper of smoke came from the tiny cabin, so he turned his chopper down Seventeen Mile Lake, heading northwest. He hung low, curving around the creek bed, his eyes on the trail that ran beside it, then ascended as the land rose, snow-clothed granite dotted with pine. He spied tracks, but they looked like ATV wheels rather than the pucker of dogs' feet or the thin track of a dogsled.

He followed the creek north for a bit, then crossed over and headed west, remembering their trek to cabin 63.

Their trek, and their night, and the way she'd felt in his arms. *Please be okay.*

The ski marks from the Remingtons' de Havilland Beaver cut into the lake, along with the snowmobile treads leading away, to Remington Mines, but otherwise the place looked cold.

His father had said she was heading toward Cache Mountain, and he remembered a hunting cabin near there, but he headed toward the PLB location.

He turned northwest, an eye on his instruments as he cut down into a gorge, following another riverbed, rising to crest the ridge. He spotted a dead moose, its antlers gone, lying in a bloody splotch on a hillside near the river. Beyond that, the river sheeted out white, except for an open patch that ran icy-gray over rocks and boulders.

An ATV was half submerged in the water.

He hovered over it a bit, noting the location. The PLB indicator was beeping, signaling its presence, and he flew north, hovering overhead.

The tracks here seemed blemished, but he made out the definite press of dogs' feet, a trail of thin skids—

She'd fallen here. Gotten back up and headed into the forest. But most likely had dropped her PLB. Yes, that made sense.

Maybe she didn't even realize it until too late.

His fuel gauge had fallen, but he always left ten percent in the tank, so he pushed forward, through the forest.

Sitting over the crest, near a tiny lake, he spotted a cabin, the finest wisp of smoke curling from the pipe, and the fist in his chest eased.

He put down on the shore and got out.

The sun was warm, his feet breaking through icy layers, crunching hard through the snow onshore.

As he drew closer, he spotted a couple ATVs outside the cabin, and slowed.

The door opened. "It's about time. We could use those parts." A man stepped out, wearing a flannel shirt, a pair of jeans, and a fur hat. He had long brown hair and a matted beard.

It was the .338 Winchester Magnum that caught Dodge's attention. He stopped walking.

The man stared at him. Then smiled. "You."

Dodge held up his hand. "Hey there, Idaho." The last time they'd chatted flashed through his head, and he mentally measured how far he was from his chopper. "Sorry, wrong pilot," he said. "I don't have your parts. My guess is the ATV I saw in the river back there is yours?"

Idaho rested the gun in the crook of his arm. "Blew a tire and the axle got messed up in the river."

"I was just flying by and saw the smoke." He was backing up now.

Another man came out on the stoop. He was big, over six feet, short brown hair. He wore jeans, no shirt, and stood in the cold like he might be part polar bear. He held a cigar in his hands and smiled at Dodge. A gold tooth glinted in the sun. "Чего он хочет?"

He didn't speak Russian, but he didn't have to. He was clearly trespassing, of a sort.

Still, what was Idaho doing with a Russian man?

Another man stepped out, this one shorter, beefier. He was eating out of a can.

"Sorry I can't be of help," Dodge said.

"You're looking for her, aren't you?"

He stilled and stared at Idaho. "Her?"

"Your girlfriend. Grizzly Adams's girl."

Dodge swallowed. Found a smile. "Have you seen her?"

Idaho looked at his cronies, one, then the other, and they laughed. "Last time we saw her, she was running like the world was on fire with her doggies."

Dodge couldn't stop himself. "Why would she be doing that?"

Idaho shrugged. "Dunno. She must scare easily."

Not hardly.

"Sure." He glanced at the sky, then back to Idaho, who'd walked out to the edge of the porch. "Be careful out there. The temperature is rising. You know how it gets out here in the spring. The rivers rise fast, the earth turns to mud. And Alaska is dangerous."

"It is, boy. It is. People get lost here all the time." Idaho just stood there, watching as Dodge backed up, all the way to his chopper.

He was still standing on the porch, the wind blowing the fur from his face as Dodge lifted off.

Something was wrong. Very, very wrong.

Dodge glanced at his fuel tank, at the world below him, lush with pine trees and deep gullies and rivers starting to awaken. Somewhere down there, Echo was lost. Maybe hurt.

And worst of all, alone.

FIFTEEN

Her father was dying. Echo could see it in his eyes, in the pale hue of his face, in the slowing of his breath, and especially in the sluggish refill of his color when she pressed on his wrist to find a pulse.

He'd lost a lot of blood in the night, too much, despite his reassurance that he'd stopped bleeding. She'd tried to clog it with a mitten, then her thermal shirt, which she pulled off and tied around him.

She had to move him.

She'd debated leaving in the middle of the night, but the fact that the poachers were still out there somewhere had her father grabbing her arm, practically ordering her to stay.

And frankly, she was scared.

But not so scared of Idaho that she was going to let her father die in an old bear cave. Although, honestly, it might be his preferred choice of final resting places.

Clearly, she was turning dark and grim.

"We need to get you home," she said sometime around 5:00 a.m., when the slivers of dawn started to creep into the cave. "We can take your machine, and I'll come back for the dogs."

He shook his head. "The sled is gone. When they shot at me, they burst a fuel line. I didn't see it until I found Elsa. I managed to stop it up, but the tank is drained. It won't get us a mile."

Perfect.

So she'd just have to come up with another plan.

It was warm out, so warm that she worked up a sweat lugging him out of the cave and down the hill, onto the dogsled, which she'd uncovered and tied the dogs to. They were yipping, barking, whining, and pulling at the sled. Good thing she'd tied it to a nearby birch tree.

If Idaho were out here looking for them, he'd only have to follow the sounds of her excited dogs.

She didn't like the texture of the snow, the way it clung to itself. Mushing through this would be like glue.

"We're not going home," she said as she tucked a sleeping bag over her father. She'd already packed their belongings and added them to the sled. Too much weight, maybe, for the dogs, which meant she'd have to help push. Or run along behind.

"We can't make it thirty miles home, or however far it is in these conditions, so we're taking the creek over to Cache Mountain and the cabins beyond. I figure it's about five, six miles, at the most."

"You'll have to cross the lake," he said. "And then the ridge."

"I know."

Around her, the forest was dripping. It always amazed her how quickly the winter transformed once spring decided to hit. How the ice cap on the mountaintops melted away, forming into the raging rivers, the lakes growing weak, then opening up from the edges, and finally the trees reaching out to push forth buds.

They were at least a month away from any color, but already, in the last two weeks, the sun had started to shine longer, giving them almost twelve-hour days. It would stretch out quickly until at the height of summer, it would burn all day, until they had no more than four hours of darkness.

How she loved the sunrises of spring in Alaska.

But not today. "Hike!" The dogs leaned against their harnesses, and the sled broke free, heading down the ravine toward the creek bed that would take them west, toward Cache Mountain.

But first, like her father said, they'd have to cross the lake, which sat at the bottom of the mountain, blocking the pass.

She lifted her gaze to the blue sky, the parting of the trees ahead. She whistled to her dogs, and their pace picked up, the quiet thunder of their feet on the snow and her heaving breath evidence of their labor.

Her father tried to hold in his groans, but the ground was uneven and jostled and bumped him.

"Hang in there, Dad." She put her hand on him when he went quiet. He was still breathing.

They followed a deer path in the forest along the creek. The dogs slowed to a walk, and she helped push as they fought the tiny pathway. She finally stopped, reeled out the gangline so they could go one by one, and re-hooked them.

They moved easier, snaking through the forest to her occasional "Yip, yip," and "Good job."

He father had gone terribly, awfully quiet.

She wanted to shed her jacket. Instead, she unzipped it, sweat tunneling down her spine.

This was a terrible plan.

Her eyes filled, and she didn't even bother to stop the tears as she continued to push the sled. They finally broke free of the forest and stood at the edge, on a slope overlooking the lake.

She set the brake, then dug out water from the supply that she'd melted last night. She tried to wake her father, but he wouldn't rouse. Her breath was shaking as she pressed her fingers to his carotid artery.

Weak. But still alive.

She took a drink, then watered the dogs, letting them rest a moment.

Below her was the lake, a long stretch of ribbon at the base of the mountain, some two miles across, ten miles long. More of a river, really, but in the winter, it was frozen solid.

Except it wasn't winter anymore, and she feared the flux of the recent weather would have weakened it.

What choice did she have?

She was scanning the horizon, the great rise of mountains on the other side gray-black, with steep washes of snow and glacier. At the base, pine covered walls all the way down to the vast whiteness of the lake. It fell to a V at the southern end, where it formed into a white-capped, lethal river.

And—her breath caught.

In the hills beyond the lake, spiraling into the sky, just barely, was a wisp of smoke.

She pulled out her monocular from her pack and tried to find the source. Hidden, but surely there.

Or maybe not. Because the smoke seemed to have vanished into the blue of the sky.

Maybe she'd imagined it.

She took off her gloves and ran a hand along her brow, pushing back her hat.

If she crossed the lake, she knew the Cache cabins lay on the other side. It would mean climbing the pass, crossing the ridgeline, and then somehow keeping the sled from tumbling down the other side. But there, at Cache, she'd find help. Six or so miles away.

Hopefully. Please.

Or she could go south, along the lake, three, maybe more miles to the imaginary wisp of smoke.

From his position, Granite walked over to her, licked her face. She sat down in the snow, put her arms around him, and buried her face in his fur.

"I don't know what to do. I just don't know."

"The Lord himself watches over you."

Barry's words settled into her head, and she sat back in the snow, looking heavenward.

The dogs were breathing hard. Her father was silent, unconscious.

"Please. God. Tell me what to do."

Silence. But inside it, the sound came to her like a pulse, a beating of her heart, then louder, a deep rhythm that shook the hills and shivered the pine trees around her, until it turned deafening.

And then it washed over her, a thunder that swept out her breath.

A deep-blue chopper, flying low and fast over the trees.

Heading for a destination at the south of the lake.

"Hey! Hey!" She wrestled herself to her feet and stumbled out of the cover of the woods, waving her arms. But the chopper was long past by her. It swept down, around the horizon.

She stood, stuck in the grip of snow up to her knees, watching help vanish.

Then it turned around.

Her heart filled her throat as the chopper dipped and sped back in her direction. She waved her arms, watching it barrel toward her.

And there he was at the helm, flying like he might be going into battle. Dodge.

She kept waving, but it wasn't necessary. As he grew closer, his expression was almost unnerving in its fierceness.

Had he been searching for her?

He put down near the shore of the lake, and she unhooked her sled. "Hike! Hike!"

Granite was already moving. They bounded down the hill, and she rode the drag to keep them from going over. As it was, the sled sunk into the snow, slow and arduous.

Dodge was out of the chopper by the time she reached him.

She dropped the anchor and didn't care what she'd said to him before. Sure, she could take care of herself . . . but she didn't want to. "Dodge!"

He caught her up as if she wasn't wearing a thousand layers, his arms around her, pulling her to himself, lifting her into his embrace.

"E," he said, his voice ragged. "You really freaked me out."

He put her down, clasped her face in his hands. "I thought . . . I don't know why, but I thought you were hurt or in trouble or—"

Yes, to all of it. But she didn't correct him.

She kissed him. Just pulled him down to her and held on. Because he was here—*of course* he was here.

He tasted of coffee and smelled of his morning shower and was exactly the man she'd waited for. Needed.

And he kissed her back, diving in with a touch of relief, maybe even of possession.

Yes.

She grabbed his lapels. *Dodge.*

He finally pulled away. Met her eyes. Aw shoot, she was crying again. "I'm sorry I went without you. I should have waited for you—"

"Babe, what's wrong?"

"It's my dad. He's been shot."

The word changed him, right before her eyes. He let her go, started for her dad. "How bad?"

"He's lost a lot of blood." She followed him to the sled, mired now in the shoreline mud. The dogs were eating snow and lapping at a puddle of lake water.

Dodge pulled back the sleeping bag from her dad, took a peek at his wound, still bandaged. Pressed his fingers to his neck. "I'm not a medic, but he's in bad shape. His pulse is thready."

"I know. Let's get him in the chopper."

Dodge looked at the machine. "I'm nearly out of fuel. I followed you to your PLB, but you weren't there, so I, uh, kept going. I don't have enough to get him home. Or even down to Remington Mines."

She stared at him, the realization creeping over her. "No— see, I told myself that this would work. That I could get him to the Cache cabins, and then . . ." She pressed her hands over her face. "This is my fault. I should have left last night, when it was still cold out, gotten help—"

She bent over, her breaths tumbling over each other—

"Echo!" Dodge grabbed her arms, pulled her up. "You're hyperventilating. Breathe. Stop. I know you're scared. Me too. Let's just take a moment here." He put his forehead down on hers, closed his eyes. "God. Please . . . help us."

She closed her eyes too. Because what choice, who else, did they have?

God . . . please.

A sound behind them lifted his head, and he turned as Echo looked past him.

In the distance, a snow machine was headed along the shore-line.

What?

Dodge stiffened, then stepped in front of her.

"What are you doing?"

"Nothing," he said, but he took her hand.

The dogs began to bark and whine, and Granite pulled at his harness, leaping at the sled. Especially when the machine stopped not far away.

The driver got off—a man, from the cut of his form. He pulled off his helmet.

Nash Remington, in all his long, tawny-brown-haired, studly glory, emerging from the hills like some backwoods trapper. "Dodge. I thought that was you," Nash said. "I saw your chopper come over the cabin and thought maybe you were in trouble."

"We are," Dodge said, recovering faster than Echo. "Charlie's on the sled—he's been shot."

Nash tromped through the snow over to them. "What happened?"

"Poachers is my guess," Dodge said.

How—? But it didn't matter. "Yeah," she said. "It's a through and through, but he's lost a lot of blood."

"Let's get him back to the cabin." He started unstrapping her dad.

"Can we get someone on the radio?" Echo said.

Nash made a face. "Radio's out."

"Mine isn't," Dodge said. "I'll call from the chopper. But we should get him to the cabin first, see if we can get that bleeding stopped. Let's get moving."

Dodge zipped up the sleeping bag around her dad, and then Nash and Dodge lifted him into the bed of the chopper.

"Echo." He came over to her. "You come with me. Let Nash tow your sled to the cabin."

"But the dogs—"

He caught her hands. "Unhook them. They'll follow the sled. No, they'll follow *you*. Trust me—they know to come back to the one they love."

Dodge knew the look of death, and Charlie bore a gray, pallid hue that had Dodge rethinking his hop to Nash's cabin. Remington Mines was a mere ten miles away.

But he'd already used up his fuel reserve searching the mountains and valleys for Echo, and unlike a plane, without fuel the chopper would simply drop like a brick from the sky.

No gentle landing to a nearby strip of lake or highway or a soft snowy field.

Echo knelt next to her father in the back of the chopper, tears drying on her face. Nash had unhooked her dogs from the sled, letting them run free, and loaded her gear into the back of the chopper.

Nash tied the sled to the back of his snow machine for easy hauling.

Dodge still couldn't believe he'd spotted Echo. Wouldn't have, really—he'd been aiming for the wisp of smoke he'd seen on the horizon and then the tiny cabin nestled on the hill behind the lake.

But out of the corner of his eye, he'd spotted a blur of red.

Echo. And her dogs, barking, jumping, and straining to get his attention.

Thank you, God, was the first thought out of his brain as he'd turned the chopper and headed toward her. Because frankly, he'd abandoned any flight plan, and really, common sense. If he hadn't seen her, he might have kept flying all the way until he ended up as a splat on the side of a mountain.

See, his father was right. Maybe he didn't always have to be in charge.

Or rather, maybe God had simply saved him, again.

Nash was riding back, ahead of him on the shoreline, as Dodge took off. The chopper rose over the great plain of white, toward the ridge, where he spotted a well-trampled cutout to the lake.

The cabin sat just over the top of the hill, overlooking the lake. Behind it, a field sloped down to the south, into the canyon and river basin that flushed gold to the Remington Mines.

The spike cabin that Jude had mentioned.

It was a small affair, with planed timber walls and a tiny smokestack protruding from the slanted metal roof. A trail led to an outhouse, and a gravity-fed water tank was built on the back of the cabin. A front door and porch faced the lake, but Dodge put down in the yard behind the cabin.

A massive open-air shed near the house held firewood and a small Wood-Mizer sawmill, wood chips scattered around the base.

Clearly, Nash had been hard at work setting up shop.

Dodge turned off the bird and came around to open the door. Charlie wasn't a large man, but he was tall, and as Dodge pulled him out, he knew he'd need Nash's help to carry him inside if he didn't want to throw the man over his shoulder.

The buzz from the snowmobile hummed in the air—he was close.

"Echo—go inside and find us a place to put him."

She grabbed her father's bivouac bag and her pack and hiked up to the cabin.

Nash came into the yard, the dogs yipping behind him. They clustered around the chopper, clearly drawn by the rank smell of the deck. He hadn't had time to wash out the blood and other previously frozen fluids from Nola's emergency trip to Anchorage. The warmer weather was thawing it into a pungent odor. Charlie's blood only added to the mix.

"Get his legs," Dodge said to Nash as he ran over. Nash grabbed the bottom of the sleeping bag and Dodge held it near Charlie's shoulders as they heaved him off the deck.

They were halfway to the cabin when a scream lifted from inside. Quick, more of a startled scream than one of terror, but Dodge nearly dropped Charlie. "Echo! Are you okay?"

Nash picked up his pace. "Maybe the bear got in."

"What bear?" They'd nearly reached the deck.

"There's been a bear roaming around here. I think he's looking for food, but I have it up in the cache, and it's secure. He's tried to climb it a couple times."

"Echo!"

She still hadn't emerged from the cabin.

"Are you okay?"

And then a dog raced out of the cabin door, a beautiful husky, white legs, black topcoat, his tongue dangling from his mouth. He darted through the snow to the dogs now wrestling near the chopper.

"I'm okay!" Echo said as she appeared in the door, her eyes wide. "That was Maverick, one of my dogs."

"You found her dog?" he said to Nash.

"No. He found *Peyton*!" Echo said. "She's *here*."

"Oh," Nash said. "I guess I should have mentioned—"

"What?" Dodge glanced at her over his shoulder as he climbed the deck. "Peyton is here?"

"Yeah," Nash said, maneuvering Charlie through the door. "It's a long story. She showed up after the storm a few days ago. Scared me to death. Hurt her ankle."

They carried Charlie into the house. "Peyton Samson. Is *here*?"

Nash frowned. "Yeah. So?"

"Are you kidding me? We've been searching for her for days."

"I made a place for him in the back bedroom," Echo said, interrupting their conversation and opening a door in the small cabin.

The cabin was rough-hewn but cozy, with a small main area with camp chairs surrounding the stove, a waterless kitchen, a table, a camp stove on the counter, and a back bedroom with a twin bed. A loft, accessed by a wooden ladder, overlooked the room and the view of the land through the windows at the front of the cabin.

Not a bad place to hibernate.

Peyton sat in a chair near the stove, her foot up, her ankle deeply bruised, purple and green and gray, her hair fluffed out.

No wonder Echo had screamed.

He followed Echo into the room. Inside, a mattress on a wooden frame was covered with blankets. They set Charlie on it, and Dodge took it as a good sign when he moaned.

"Let's get his feet up," Dodge said. "Keep shock away and the blood closer to his heart."

"I should have thought of that last night," Echo said as Nash built up pillows around his legs. Echo opened the sleeping bag and then his shirt. The wound still seeped, although the bleeding might have lessened. The bag and all his clothing were sopping with blood.

"He's a survivor, E," Dodge said, pulling her against him. He kissed the top of her head. "I'm going out to the chopper to radio in for help."

She held on a moment longer, and then let him go. "Do you have any more bandages, Nash?"

"I have a few towels we can use."

Dodge headed into the main room.

"Are the dogs okay?" Peyton asked as Dodge headed through the room. She looked wan and thin, as if she'd lost weight. So, maybe she had been through an ordeal.

"Granite ran off the night we rescued Holly," Echo said, coming out of the room. "But he made it home. So did Jester and Merlin. And we found Goose and Iceman but Viper is still missing."

Dodge glanced at Echo just as he left the house, saw worry play over her face.

He'd get the story later. It occurred to him that Peyton's disappearance was exactly the kind of panic he might have put his family through when he enlisted without a word.

He owed them all an apology. Especially his father, even though he'd known about his enlistment.

Dodge got inside the chopper, put on his headphones, and turned on the radio. Picked up the mic. "Sky King Chopper to base. Come in."

His father answered—probably was sitting by the radio, as promised. "Base to Sky King Chopper. I'm here, Dodge. Did you find them?"

"Affirmative. Echo *and* Charlie. But Charlie's hurt—he's been shot. We need rescue. A plane."

"Affirmative. Where are you?"

"At a cabin near Cache Mountain, on the east side, south end of the lake."

"Roger. Help is on the way. Over."

Dodge pressed the mic to his forehead, exhaling hard. Then, "Thanks, Dad. Out."

He hoped Winter or Sheldon was around to fly. They couldn't wait for Air One—Charlie didn't have that kind of time.

He hung the mic back and got out, going around the chopper to close the door.

And that's when he heard the motors. He spotted two ATVs tear up past the house, into the backyard.

What?

Idaho and his Russian comrades. One of them rode behind Idaho. The air soured with the smell of oil burning.

Dodge glanced at his .357 Taurus, back in its holster behind the door, drew a breath against his impulses, and crouched down behind the chopper.

Then Echo walked outside. She looked at Idaho, glanced at the chopper, then back to the guide. "What are you doing here?"

The man behind Idaho held a Winchester against his hip and now got off and pointed it at Echo. He said something to her in Russian, then spat on the ground.

She didn't move.

Idaho got off the machine. "I thought we'd find you here. Saw that chopper go down and figured we'd follow it. Your boyfriend around?"

Dodge crept up inside the open deck and grabbed the hand-gun out of the holster.

"No. He went for help. Because you *shot* my father."

She stood on the porch, her blond hair blowing around her shoulders, her hands on her hips, looking like some Nordic Viking. Dodge's heart nearly exploded.

Wow, he loved her. Loved her strength, her convictions, her fearlessness, loved her loyalty.

Loved her courage against the darkness. Despite her wounds, she survived—no, more than that, she thrived.

She'd been more than his best friend. She'd been his light.

She'd been hope for a tomorrow he still thirsted for.

This was his answer—her. Anything he did had to include her, and if she was leaving Copper Mountain, then he was also.

"You need to go," she said, coming down the stairs. "Because when Hank and Deke find out what you've done, you'll never hunt in Alaska again. And frankly, when I'm done testifying, you might never see another sunrise."

Aw, Echo—stop talking—

It happened so fast—but he could almost slow it down, predict it.

One second she was standing fiercely in front of them, the next, the taller man had grabbed her.

She screamed, and he threw her down and pointed the gun at her. "Shut. Up!"

Dodge came around the chopper. "Back away from her!"

The other guy, a short and beefy man—got off his own ATV. He pointed a gun—not a hunting rifle, but a handgun—at Dodge, backing up to Echo. He shouted something in Russian.

"Igor—" Idaho said, a hint of panic in his voice. "Don't—"

Igor grabbed Echo by her hair, dragged her to her feet. She tried to kick him, but he shook her hard and she shouted.

Oh, God, help.

Nash had come outside now, and held his own gun, pointing it first at the Russians, then Idaho, who looked between Dodge and Nash, as if suddenly undone.

"So, we're at a draw," Nash said. "Tell your clients that this is America. You don't get to just shoot people in the woods and leave their bodies behind."

"Or animals!" Echo said, for some reason. She had her hand gripped around Igor's in her hair.

Please, Echo, stop. Because he'd seen guys like this before. The kind of guys who would track down a group of wounded SEALs and murder them. The kind of guys to whom a kill meant nothing but power.

And right now, they had the power.

Dodge trained his gun on Idaho, and for a moment, the urge to simply pull the trigger, to end this, swept through him.

But then he'd end up right where he started—in jail.

Echo's gaze clung to him. She was shaking her head, as if saying, "Don't."

Don't what? Give his life for her? Do *anything* to make sure she was safe?

"God always answers. It's just a matter of how."

He blew out a hard breath. *Please*—

Igor pushed Echo over to his ATV, his gun at her head. Made her get on. "Drive," he said and put the gun at the base of her skull.

Dodge went cold.

The other Russian got on the second ATV. Glanced at Idaho, who shook his head, backed away.

Then the man gunned the ATV, spitting dirt and snow in his wake.

Echo yipped, and Dodge guessed Igor had nudged her.

"No!" Dodge said, stepping toward them.

Igor turned his gun on him, and Dodge stopped just as a bullet bit the snow near his feet.

Echo screamed and pulled back on the throttle. Her ATV took off after the first.

Dodge stood there, his heart a fist, slamming in his chest as he watched the snow plume in their wake.

"Sorry—" Idaho said, and Dodge turned and flattened him. Then he sprinted for his chopper. His brain had simply shut down on one thought.

Rescue Echo.

He jumped in, powered it up, not even bothering to shut the bay door, and lifted into the sky. Nash had come off the porch and was running around to the front of his house, maybe on his way to get his snowmobile.

Dodge glanced at his fuel tank, his jaw tight.

He spotted the poachers just emerging onto the lake, skirting around the lakeshore, Echo's ATV behind the other.

Hang on, honey, I'm coming.

He throttled down the slope, hard on their tail.

Igor glanced behind him as Dodge rode hard up his flank. But Dodge rose as he passed them, just enough to slow them down, and then barreled hard toward the first ATV.

The rider turned, his hand up as if to shoo him away as Dodge buzzed the machine, flying so close the man could have grabbed hold of his skid.

Dodge veered away, flew forward, and turned around.

And sighted the ATV in front of him.

He had to be flying on vapors now. *C'mon, give me just a bit more.*

He centered on the front machine and throttled forward.

Chicken. He kept his eyes on the driver, unmoving.

The man sat down on his ATV, ducking, digging in.

They were going to collide. Dodge didn't move from his course.

Behind the first machine, Echo had slowed, but Dodge didn't look at her.

Fifty feet, forty, thirty—

The man glanced behind him, as if looking for guidance.

Twenty—

"C'mon, man, give!"

The driver turned back—

Ten.

He veered from the path, jerking hard. The soft snow grabbed the wheels, slowing the turn—

The ATV jerked, rolled, and he went flying.

Dodge throttled forward, his eyes now on Echo. She'd slowed, and Igor was waving his arms as if to warn Dodge away, his gun no longer aimed at her.

Echo met his eyes, then suddenly jerked the ATV hard, gunning it, and her captor went flying off the back.

Attagirl!

Except the machine turned so hard, Echo too flew off.

Igor lay twenty feet away from her, sprawled in the snow. Dodge's chopper drank the last of his fuel.

It coughed, and Dodge set it down, hard, pitching nearly nose-first into the snow, fifty yards away.

The rotor spun, the engine wheezing, and Dodge tumbled out. He spotted Igor searching through the snow for his gun.

Dodge advanced, his feet breaking through icy layers. "Stay down!"

Not a chance. Igor got up.

He wasn't a big man, more solid, bullish, but he had a good twenty pounds on Dodge.

Dodge recognized a foul Russian word that emerged from him as he reached onto his belt and palmed a hunting knife.

Super.

Igor advanced on Dodge, something wild in his eyes.

Echo's scream lifted, piercing the air.

He searched for her, and his breath caught as he spotted her, the other Russian holding on to her jacket.

And now he'd done it.

His stupid, maybe impulsive actions getting them all killed. Again.

He blew out a breath. Fine. He'd go down fighting.

"Dodge!" Echo yelled.

He couldn't look at her, his gaze only on Igor.

The thing about knives was that you didn't escape without injury.

In the distance, Dodge heard a motor—Nash. Maybe if he could slow down Igor, Nash had a chance of getting to Echo.

And right then, something fierce and powerful and *right* swelled inside Dodge. Not impulse, but surety. The same feeling he'd had when he spotted that nest of snipers.

"Okay, buddy, let's go."

Igor smiled. He stood just a few feet away, the bowie in his hand, as if trying to figure out where to start.

Dodge kept his eyes on the knife.

Igor lunged, and Dodge stepped to the side, turned, grabbed his wrist, and trapped it against his thigh.

Get rid of the knife!

Igor slammed his fist into Dodge's temple, but he kept his grip and yanked the man's thumb back, tearing the knife free. It dropped into the snow. Dodge kicked the snow, sending the knife flying.

Dodge elbowed the man, hit pay dirt, and Igor fell back, swearing.

Blood gushed from his nose.

Dodge rounded, hot and ready. "Still wanna go?"

And that's when Dodge heard it. A familiar snuffle and grunt. And on the wind, the rank, feral smell of something wild.

Everything went cold.

He looked at Echo, who met his eyes. Still struggling with her captor, she'd heard it too. Paused.

And then she screamed again.

Because right then, the bear came out of the woods. Thick brown hair, teeth bared, he roared as he charged straight at them.

Dodge just had to be faster than Igor, who was still lying in the snow.

Dodge sprinted toward Echo. The shock of seeing a grizzly barreling down at him seemed to release the man's grip on her.

Dodge slammed his fist into his face, and he went down, bloodied. Dodge grabbed Echo's hand. "Get to the chopper!"

It was out of fuel and would hardly hold off a thousand-pound, angry grizzly. Still—

"Dodge—wait!"

He turned. Igor had suffered a brutal swipe across his body that had sent him sprawling. Now the bear fell to all four feet, rocking.

It roared at her.

"That's a warning," she said.

"You think?" Dodge was pulling at her. She grabbed his wrist and stayed planted.

"Black, fight back. Brown, get down."

"What?"

She looked at him, her eyes earnest. "Don't. Move."

Moving was the only thing he could think of.

In the distance he heard the hum of the motor and the sound of dogs barking. Too far.

"Hey there, big boy," she said, kneeling.

"What are you *doing*?"

"It's George, Dodge. Get *down*." She pulled his jacket.

This was crazy.

The bear stood thirty feet away, still rocking back and forth, roaring, his claws digging into the snow and dirt, angry, as if getting ready to charge. Again.

That's when Dodge spotted the nearly black, fraying collar, the white tuft of hair between the bear's ears.

No, it couldn't be.

"He knows me, Dodge."

"Doesn't mean he won't eat you—"

"Away!" she shouted.

The bear roared again, and Dodge very much wanted to leap at Echo, drag her to the chopper.

But it was probably too late for that, given the distance to the bird, the snow cover.

And his own paralyzed limbs.

The bear continued to rock.

"Away, George!" Echo yelled again from their submissive position.

Then, the animal rose, pawing the air, and Dodge's heart just stopped.

Enough of this. He threw his arms around Echo and pulled her to the ground, his body over hers as he kneeled. *Please, God, let Echo live.*

He pressed his face close to hers. "I love you, Echo. I love you."

"Shh. It'll be okay." But she didn't fight him.

Dodge closed his eyes, bracing himself, waiting for the first swipe.

Nothing. He heard the bear grunt. Huff.

Beneath him, Echo pushed up onto all fours. "George. Away!"

Dodge had to look.

The bear seemed to be considering her words, and the world stopped moving, all of nature holding its breath.

Away! He willed him with his every heartbeat.

Then, chaos erupted.

The dogs appeared from behind the chopper, running hard. Maverick and Granite ran right up to the bear, who rose and tried to bat them away. They bared their teeth, growling, dodging him.

"Merlin! Jester! Goose!" Echo called, and the other three animals came over to her, barking and whining.

The bear took a swipe at Maverick and missed.

The dog barked, fell back.

And that's when Echo scooted out from under Dodge and stood, her hands up. "George! Away!"

The bear fell back on all fours again. She grabbed Merlin and Jester. Dodge grabbed Goose.

"Go!" she shouted.

He rose again, his claws scrubbing the air. Then he dropped and ran off into the woods.

Dodge was still on his knees, and maybe he'd just stay there while he found his bones again.

Good place to retch too.

Nash parked his snowmobile beside the chopper, walked over to Igor, who lay on the ground, and rolled him over. His jacket was shredded, but there was barely any blood. Igor jerked away.

As Dodge watched—and tried to climb to his feet—Nash sent his fist into the man's face. Igor fell back, holding his nose. The other man had taken off.

"I got this," Echo said, and Dodge turned, his breath tight when he spotted Echo holding Igor's gun, finally located in the snow. She held it on him.

"Honey. It's not . . . don't do it."

She looked at him. "I'm not going to shoot him. Not unless he tries to hurt you."

Oh. "Okay."

"Let's tie him up," she said, and Igor, who still bled from his nose, swore at her.

"I have rope on the sled," Nash said. "You guys okay?"

"Barely," Dodge said.

Nash glanced at Igor, then back to Dodge. "Was that a grizzly I saw?"

"Just came out of nowhere," Echo said.

Dodge very much doubted that.

He held Igor down as Nash tied his hands and rolled him over.

Then he looked at Echo. She was breathing hard and only now lowered the gun.

"E? You okay?"

She wore a faraway look, something unfamiliar in her eyes. "He saved us."

Dodge frowned.

"George. He saved us."

Huh. Dodge wouldn't quite put it that way, but maybe.

He walked over and pulled her to himself. She put her arms around him, holding tight.

He might still be shaking a little.

When he pulled away, she looked up at him. "Thanks for staying with me. Thanks for not running."

He took her face in his hands. "Never." Then he kissed her.

And now wasn't the time for passion, but for trust, hope, promises.

All that he planned to keep.

Still, he lingered, kissed her long enough to know she was his. Always had been.

Overhead, he heard a hum, and as he pulled away, he spotted a deep-yellow Piper Family Cruiser dipping down over them. It wagged its wings and Dodge's heart just about stopped.

His *father* was at the helm.

What?

He ran to the ridge and watched as his bird came around for landing and settled perfectly on the glistening surface of the lake. The plane's massive tundra wheels rode the snow and ice to the shore.

Dodge couldn't breathe. What was he *doing*?

Except maybe he knew.

Risking everything for someone he loved. Dodge's chest tightened, heated. "Let's get Charlie," Dodge said.

They loaded Igor onto the back of the ATV, tying him to the backrest and footpads.

He drove his prisoner back to the cabin, Echo behind Nash. Idaho was gone.

Peyton came out onto the porch on makeshift crutches, a blanket over her shoulders, as they drove up. "Where did you say they killed that moose, Echo?"

"And shot my father? At the far end of the Cache River basin. Near the hunter cabin on Kayuh Lake."

"I have a camera there. It's a wide angle, on an old wolf den."

"You can run, Idaho, but you can't hide!" Echo yelled into the woods.

"Let's get your dad," Dodge said and headed to the front porch. He passed Peyton as he went inside, Nash right behind him. "Why didn't you contact us, Peyton? Let us know you were okay?" Dodge couldn't help the edge to his voice.

"The radio is out," Nash said.

Dodge turned to him. "But you went down to the mine a few days ago—why didn't you say anything to Jude, or call in then?" He walked into the bedroom.

Nash followed him in. "I didn't realize anyone was looking for her."

Dodge gave him a look. "You didn't think that the dogs showing up would have alerted Echo to trouble?" He cast a look at Nash, then Peyton, who had limped to the doorway.

"I didn't realize Granite was gone until the day after the storm," Peyton said. "I thought he was sleeping with the pack. I should have turned back then, but I thought he'd find his way home, and I was worried about the wolves with that grizzly around. So I kept going to the next cabin, stayed there, and then the next day took off for the hunting cabin, before the storm could set in."

Nash and Dodge bundled Charlie up again as she spoke.

Echo came into the room to grab his stuff. "How did you end up here?" she asked.

"I'm not sure what happened. All I remember is the sound of a gunshot—I'm not sure if someone was shooting at the dogs, but they panicked, and I lost control. We ended up going over a ledge."

Dodge looked at Echo, his mouth a tight line. He'd bet Idaho and his sportsmen had something to do with that.

Or maybe he was just jumping to conclusions. Again.

He took Charlie's feet at the base of the sleeping bag, Nash took the top.

"I was thrown off the sled," Peyton said. "I hurt my ankle, and the sled was destroyed. I tried to get to the dogs, but the storm was closing in. By the time I got to them, a couple had chewed through their harnesses. I cut the rest free.

"Somehow, I found shelter and hunkered down for a couple days. Maverick kept me warm. Probably saved my life."

"We're going to move you now, Dad," Echo said and kissed his forehead.

"How'd Nash find you?" Dodge asked as they picked him up. They eased him off the bed, then around to the main room.

Peyton moved to the side as they carried Charlie, following the group as she answered. "I saw the cabin when I was mushing, so I must have been way off course. I kept thinking if I could get to it . . ."

"I found her in the yard," Nash said. "Maverick was standing over her, barking in the middle of the night. Any longer out there, and she would have died."

Nash cast her a look, something of worry in it.

Oh. And Dodge remembered Spike's comment about Nash not seeming quite so lonely.

Aha.

By the time they reached the door with Charlie, Dodge's father had climbed the hill, breathing hard. He met them on the porch.

"How's he doing?" his father asked as they trundled down the hill, their footing slick.

"Not great," Dodge said.

Echo hustled behind them, carrying their gear.

The sun hung over the mountains, still bright upon the day. "What are you doing, Dad?" Dodge cut his voice low. "I mean . . . you can't see—" He looked at him. His dad wore his aviator glasses, his leather jacket, his gimme cap, every inch the pilot he remembered, the Barry Kingston who owned the skies.

"I can see just fine when my son is in trouble," he said. "You needed help. Of course I showed up."

Dodge's throat thickened. They reached the plane, and Dodge saw that his father had removed the middle seats. They settled Charlie inside and he roused, breathing in hard, moaning. Opened his eyes.

"What's going on?" He looked at Echo, then Dodge. "Oh. Okay." Then he closed his eyes again.

"Dad?" Echo said.

"Get in, Echo," Dodge said, then turned to his father. "I got it from here."

"I know." He backed away. "I contacted Hank and Deke, by the way. They're on their way. I think Winter is flying them out."

"Idaho and another Russian man are somewhere in the woods, so watch your back." Dodge climbed into the cockpit, reached for the headset, then the door. His father stepped back, but Dodge met his eyes. "Thanks, Dad, for coming for me."

He lifted a hand, smiled. Nodded. "Fly smart."

Dodge closed the door, turned the plane, and took off into the blue sky, Echo strapped in the seat beside him.

As he arched over the lake, he saw the giant bear emerge from the woods on the north end of the lake, as if following their shadow.

SIXTEEN

Echo didn't care what Dodge said—they *had* been saved by a bear. Which had come out of nowhere.

And not just any bear, but *George*.

If anything, her father had to live just so she could tell him that, in the end, George wasn't lost.

A strange bubble of disbelief-slash-hysteria had built inside her, even as Dodge had flown them—without running out of fuel and dropping out of the sky—to Anchorage.

Right back to the ER where they'd brought Jane Doe.

And where Echo's life had sort of imploded. Except, maybe that had been a catastrophe of her own making. She'd been upset and had read into Moose's conversation, and maybe Dodge *wasn't* leaving.

And then there was the conversation with her mother that had stirred up all her fears.

"I need coffee," Dodge had said as they sat in the surgical waiting room. He ran a hand behind his neck, squeezed the muscle there.

"I'm on it."

"No, I'll go." He started to get up, but she pushed him back. "You wait just in case the doctor comes back. I have to walk."

He caught her hand, his blue eyes thick with concern. "Fine. Don't wander off." Then he tugged her down and kissed her.

Aw, what was she supposed to do with that?

She'd left Dodge there, keenly aware that not only had he shown up for her, he hadn't let go of her hand since the doctors had taken her father into surgery.

Her dad had internal bleeding, of course. She understood—she felt like maybe she'd been bleeding internally for the better part of a decade.

Maybe even before Dodge left.

Now, Echo looked into the mirror of the bathroom, at her tired, bloodshot eyes, her pale face, and tried to shake off the memory of the Russian man's hands in her hair. His rank breath on her face, acrid and smelling of drink. Tried to blink away the sight of Igor about to kill the man she loved and, most importantly, Dodge standing there, unarmed, ready to take him on. Ready to die, for *her*.

And it hit her.

This was love. Love showed up. Love stayed. Love sacrificed.

She knew love. She knew love through her dad.

She knew love through Dodge.

"We don't know how God protects us. How he is there for us, but he is."

Maybe she just needed to step back and open her eyes. Look for a different perspective.

See.

"My point is that we found you. *Practically a miracle."*

And it hadn't happened only once, but twice, and how many other times, she couldn't know.

"But what if we judged God by what didn't *happen to us?"*

What didn't happen. So much, it was breathtaking.

This could have ended so differently.

She splashed water on her face, drew out a couple paper towels, and headed back to the waiting room. When she stopped by the coffee vending machine, she realized she hadn't brought her wallet with her.

Outside, through the big picture window at the end of the hall, the sun had just fled the day, long gray shadows hovered over the valley north of the hospital, the faraway mountains an eerie blue-black. She was hungry, tired, and edgy, and probably in no mood to walk into the conversation between Dodge and Moose.

Again.

Dodge had risen from his chair, his hair mussed from where he'd been folding his hands behind his neck, leaning forward, trying to manage his worry about her dad. He wore a black thermal shirt, the sleeves shoved up past his elbows, as if he wanted to slam open the double doors to the operating room and have a go.

Maybe she would like that too.

Except, there he was, talking to Moose, who stood with his back to her, hands in his pockets. What, did he have some sort of homing beacon on Dodge that whenever he showed up in town, so did Moose?

Dodge was nodding, and it did something to her gut, and no, she didn't want to hear about his plans to move to Anchorage. Not now.

Her eyes filled, gritty, and she turned, heading the opposite direction, toward the lounge where she'd seen—and smelled— coffee earlier.

She found the small lounge that probably served the nurses on the floor. Sneaking in, she grabbed a couple cups and filled them at the machine.

"Echo?"

She turned, and Winter Starr stood at the door. "I was on my way to check on your dad. I flew in the poacher who was mauled. He's in cuffs down in the ER. Not badly hurt though." She stepped into the room and gave Echo a hug. "How are you?"

Echo let out a shaky breath. "I don't even know."

Winter gave her a sad nod. "I can't believe your dad was shot."

"He saw those hunters poach a moose."

"So amazing that you found him."

Actually . . .

Just another way, maybe, that God had intervened. Allowed her to be in the area where her dad could find her and she could bring him to help.

Huh.

Yes, she needed to open her eyes.

Winter grabbed a cup of coffee too. "I saw Dodge. Are you two . . . ?" She raised an eyebrow.

Echo looked down at her two cups, not sure what to say.

"Oh, please. You're not going to let him go, are you?"

She sighed. "Moose wants him to fly for Air One, and I can't hold him back."

Winter took a sip of her coffee. "This is easy, Echo. You go with him."

Echo stared at her. Winter had always possessed a fearlessness that Echo envied. She'd become one of the best bush pilots in the area over the past ten years.

Easy. "And what about my dad?"

"What about your dad? Your father's decisions don't have to hold you hostage. I know you love your dad, but maybe it's time to see what your future might be if you let him go and stopped worrying so much."

"I'm not sure what my life would look like without worry." She grinned, but the question dug into her soul.

She did spend her life worrying. Afraid of losing. Afraid of living, maybe.

Afraid.

"The Lord himself watches over you, and you can trust him."

"I think it might look like how it does from the air. Open, free, and beautiful." Winter winked at her. "C'mon. Let's go check on your dad."

Winter walked out, but Echo stayed for a moment, the words sweeping through her.

Open, free, and beautiful. Like she felt when she mushed

her dogs, the quiet, peaceful silence inside a brutal, harsh landscape.

Lord, I don't want to be afraid anymore. The thought pulsed inside her.

She followed Winter out and down the hall.

Maybe Winter was right. Her dad would be fine.

She turned the corner to the waiting room and slowed.

Winter had stopped next to Moose.

But no Dodge.

She spotted movement down the hall. Dodge came out of a room.

The stricken, almost horrified expression caught her breath.

No! "Dodge?"

"I'm sorry, Echo—"

"No!" She took another step, her legs shaking. They nearly gave out then, and she dropped the coffee.

Winter moved toward her, but Dodge broke out into a run. "Echo—no—your dad is fine. He's"—he grabbed her arms to steady her—"he's fine. I'm sorry. He's awake—"

She looked up at him. "What? Then why did you—"

"Your *mom* is with him."

She just blinked at him. She'd gotten coffee on her pants, but it hadn't soaked through. She looked at the mess, back at Dodge.

"I'll get this," said Winter.

Shoot. So much for all her brave words. "Thanks."

Then she turned and stalked down the hall. If Effie thought she could just slip back into her dad's life to decimate it again . . .

Echo banged through the door, not caring that she might be making a scene, and barely hesitated at the sight of her father lying in the bed, bandaged, an IV in his arm, under an oxygen cannula, a heart monitor beeping. In his flimsy gown he almost looked . . . fragile.

Well, that's why she was here—to protect him. She pinned

her gaze on the woman sitting in the chair by his bed *holding his hand.*

What on earth?

"Dad. What is going on?"

"Calm down," said Effie, who got up. "I heard your dad was here, and I had to see him."

"You *had* to see him?" She just stared at Effie, who wore her hair back in a surgical cap. She had on a pair of orange scrubs, as if she'd just come from delivering a baby.

"Yes. I had to see him." Something almost tender crossed her expression as she turned to her former husband. "I missed him."

He smiled back at her.

No, no—

Effie looked up at Echo and took a breath. "You were right—what you said to me. I was the poorer for not having you or your father in my life. I was scared of a future I couldn't see an end to, and I ran. And thought—I *always* thought—I could never come back."

"You can't."

"Echo," her father said quietly. "Listen to her."

"But I wanted to," Effie said. "I think that's why I kept reaching out to your father. And why he kept reaching back. Because love doesn't stop just because you run. Love keeps reaching out. Keeps believing, even when it feels impossible." She drew in a breath. "If there is one thing I've learned in my career, it's that true love is at once painful and freeing and so worth the effort. And in the darkness of my world, I forgot that."

Whatever.

"And I let her go," her father said. "When you went after her and got lost—and nearly died—I wanted to hate her for it. But I couldn't convince my heart of that. The love inside just kept wanting out."

She stared at them, hollow.

"Forgive us," her mother said. "Please forgive us."

What? "No—"

"Listen, honey," her father said. "I'm so sorry. I kept you two apart because I feared losing you to her world too." He swallowed. "I wanted you in mine."

Her eyes burned. "Are you *kidding* me?" She looked at her mother, her father. "What you did—what you *both* did— eviscerated me. My entire life I grew up thinking that you left because of me." She turned to Effie. "I get it, really. It *is* dark— so dark—in the winter that it's easy to forget the sunrise, and even when the sun does come up, it never really dents the darkness. But then comes spring, and Alaska awakens and suddenly everything comes alive, and it's then that you know there was a reason to keep living, keep hoping."

She took a breath. "But see, you took that away from me too. Hope. You inflicted chaos and destruction on my soul. Every day that you didn't come home, every day my prayers weren't answered, all I heard was God's silence. God telling me I didn't matter." Her voice dropped. "What you did made me believe that God hated me."

Her mother swallowed. "Echo—"

She held up a hand. "Stay. Away. From. Me."

"Please. I love you. I'm sorry I left you." Her mother's expression was wrecked, sincere sorrow on her face.

Inside Echo sounded a terrible roaring, something tearing, a pulse of compassion—

No.

She backed away.

"Echo?"

Then she turned and pushed out of the room.

Dodge stood in the hall and took off after her as she stalked past the janitor mopping up her coffee. She ran all the way to the stairwell, hit the door, and took the stairs down.

Dodge was hot on her trail. "Echo!"

"Leave me alone!" But her voice had cracked, and she could hear her own choked sobs lifting, echoing.

"No!" He took the stairs two at a time and met her at the bottom, right after she slammed her way outside, into the cold.

He caught her arm, turned her. "Echo!"

She rounded, her breaths hiccupping, tears running down her face.

"What?" he said, cupping her face in his hands. "What did she say?"

"She . . . wants me to *forgive* her."

"Oh."

"She stood there and said that she never stopped loving me. Hello—I was *two hours away!*"

He said nothing, just nodded.

"After everything she's done, all the chaos and pain she's caused . . . The crazy, horrifying thing is that there's a part of me that—shoot—that still loves her. That *wants* to forgive her." She tore herself away. "What is wrong with me? I'm not a child, desperate for her mommy to come home. I'm an adult and she . . . she left us. Left me!"

She wrapped her arms around herself. "I don't get it."

The night was crowding in, the air brisk but carrying the faintest edge of spring.

He pulled her back against himself, his arms around her. "I do."

He was warm and she turned in his arms.

"It's love breaking through."

"I don't love her anymore."

"Echo. Of course you do. She's your mother."

Echo looked away.

"What if you let it go? Your anger, even the injustice of it."

She raised an eyebrow.

He took a breath. "Okay, yes, I hear you. Maybe I need to listen to myself. But what if we let God take over? Let him be angry for us, protect us. Then we don't have to choose who to love, and why. My father used to say that love doesn't come from us—it's born in us, a birthright from God. We can't manufacture it, we can only release what he's given us. That nudge to forgive? I told you—I think that's love trying to break free."

"I don't even know what that looks like."

"Yes, you do."

She met his eyes, so piercingly blue, fixed on her.

"When you get on your sled, and yell *hike*, what happens?"

"The dogs start to run?"

"They *explode* with so much power, you just have to hold on. Love is like that. You don't have to create it, you just have to open your heart to it and then let it pour out. Let God take care of protecting you."

Even as he spoke it, the pulse lit in her heart.

Forgiving might be the first step to tomorrow.

"Oh, and Echo? I heard what you said in there." He cupped her cheek. "God doesn't hate you. He loves you—even more than I do, if that's possible. Maybe it's time to let yourself believe that."

She looked at him. In his smile she saw a fourteen-year-old boy who took her in his arms and held her as she wept, terrified and hurt. And saw the brokenhearted teenager who'd fought his own brother for her. And the wounded hero who had come home angry, but longing to find the woman he loved.

Yes, God loved her.

"Forgiveness isn't for the person you're forgiving, Echo. It's for yourself. It's what you do to be set free."

She closed her eyes.

Free.

Free to heal.

To love.

To live the life she saw beyond the horizon. The one that included Dodge.

She didn't need to know the end of the story to know that

she would never ever stop loving Dodge. Never stop needing Dodge. Never stop hoping he'd show up.

Never stop believing that he was the only man for her. "I love you, Dodge."

He blinked at her, then smiled. "That's a good start."

"No, that's the happy ending too. See, I know you're going to Anchorage to work for Moose. I overheard you when you told him to hold your spot."

"What?"

"Yeah. And I . . . I sorta freaked out. I thought . . . I don't want to leave Copper Mountain, but . . . I don't want to lose you either. I waited for you for ten years. And I tried to tell myself that I was over you, and sometimes that I deserved you walking out of my life, and I tried to just stopper up all the hurt and pain, but the fact is . . . you're the only man for me, Dodge. You're brave and smart, and in the darkness that can be my life . . . you're the sunrise. So . . . okay. Let's do this."

He was grinning at her. "Let's do this?"

"It doesn't matter where you go, I'm going too."

He laughed, a deep sweet burst that she felt to her soul. "Oh, Echo. I'm not moving to Anchorage. I'm starting an Air One Rescue branch in Copper Mountain."

"What?"

"Yeah. After the last week, it's clear we need SAR a little closer than Anchorage." He turned her, and now the chill of the wall was at her back. "And, I'm thinking that we might need a good dogsled team, and a musher."

"Me?"

"Oh, please." He braced an arm over the top of her shoulder and leaned in. "I can't think of anyone who knows Alaska better than you do." He bent down, his mouth inches from hers. "So, sweetheart, I'm afraid I'm here to stay."

She put her hands on his chest, found his beating heart, and lifted her face to his. "Really?"

"Just try and get rid of me."

Then he kissed her, and as usual, he tasted of home, of the happy ending she'd been too afraid to wish for, of the big, wild man who was hers.

"Never," she whispered, and kissed him again.

She could stay here forever, but after a moment, she pushed him away. "C'mon." She took his hand.

As Echo walked back inside and reentered her father's hospital room, she spotted Effie sitting in the chair, her face in the bedclothes, her father's hand on her as she sobbed.

Okay, Dodge was right. Echo took a breath and let go. And into the hollow space inside slid compassion.

Love.

A love that really didn't belong to her. A love that she could give away.

Her mother lifted her head, her eyes reddened.

"Okay, listen," Echo said, her hand tight in Dodge's. "You wreaked havoc in my life in countless ways. Never mind that I was afraid to leave my dad—I was afraid to accept love. Instead, I sabotaged it." She shook her head. "Effie, I will never forget the choices you made that destroyed me, but I refuse to let the past hold me hostage. I choose hope. I choose freedom. So, yes, I'll try to forgive you. That's the best I can do right now. It'll have to be enough."

She looked at Dodge. "Take me home."

Two weeks later Echo sat in the belly of Dodge's chopper, the magnificent Denali range beneath them streaked in white, the floor of the park turning green and lush with a massive, untouched spread of blue alpine forget-me-nots, purple lousewort, deep-pink fireweed, and yellow poppies. From her vantage point, the horizon stretched to forever.

The park was coming alive, and seeing it at two thousand

feet lit a fresh awe in her. She loved Alaska, but never more than when she let the vastness of it sweep over her—the rugged, almost harsh beauty of a land that fought through the darkness to survive.

"If that thing wakes up, we're all dead."

Dodge's voice came through the headset, and she glanced up at him in the pilot's seat. He wore a denim Sky King Ranch jacket, a pair of gloves, his aviator sunglasses, and was handling the chopper as if he were born in the cockpit.

"He's sleeping like a baby." She put her hand on George's sedated body, just to confirm his breathing.

Oh, the animal smelled rank. Not just from the earthy scent of him but also the odor of decaying flesh from the bullet wound Anuk had found on his shoulder.

Dodge and Hank and Deke had spent the better part of a week tracking down George. They'd found the animal not far from Erv and Joann Nickle's place, scavenging a caribou that a pack of wolves had brought down.

They'd darted him then and brought him into Anuk's clinic, where she cut away the infection, dressed the wound, and administered an antibiotic. He'd been penned for another week while Anuk watched his healing.

A tense week where George prowled his enclosure. But he'd taken to the feed Anuk gave him, and when she declared him fit, Echo had volunteered to accompany Dodge as he transported him to a location deep in Denali Park.

Hank had recollared him and now checked the transmitter from where he sat buckled into one of the seats.

"Where are we going?" Echo asked.

"Northeast corner of the park," Hank said. "We found an area that we think is fairly free of other bears—at least those on our radar. He'll be able to establish his territory."

She could hardly believe this was the same bear she'd helped raise, the one who'd stared her down just two weeks ago. He looked . . . fallen. His shoulder shaved, the stitches—which would dissolve—evidence of the pain he'd suffered. Like this, asleep, he looked almost docile.

Awake, he was terrifying.

"How long until we get there?" she asked Dodge through her headset.

"Twenty minutes."

She checked her watch—they still had plenty of time on the sedative.

Hopefully.

Hank had another dose in his pack, but an angry grizzly in a chopper was sort of like snakes on a plane.

She climbed up into the other cockpit seat, glanced again at Dodge, who smiled at her, and for some reason, his father's words sifted through her. *"Forgiveness isn't for the person you're forgiving, Echo. It's for yourself. It's what you do to be set free."*

Maybe, yes. But somehow Dodge's forgiveness of her had also set her free. Released the terrible ache, the horrible regret inside.

They passed over the Alaska Range, Mount Mather to the west, its ridged back not unlike old George's, gray and slumbering, then the now-running McKinley River, sluicing down into the northern Denali basin.

Yes, up here in the wild, great alone, George could find a new home, away from people he might hurt.

"That's Wonder Lake, out the port window," Dodge said.

She spotted the lake sitting in a pocket beneath the mountain. The sun sparkled on it, already picking up the rose gold of the late hour.

"We'll set down near the shore, offload him, then cross the river to wait until he wakes."

Dodge was already descending into the river basin. It spat and frothed its way free of the Muldrow Glacier, flowing northwest to the Kantishna River, on its way to the ocean. Dead logs and ice floe still clogged the water, the tundra spongy along its banks. Dodge searched for a landing zone and finally found a patch of barren ground. He set the chopper down.

"Let's get that bear off my deck!"

Hank was already up and attaching the straps to the lift they'd devised to move the bear. He lay on a massive canvas sling, still snoozing. Hank checked his vitals, then Echo got out as Dodge extended the lift arm and secured the bracing post to the ground. He nodded at Echo.

She worked the lift. The pulleys raised the animal, the sling holding George like a massive hammock. Dodge and Hank guided him out of the chopper as the winch moved slowly, and then Echo carefully lowered the animal to the ground.

George groaned and moved his head.

She shot a look at Dodge, who was already unhooking the straps. "Let's leave it and get out of here," he said. "We'll come back for the hammock."

Hank had unhooked the other straps and Echo retracted the arm as, again, George emitted a deep rumble.

"Get in, Echo," Dodge shouted as Hank took the back.

But Echo couldn't move.

Her father should be here to say goodbye. Despite the danger, they'd needed George for a while. He'd been something to care for, something to focus on.

Something dangerous and feral as he grew, that needed to be set free.

"Echo! Now!"

Right.

She climbed in just as George rumbled to life, shuddering.

Dodge was airborne by the time George found his feet.

The bear lifted his head and let out a bone-shearing roar of anger.

"I'm not sure we should put down," Dodge said.

"The river will slow him down," Hank said.

"I need a shot, Dodge," Echo said, digging out her camera.

He glanced at her, then found a place across the river, some hundred yards away.

George prowled the shoreline, still trying to get his bearings.

Echo stepped out of the chopper and she found him in the viewfinder.

He stopped prowling, the river wild between them, casting up in frothy sparks of foam, caught in the sunlight. He stood on all fours, the sun at his back, capturing the tuft of white between his ears, turning his fur to a shade of deep amber. Behind him the greening grasses shifted slightly in the wind. A new world, beckoning.

She took the shot.

He rose. Pawed the air. She took another shot.

Then she lowered her camera.

George still stood on his hind legs.

"He's going to cross the river," Hank said.

Dodge had come up behind her, his hands on her shoulders.

"No. He's not," she said as the animal pawed the air again. "My father taught him that. He's waving."

She knew it sounded crazy, and maybe it was, but she lifted her hand to him.

He landed on all fours, then with a shake of his head, he turned and lumbered away from them, down the riverbed.

"Let's never do that again," Dodge said.

Hank laughed.

Echo watched the bear disappear into the horizon. *Bye, George.*

Then she got into the chopper, and as the sun fell into the purpling mountains, Dodge flew them home.

"Are you sure this is what you want?"

The question came from his father as Dodge leaned over the papers that Guy Roberts, their lawyer, had slid across the conference room table.

"The surest about anything I've ever done," Dodge said. Except one thing, but the timing hadn't been right the first time.

This time, he'd wait. Wait on Echo. Wait on God.

Wait, because he didn't have to be in charge of everything.

It was enough to be in charge of Sky King Rescue, the northern affiliate of Air One out of Anchorage.

Dodge finished the last page of the contract, pushed it back over to Guy, then took out his wallet and handed him a dollar. "To make it official."

His father laughed. "At least I got to keep the house."

"And the land," Dodge said. "I just need the runway, the planes, the chopper, and the hangar."

"Just." But his father grinned, despite the melancholy in his eyes. Eyes that were clouding every day with more darkness, according to the ophthalmologist, although he signed off that his father's eyesight probably had not contributed to the accident.

Still, his father couldn't take the helm any longer, in good conscience.

They'd informed their insurance company of their plan to turn the operation over to Dodge. The insurance had totaled the Otter, leaving Dodge with a check.

He had his eye on a particular de Havilland Beaver that still needed repairs.

Now, Dodge rose and shook his father's hand.

"Copper Mountain is in good hands," Guy said, his smile bright against his dark skin as he also shook Dodge's hand. He had a wife and two daughters and had recently moved to Copper Mountain from Georgia, his Southern drawl a reminder of the mix of residents in their tiny town.

"I hope so," Dodge said.

"I know so," his father added.

"I read about the poachers and Charlie in the *Good News*," Guy said as he walked them to the door. "How is Charlie doing?"

"He was discharged a week ago," Dodge said. They stood in the entryway, icicles hanging from the roof of the timber-framed building. Outside, the town had been festooned with all the trappings of this weekend's Rowdy—twinkly lights on the outside-eating decks with giant outdoor heaters pumping out a homey warmth. On the porch of the nearby town hall—an old church converted to a gathering place and theater—a handful of local bands took the stage, adding a folksy ambiance for the tourists who roamed Main Street. Local shops had flung open their doors, with sales signs posted outside. The public parking lot was jammed with cars, and a couple local sled dog groups had lines in front of their barking teams, children waiting to take a ride behind a team of huskies.

But the locals were congregating around the nearby hockey arena, and Dodge glanced at the wall clock in the office.

His father must have seen him. "I'll see you at the game."

Dodge lifted a hand to Guy, walked out onto the street, and got into his truck. He'd dug his hockey gear out of the basement closet a few days ago, gotten his skates sharpened at Ace's, and picked them up this morning.

He couldn't wait to face down Moose and Axel Mulligan, Topher Dahlquist, and the other townies, an old competitive spirit igniting inside him.

Wow, it felt good to be back. He'd even found his own Copper Mountain Grizzlies jersey.

The smell of pizza and caribou barbecue seasoned the air, and country music filtered down the street.

Dodge dearly hoped Echo would attend tonight's breakup dance. He hadn't seen her since they dropped off George over a week ago. She'd been spending time at the hospital, then at home, helping her father settle back in.

Effie had moved home with him.

Dodge still couldn't believe that Echo had stood in front of her undeserving—at least, in his opinion—mother and said she'd try to forgive her.

He'd never loved someone so much as he did Echo when she offered her mother a second chance.

It felt, in a way, that she was offering *them* a second chance. Forgiving him. Loving him. But maybe that was the way it was when someone reacted in love . . . it swept over everyone around them. Allowed them to love too.

Dodge had come home, walked into his father's study, and forgave him too. Said the words out loud.

And for the first time since his mother died, he saw his father cry.

Shoot, even he'd teared up. Because like Echo said, he chose freedom.

He drove over to the rink and pulled up next to a Remington Mines truck. Retrieving his gear from the back, he heard his name in greeting and turned to see Hank Billings headed his direction.

Dodge threw his duffel bag over his shoulder, grabbed his stick, and closed the tailgate. "I didn't know you played hockey."

Hank wore a Nashville Predators jersey and carried skates over his shoulder. "Enough to get myself in trouble. But the guys told me there was free pizza involved, so . . ."

"Only if you win." They headed for the warming house. The ice was still sharp from last night's dip into the lower teens, despite the warmer weather that seasoned the air. He put today's temps in the low forties. "How's our favorite bear? Is the tracker working?"

"Yes. He's exploring his new territory. Seems to be okay."

"And Idaho and the other poacher?"

Hank shook his head. "No sign of the hunter who got away, but Alaska Fish and Game officials apprehended Idaho in Anchorage, about to board a flight to the Lower 48."

"Wow."

"Peyton told us where to retrieve one of her cameras, and it shows all three of them surrounding the moose on their four-wheelers and killing it, so he's going to jail. As for the poacher in custody, he didn't have a permit or a visa, and frankly, we're not sure he's in the country legally. Deke feels like maybe there's something else going on. He's alerted the local FBI."

They entered the warming house, and Dodge sat down next to Goodwin and Malachi, who already had their pads on and were lacing up their skates. "Hey," Mal said. "I wasn't sure you'd be here."

"Oh, I'm here," Dodge said, opening his bag.

"Yeah?" Mal stood up. "That mean you're staying?"

"Yep."

"He's turning Sky King Ranch into a rescue operation," Moose Mulligan said behind him. He stood even taller in his skates, and beside him, his brother, Axel, grinned at Dodge with a little friendly competition in his eyes.

"Really?" Mal said. "And you and Echo—you back together?"

"Why?" Dodge asked. "You thinking about cutting in?"

Mal held up a hand. "Not going there."

Dodge grinned. "Smart man."

He laced up his skates, then grabbed his stick, his helmet, and his mouth guard and headed out onto the ice.

The sun was high, warm, and he'd worn only a thin shirt under his jersey, but he wouldn't need more. He stretched and did a couple warm-up laps, and only then did he glance over at the stands.

Peyton sat next to Shasta and Winter and raised a hand to him as he glanced her direction.

But no Echo. Which felt weird.

Dodge circled the ice again, and then the rest of the team came out, and they warmed up.

Still no Echo.

By the time he found himself on the line, ready for the puck drop, he'd surrendered to the idea that she wasn't coming.

He glanced up two minutes into the first period, though, and spotted her sitting next to Peyton, wearing an oversized Copper Mountain Grizzlies sweatshirt, her blond hair down under a white hat with a pom-pom. She waved, and something swelled inside his chest.

His very own cheerleader.

He focused back on the game just in time to see Axel headed his direction, grinning, playing with the puck, and nope, no one was getting past him today.

Dodge spun, came around, and slammed Axel into the boards.

It shook the puck loose and Dodge shot it down to the far end of the ice, where Mal caught it.

Slapped it in.

And that's how it was done. *Hooah.*

Dodge high-fived his team and kept his mind on the ice all the way to the end of the game.

The bush team won, three goals to one.

Grabbing a towel from the sidelines, Dodge skated over to the bleacher area. Echo stood with Peyton, who was on crutches and seemed to be waiting for Nash.

Indeed, Nash came over, leaned down, and popped Peyton with a kiss. Interesting.

Echo wrapped her arms around herself, obviously shivering. "Great game."

He wanted to reach out for her, pull her in close by her scarf so he could kiss her. But she stood strangely away, her gaze not quite meeting his.

"You okay?"

"Mmhmm."

"Am I going to see you tonight at the breakup dance?"

Her eyes lifted. "Really?"

He laughed. "Only if you say you'll go with me."

She grinned then. "It's against the rules, but I'll go with you." She left with Winter and Shasta, and he skated back to the warming house, changed, grabbed some free pizza with the guys, then headed home.

He spent about an hour trying to figure out what to wear. He'd never actually been to the breakup dance. Oh, how he hated dancing. In his worst fears, he ended up on the floor, in a tangled mess, maybe on top of Echo. Nice. But Echo always had this thing for it, loved dancing movies . . .

And that's what love did—it ignored the what-ifs.

He decided on a pair of jeans and one of his old dress shirts and headed back to Copper Mountain.

The town was packed, dusk falling like fairy dust, the place almost magical thanks to the twinkly lights that lit up the shadows. The decks of the local establishments were packed, heaters chugging out blasts of warm air into the night.

The old community center had flung open its doors, the music rolling outside. The Yankee Belles were rocking the house with a song that had everyone on their feet. Locals and tourists, all two-stepping and line dancing, packed the dance floor.

Oh, this would be a disaster.

Dodge pushed his way inside, spotted Malachi dancing with Shasta Starr, and Jude Remington with a cute redhead he didn't know, and tried to find Echo.

No sign of her.

Dodge stood a moment, searching the crowd, the dance floor. Huh. She *had* been acting strange today.

He was about to head toward his truck when he spotted Charlie and Effie. Effie had her hair down, behind her ears, and wore a flowing bohemian dress with cowboy boots. She was laughing at something Charlie said. He sat in a chair, holding court with a few locals, Ace Mulligan, and Ox Remington. Charlie held a glass of lemonade, clear-eyed.

Dodge walked over to them and got Effie's attention, and she scooted out.

"Have you seen Echo?" he asked.

"She was at the house today when Charlie and I left," Effie said. She gave him a strange smile.

Weird. Dodge got back in his truck and headed for the homestead. Down the darkened drive, lights lit up the house like a beacon. Granite came off the deck and ran out, barking at his truck.

Dodge got out and crouched, petting the dog. The other dogs rose from the beds inside their massive pen, then came to the fence to stick their noses through. Dodge stuck his fingers into the fencing and petted them. "Hey, guys. Where's your mama?"

Echo hadn't come out of the house, so he went to the arctic entry and let himself in. "Echo, are you here?"

No answer, so he went inside to the kitchen, then the great room. A quiet fire simmered in the hearth.

"Echo?"

He spotted her on the porch, overlooking the river, and went outside.

She wore a pretty black dress. That alone stopped him, and as she turned, her golden-blond hair down, her beautiful green eyes on his, he couldn't move.

"Wow, you're beautiful."

She smiled then, something sweet, albeit sad in her expression.

"Hey," he said, coming close and wrapping his arms around her. "What's going on? I thought you said you were coming to the dance."

She nodded, and then, weirdly, her eyes filled.

"Echo—?"

"I did it, Dodge. I . . . I forgave her."

His mouth opened.

"My mom."

"Yes, I figured—"

"It was George."

"Huh?"

"I don't know why, but letting him go . . ." She shook her head. "It was like you said. The more she was here, the more I realized that there was no room anymore for the anger."

"You forgave her."

"Yes. And . . . I started calling her Mom."

He touched her face. "Really?"

"It feels strange. Like she never really left. She's starting an OB-GYN practice in town. And last night, she popped popcorn in the fireplace. And . . . she bought me this dress."

"I like it." He stood back and let his gaze travel over her. "A lot."

"It feels weird."

He tucked her hair behind her ear. "Let love guide you."

She pushed him away. "Dodge. That's the thing. I sat in the bleachers, watching you—great game, by the way—and . . . what if I'm *too* happy?"

"Isn't that the point?"

She made a face, but a tear spilled down. "What if I love you too much? What if—"

"Stop what-iffing." He pressed his forehead to hers. "What if we just promise that we're going to live happily ever after . . . and we do. And we trust God to help us keep that promise."

She searched his eyes. "Even when the grizzlies show up?"

"Especially when the grizzlies show up."

She smiled and ran her hands up around his neck, played with his hair. "You really went to the dance?"

"Of course I did." He began to sway. "I think this is as good as it gets."

"Impressive."

"Mind-blowing. I could probably even dip you."

"Let's stay on our feet."

"Chicken."

"Oh yes." She smoothed her hands on his dress shirt. "Did you *iron?*"

"Is that a dress you're wearing?"

She wound her hands around his neck again and brought his head down to hers.

Kissed him. It was soft, gentle, at once a surrender and a gift. She stepped closer, into his arms, as if his entire body could absorb her, draw her into his heart. Desire shot through him.

Oh, he needed this woman. Not just in his arms, but in his life. In fact, he didn't know where he stopped and she started. Just that he hadn't been whole since he'd left.

She pushed away, looked up at him, her skin flushed. "I think it's time."

"Time?" Right. They should leave. He took her hand. "I think we can get back while the band is still playing."

But she didn't budge. "No, Dodge. It's time."

Time?

He stilled, and suddenly Effie's words returned to him. "*We talked about dreams, and a bigger life and . . . maybe she realized that it's time for her to move on.*"

He took a breath. Okay, then. "So, you're thinking of moving to Anchorage, to get that degree? I get it. I shouldn't expect you to stay. But you should know that I'll wait for you . . ."

She smelled good, like a fresh shower, and maybe perfume, and he was trying very hard not to let it go to his head.

"What? Where do you think I'm going?"

Oh. "I don't know—"

"What does a girl have to do? It's *time.*"

His eyes widened and he swallowed.

She laughed. "Not that." She sighed, shook her head, stepped away from him.

He stared at her, the way the simple black dress fit all her curves, that dark, golden hair filled with moonlight and—was she wearing makeup? It only made her eyes larger, her lips—

He blew out a breath, his heart thudding, very aware, suddenly, that they were alone here. Alone, and longing rose inside him and—

It's time.

Oh.

"Yes, it's time," he said softly.

She drew in a breath and he took her hand, got down on one knee.

"Wow. Last time you didn't—"

"Stop talking. I got this." He ran his thumb over her hand, his throat suddenly thickened. Ah, he might even cry. "E," he said quietly, "you are so much a part of my world that I don't know if my dreams are yours or mine. You've been in my heart since before I knew what love was, and every single day I spent apart from you was agony. I love you with every breath, every heartbeat, and I don't want to spend another moment without you. Please, please, marry me. I promise to take care of you, to support you, and most of all, to never leave you again."

She stared at him, and in that eternal moment he tasted his heartbeat, the tomorrows he longed for. Please.

"Yes." She cupped his face with her hands. "Yes, I will marry you."

"Finally."

They turned and he spotted her father standing in the great room. Her mother stood beside Charlie, holding his hand, tears streaking down her cheeks. They must have followed him here from the dance.

Charlie gave him a thumbs-up. "Good job, son," he mouthed.

Dodge laughed, got up, then caught Echo up in his arms and swung her around.

She laughed, the sound of it like sunlight, sweeping away the last vestiges of darkness.

Good job, indeed.

He put her down, wound a hand around her neck to kiss her again when a bark sounded in the night.

Echo pressed her hands against his chest. "Wait—I think that's Viper!" She stepped off the porch and called for him.

The barking grew louder.

She whistled, and after a minute, an animal launched at her out of the darkness. He nearly took Echo down, but Dodge bent next to her and helped catch the dog. His fur was matted and grimy, his harness gone, but he lathered Echo with kisses.

"Viper!"

"Where did he come from?" Charlie said as he came out and also crouched to pet the dog. Viper went to him, his entire body wiggling with joy.

"I can't believe it," Echo said as Dodge pulled her up.

He caught her face in his hands. "I can. Didn't I tell you? The ones who love you always come back."

She smiled, her eyes sparkling, and looked at Charlie, Viper, and even her mother. And finally, back to Dodge. "Yes. I guess they do."

And then, as the northern lights arched over them, and the massive hulk of Denali watched, he kissed her.

Because Dodge Kingston was finally home.

Someone had turned on the television.

She knew because of the ads—they played over and over, with funny jingles that now, unfortunately, stuck in her head.

Like the one for MyPillow.

And, "Like a good neighbor" . . . If she heard the State Farm song again, she might throw a pillow at the television.

If she were awake. If her body didn't feel like glue under layers of gauzy film. If she didn't constantly succumb to the sense that she had her fingers around something, grasping freedom, only to fall back into the shadows.

If the darkness didn't feel so . . . enveloping. Because she could hide in the darkness. Didn't have to wake and face it all.

"It's up to you."

Roy again, his voice soft and deep in the folds of her mind. Stop.

She focused on the television and recognized the game show *Jeopardy.* Listened to the chosen category. "Figures in History for two hundred."

"After the deed, he leaped to the stage, shouting, '*Sic semper tyrannis!*'"

She knew this one. *Who was John Wilkes Booth, after he shot Abraham Lincoln?*

"Who was John Wilkes Booth?"

Latin. She knew Latin. Thus always to tyrants.

Of course she knew Latin. She hadn't forgotten everything lying here.

"What's Up, Doc, for one hundred."

Yes. This was her category.

"Some algae have been classified in this kingdom, neither fully plant nor animal."

Oh, oh—what is Protista?

"What is Protista or protists?"

Biology 101, people.

She could smell dinner, or something like it—chicken soup, mashed potatoes—filtering in from the hall. It was clearly after 5:00 p.m., which meant the nurse with the soft hands would be coming in soon. The one who sometimes stood at the foot of her bed, her hand on her leg, humming. Maybe praying.

The one who took her hand, deep in the night, when the past found her, haunted her. The soft-handed nurse comforted her and told her it was okay to wake up.

Maybe. Maybe not.

"In 1816 French physician René Laënnec fashioned the first one of these instruments from a hollow wooden tube."

What is a stethoscope?

"What is a stethoscope?"

"Good evening, Jane." The voice spoke over the television, and she tried to ignore it, listening to the game show host.

She could feel something awakening inside her.

"Often found in areas with large deer populations, this bacterial inflammatory disease was first identified in 1975."

"You're looking well today. How do you feel about waking up?" The nurse touched her arm, picking up her wrist to take her pulse. Yes, soft hands.

What is Lyme disease?

"Jane? Did you say something?"

"What is Lyme disease?"

She knew it.

"Jane?" A hand pressed her forehead. "I can hear you. Try again."

The host read the next prompt. "In 1910 physician James Herrick became the first to identify this blood disease that affects many African Americans."

"What is sickle cell anemia?"

"Jane, that's right. That's"—the nurse raised her voice— "Can I get some help in here?"

The bed was moving, the nurse sitting her up.

"What is sickle cell anemia?" said the contestant.

She knew it. She could almost see the room, she'd drawn it so often in her mind. The television centered in the corner, a window overlooking the mountains, and—

A woman was looking at her. Long dark hair, Native American features. She wore a kind smile as she held her hand. "Jane?"

She blinked at her, clearing her vision.

"Latin for poison, it's a submicroscopic agent infecting living organisms and causing disease."

A *virus.*

"What is a virus?" said the woman on the screen.

Jane stared at the nurse, her heart slamming against her chest.

Awake. She was *awake.* And that meant—

She looked at the television. Took a breath.

And screamed.

WHAT COMES NEXT . . .

I t felt good to finally sweat.

"Hey, Echo, got another sheet for me?" Dodge walked over to the edge of the roof, where the sun had heated the tin and puddled any remaining snow long ago. Around him, the ranch was coming alive, the grass greening with increasing sunlight hours, the baby fir and white pine dotting the valley amid budding purple shooting stars and white chickweed. The lake had opened, too, deep-blue water lapping quietly against the seaplane dock.

Dodge wore a thermal shirt, pushed up at the elbows, but with the sun high and the sweat prickling his spine, he pulled it off and dropped it on the roof as he reached down for the sheet of tin Echo held up to him. She had shucked her sweatshirt and wore a short-sleeved shirt, her blond hair back in a red bandanna.

"That's the last piece," she said. "Hope it's enough."

He brought the piece over to the massive hole he was repairing and fitted it over the gap. "It's enough. But I'll need to replace this entire roof sometime soon."

Right after he inspected and patched the other roofs, as well as rebuilt the deck on cabin 4. And then there was the supplying of Sky King Rescue. Although Nash hadn't let him purchase his beautiful DHC-2 Beaver, Dodge had found an equally perfect model, rebuilt in 2018 with a Hartzell Prop, Sky Force GPS, and plenty of cargo space.

Durable and exactly what he needed for his fleet.

His fleet.

He could hardly believe how his world was coming together. Echo, ready to marry him as soon as their house was finished—he had plans to rebuild his grandparents' place at the end of the lake—Sky King Ranch back in the black, and Larke had even called and said that she'd made it past twenty weeks and felt the baby kick. His father might be going blind, but Dodge could still see the sparkle of joy in his eyes.

Larke promised a trip home as soon as the baby was born.

He nailed the last sheet down and stood up, stretching. Below, Echo threw a stick out for Iceman to play catch. He'd been living at the ranch since Dodge found him, and it seemed like he didn't want to leave.

Dodge's stomach growled and he headed toward the ladder, but a glimmer of light against a red truck motoring along the drive to the lodge stopped him. He watched it pull up, and although he couldn't make out the model, it looked a lot like the truck that belonged to Dwayne, their NATB agent.

What now?

He grabbed his shirt and climbed down the ladder. "NATB is at the house," he said to Echo as he took a drink of water from his thermos.

"Really? Why?"

"Dunno. Maybe they're lifting the probation." He pulled his thermal over his head and tugged it down. Echo came over to him.

"Shoot. I liked the view."

He laughed but wrapped his arms around her shoulders and kissed her. She smiled under his touch. "I see a lot more projects in your future."

"You got it, babe," he said and winked, then he took her hand as they headed up to the lodge.

Please let Dwayne not be yanking their FBO license.

Iceman bounded into the arctic entry ahead of them, barking, then running into the great room. The lodge smelled of fresh coffee, probably his father being hospitable. Dodge could hear his father even as he came into the office.

"How long?"

Dodge's heart fell. Shoot. Now he'd have to go the route of reapplying for status, the paperwork, the inspections, the ride-alongs, the scrutiny . . . Dodge walked into the room, ready to protest, plead his case, anything to save his operation—

"About three weeks."

Dodge stopped as the speaker turned, looked at him.

"Range," Dodge said softly.

They used to call them the bookends, he and Ranger, although Ranger was shorter than Dodge by an inch. Still, he had the same dark hair and blue eyes, wide shoulders, and even-handed demeanor as his oldest brother. However, he'd been the one who didn't let his temper off its leash, the one who had a goal and let nothing deter him from it.

"Dodge," Ranger said, walking over, his hand outstretched. Dodge took it and then Ranger pulled him into a hug. Slapped his back. "Good to see you."

A warmth went through Dodge, something he hadn't let himself feel in years, although he had no real beef with Ranger.

"Last time I saw you, you were in Afghanistan. When did you get home?"

Ranger gave a half smile, but something hooded came over his eyes. "A while ago," he said. "Hey, Echo."

Echo had come in beside Dodge and now stepped up to Ranger to give him a hug. "Range. Glad you're back."

He hugged her too, then let her go. "Not sure I'm back, but . . ." He looked at Dodge, then his father. "Something's happened."

Echo took Dodge's hand, squeezed.

"What do you mean? What happened?" Dodge asked. He glanced at his father, who had walked over, his hands in his pockets. He met Dodge's gaze, his shoulders rising and falling.

Something—and his thoughts went to the worst. "It's Colt," Dodge said.

Ranger's expression turned grim, and he nodded.

Echo's grip in his tightened even as Dodge's other hand went to the back of a nearby chair.

It wasn't supposed to end like this. Their story wasn't over—his and Colt's. Dodge was supposed to have time to fix things, to apologize, to forgive . . . and be forgiven.

"When? Where?" He took a breath, and his voice barely wavered. "How?"

Ranger blinked, frowned, then came close and put his hand on his shoulder. "He's not dead."

Dodge didn't know why, but Ranger's words shuddered through him, turned him even weaker. He looked away, blinked back a terrible burn.

"Then what's happened?" Echo asked, probably for him.

"He's been taken," his father said, walking up to stand beside Ranger.

Dodge looked at his brother, who nodded.

"Almost three weeks ago," Ranger said. "While on assignment in Africa. Nigeria, to be exact."

"What's Delta Force doing in Nigeria?" Although with the recent violence there, maybe they'd been deployed to protect or even rescue national assets. "Have they sent in a team to get him?"

"He's not with Delta anymore," Ranger said. "Hasn't been for quite a while."

Dodge glanced at his father, who lifted an eyebrow. So, this was news, even to him.

"He was discharged a while back. There's a rumor going

around about dishonorable behavior, but I looked into it—he got a general discharge, nothing noted on his record."

But not an honorable separation, so it meant *something* went down.

"So, what's he doing in Africa?"

"He works for a private security outfit—Jones, Inc. They have a global SAR team and a private security action team. Colt is on the action team along with a former teammate of mine, Fraser Marshall. They were in Africa doing some security work when they were taken."

"By whom?"

"According to Ham—head of Jones, Inc.—he thinks it was by an offshoot group of Boko Haram. It's a jihadist organization—"

"I know who they are," Dodge said.

"Then you know they are into mass kidnappings, human trafficking, bombings, and public executions."

Dodge nodded, his chest tight.

Ranger took a breath, looked at his father, then back to Dodge.

"Unless we can rescue him, Colt is slated to be executed any day now on live TV."

Susan May Warren is the *USA Today* bestselling author of more than 85 novels with more than 1.5 million books sold, including *The Way of the Brave* and *The Heart of a Hero*, as well as the Montana Rescue series. Winner of a RITA Award and multiple Christy and Carol Awards, as well as the HOLT Medallion and numerous Readers' Choice Awards, Susan makes her home in Minnesota. Find her online at www.SusanMayWarren .com, on Facebook @SusanMayWarrenFiction, and on Twitter @SusanMayWarren.

"Warren's Global Search and Rescue series combines high-adrenaline thrills and a sweet romance."

—*Booklist*

For high-octane adventure and romance that sizzles, you won't want to miss this series from bestselling author Susan May Warren.

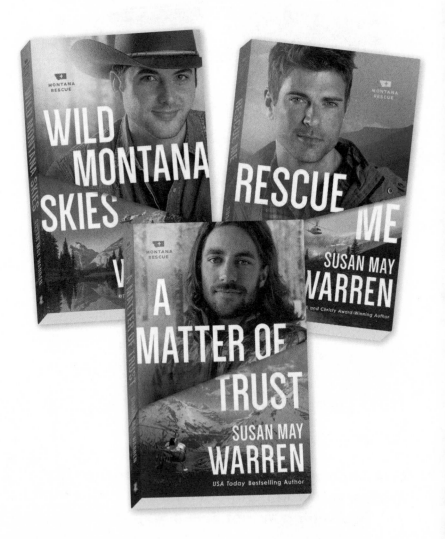

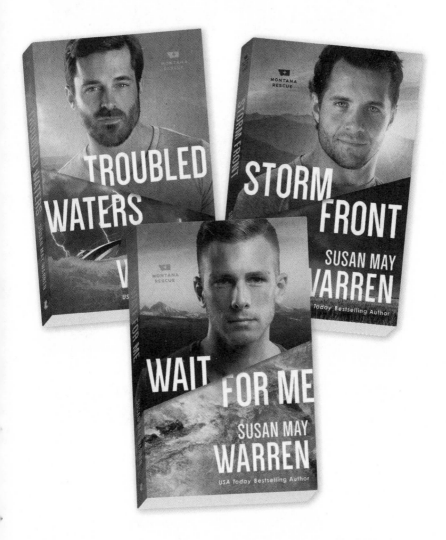

Connect with
Susan May Warren

Visit her website and sign up for her newsletter to get a free novella, hot news, contests, sales, and sneak peeks!

www.susanmaywarren.com

 SusanMayWarrenFiction   SusanMayWarren